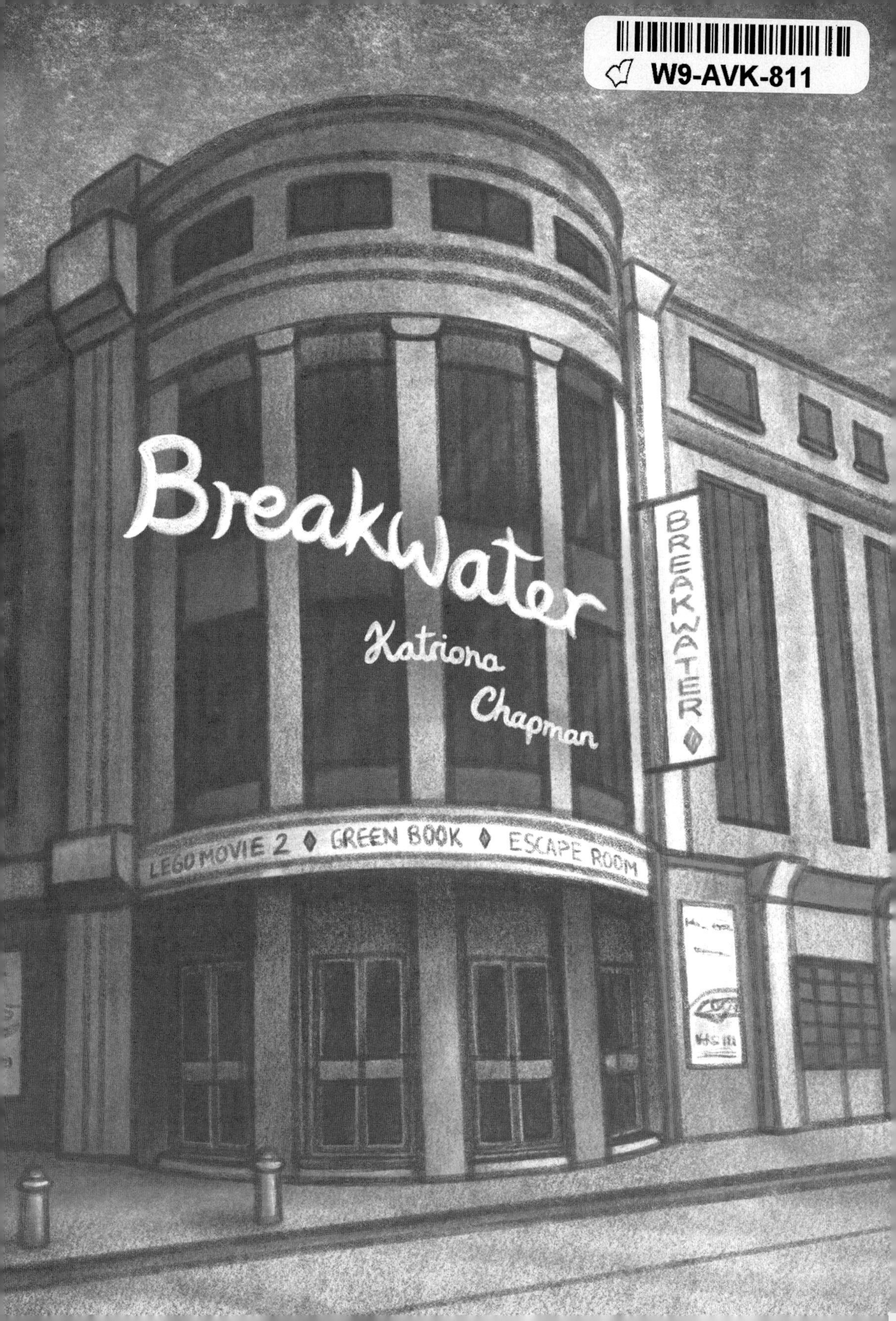
Breakwater
Katriona Chapman
BREAKWATER
LEGO MOVIE 2
GREEN BOOK
ESCAPE ROOM

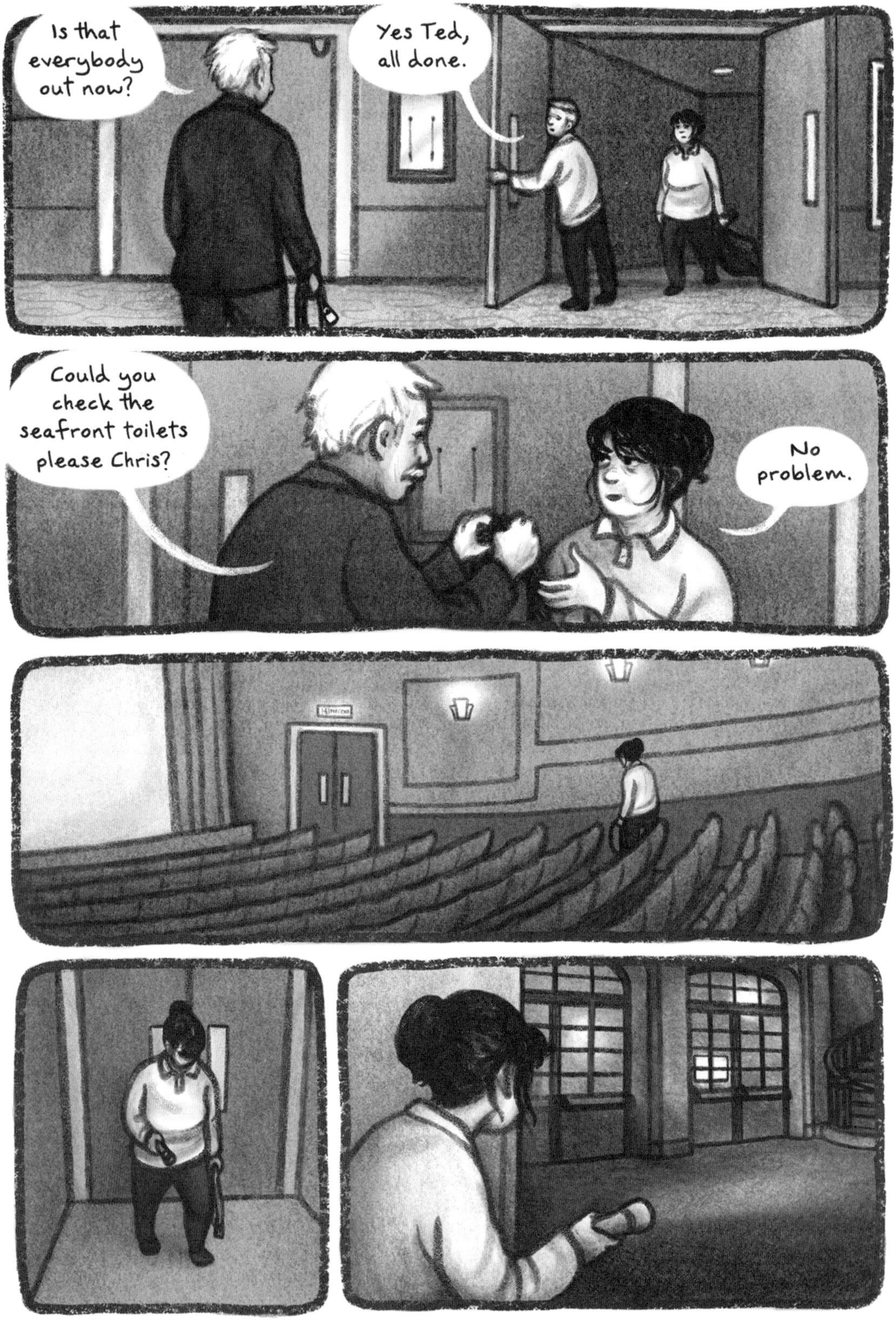
Is that everybody out now?
Yes Ted, all done.
Could you check the seafront toilets please Chris?
No problem.

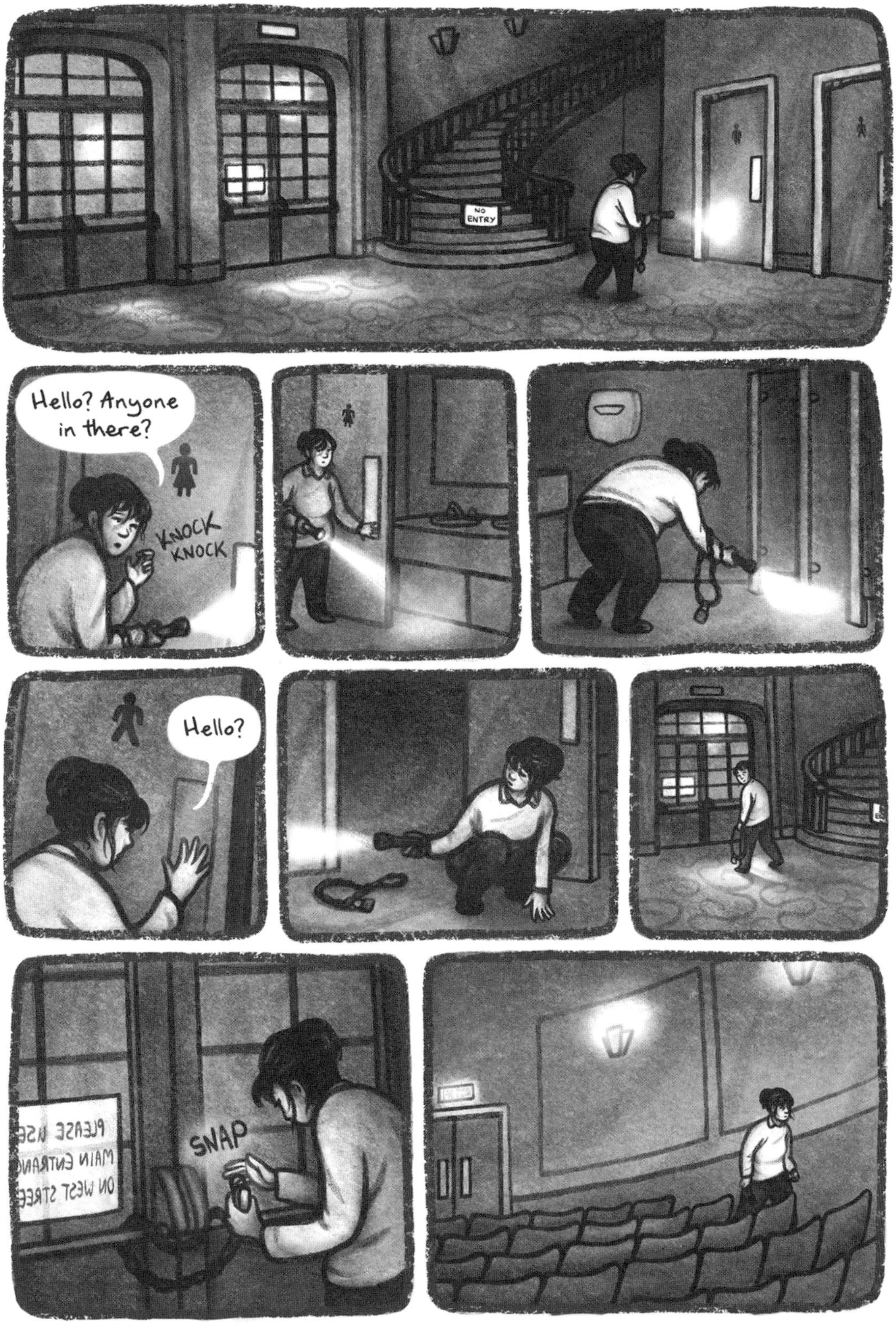
NO ENTRY
Hello? Anyone in there?
KNOCK KNOCK
Hello?
SNAP

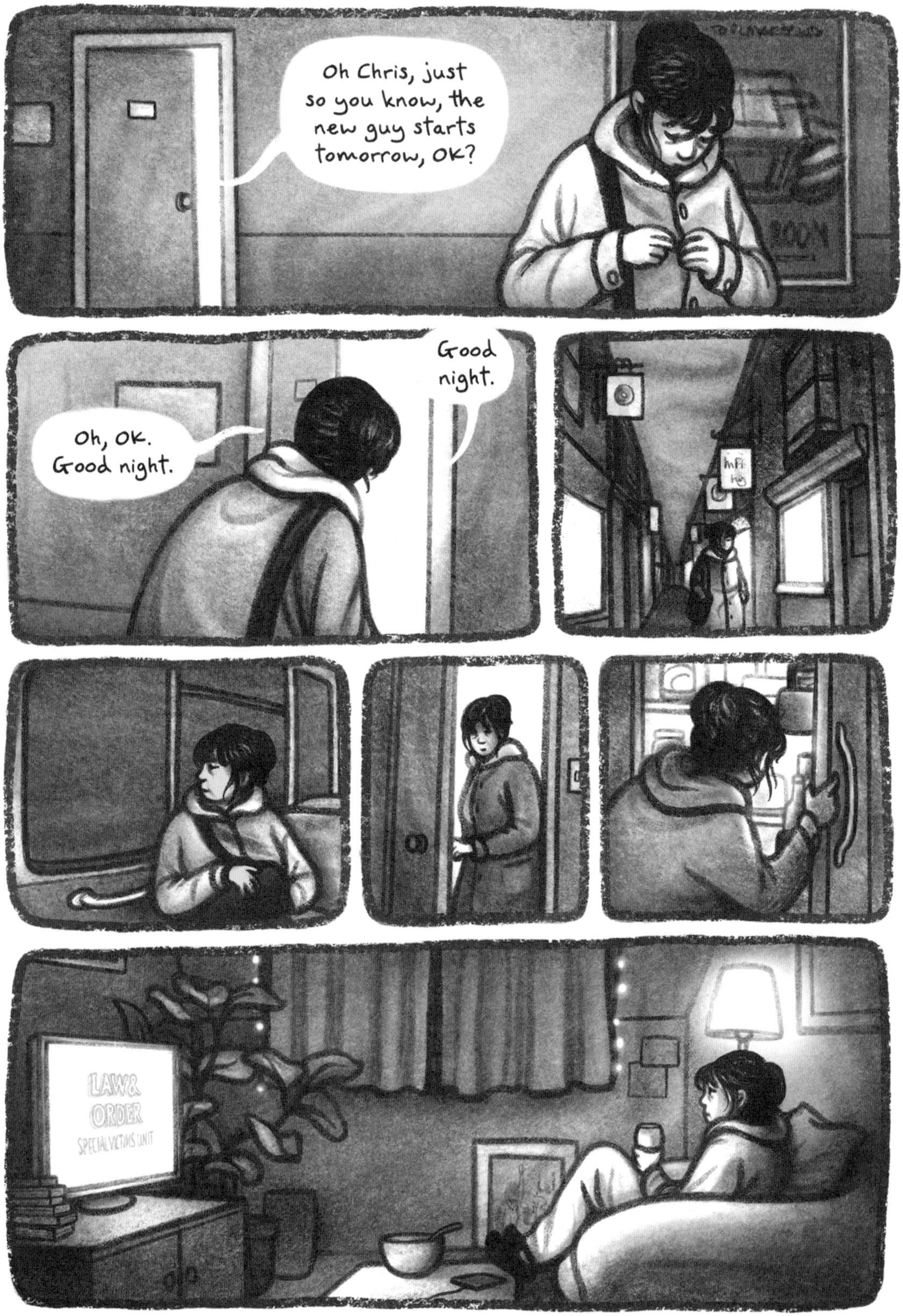
Oh Chris, just so you know, the new guy starts tomorrow, OK?
Oh, OK. Good night.
Good night.
LAW& ORDER
SPECIAL VICTIMS UNIT

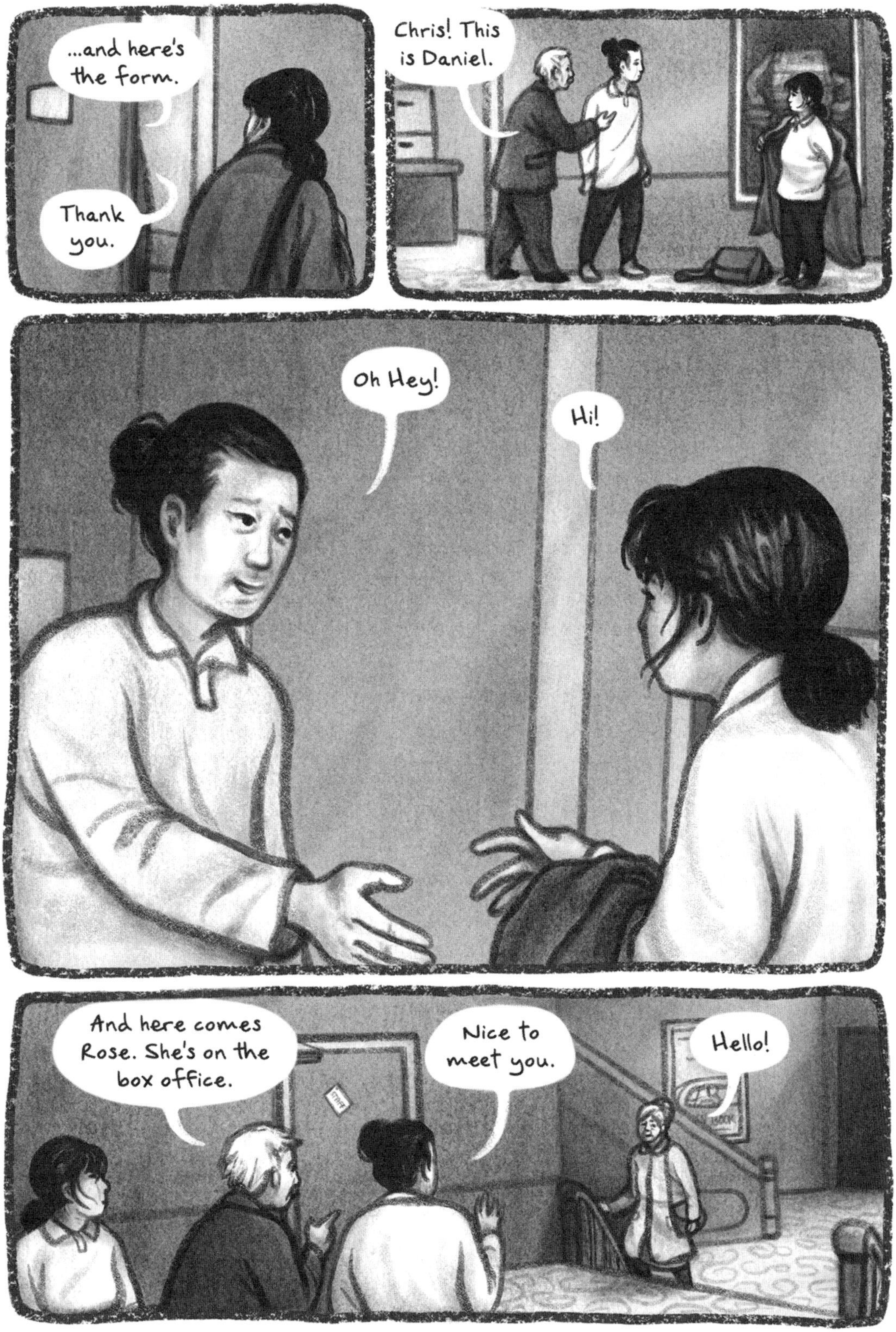
...and here's the form.
Thank you.
Chris! This is Daniel.
Oh Hey!
Hi!
And here comes Rose. She's on the box office.
Nice to meet you.
Hello!

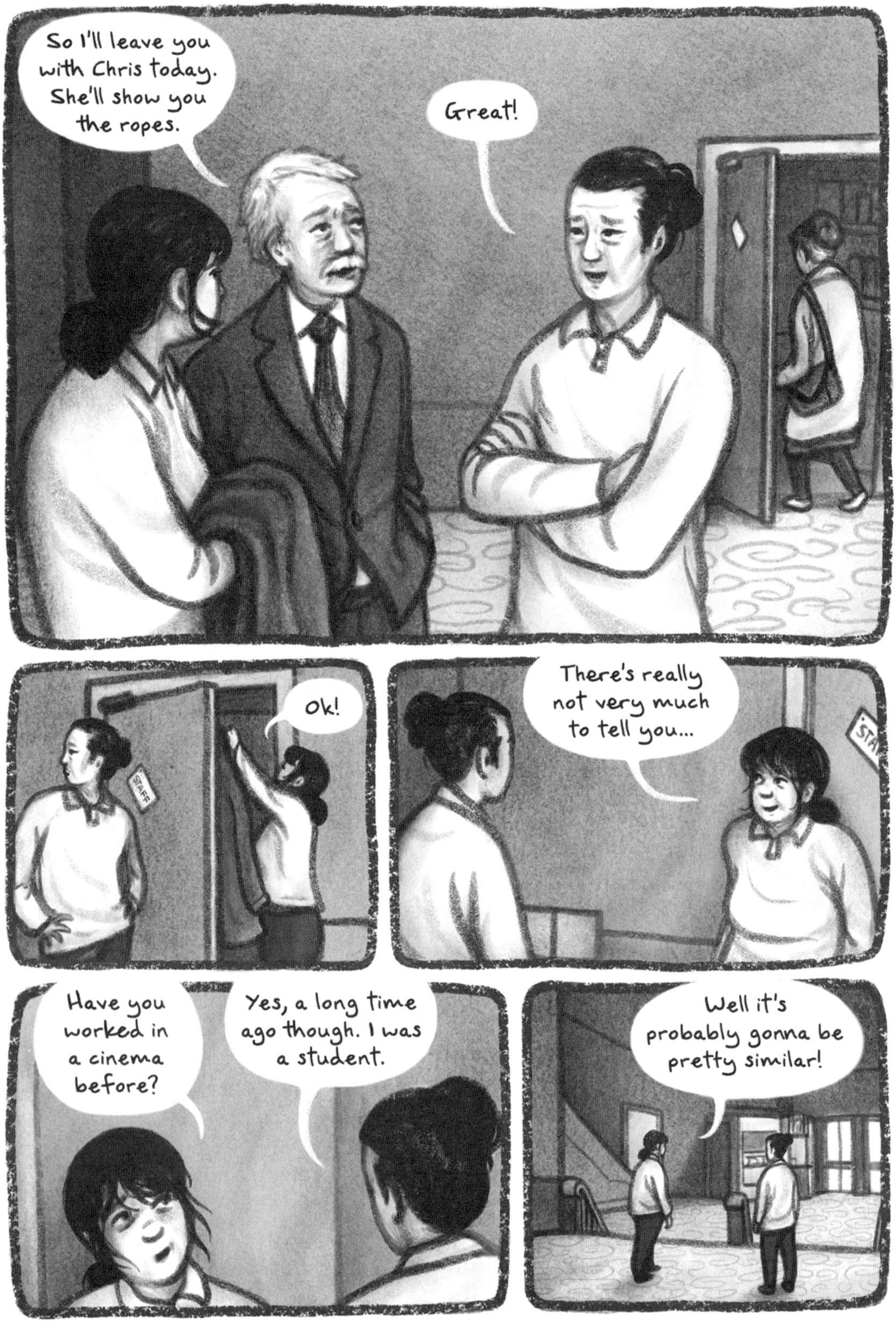
So I'll leave you with Chris today. She'll show you the ropes.
Great!
Ok!
There's really not very much to tell you...
Have you worked in a cinema before?
Yes, a long time ago though. I was a student.
Well it's probably gonna be pretty similar!

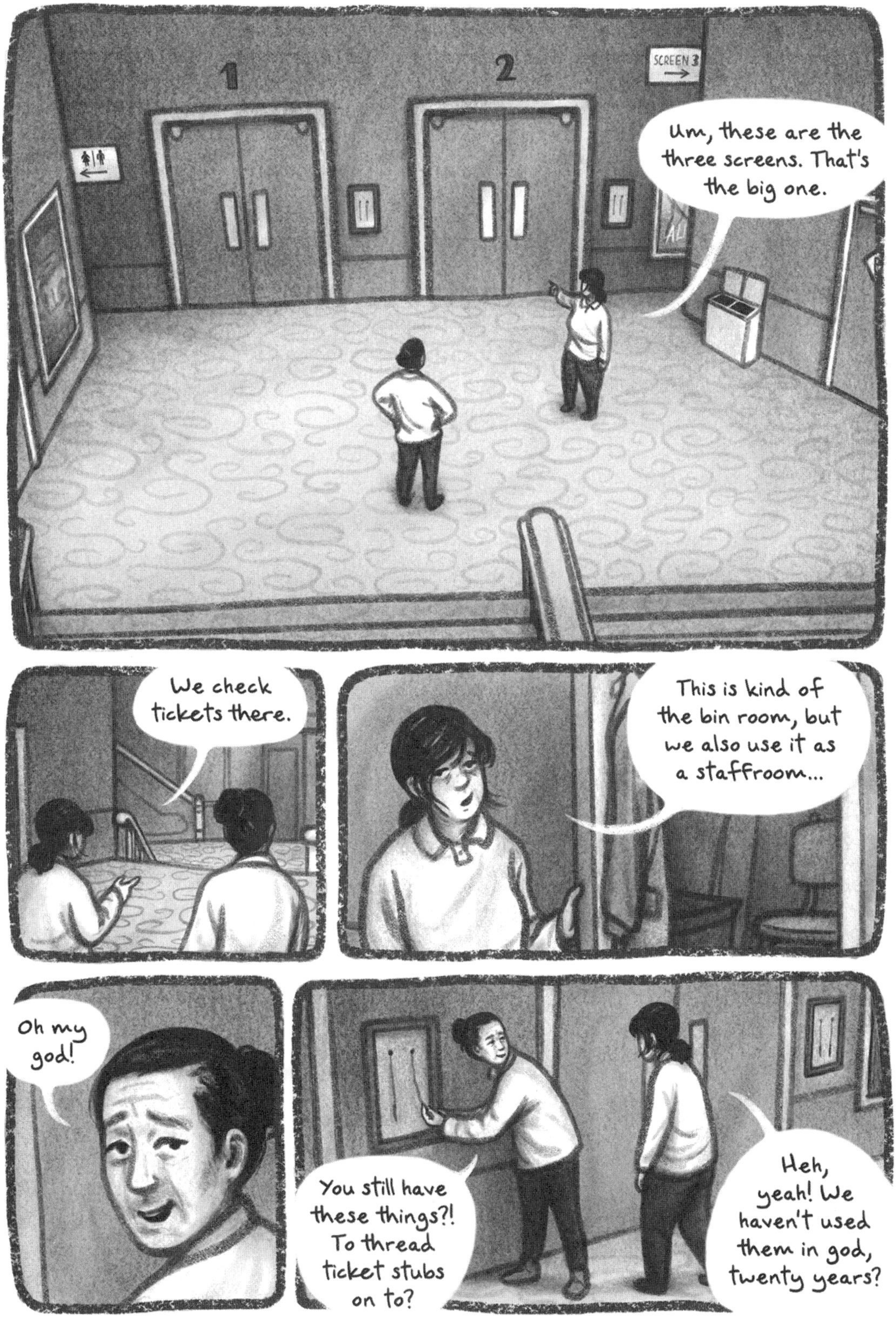
1
2
SCREEN 3
Um, these are the three screens. That's the big one.
We check tickets there.
This is kind of the bin room, but we also use it as a staffroom...
Oh my god!
You still have these things?! To thread ticket stubs on to?
Heh, yeah! We haven't used them in god, twenty years?

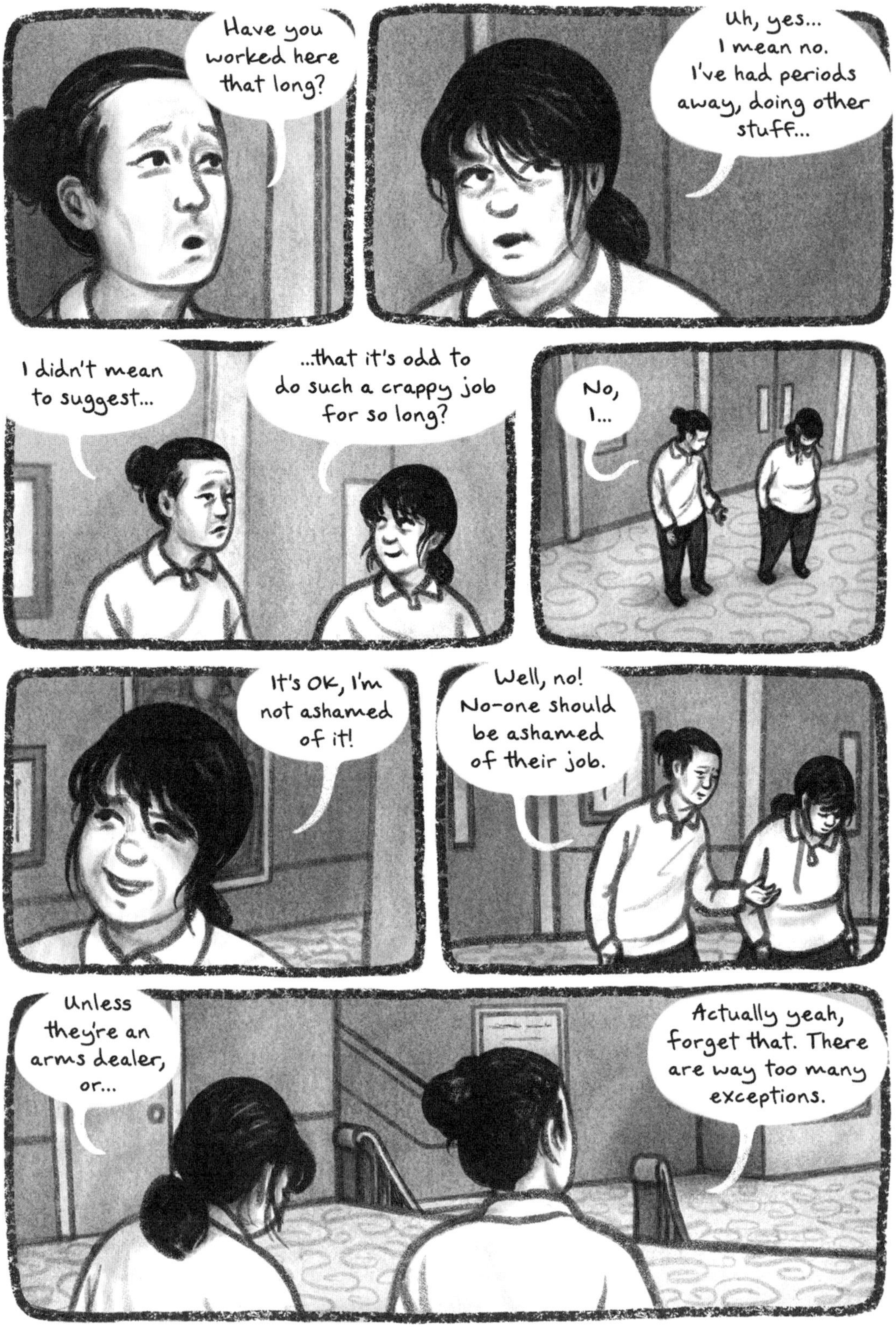
Have you worked here that long?
Uh, yes... I mean no. I've had periods away, doing other stuff...
I didn't mean to suggest...
...that it's odd to do such a crappy job for so long?
No, I...
It's OK, I'm not ashamed of it!
Well, no! No-one should be ashamed of their job.
Unless they're an arms dealer, or...
Actually yeah, forget that. There are way too many exceptions.

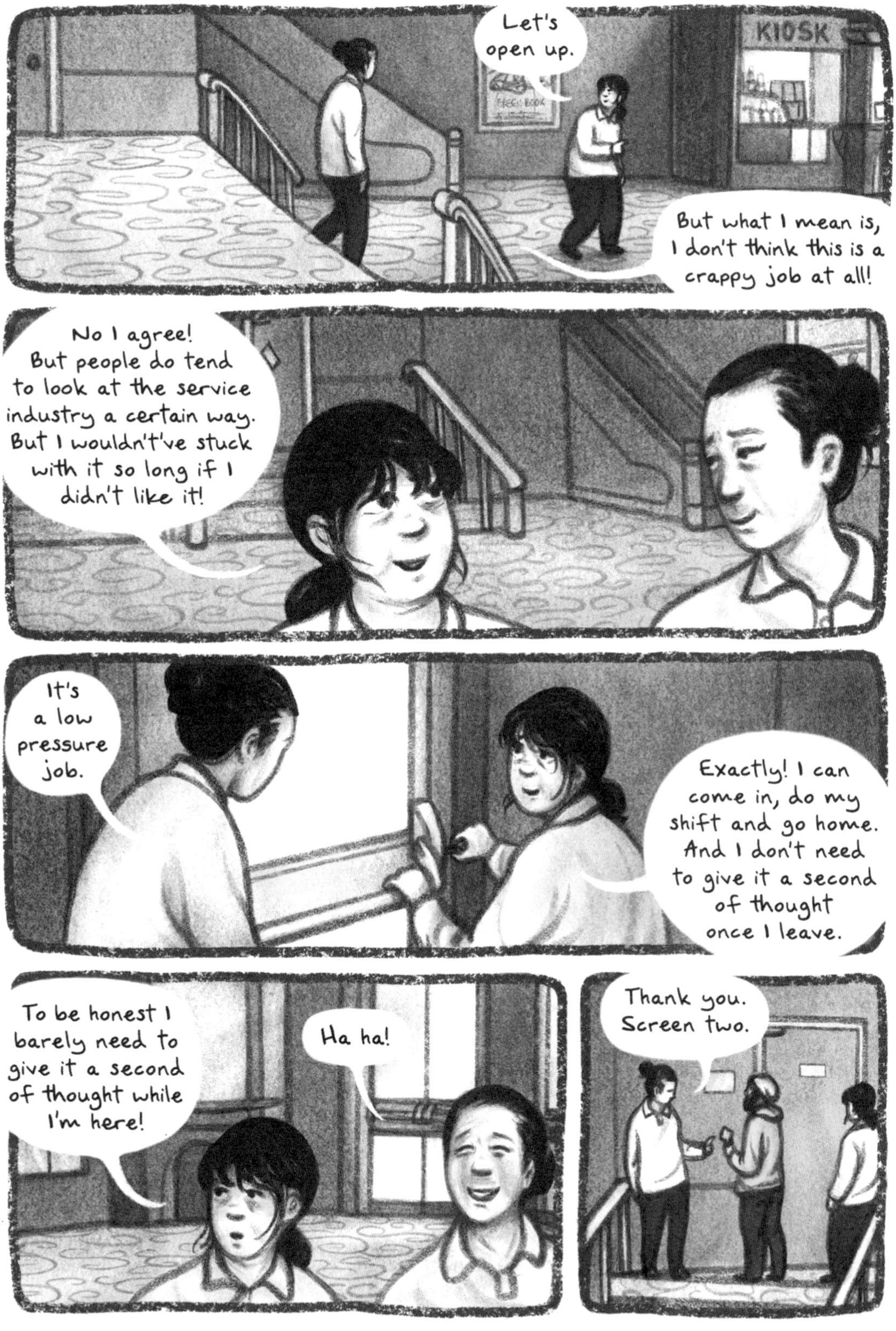

KIOSK
Let's open up.
But what I mean is, I don't think this is a crappy job at all!
No I agree! But people do tend to look at the service industry a certain way. But I wouldn't've stuck with it so long if I didn't like it!
It's a low pressure job.
Exactly! I can come in, do my shift and go home. And I don't need to give it a second of thought once I leave.
To be honest I barely need to give it a second of thought while I'm here!
Ha ha!
Thank you. Screen two.

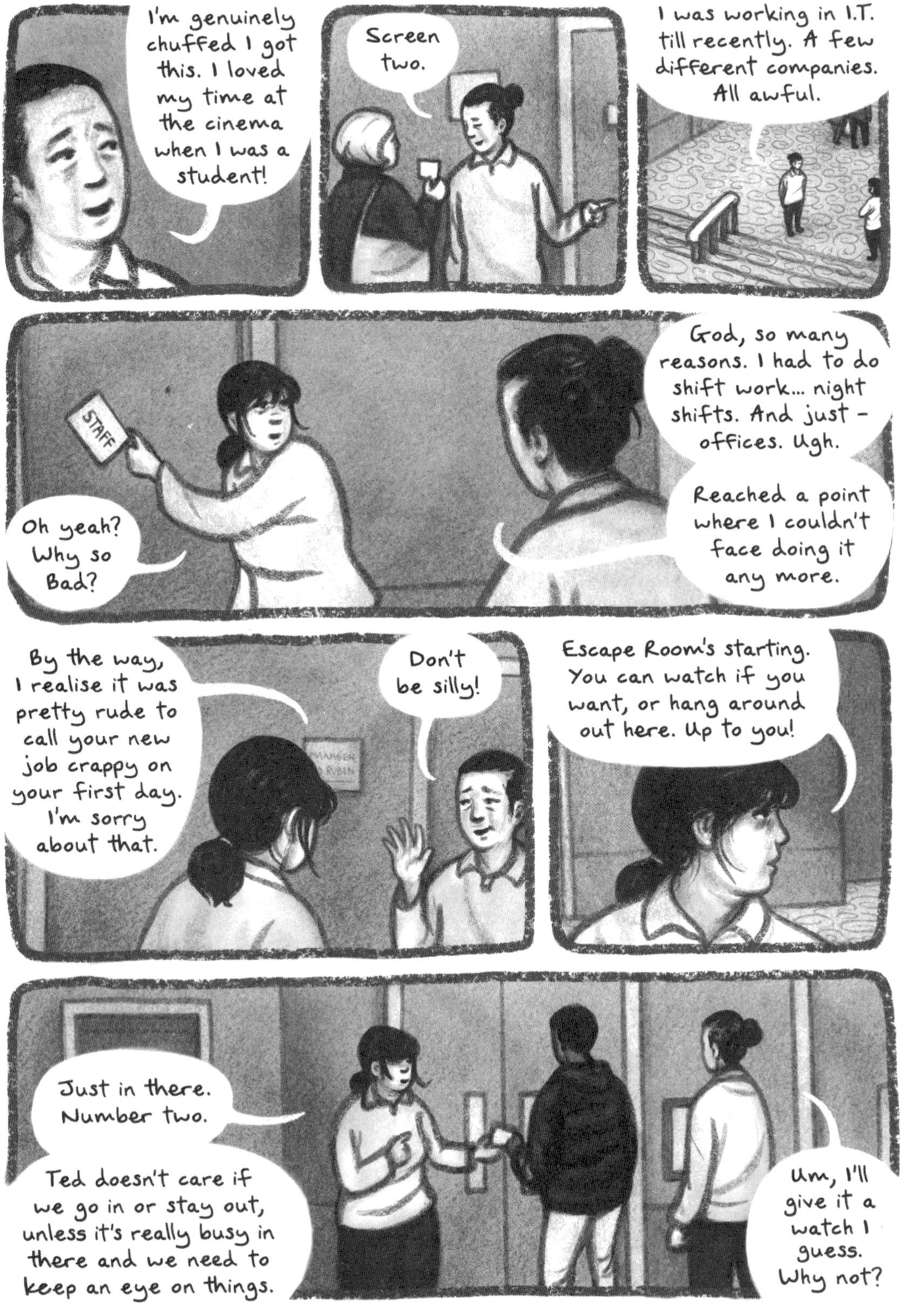
I'm genuinely chuffed I got this. I loved my time at the cinema when I was a student!
Screen two.
I was working in I.T. till recently. A few different companies. All awful.
Oh yeah? Why so Bad?
STAFF
God, so many reasons. I had to do shift work... night shifts. And just - offices. Ugh.
Reached a point where I couldn't face doing it any more.
By the way, I realise it was pretty rude to call your new job crappy on your first day. I'm sorry about that.
Don't be silly!
Escape Room's starting. You can watch if you want, or hang around out here. Up to you!
Just in there. Number two.
Ted doesn't care if we go in or stay out, unless it's really busy in there and we need to keep an eye on things.
Um, I'll give it a watch I guess. Why not?

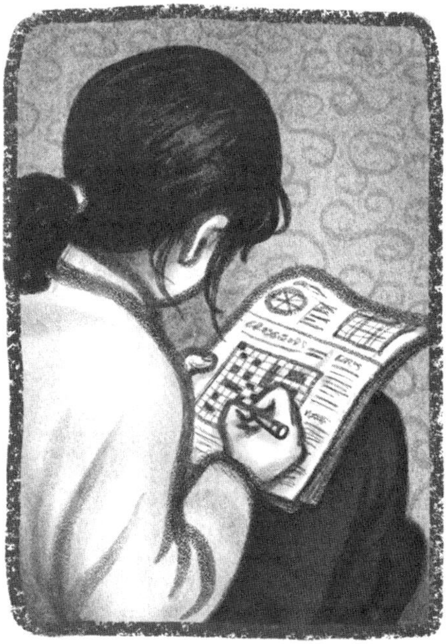

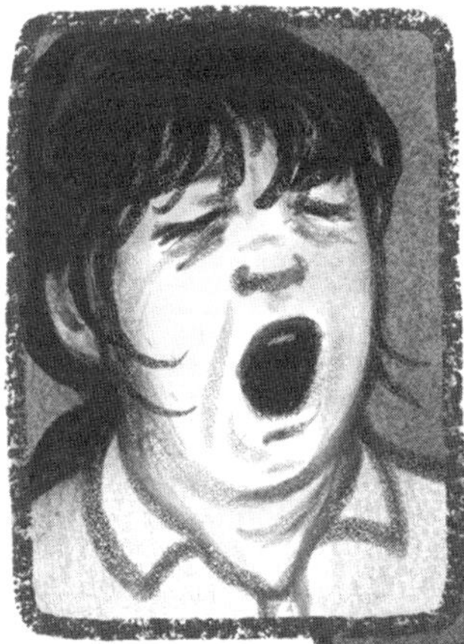

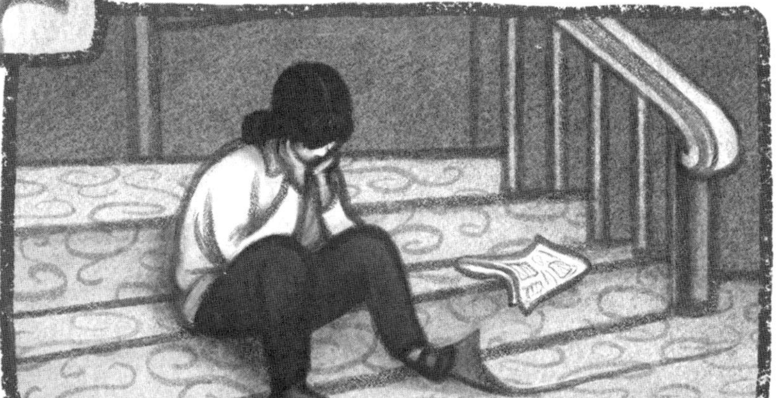

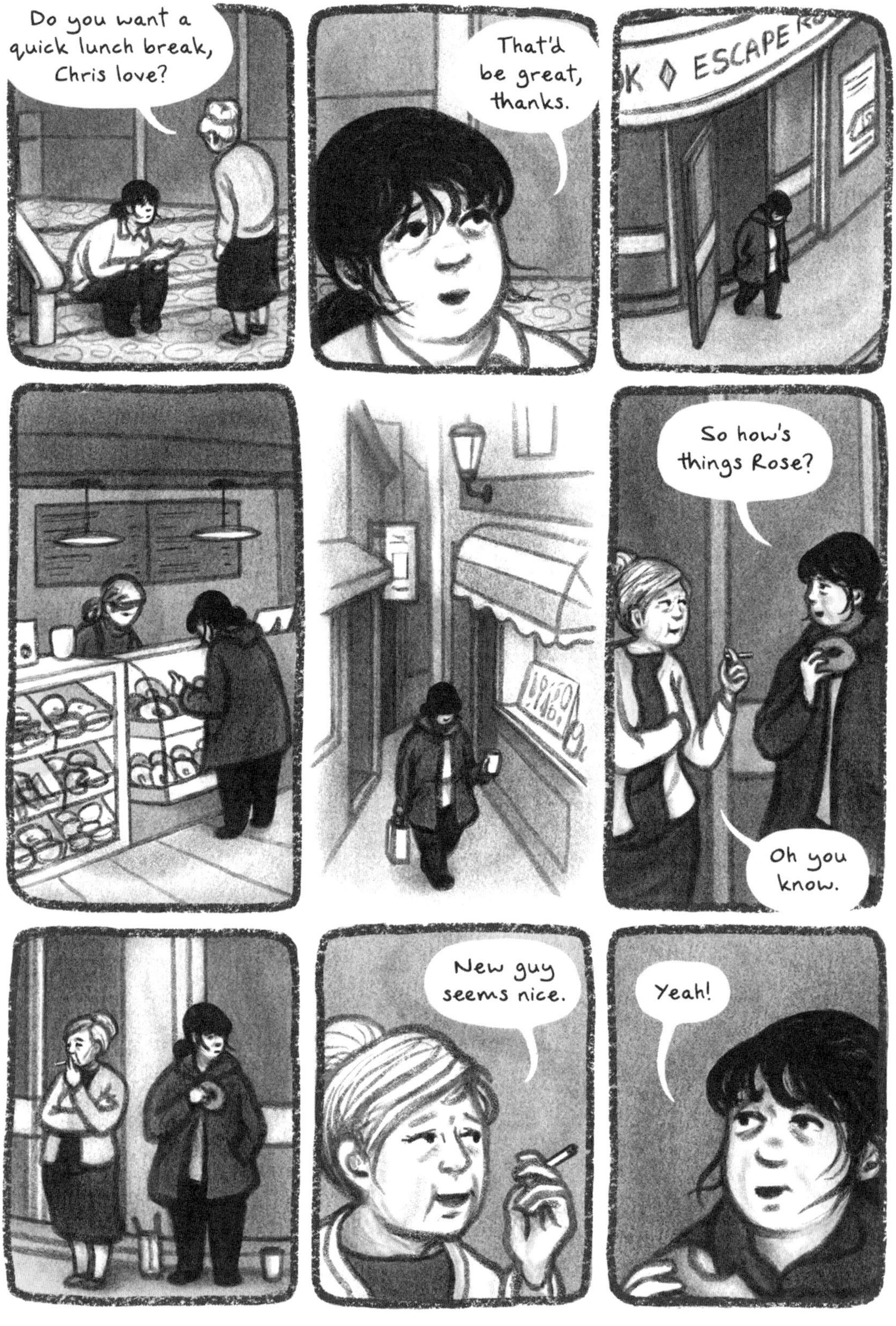
Do you want a quick lunch break, Chris love?
That'd be great, thanks.
ESCAPE
So how's things Rose?
Oh you know.
New guy seems nice.
Yeah!

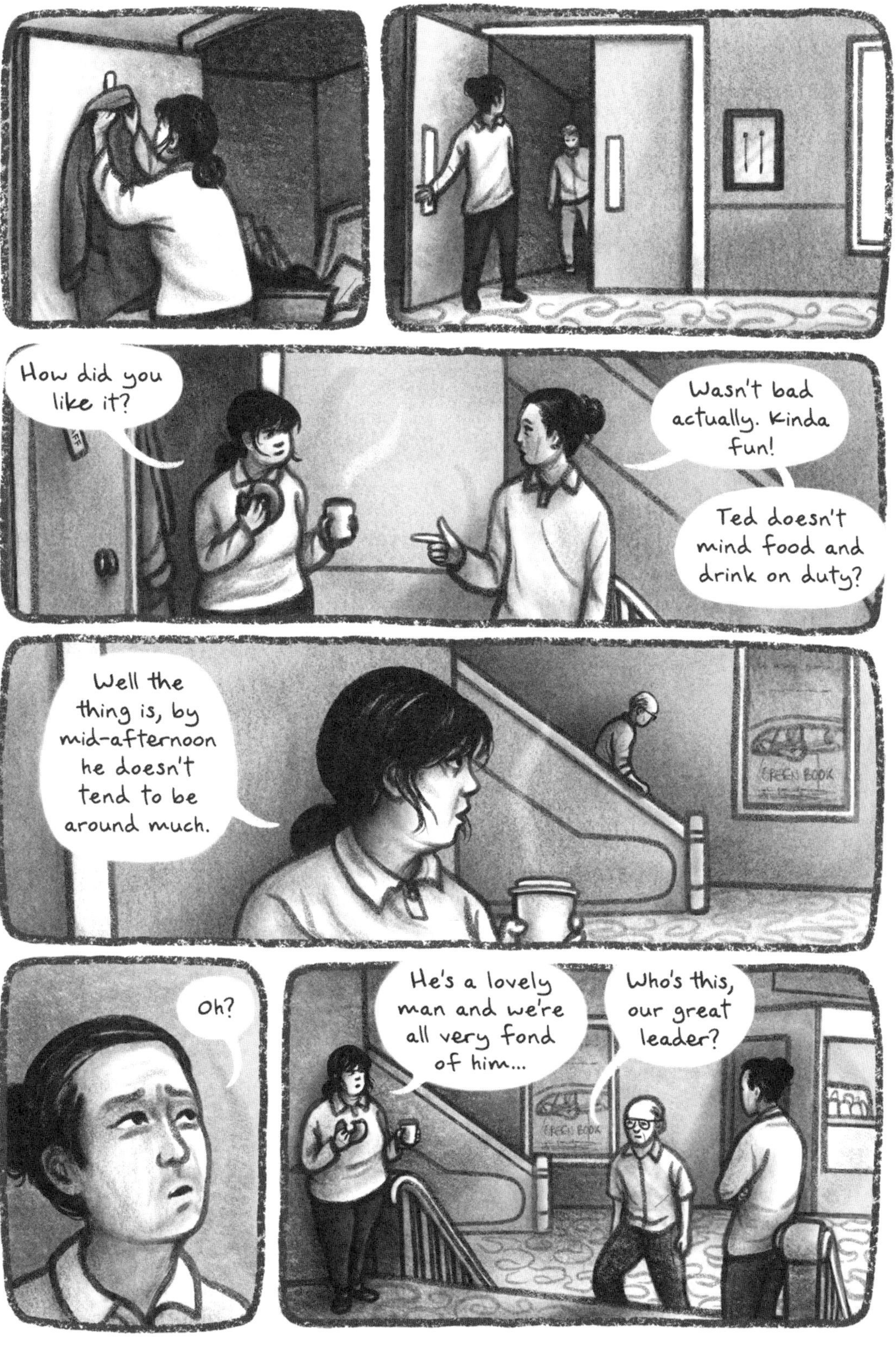
How did you like it?
Wasn't bad actually. Kinda fun!
Ted doesn't mind food and drink on duty?
Well the thing is, by mid-afternoon he doesn't tend to be around much.
Oh?
He's a lovely man and we're all very fond of him...
Who's this, our great leader?

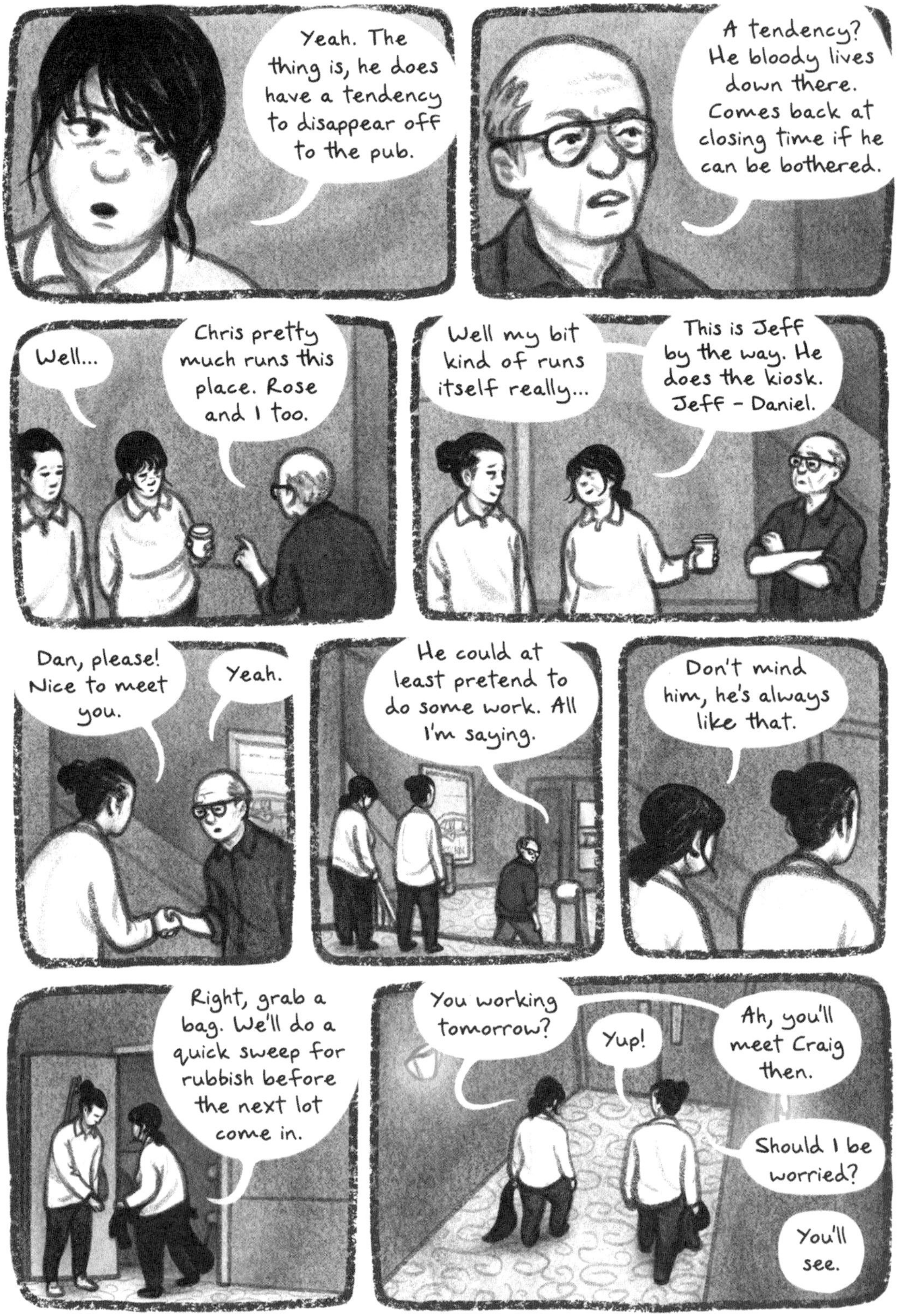
Yeah. The thing is, he does have a tendency to disappear off to the pub.
A tendency? He bloody lives down there. Comes back at closing time if he can be bothered.
Well...
Chris pretty much runs this place. Rose and I too.
Well my bit kind of runs itself really...
This is Jeff by the way. He does the kiosk. Jeff - Daniel.
Dan, please! Nice to meet you.
Yeah.
He could at least pretend to do some work. All I'm saying.
Don't mind him, he's always like that.
Right, grab a bag. We'll do a quick sweep for rubbish before the next lot come in.
You working tomorrow?
Yup!
Ah, you'll meet Craig then.
Should I be worried?
You'll see.

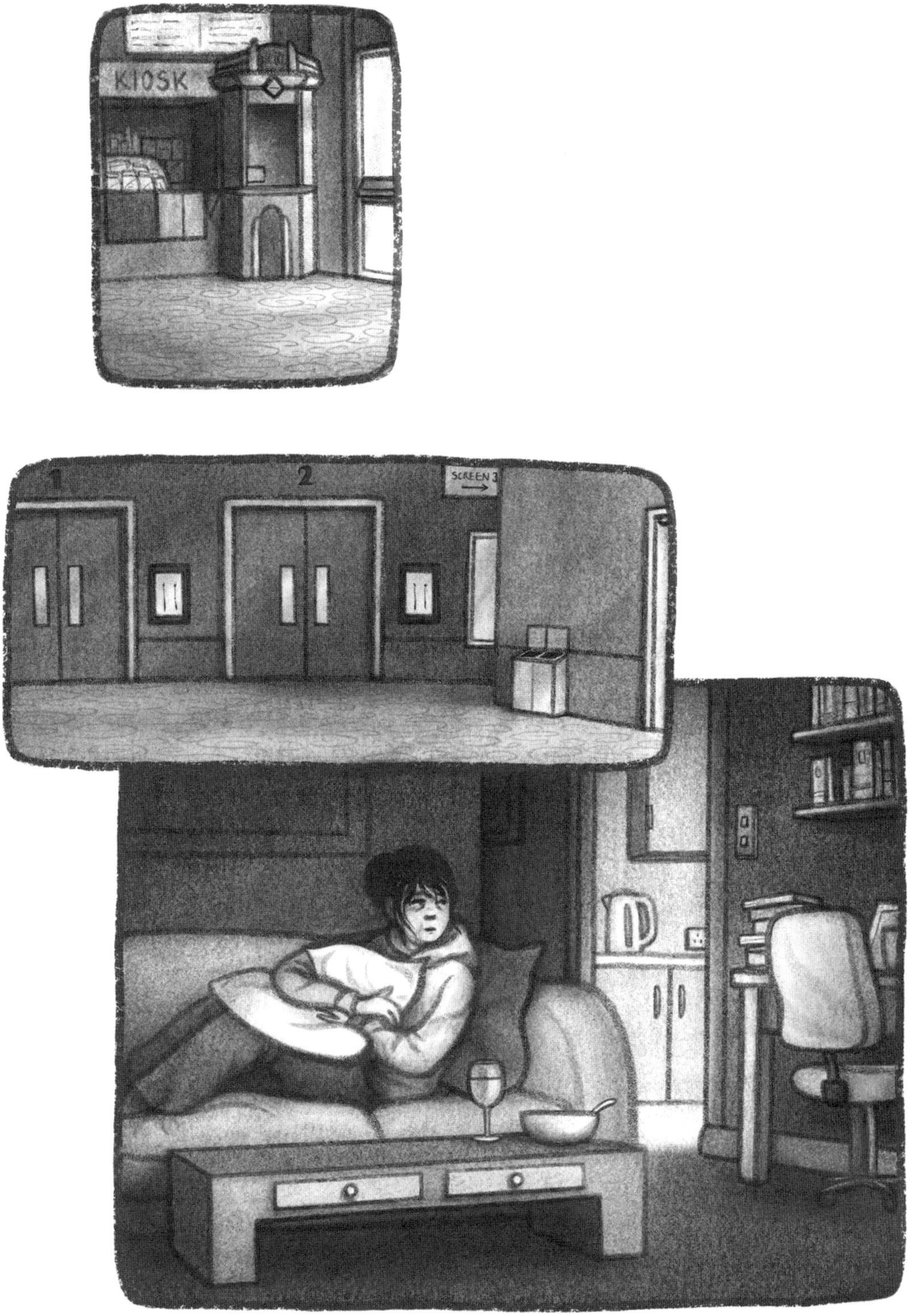
KIOSK
1
2
SCREEN 3

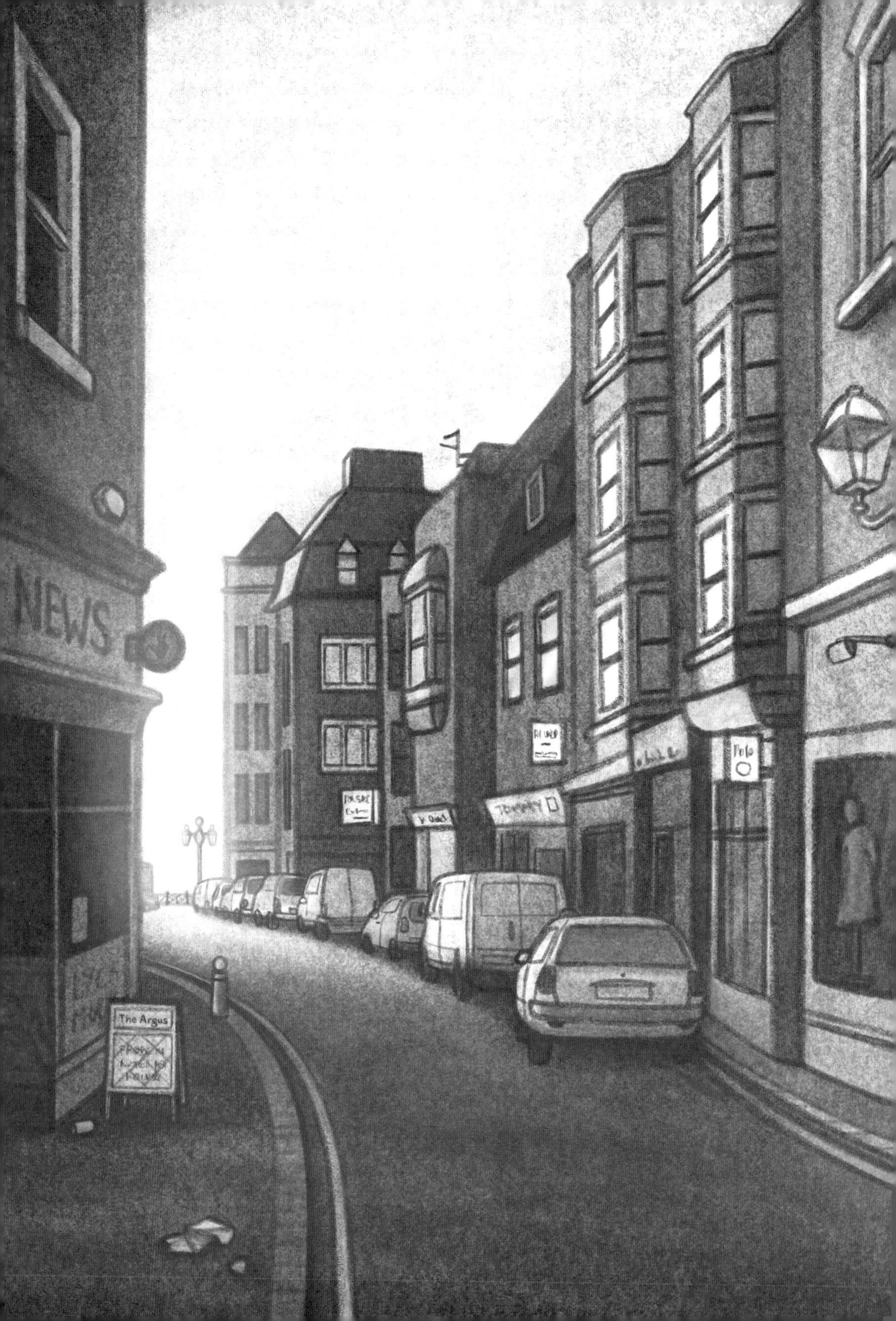
NEWS
The Argus

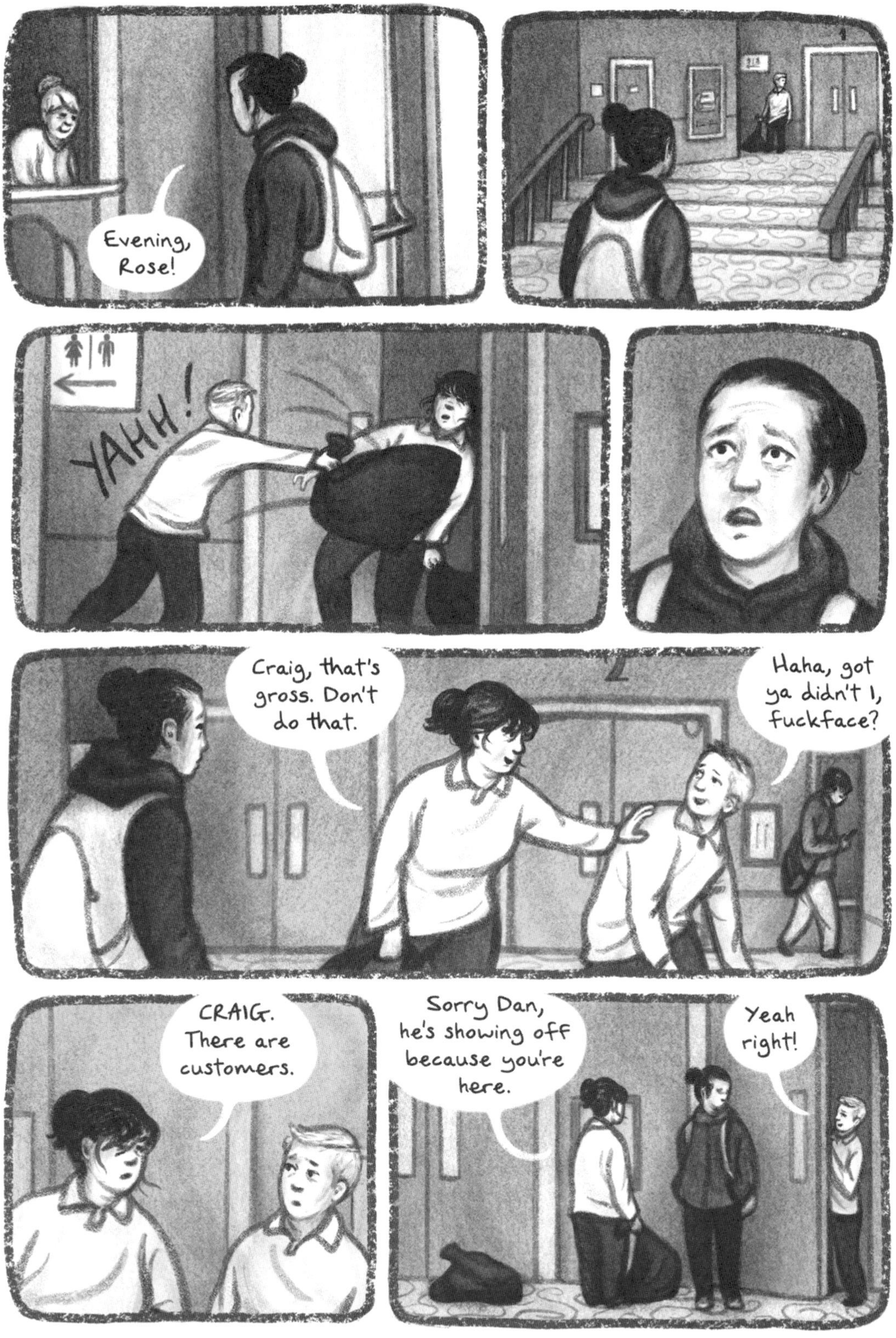
Evening, Rose!
YAHH!
Craig, that's gross. Don't do that.
Haha, got ya didn't I, fuckface?
CRAIG. There are customers.
Sorry Dan, he's showing off because you're here.
Yeah right!

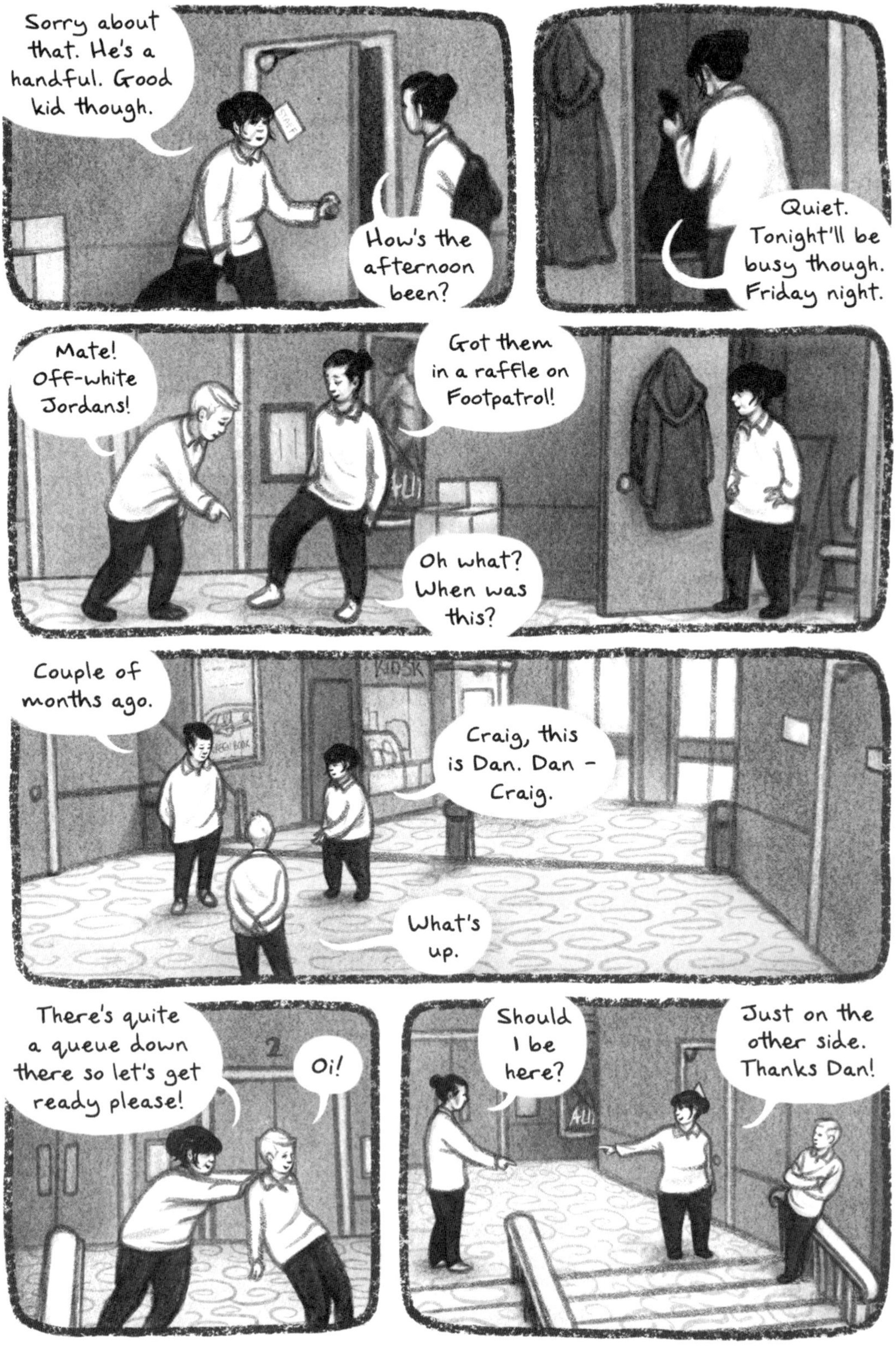
Sorry about that. He's a handful. Good kid though.
How's the afternoon been?
Quiet. Tonight'll be busy though. Friday night.
Mate! Off-white Jordans!
Got them in a raffle on Footpatrol!
Oh what? When was this?
Couple of months ago.
Craig, this is Dan. Dan - Craig.
What's up.
There's quite a queue down there so let's get ready please!
Oi!
Should I be here?
Just on the other side. Thanks Dan!

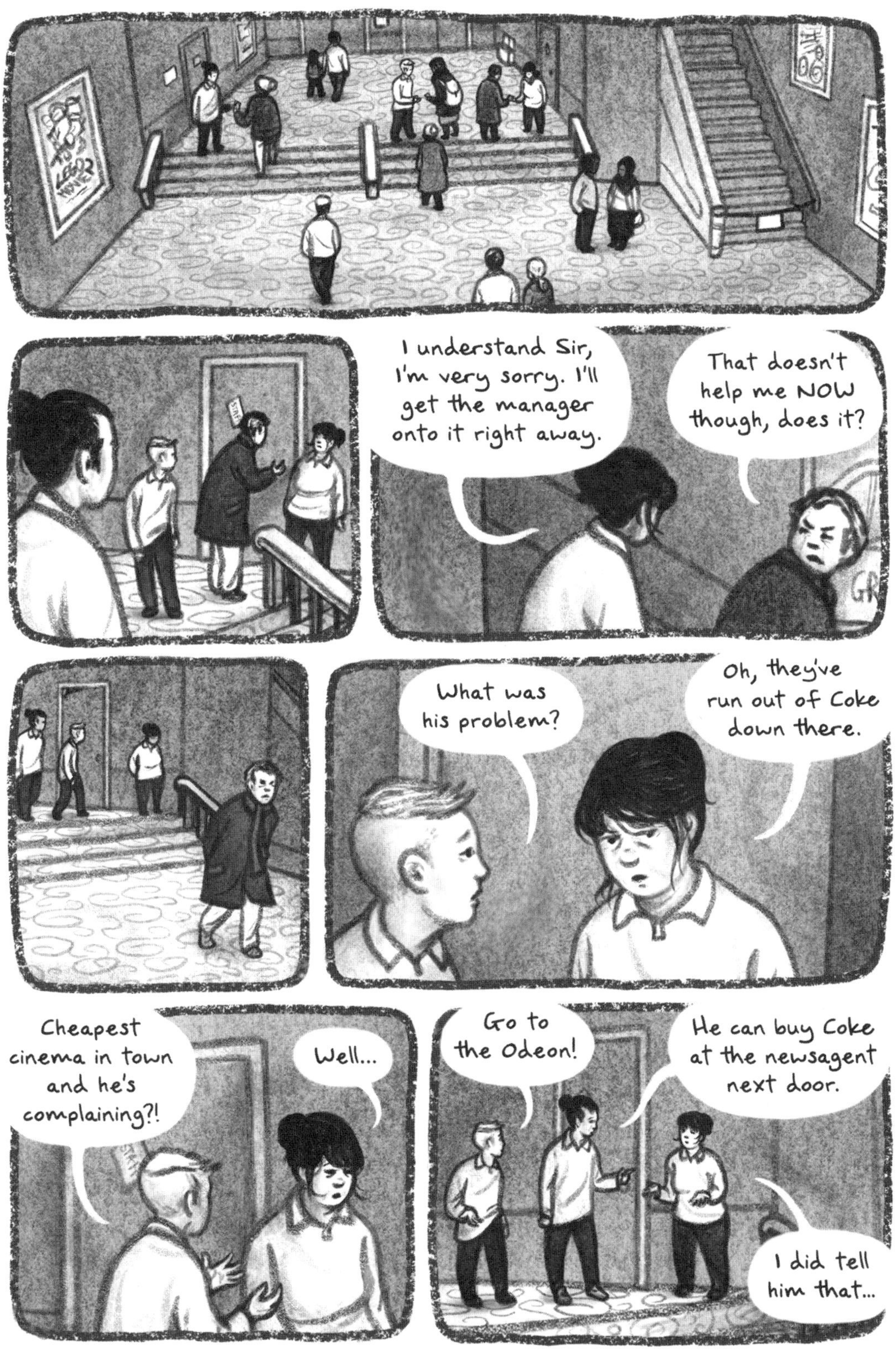
I understand Sir, I'm very sorry. I'll get the manager onto it right away.
That doesn't help me NOW though, does it?
What was his problem?
Oh, they've run out of Coke down there.
Cheapest cinema in town and he's complaining?!
Well...
Go to the Odeon!
He can buy Coke at the newsagent next door.
I did tell him that...

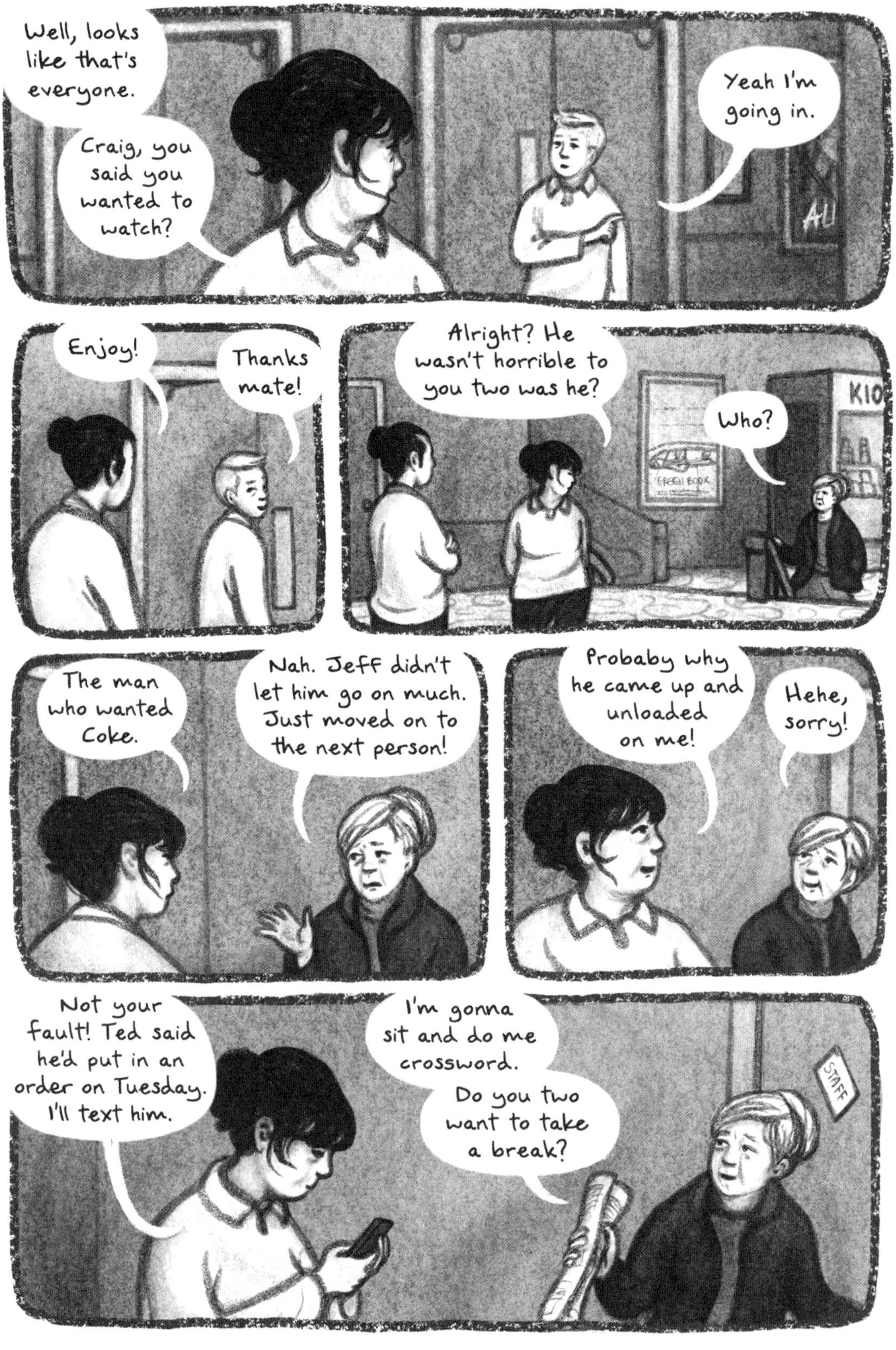
Well, looks like that's everyone.
Craig, you said you wanted to watch?
Yeah I'm going in.
Enjoy!
Thanks mate!
Alright? He wasn't horrible to you two was he?
Who?
GREEN BOOK
The man who wanted Coke.
Nah. Jeff didn't let him go on much. Just moved on to the next person!
Probaby why he came up and unloaded on me!
Hehe, sorry!
Not your fault! Ted said he'd put in an order on Tuesday. I'll text him.
I'm gonna sit and do me crossword.
Do you two want to take a break?
STAFF

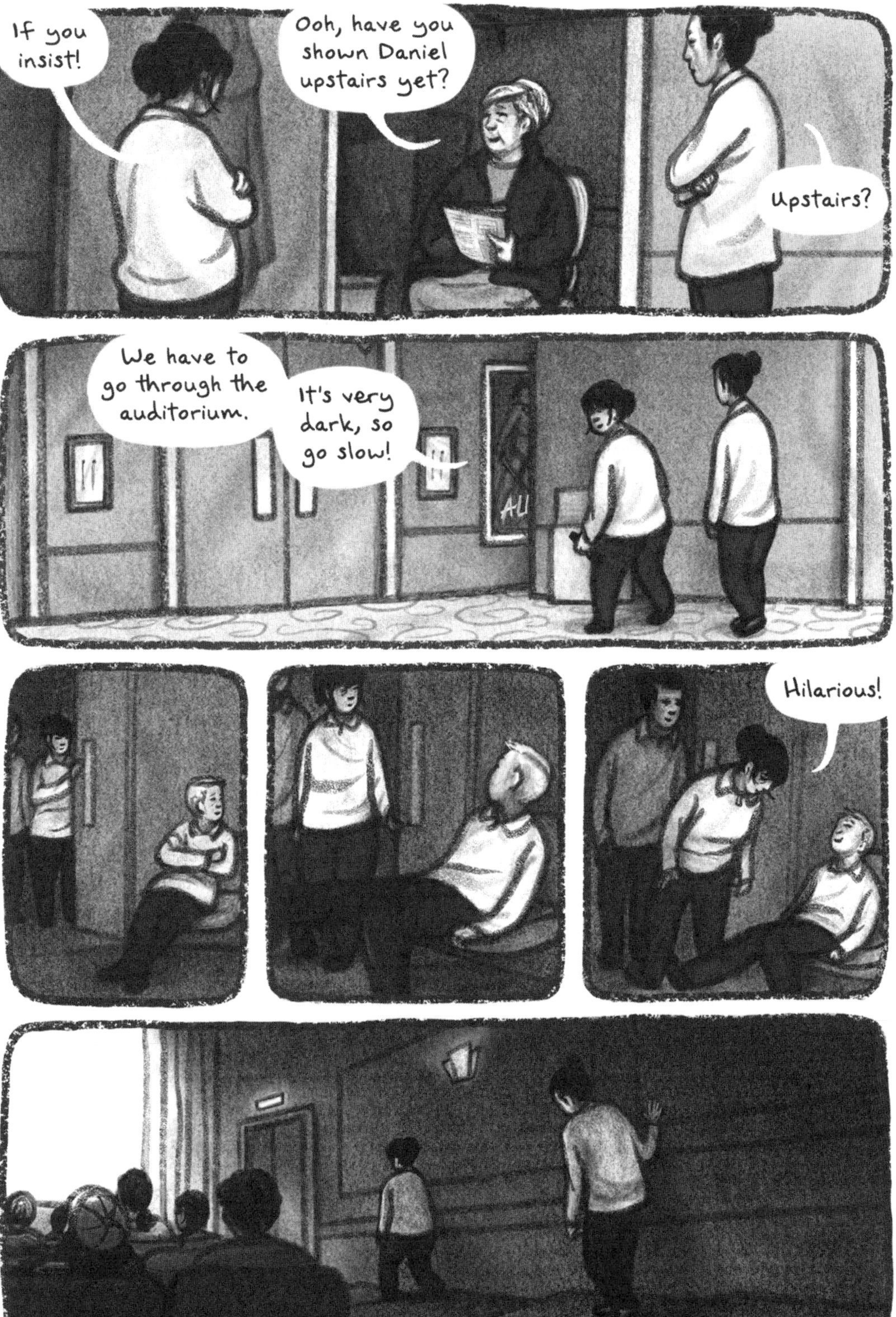
If you insist!
Ooh, have you shown Daniel upstairs yet?
Upstairs?
We have to go through the auditorium.
It's very dark, so go slow!
AU
Hilarious!

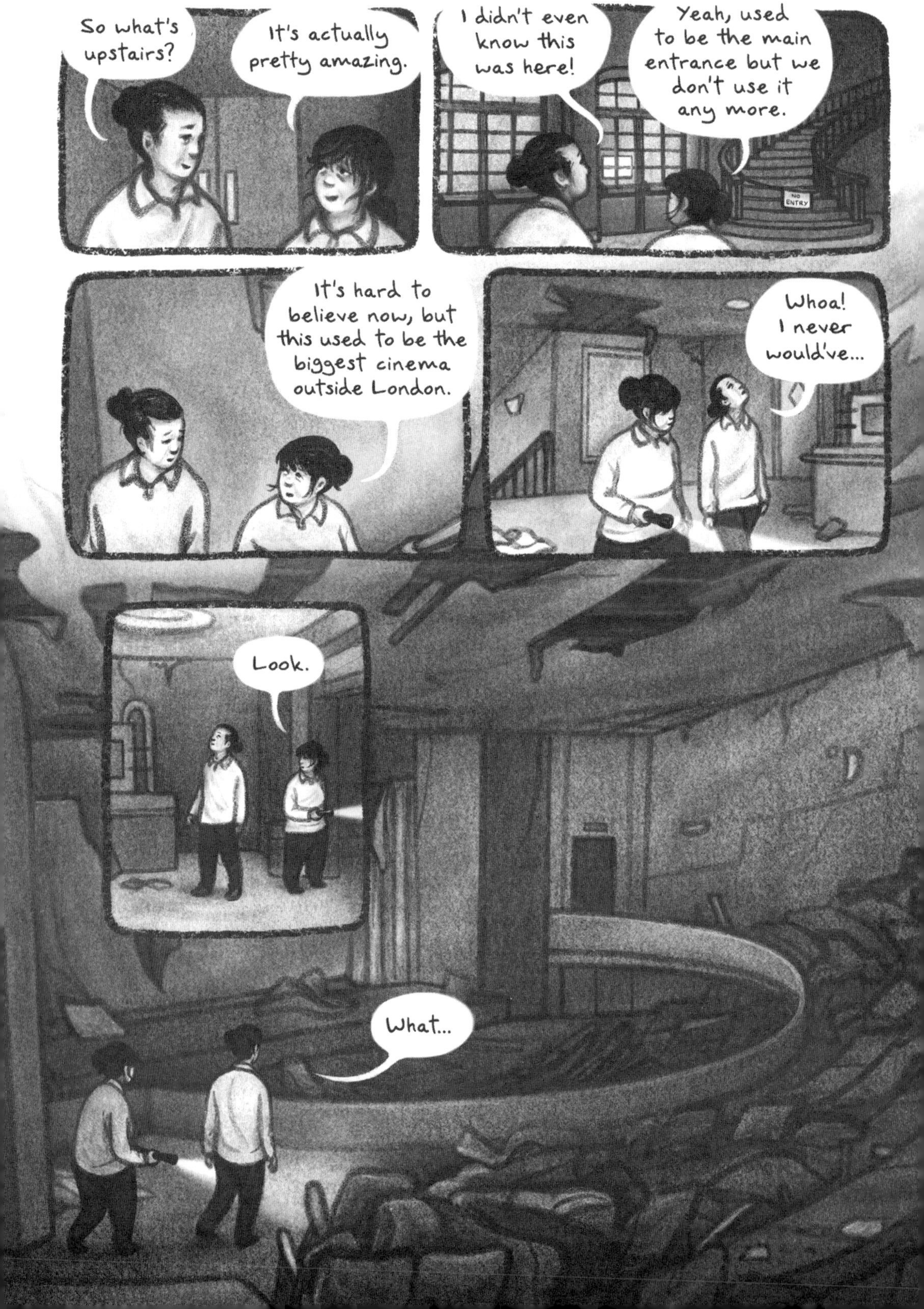

So what's upstairs?
It's actually pretty amazing.
I didn't even know this was here!
Yeah, used to be the main entrance but we don't use it any more.
NO ENTRY
It's hard to believe now, but this used to be the biggest cinema outside London.
Whoa! I never would've...
Look.
What...

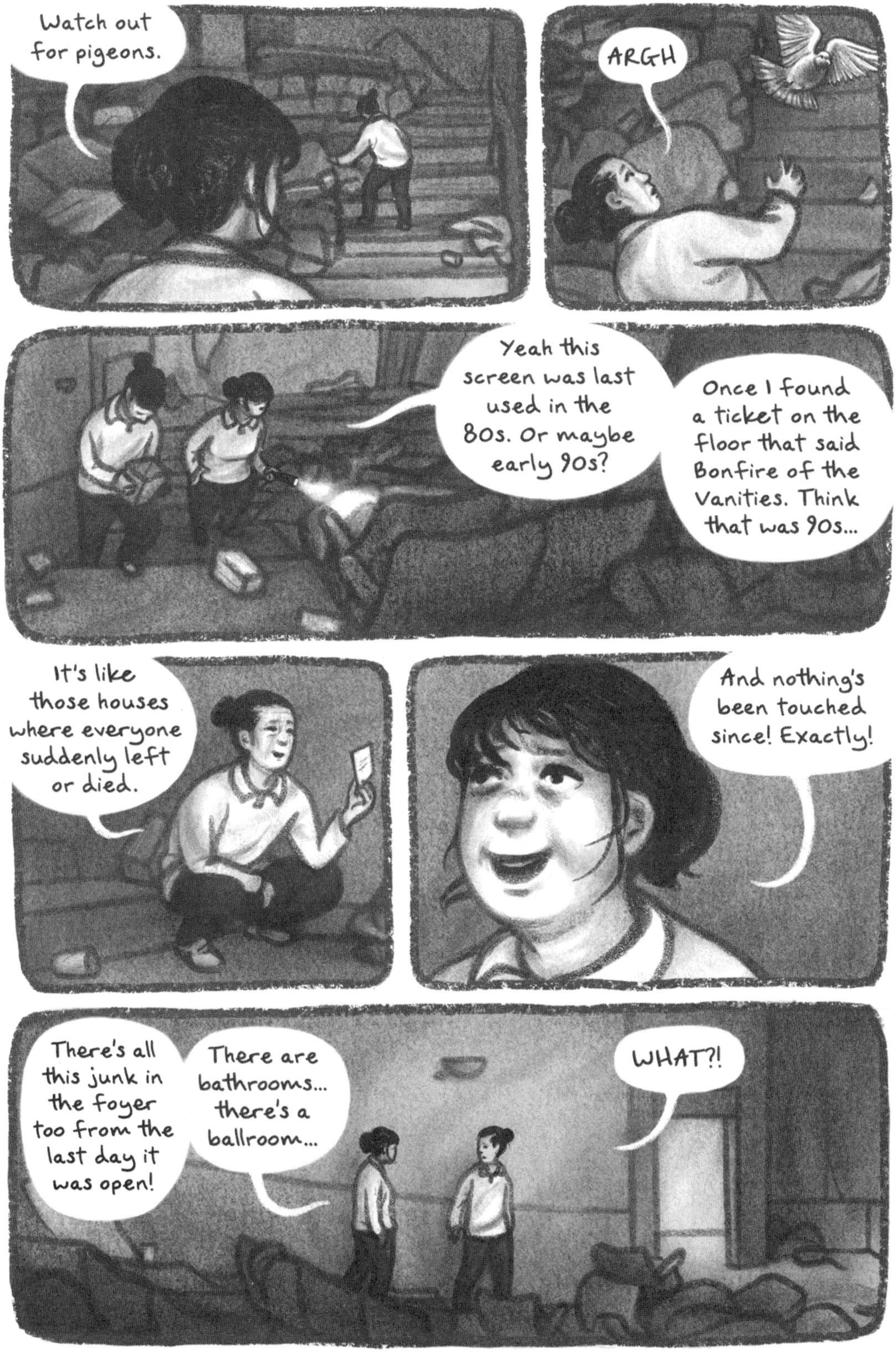
Watch out for pigeons.
ARGH
Yeah this screen was last used in the 80s. Or maybe early 90s?
Once I found a ticket on the floor that said Bonfire of the Vanities. Think that was 90s...
It's like those houses where everyone suddenly left or died.
And nothing's been touched since! Exactly!
There's all this junk in the foyer too from the last day it was open!
There are bathrooms... there's a ballroom...
WHAT?!

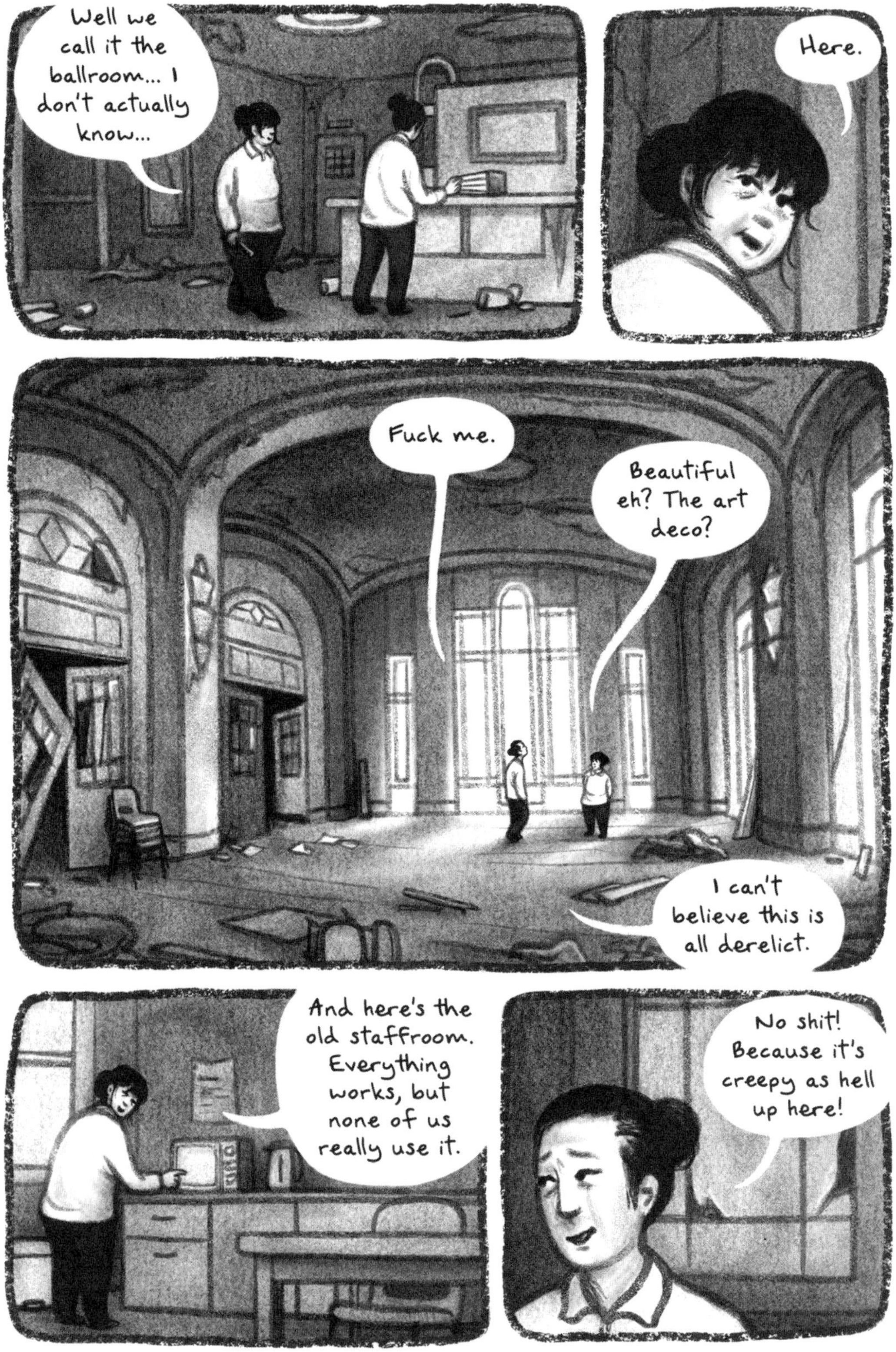
Well we call it the ballroom... I don't actually know...
Here.
Fuck me.
Beautiful eh? The art deco?
I can't believe this is all derelict.
And here's the old staffroom. Everything works, but none of us really use it.
No shit! Because it's creepy as hell up here!

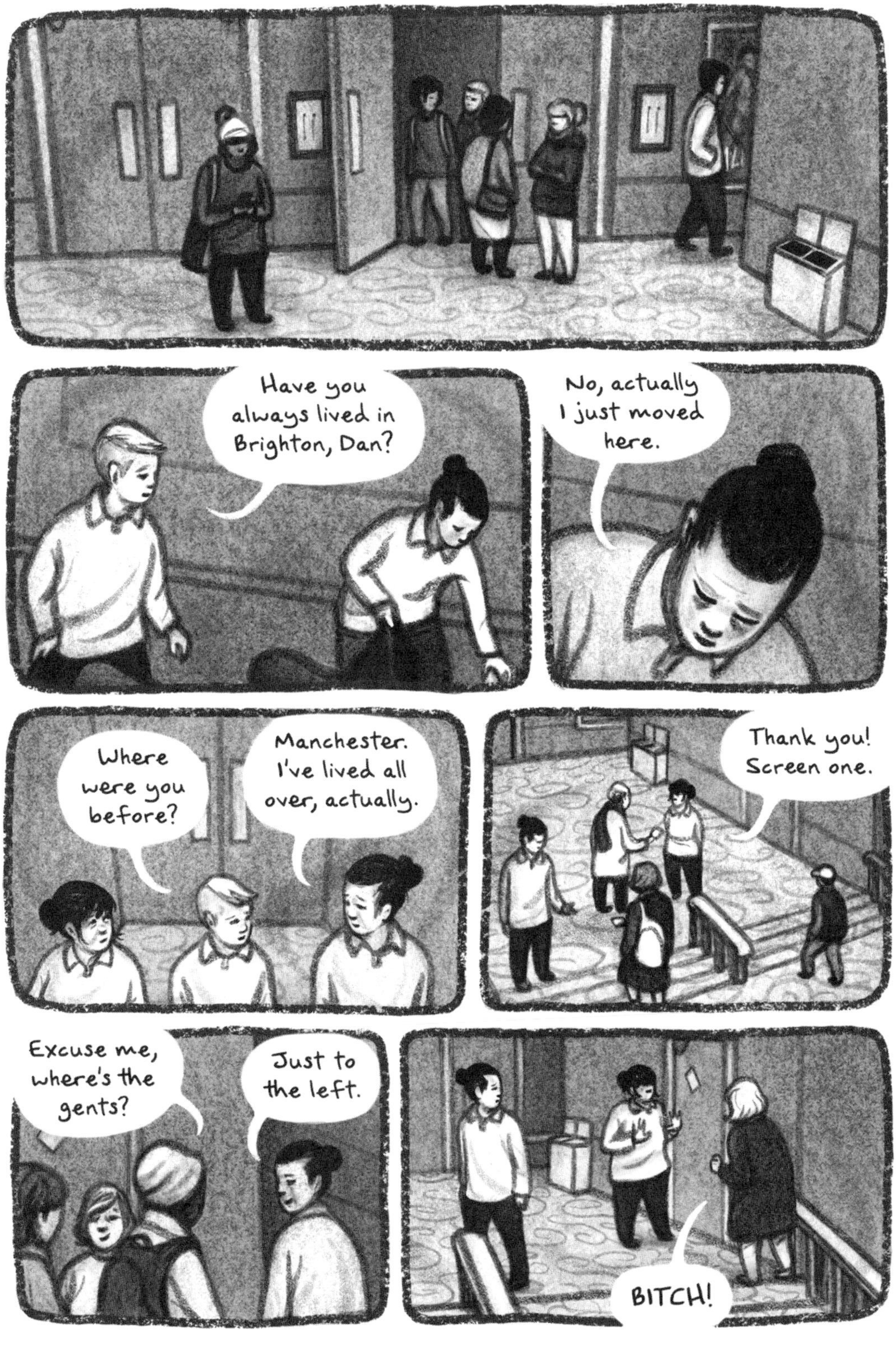
Have you always lived in Brighton, Dan?
No, actually I just moved here.
Where were you before?
Manchester. I've lived all over, actually.
Thank you! Screen one.
Excuse me, where's the gents?
Just to the left.
BITCH!

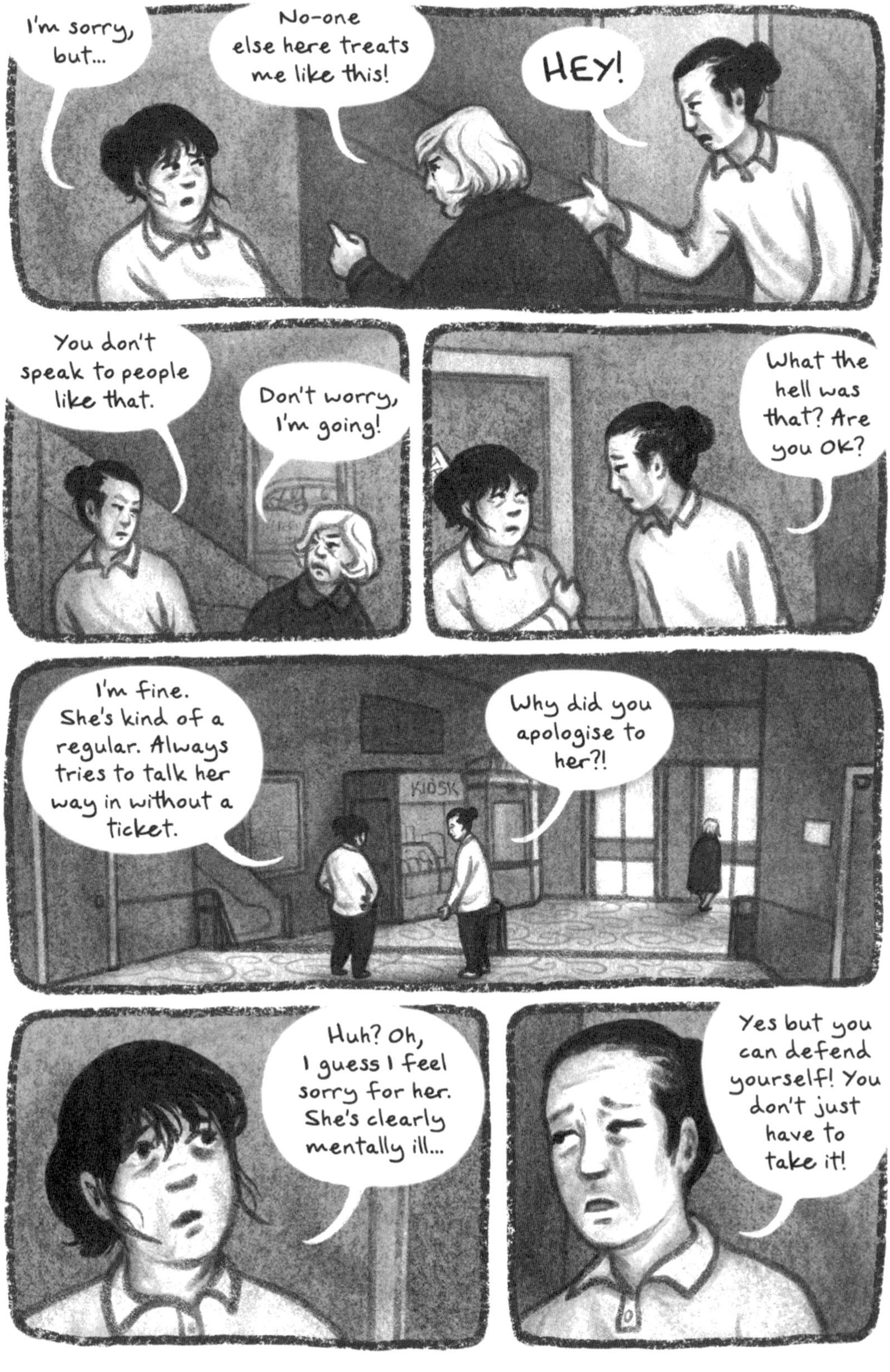

I'm sorry, but...
No-one else here treats me like this!
HEY!
You don't speak to people like that.
Don't worry, I'm going!
What the hell was that? Are you OK?
I'm fine. She's kind of a regular. Always tries to talk her way in without a ticket.
Why did you apologise to her?!
KIOSK
Huh? Oh, I guess I feel sorry for her. She's clearly mentally ill...
Yes but you can defend yourself! You don't just have to take it!

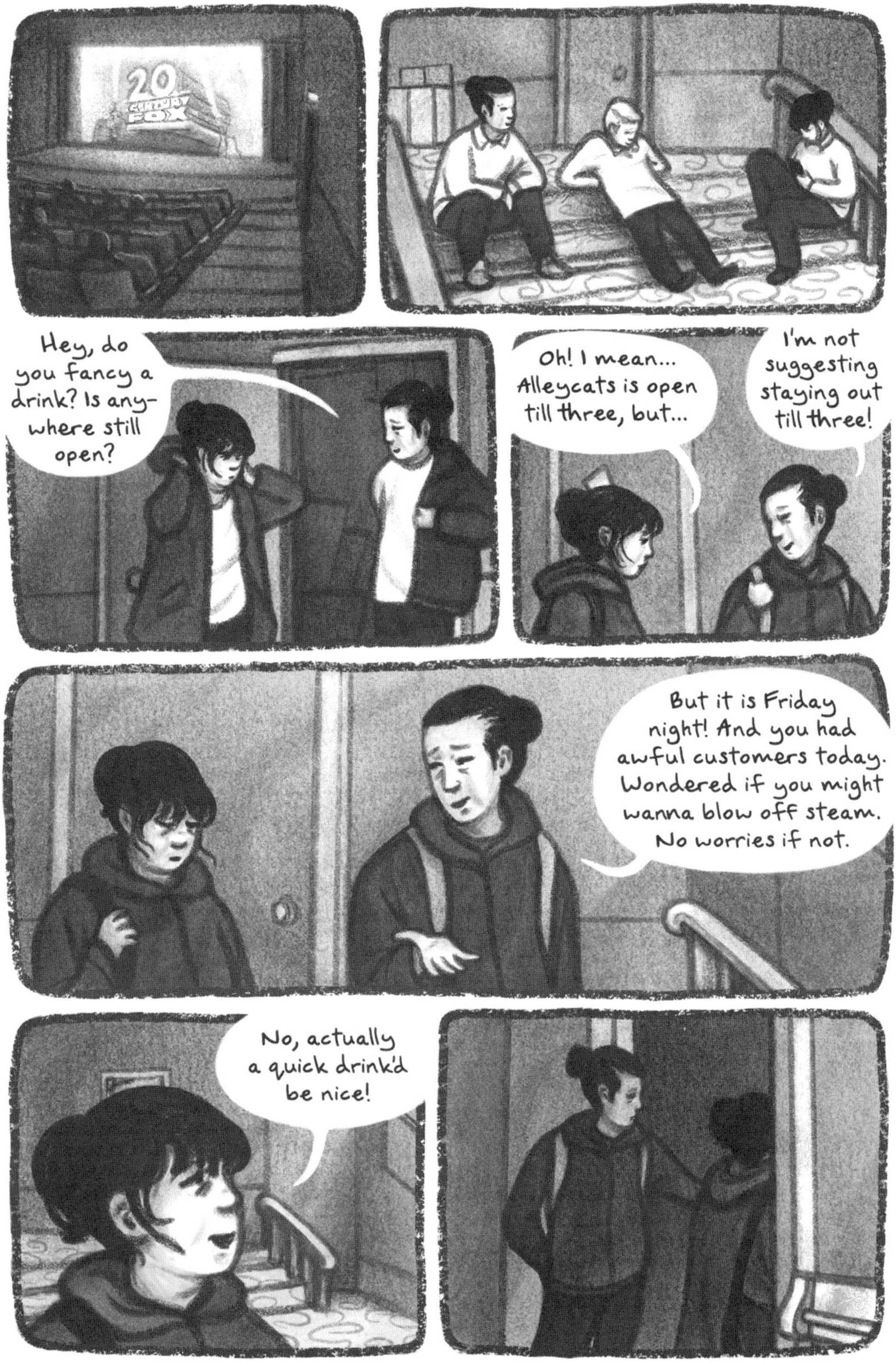

20 CENTURY FOX
Hey, do you fancy a drink? Is anywhere still open?
Oh! I mean... Alleycats is open till three, but...
I'm not suggesting staying out till three!
But it is Friday night! And you had awful customers today. Wondered if you might wanna blow off steam. No worries if not.
No, actually a quick drink'd be nice!

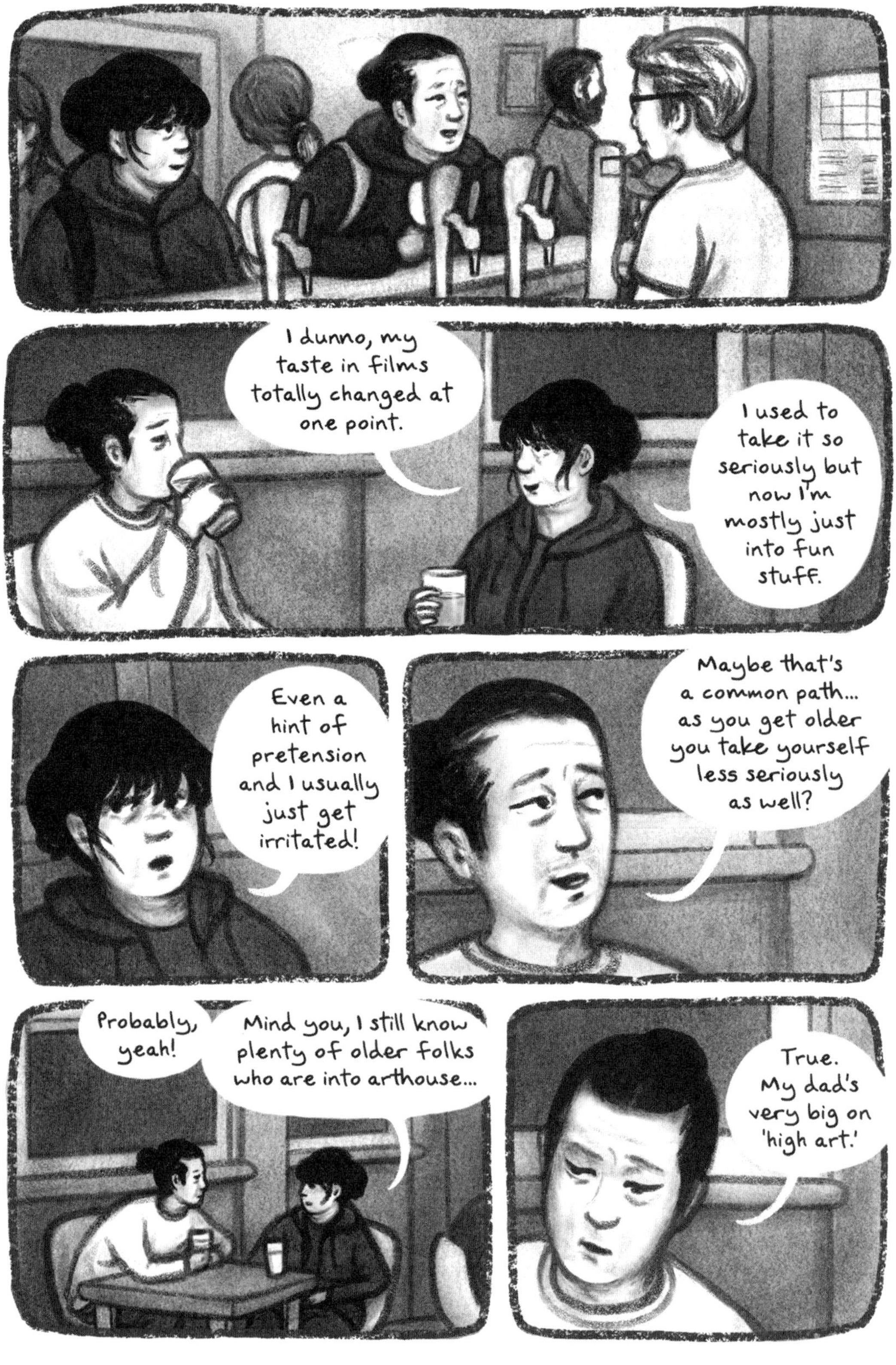
I dunno, my taste in films totally changed at one point.
I used to take it so seriously but now I'm mostly just into fun stuff.
Even a hint of pretension and I usually just get irritated!
Maybe that's a common path... as you get older you take yourself less seriously as well?
Probably, yeah!
Mind you, I still know plenty of older folks who are into arthouse...
True. My dad's very big on 'high art.'

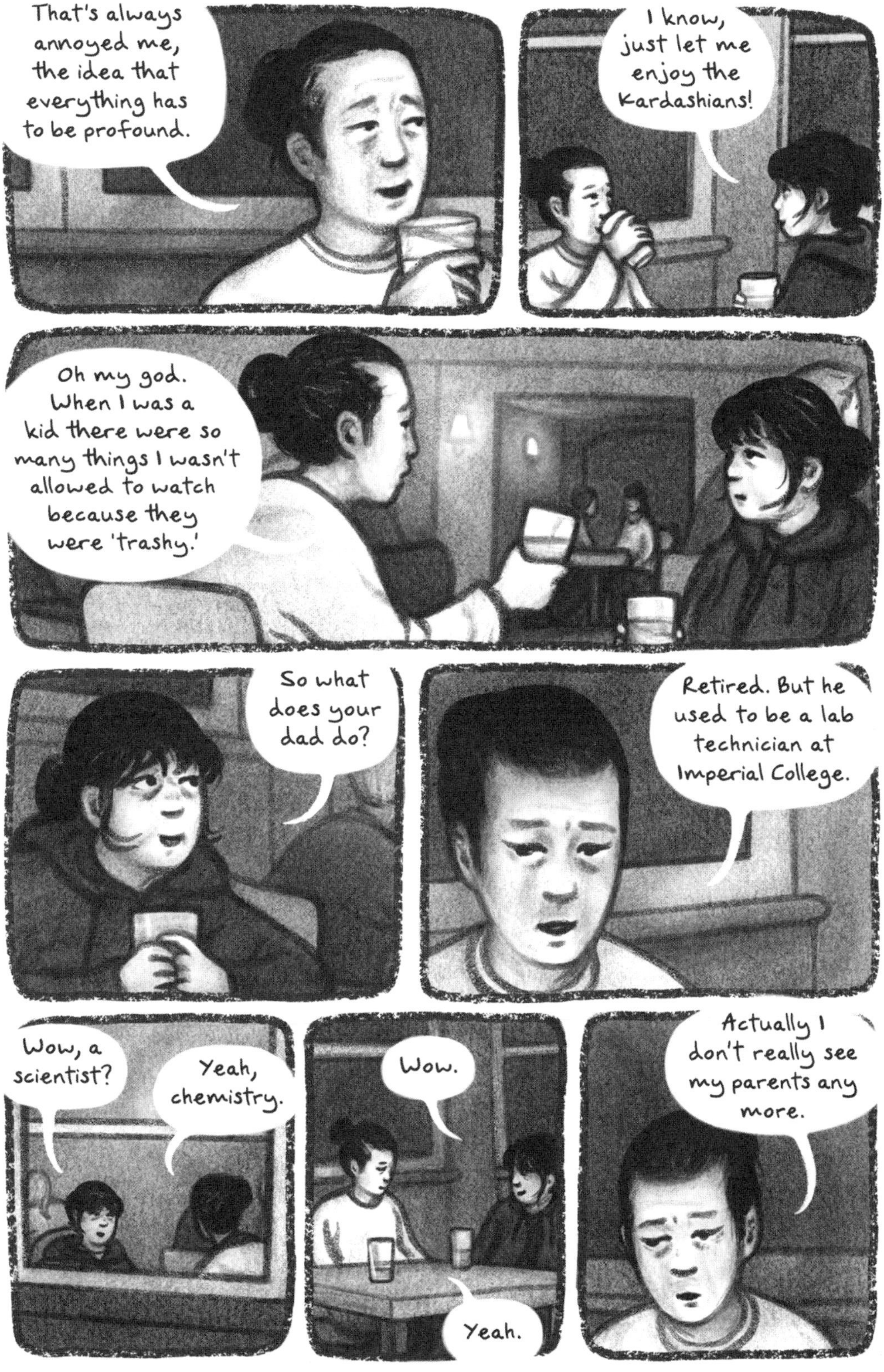
That's always annoyed me, the idea that everything has to be profound.
I know, just let me enjoy the Kardashians!
Oh my god. When I was a kid there were so many things I wasn't allowed to watch because they were 'trashy.'
So what does your dad do?
Retired. But he used to be a lab technician at Imperial College.
Wow, a scientist?
Yeah, chemistry.
Wow.
Yeah.
Actually I don't really see my parents any more.

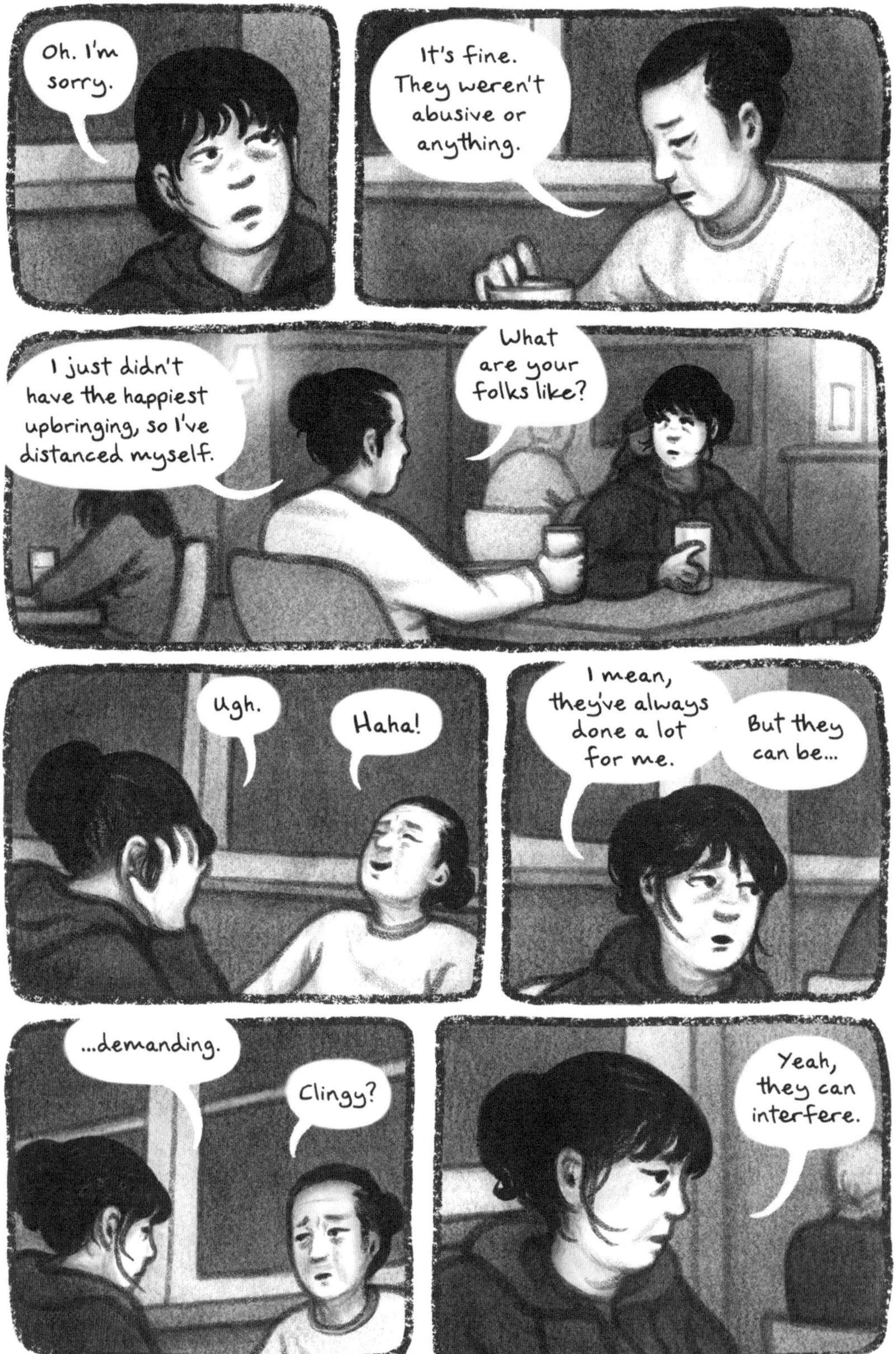
Oh. I'm sorry.
It's fine. They weren't abusive or anything.
I just didn't have the happiest upbringing, so I've distanced myself.
What are your folks like?
Ugh.
Haha!
I mean, they've always done a lot for me.
But they can be...
...demanding.
Clingy?
Yeah, they can interfere.

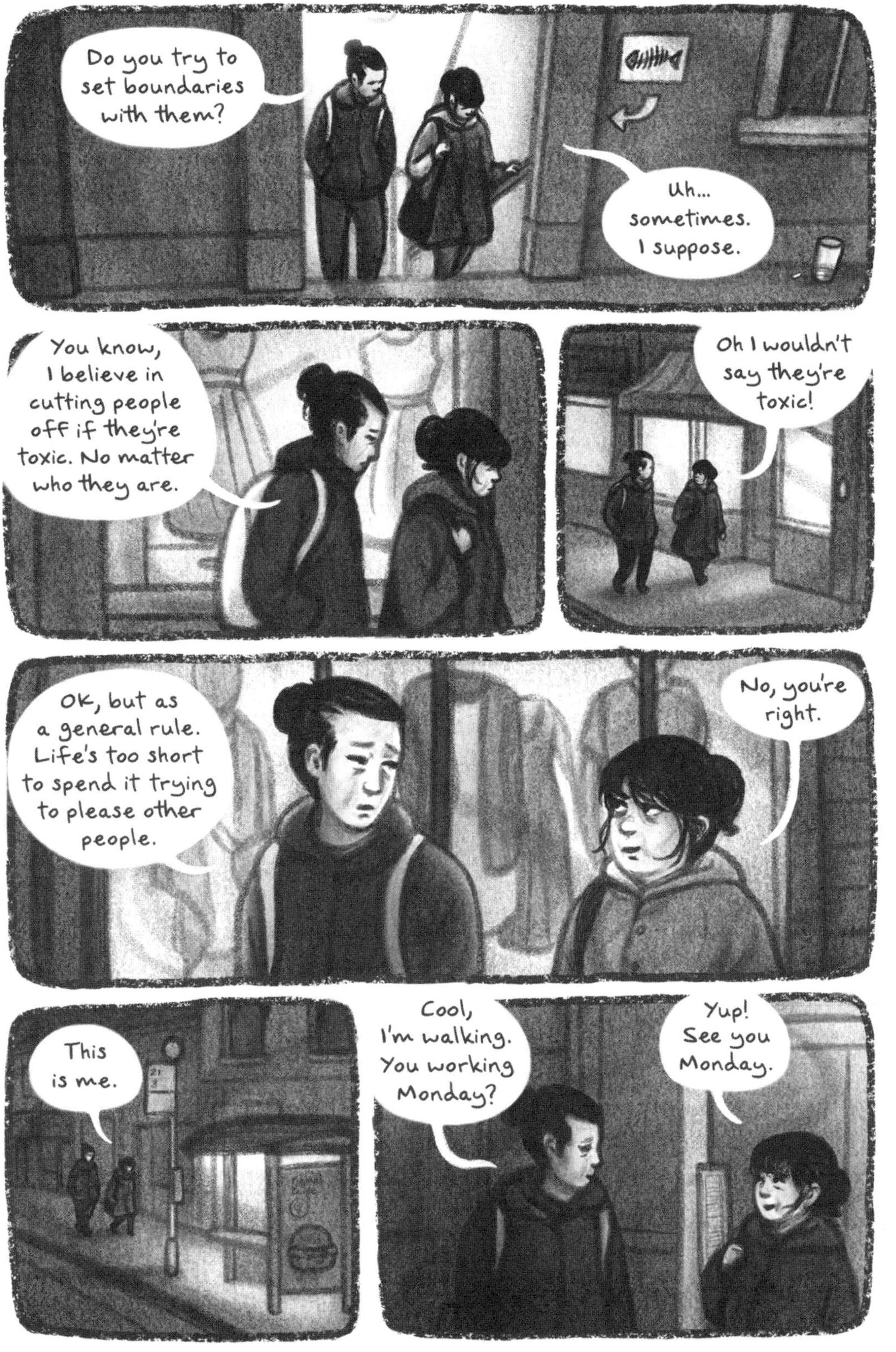
Do you try to set boundaries with them?
Uh... sometimes. I suppose.
You know, I believe in cutting people off if they're toxic. No matter who they are.
Oh I wouldn't say they're toxic!
OK, but as a general rule. Life's too short to spend it trying to please other people.
No, you're right.
This is me.
Cool, I'm walking. You working Monday?
Yup! See you Monday.

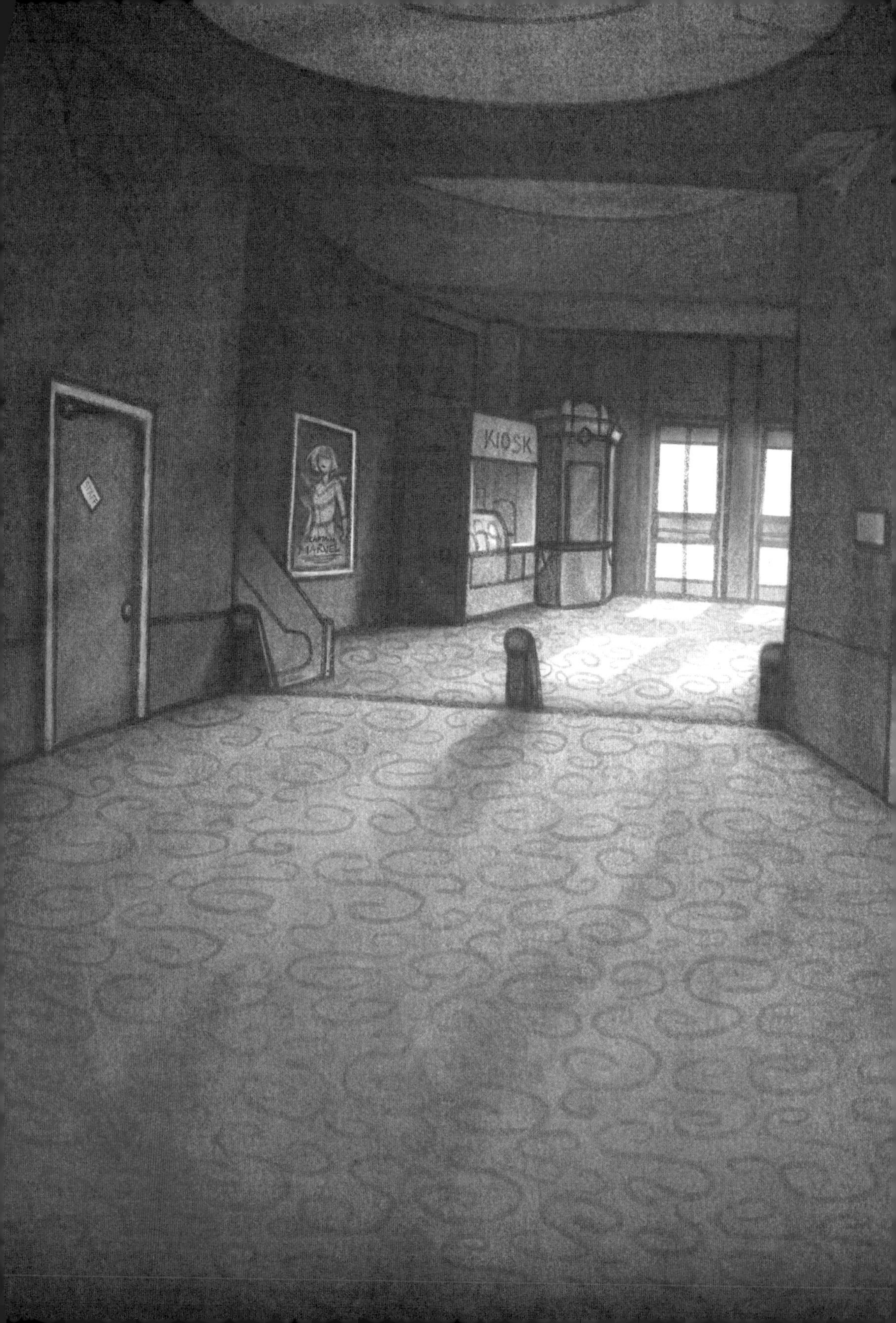
STAFF
CAPTAIN
MARVEL
KIOSK

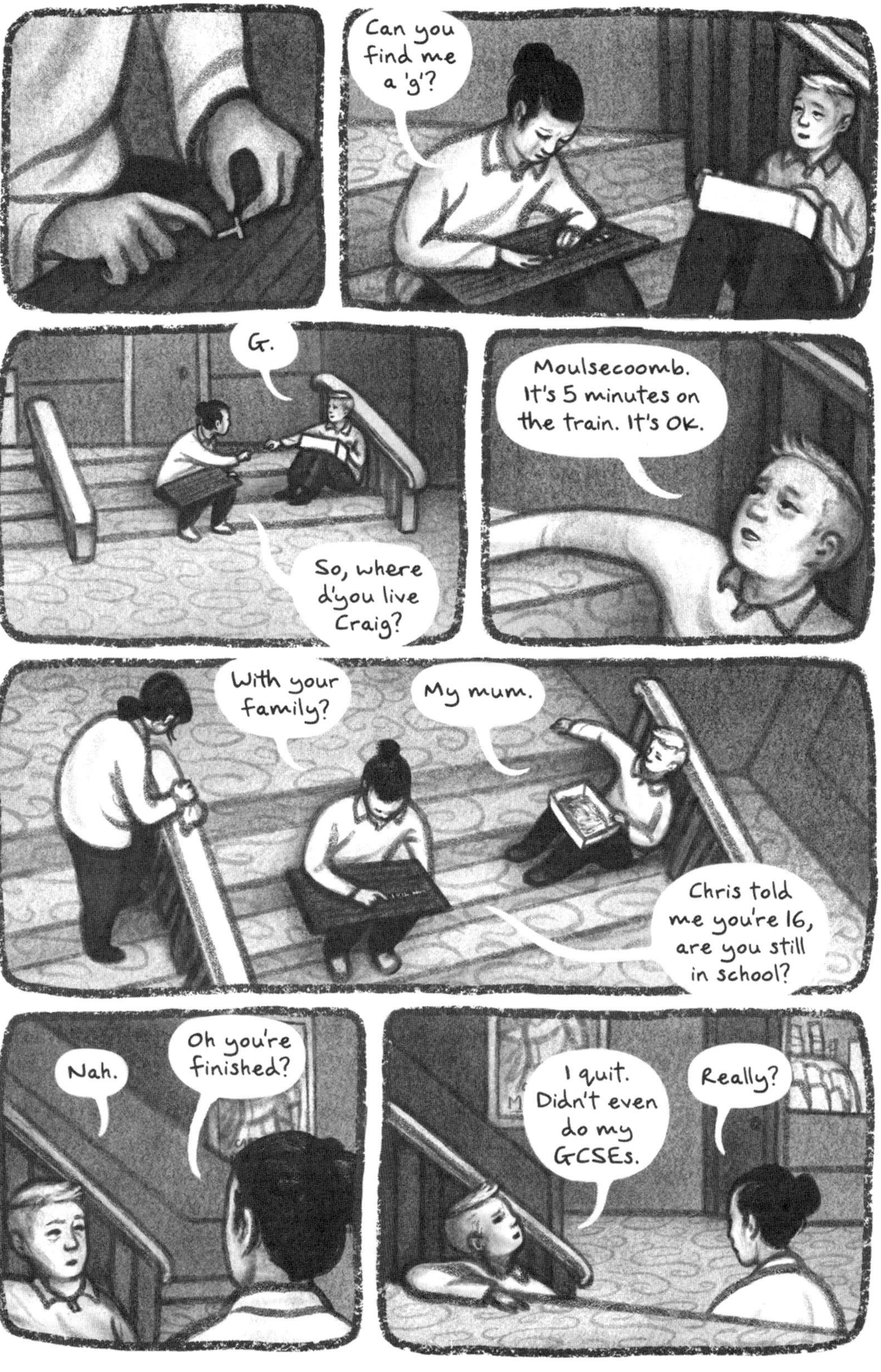
Can you find me a 'g'?
G.
So, where d'you live Craig?
Moulsecoomb. It's 5 minutes on the train. It's OK.
With your family?
My mum.
Chris told me you're 16, are you still in school?
Nah.
Oh you're finished?
I quit. Didn't even do my GCSEs.
Really?

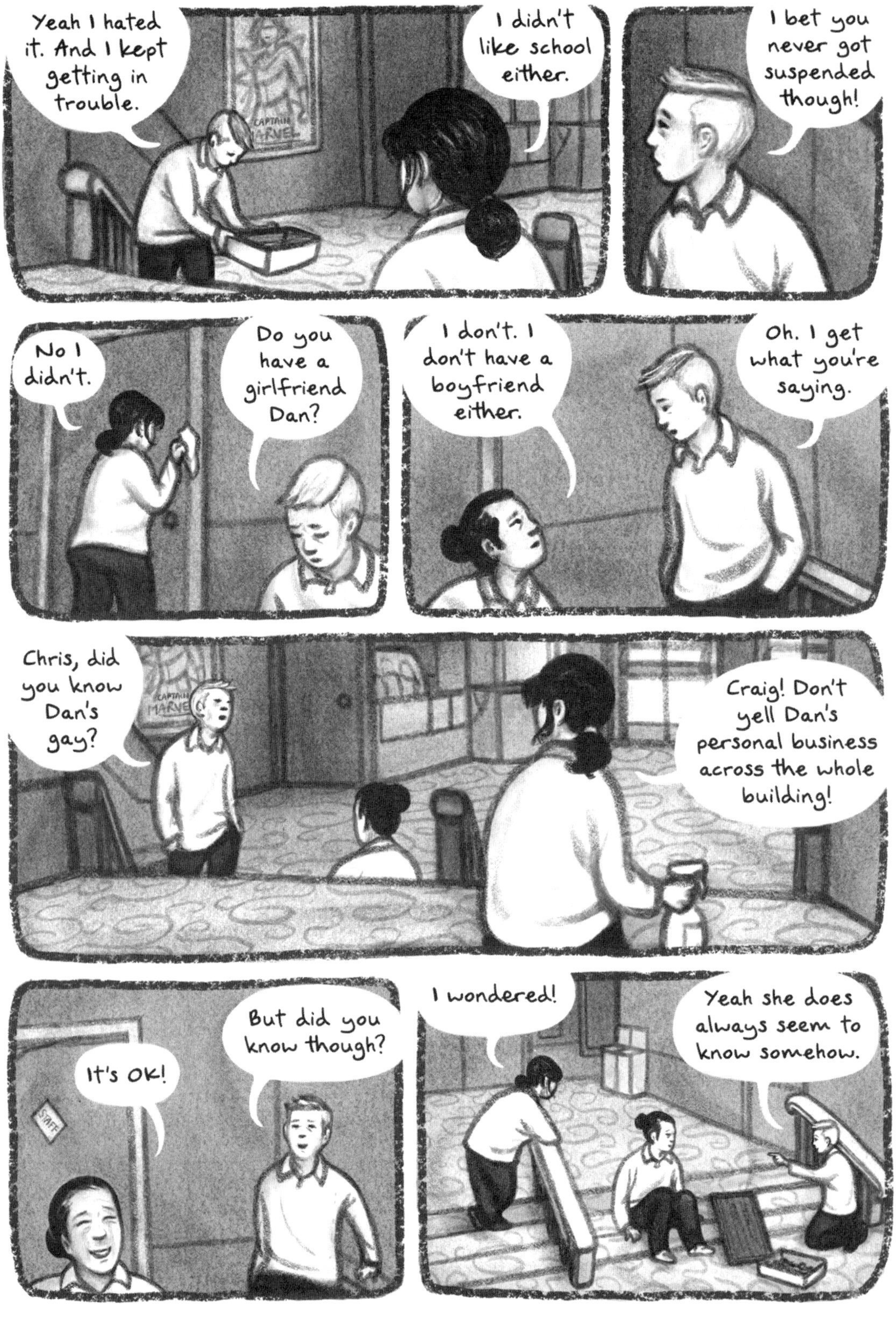
Yeah I hated it. And I kept getting in trouble.
I didn't like school either.
I bet you never got suspended though!
No I didn't.
Do you have a girlfriend Dan?
I don't. I don't have a boyfriend either.
Oh. I get what you're saying.
Chris, did you know Dan's gay?
Craig! Don't yell Dan's personal business across the whole building!
It's OK!
But did you know though?
I wondered!
Yeah she does always seem to know somehow.

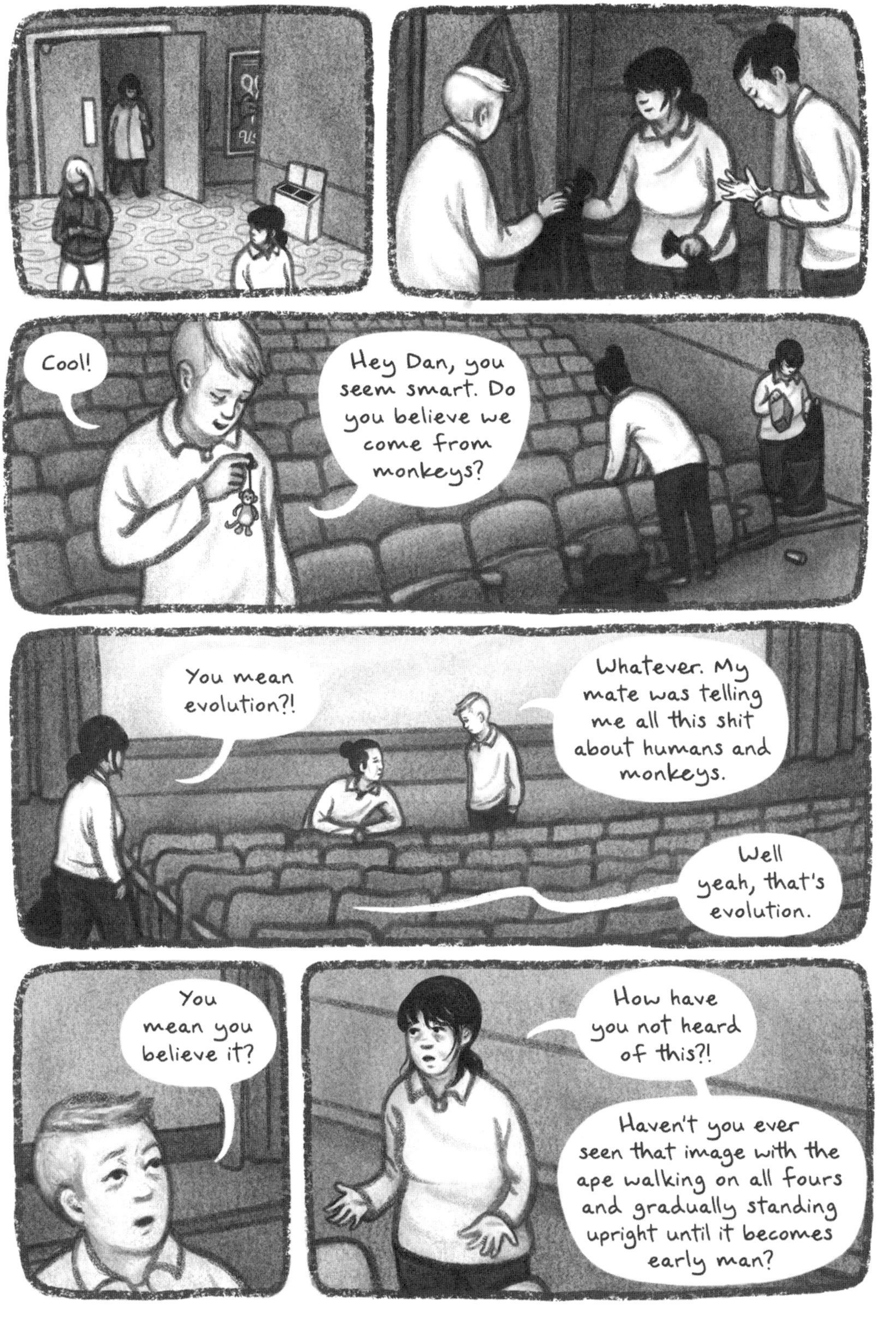
Cool!
Hey Dan, you seem smart. Do you believe we come from monkeys?
You mean evolution?!
Whatever. My mate was telling me all this shit about humans and monkeys.
Well yeah, that's evolution.
You mean you believe it?
How have you not heard of this?!
Haven't you ever seen that image with the ape walking on all fours and gradually standing upright until it becomes early man?

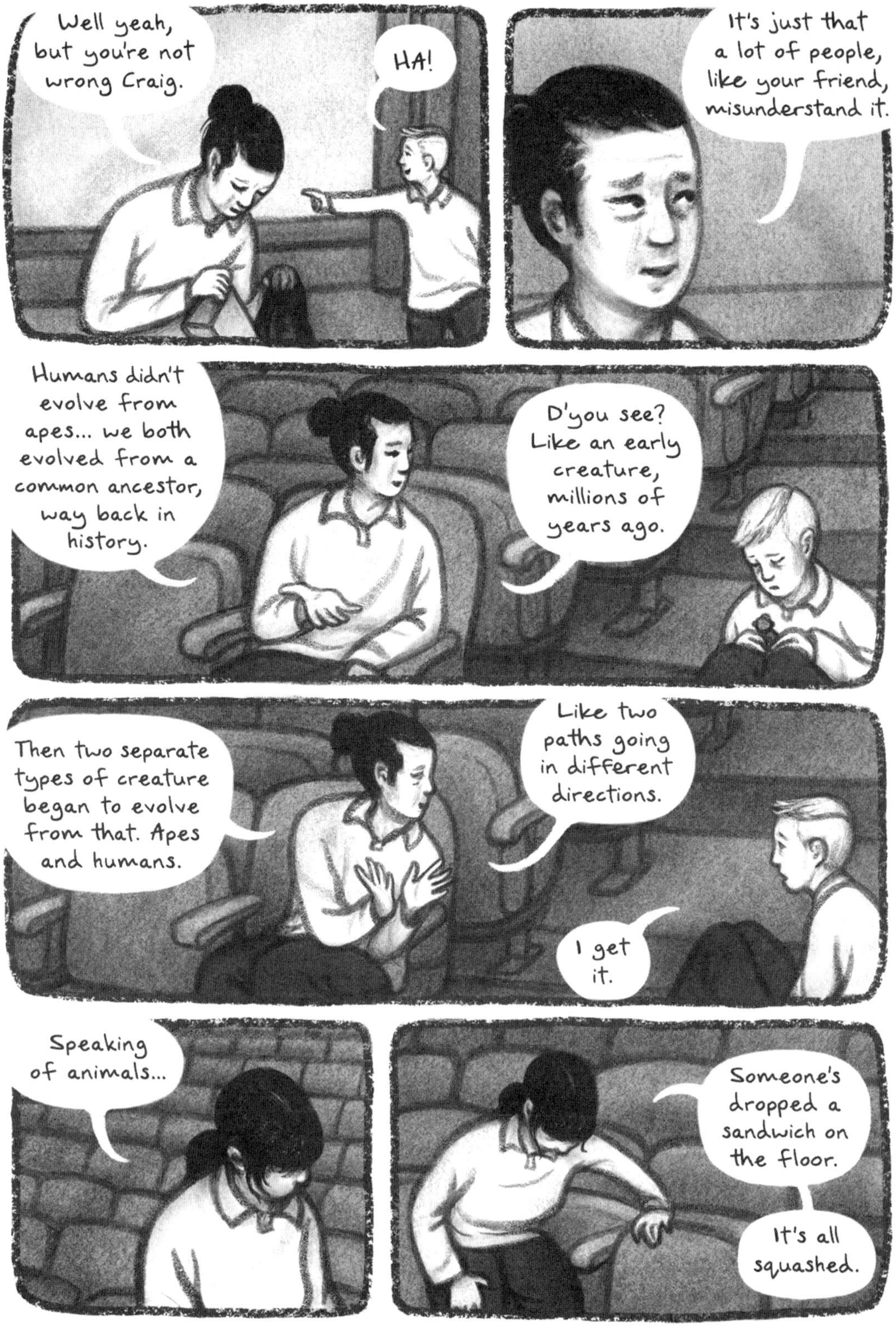
Well yeah, but you're not wrong Craig.
HA!
It's just that a lot of people, like your friend, misunderstand it.
Humans didn't evolve from apes... we both evolved from a common ancestor, way back in history.
D'you see? Like an early creature, millions of years ago.
Then two separate types of creature began to evolve from that. Apes and humans.
Like two paths going in different directions.
I get it.
Speaking of animals...
Someone's dropped a sandwich on the floor.
It's all squashed.

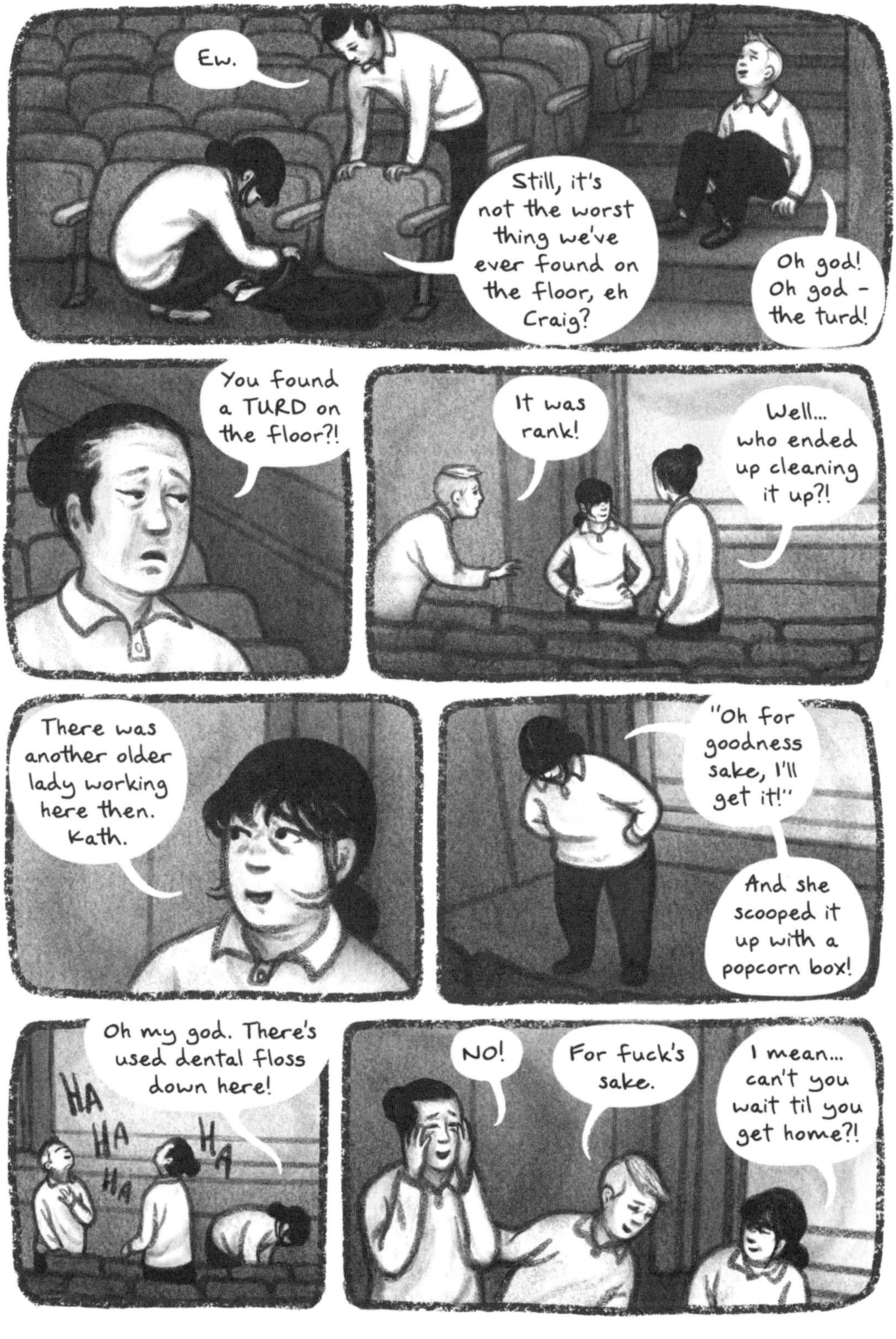
Ew.
Still, it's not the worst thing we've ever found on the floor, eh Craig?
Oh god! Oh god - the turd!
You found a TURD on the floor?!
It was rank!
Well... who ended up cleaning it up?!
There was another older lady working here then. Kath.
"Oh for goodness sake, I'll get it!"
And she scooped it up with a popcorn box!
Oh my god. There's used dental floss down here!
HA
HA
HA
HA
NO!
For fuck's sake.
I mean... can't you wait til you get home?!

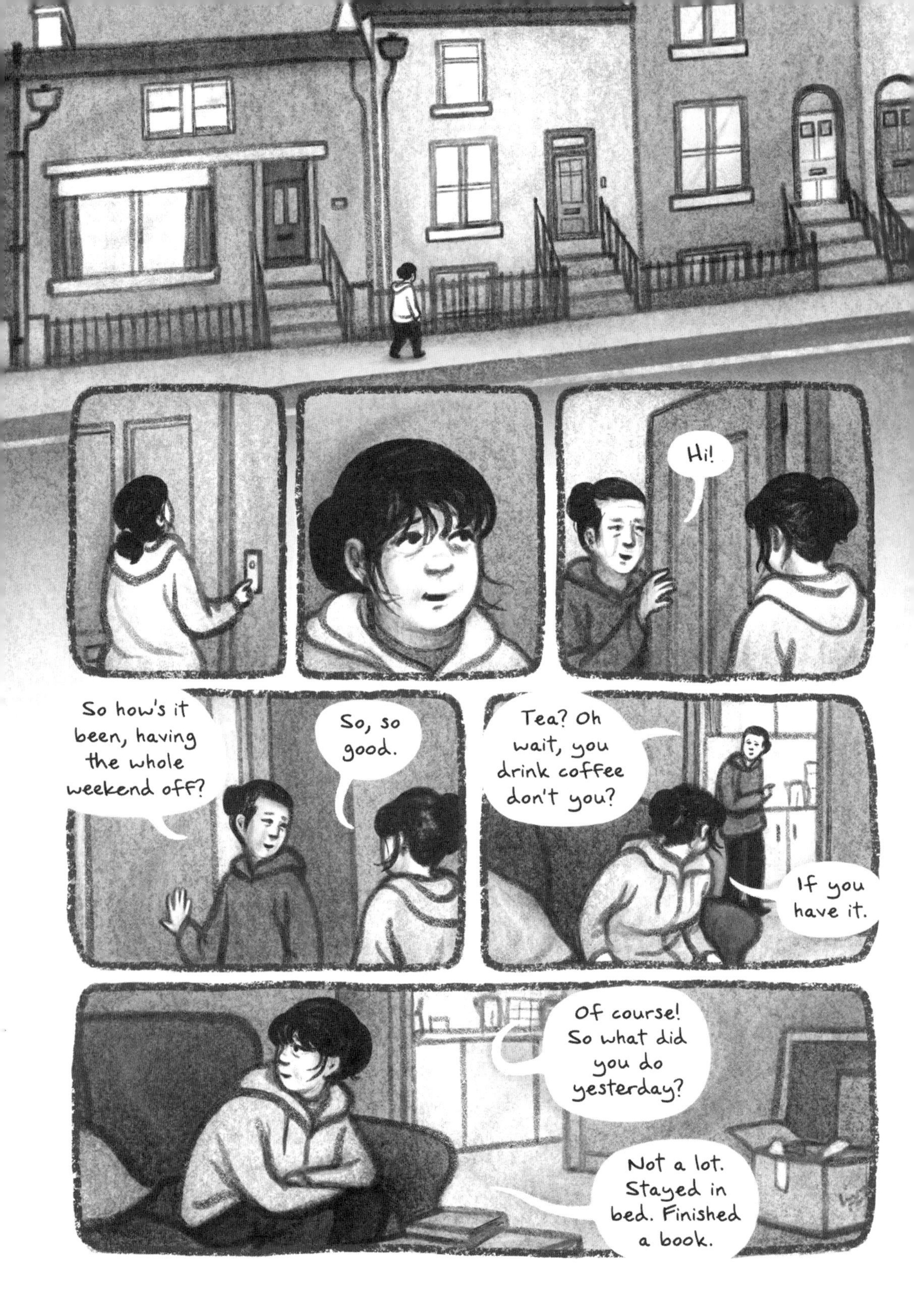
Hi!
So how's it been, having the whole weekend off?
So, so good.
Tea? Oh wait, you drink coffee don't you?
If you have it.
Of course! So what did you do yesterday?
Not a lot. Stayed in bed. Finished a book.

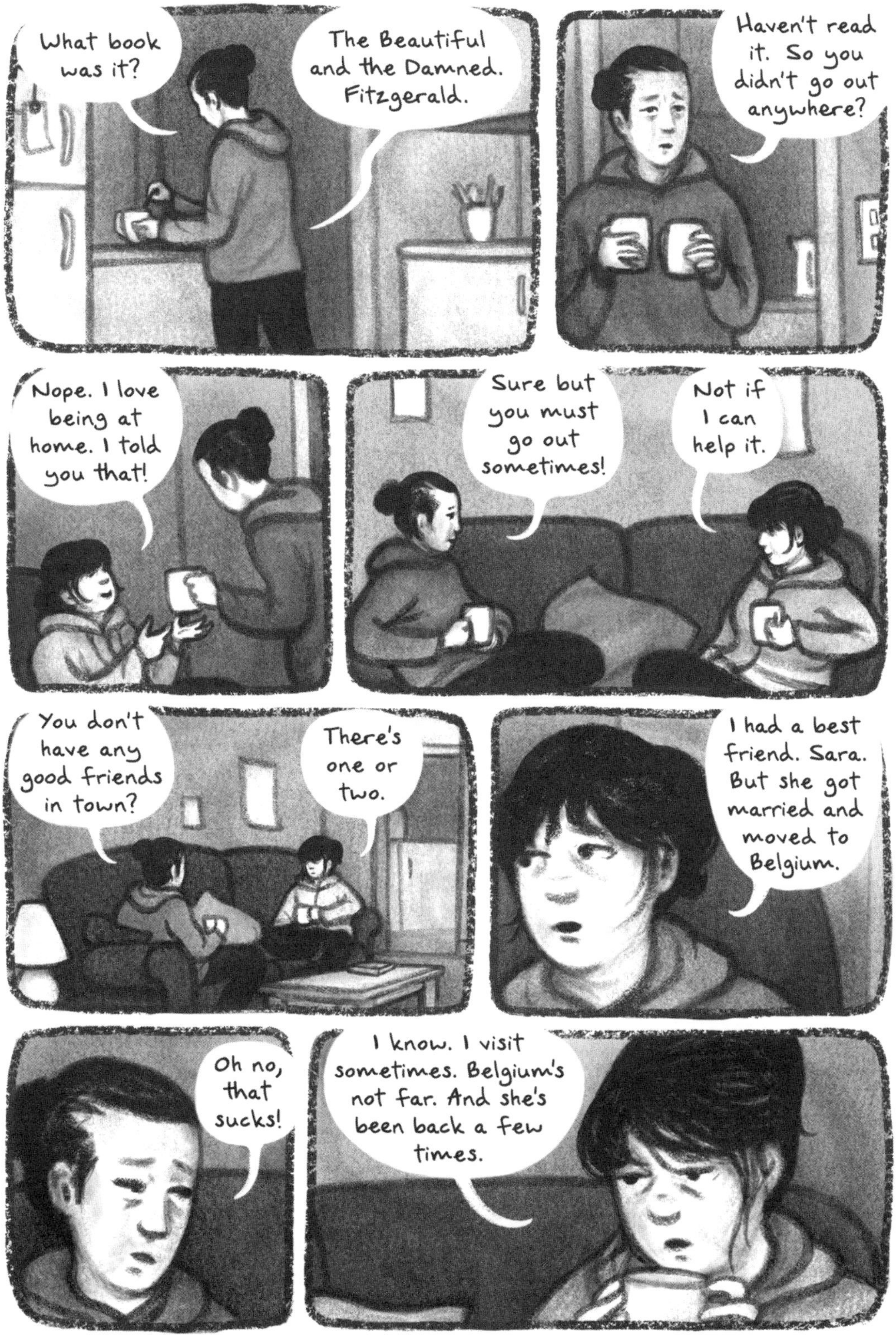
What book was it?
The Beautiful and the Damned. Fitzgerald.
Haven't read it. So you didn't go out anywhere?
Nope. I love being at home. I told you that!
Sure but you must go out sometimes!
Not if I can help it.
You don't have any good friends in town?
There's one or two.
I had a best friend. Sara. But she got married and moved to Belgium.
Oh no, that sucks!
I know. I visit sometimes. Belgium's not far. And she's been back a few times.

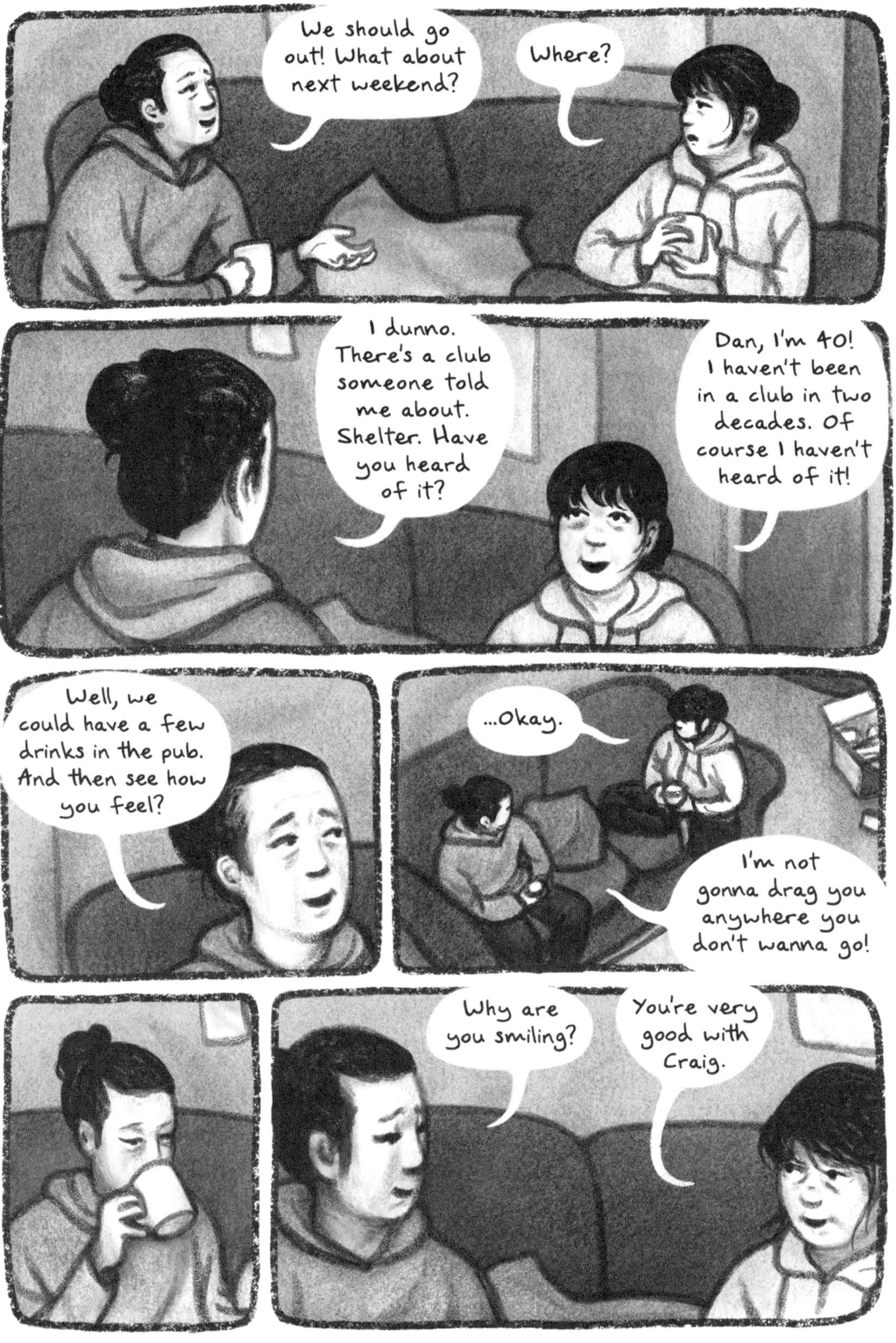
We should go out! What about next weekend?
Where?
I dunno. There's a club someone told me about. Shelter. Have you heard of it?
Dan, I'm 40! I haven't been in a club in two decades. Of course I haven't heard of it!
Well, we could have a few drinks in the pub. And then see how you feel?
...Okay.
I'm not gonna drag you anywhere you don't wanna go!
Why are you smiling?
You're very good with Craig.

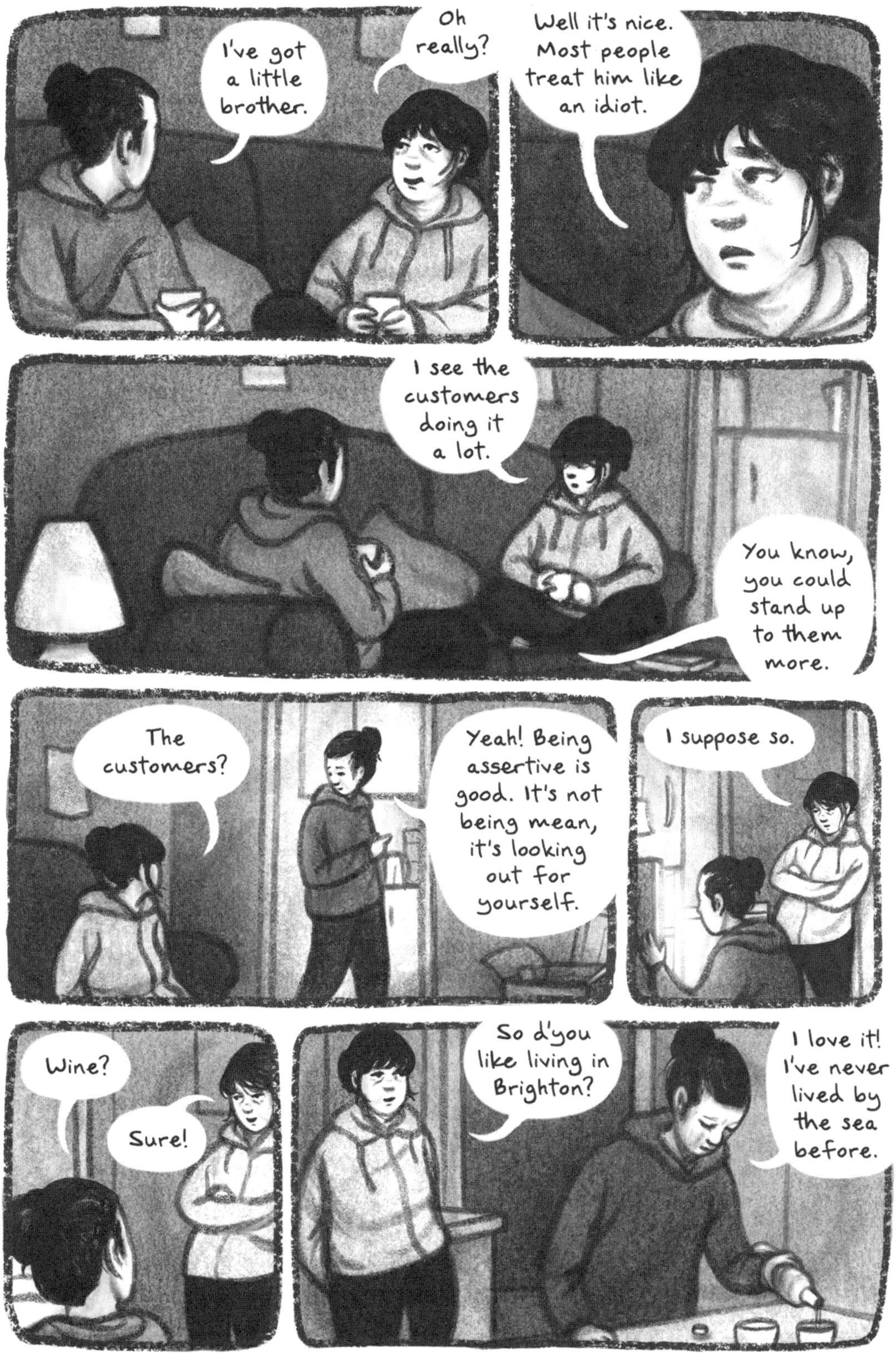
I've got a little brother.
Oh really?
Well it's nice. Most people treat him like an idiot.
I see the customers doing it a lot.
You know, you could stand up to them more.
The customers?
Yeah! Being assertive is good. It's not being mean, it's looking out for yourself.
I suppose so.
Wine?
Sure!
So d'you like living in Brighton?
I love it! I've never lived by the sea before.

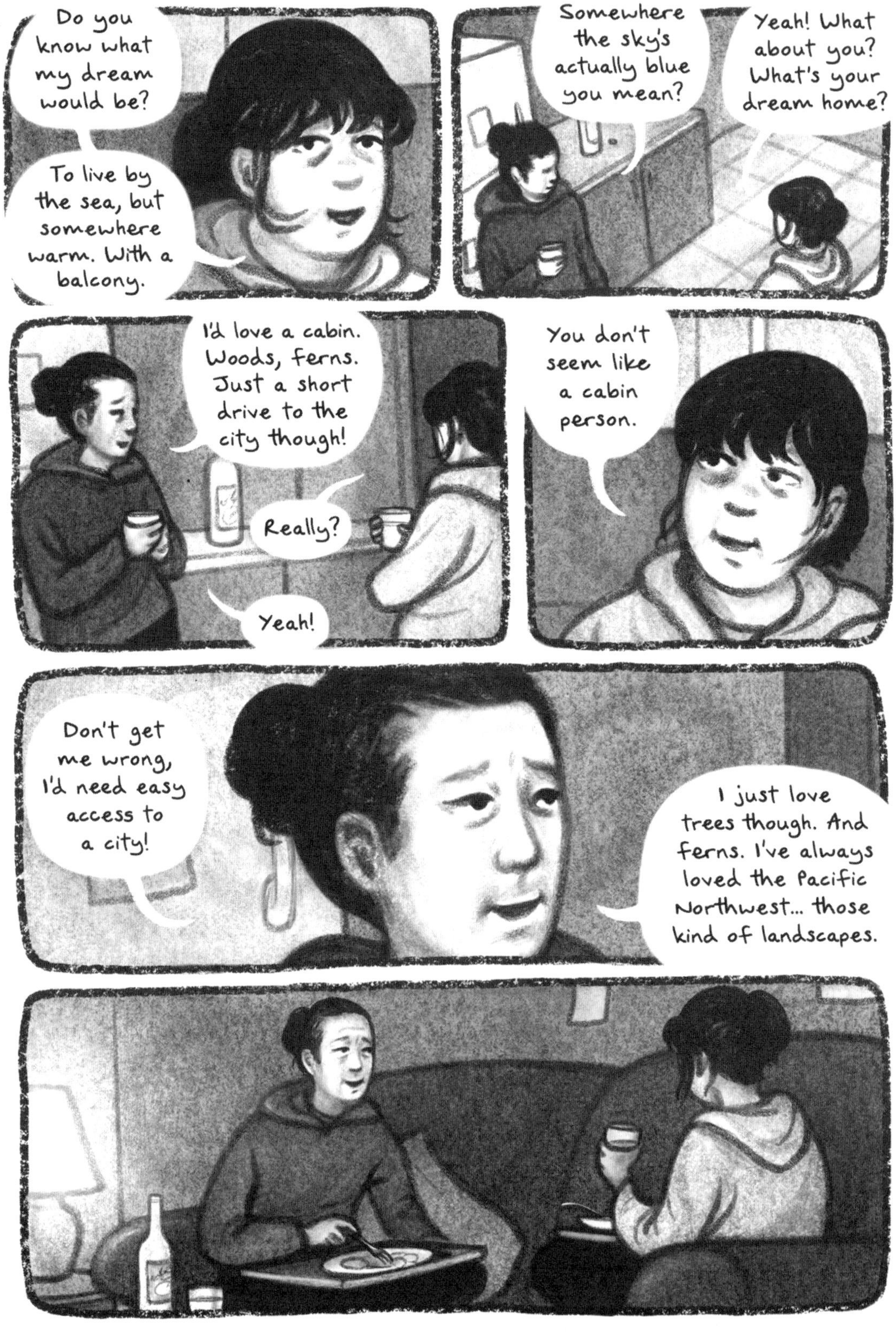
Do you know what my dream would be?
To live by the sea, but somewhere warm. With a balcony.
Somewhere the sky's actually blue you mean?
Yeah! What about you? What's your dream home?
I'd love a cabin. Woods, ferns. Just a short drive to the city though!
Really?
Yeah!
You don't seem like a cabin person.
Don't get me wrong, I'd need easy access to a city!
I just love trees though. And ferns. I've always loved the Pacific Northwest... those kind of landscapes.

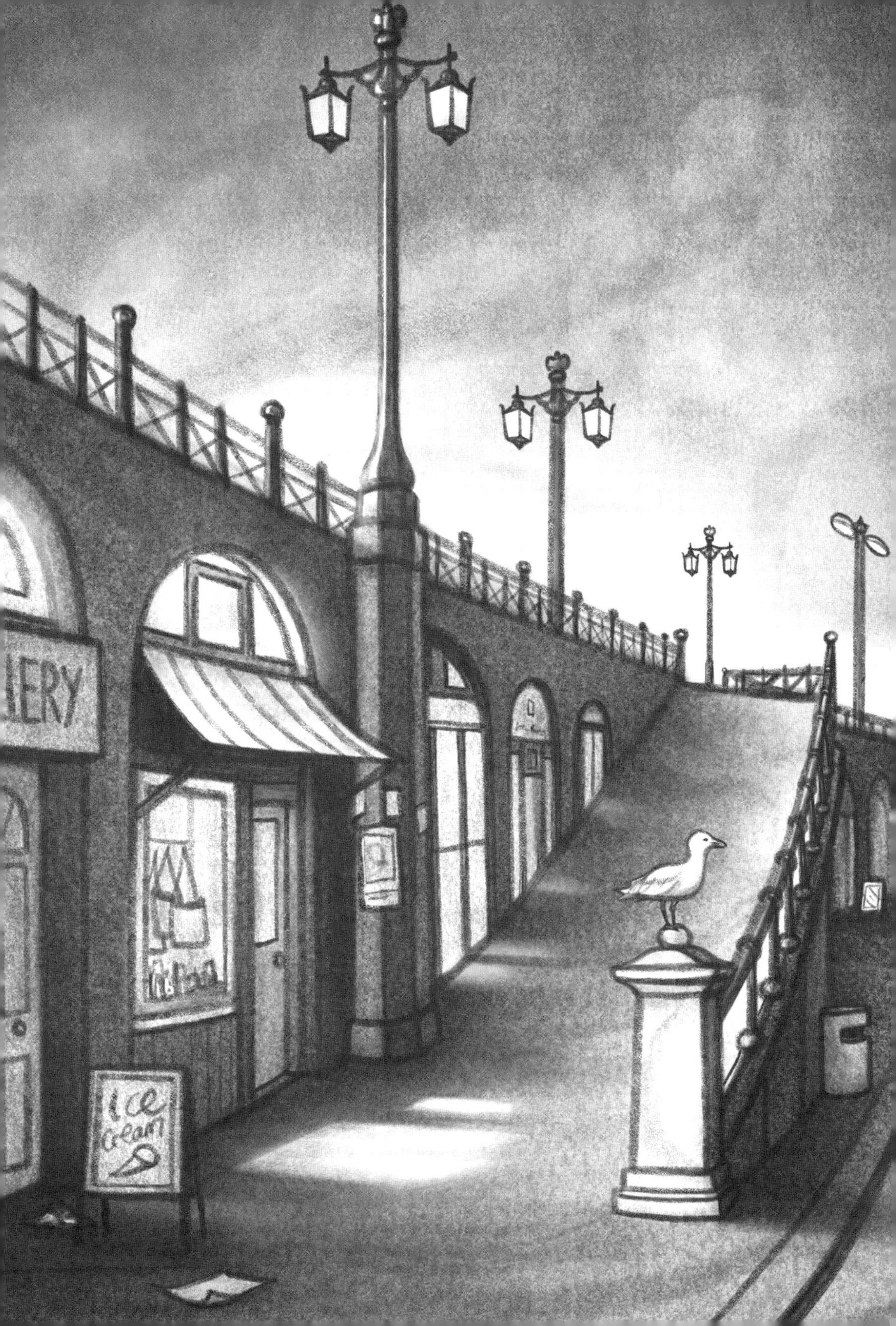
ice cream

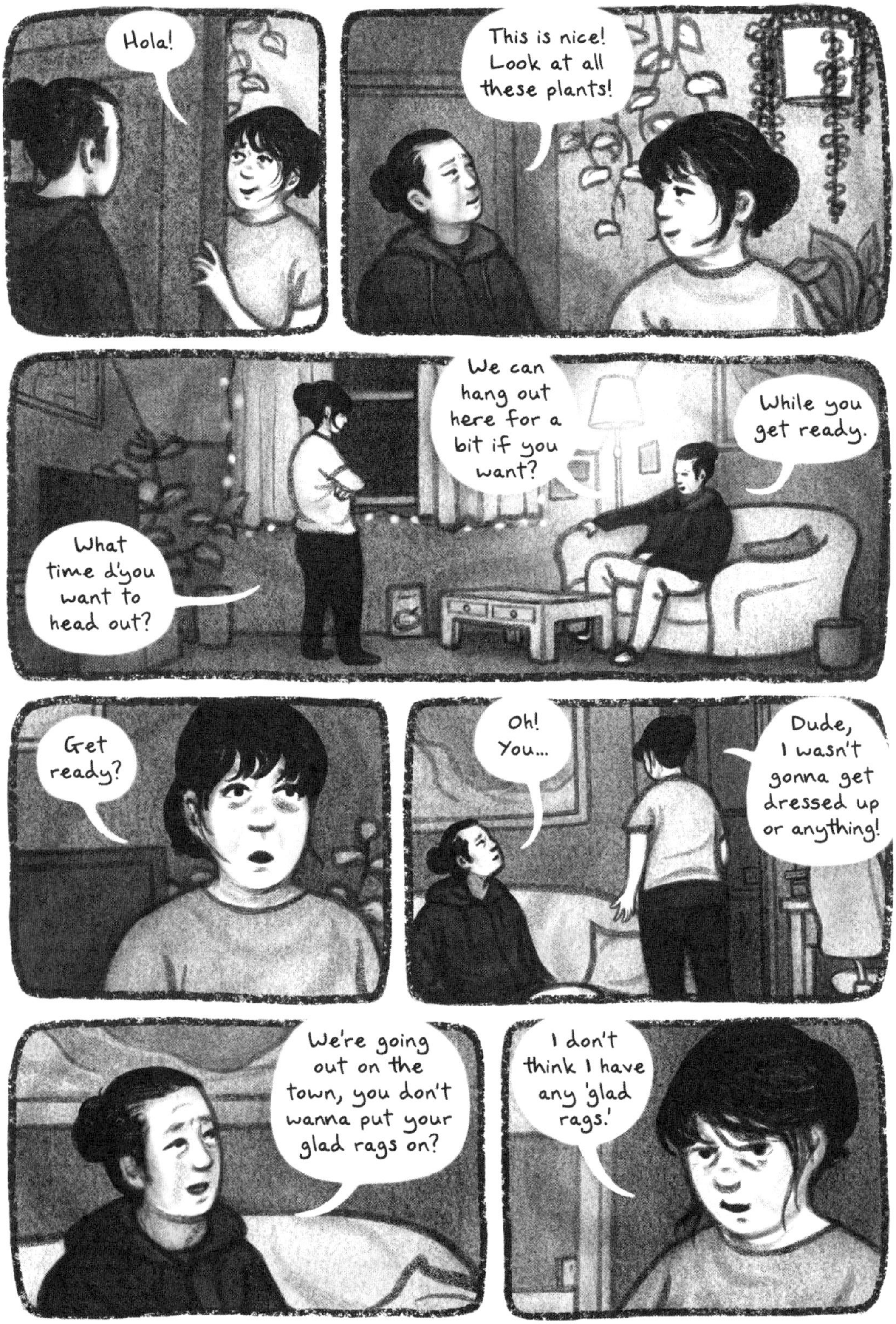
Hola!
This is nice! Look at all these plants!
What time d'you want to head out?
We can hang out here for a bit if you want?
While you get ready.
Get ready?
Oh! You...
Dude, I wasn't gonna get dressed up or anything!
We're going out on the town, you don't wanna put your glad rags on?
I don't think I have any 'glad rags.'

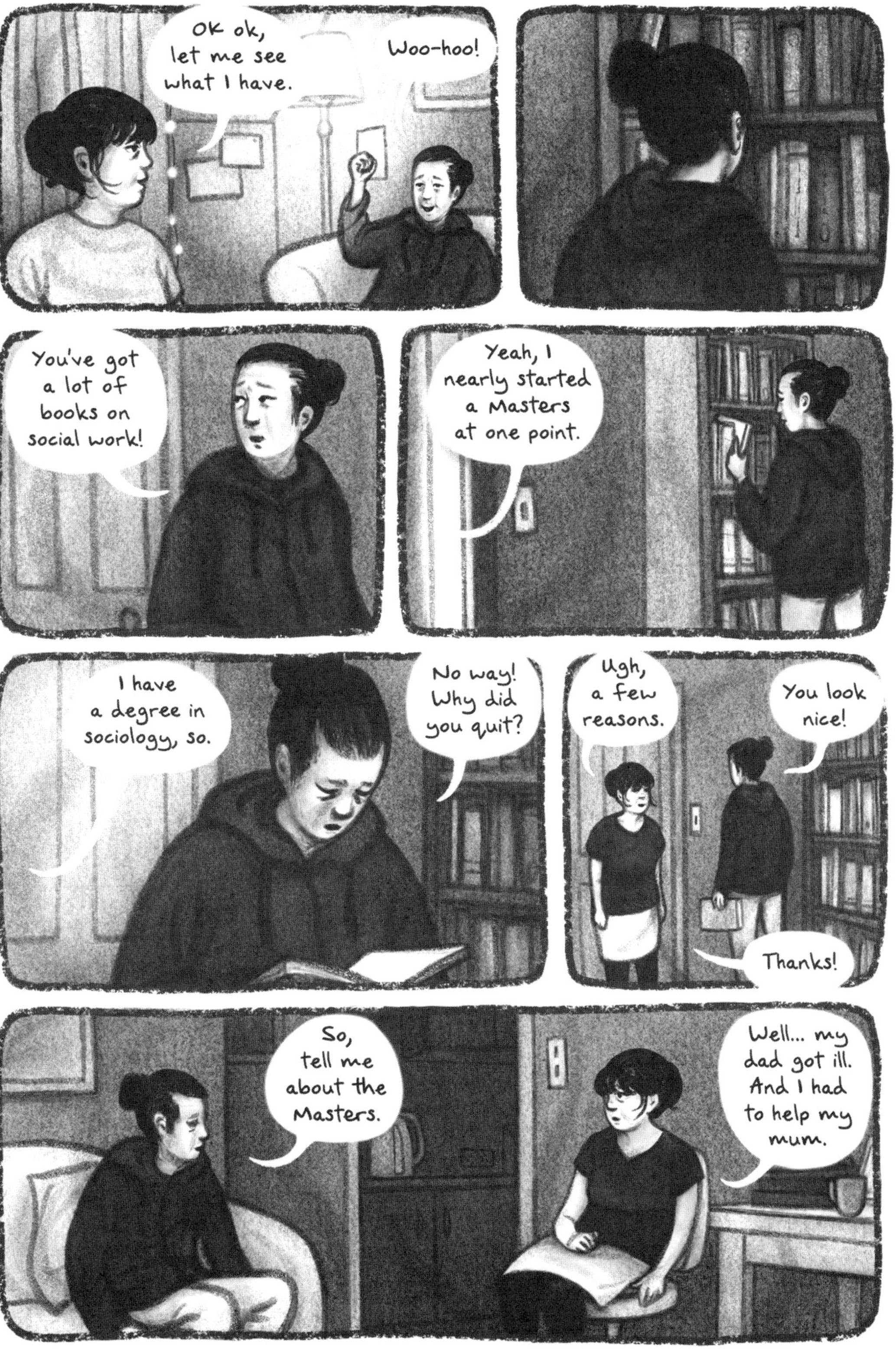
Ok ok, let me see what I have.
Woo-hoo!
You've got a lot of books on social work!
Yeah, I nearly started a Masters at one point.
I have a degree in sociology, so.
No way! Why did you quit?
Ugh, a few reasons.
You look nice!
Thanks!
So, tell me about the Masters.
Well... my dad got ill. And I had to help my mum.

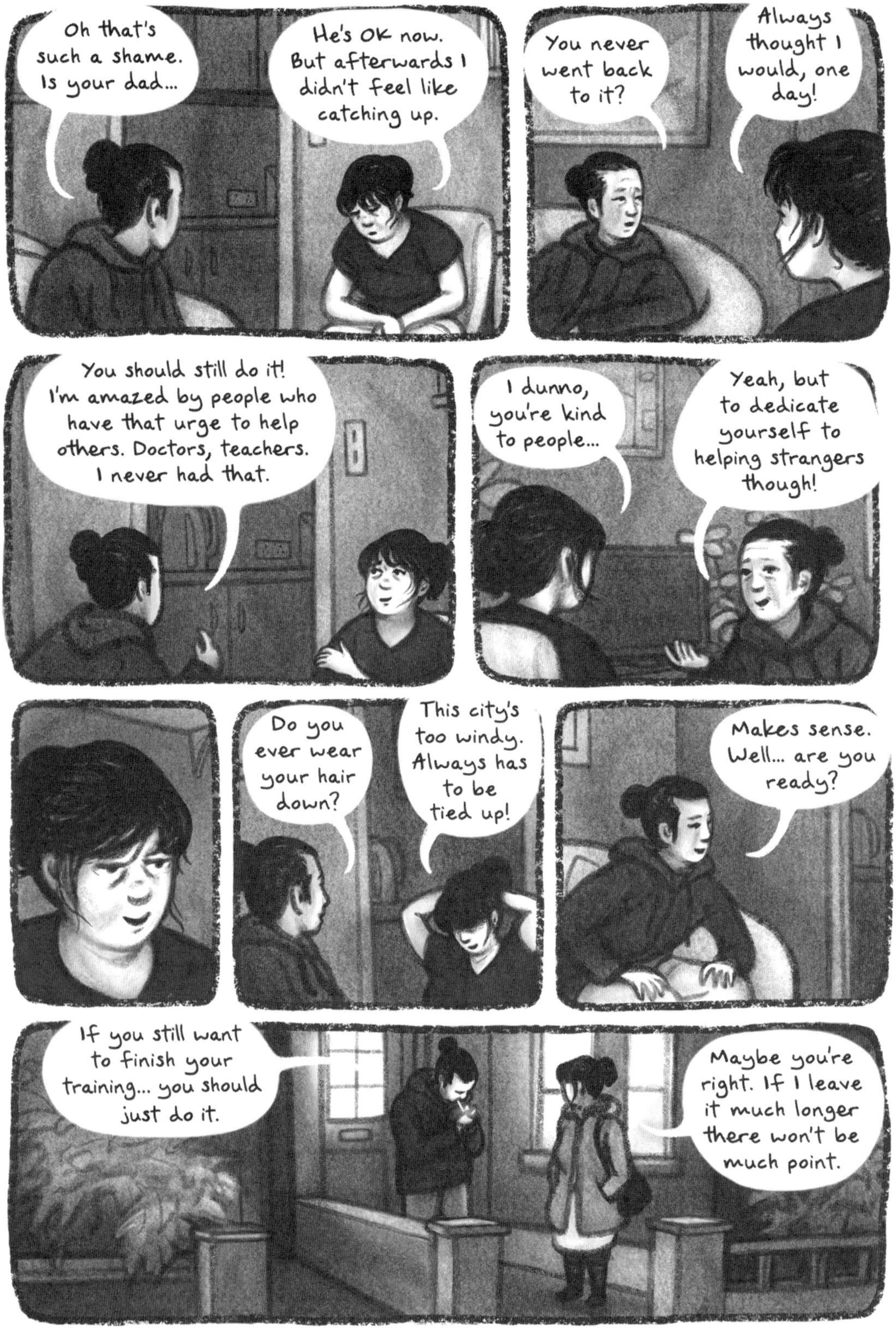
Oh that's such a shame. Is your dad...
He's OK now. But afterwards I didn't feel like catching up.
You never went back to it?
Always thought I would, one day!
You should still do it! I'm amazed by people who have that urge to help others. Doctors, teachers. I never had that.
I dunno, you're kind to people...
Yeah, but to dedicate yourself to helping strangers though!
Do you ever wear your hair down?
This city's too windy. Always has to be tied up!
Makes sense. Well... are you ready?
If you still want to finish your training... you should just do it.
Maybe you're right. If I leave it much longer there won't be much point.

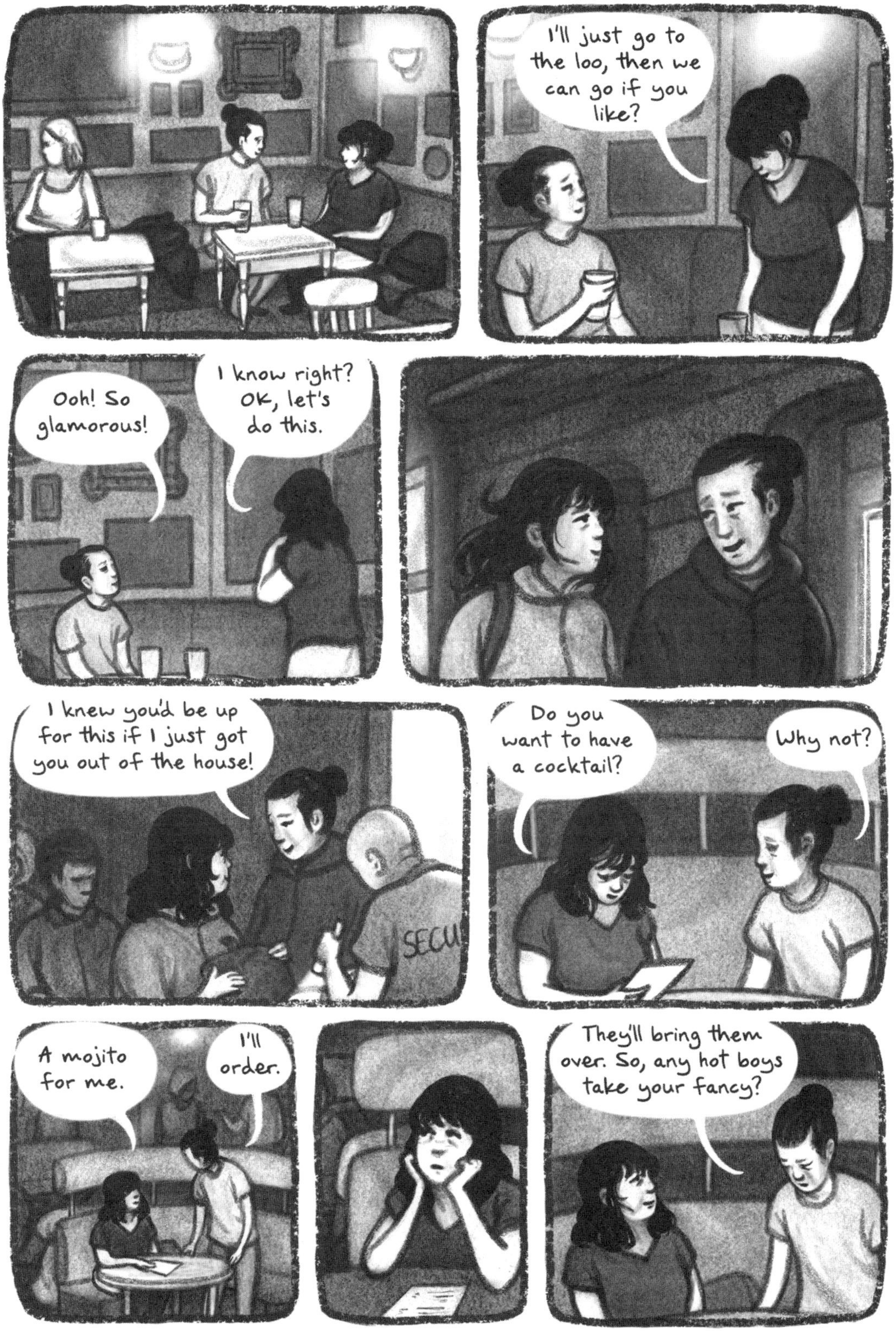
I'll just go to the loo, then we can go if you like?
Ooh! So glamorous!
I know right? OK, let's do this.
I knew you'd be up for this if I just got you out of the house!
SECU
Do you want to have a cocktail?
Why not?
A mojito for me.
I'll order.
They'll bring them over. So, any hot boys take your fancy?

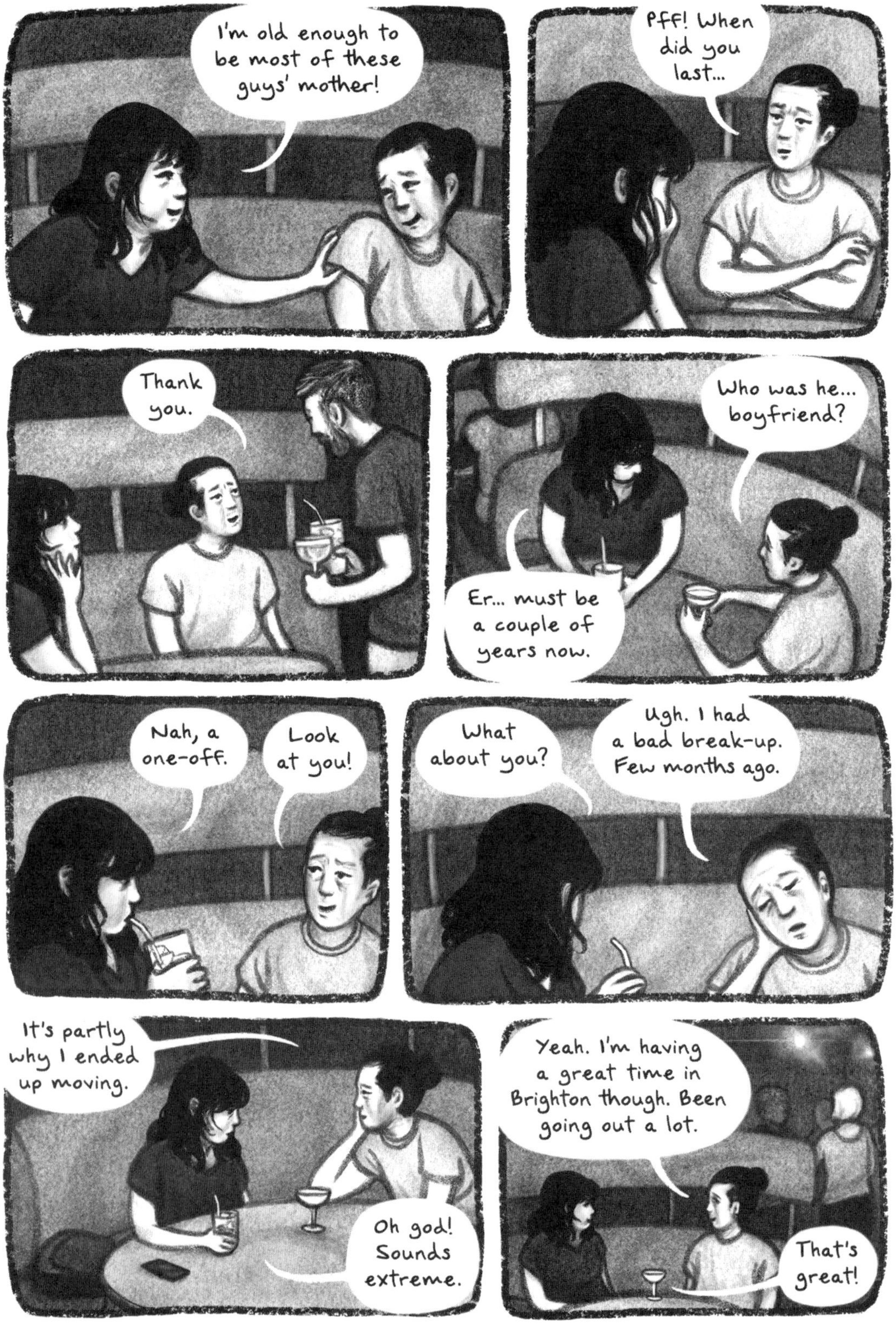
I'm old enough to be most of these guys' mother!
Pff! When did you last...
Thank you.
Who was he... boyfriend?
Er... must be a couple of years now.
Nah, a one-off.
Look at you!
What about you?
Ugh. I had a bad break-up. Few months ago.
It's partly why I ended up moving.
Oh god! Sounds extreme.
Yeah. I'm having a great time in Brighton though. Been going out a lot.
That's great!

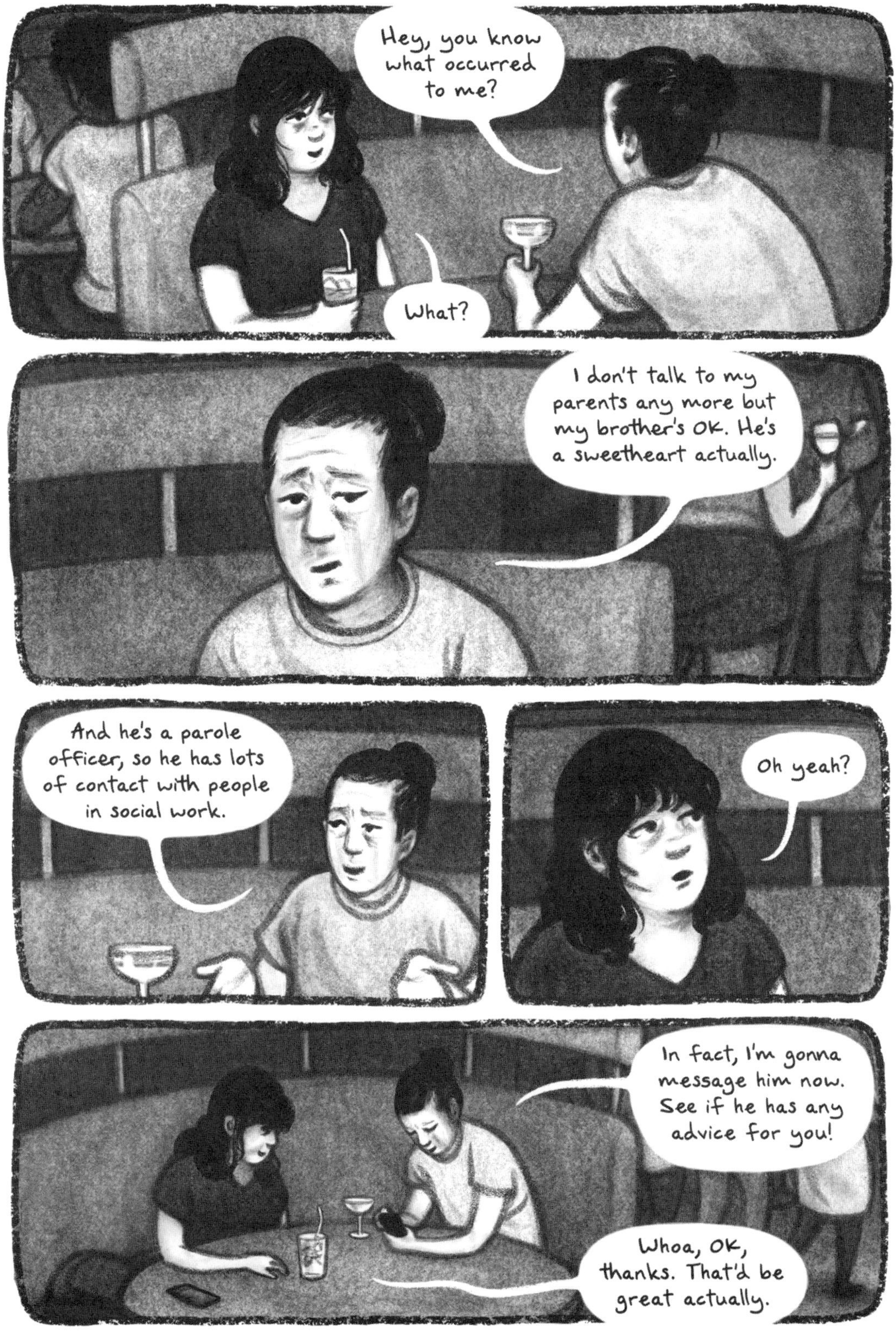
Hey, you know what occurred to me?
What?
I don't talk to my parents any more but my brother's OK. He's a sweetheart actually.
And he's a parole officer, so he has lots of contact with people in social work.
Oh yeah?
In fact, I'm gonna message him now. See if he has any advice for you!
Whoa, OK, thanks. That'd be great actually.

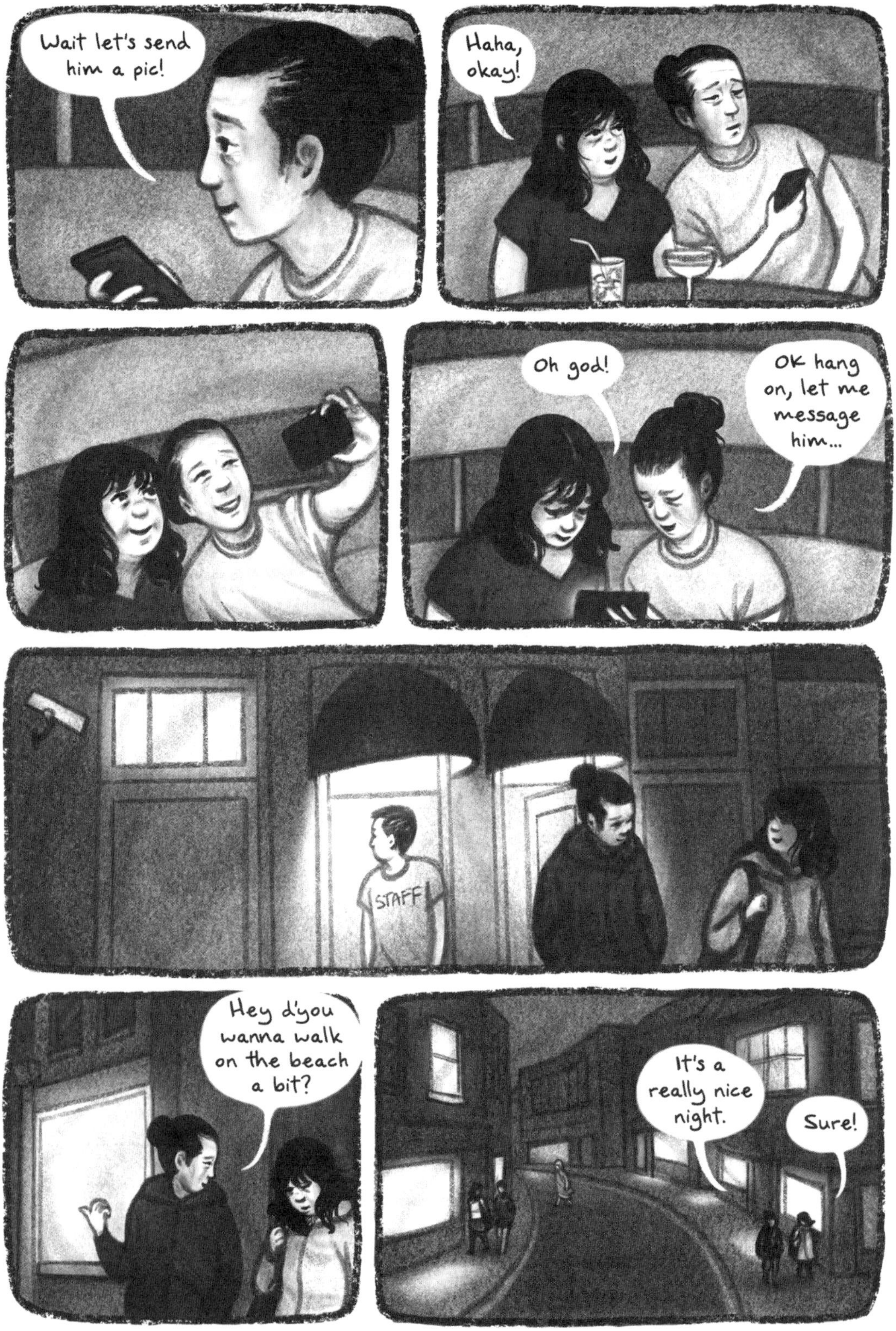
Wait let's send him a pic!
Haha, okay!
Oh god!
OK hang on, let me message him...
STAFF
Hey d'you wanna walk on the beach a bit?
It's a really nice night.
Sure!

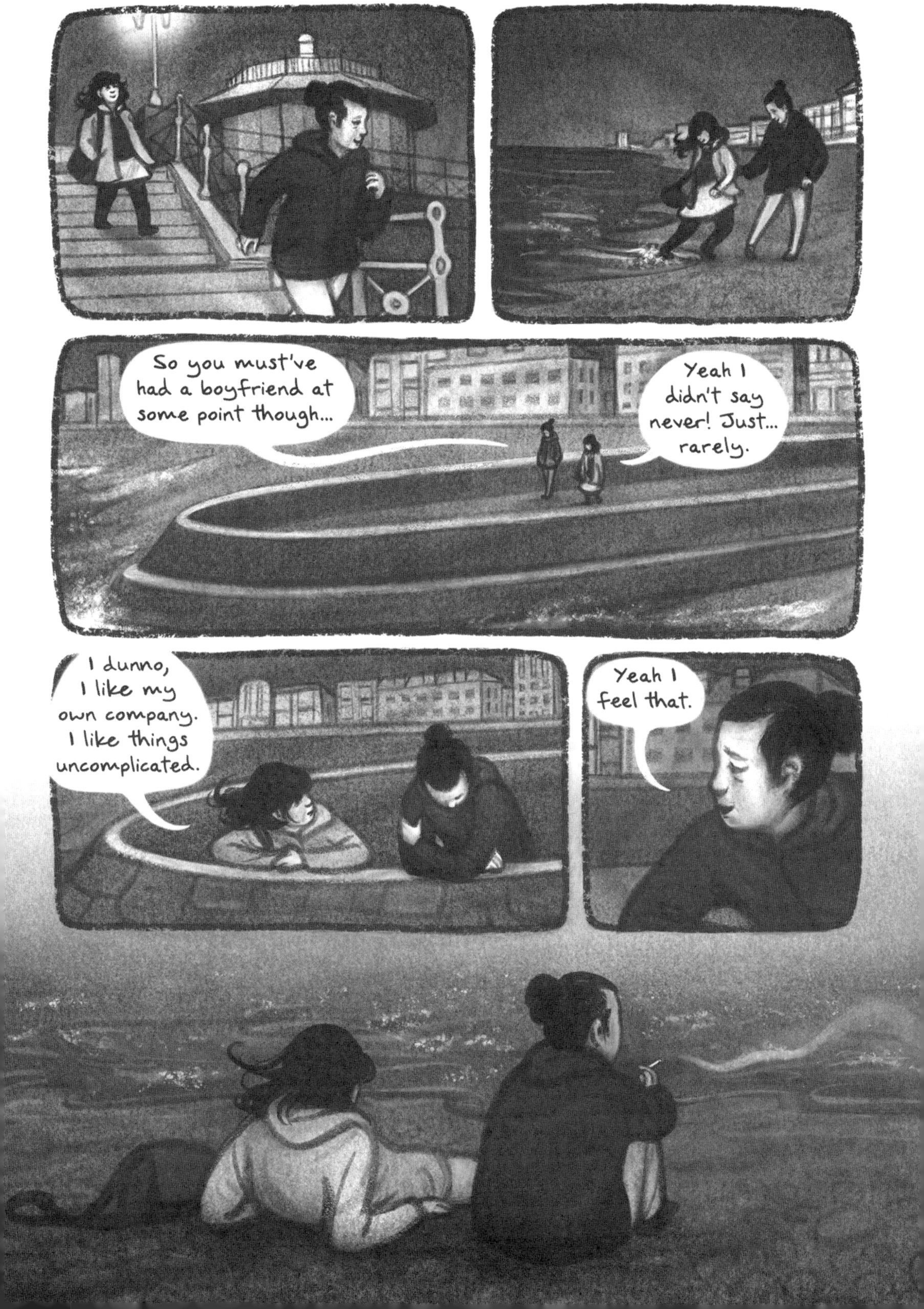
So you must've had a boyfriend at some point though...
Yeah I didn't say never! Just... rarely.
I dunno, I like my own company. I like things uncomplicated.
Yeah I feel that.

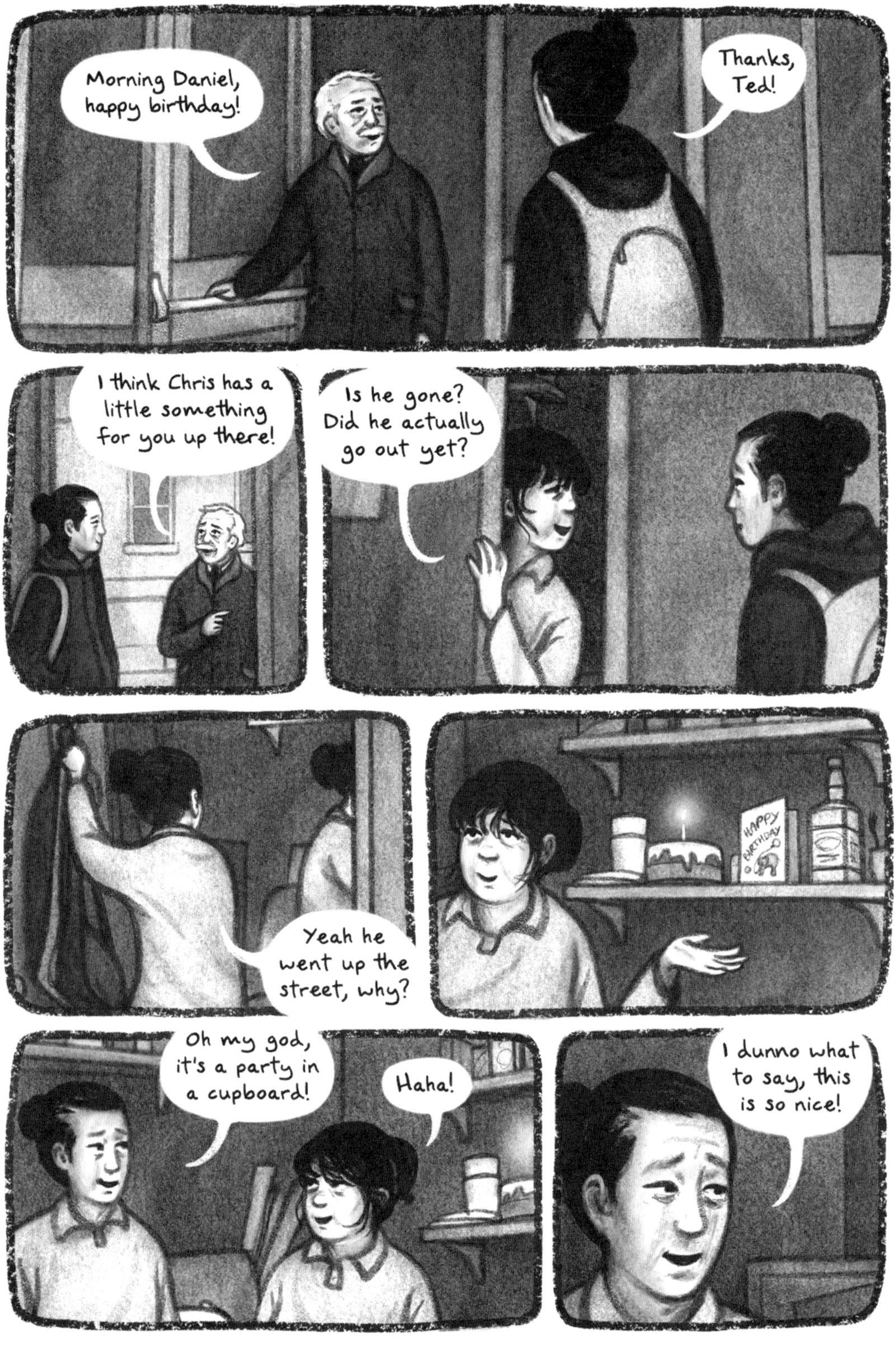
Morning Daniel, happy birthday!
Thanks, Ted!
I think Chris has a little something for you up there!
Is he gone? Did he actually go out yet?
Yeah he went up the street, why?
Oh my god, it's a party in a cupboard!
Haha!
I dunno what to say, this is so nice!
HAPPY BIRTHDAY

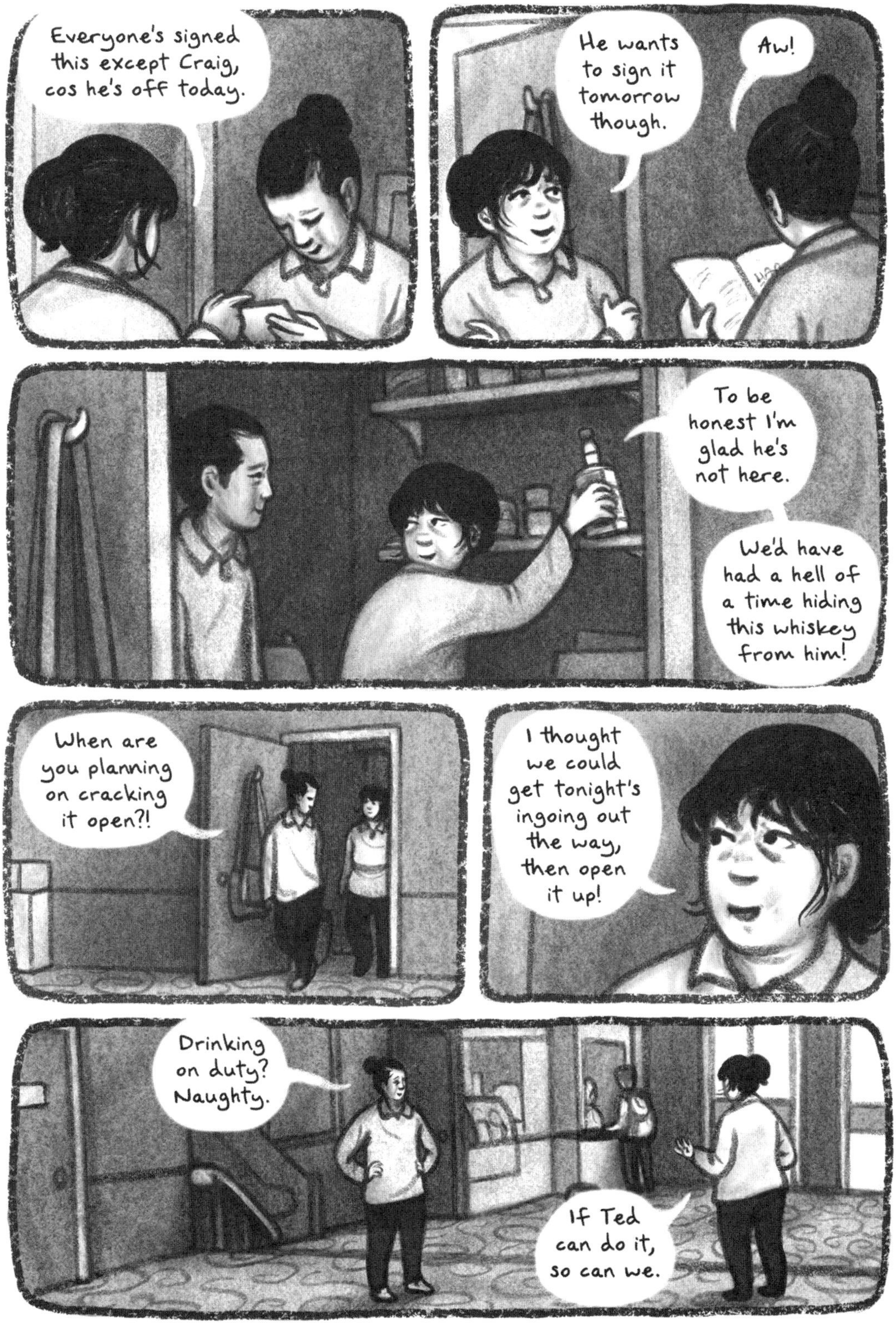
Everyone's signed this except Craig, cos he's off today.
He wants to sign it tomorrow though.
Aw!
To be honest I'm glad he's not here.
We'd have had a hell of a time hiding this whiskey from him!
When are you planning on cracking it open?!
I thought we could get tonight's ingoing out the way, then open it up!
Drinking on duty? Naughty.
If Ted can do it, so can we.

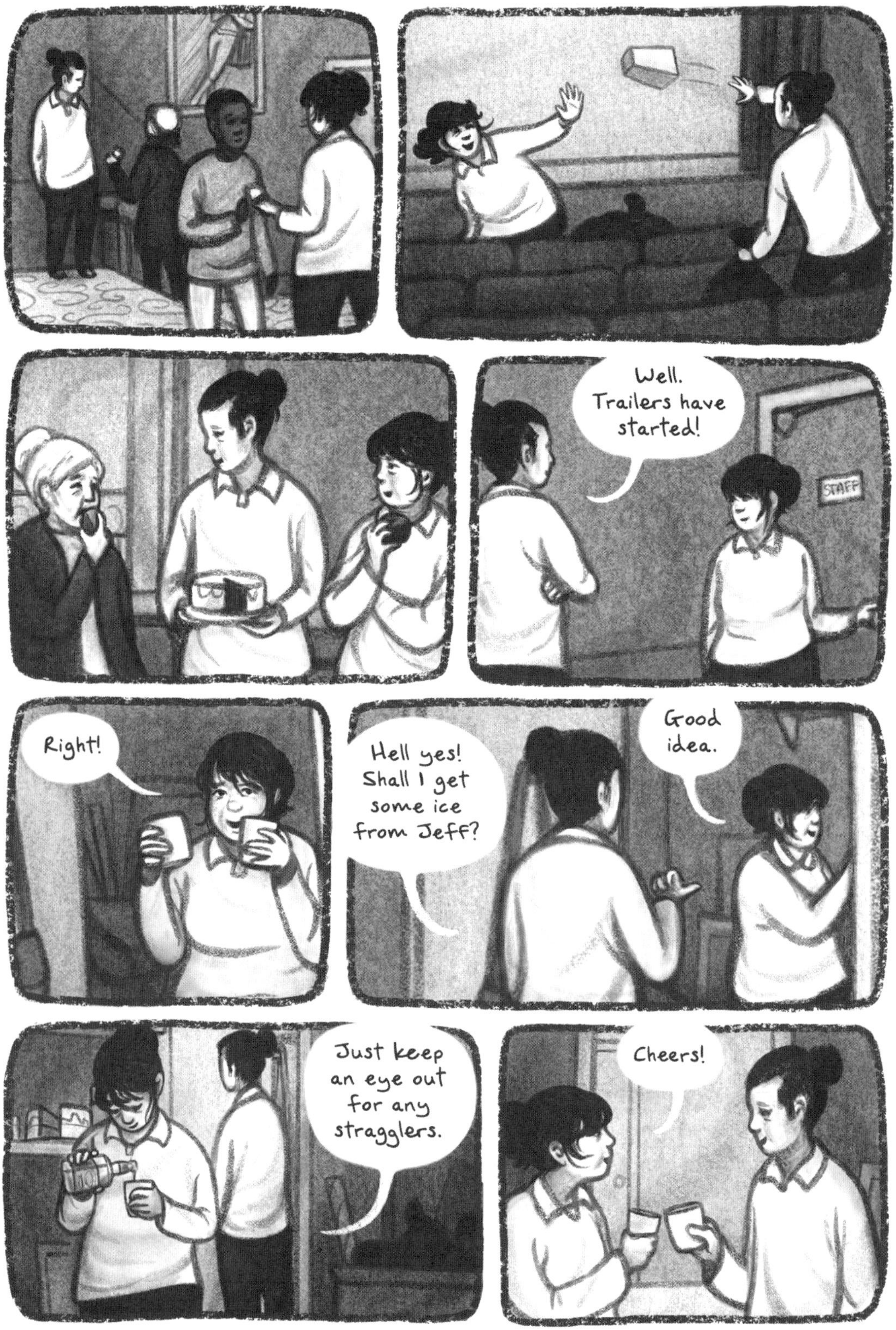
Well. Trailers have started!
STAFF
Right!
Hell yes! Shall I get some ice from Jeff?
Good idea.
Just keep an eye out for any stragglers.
Cheers!

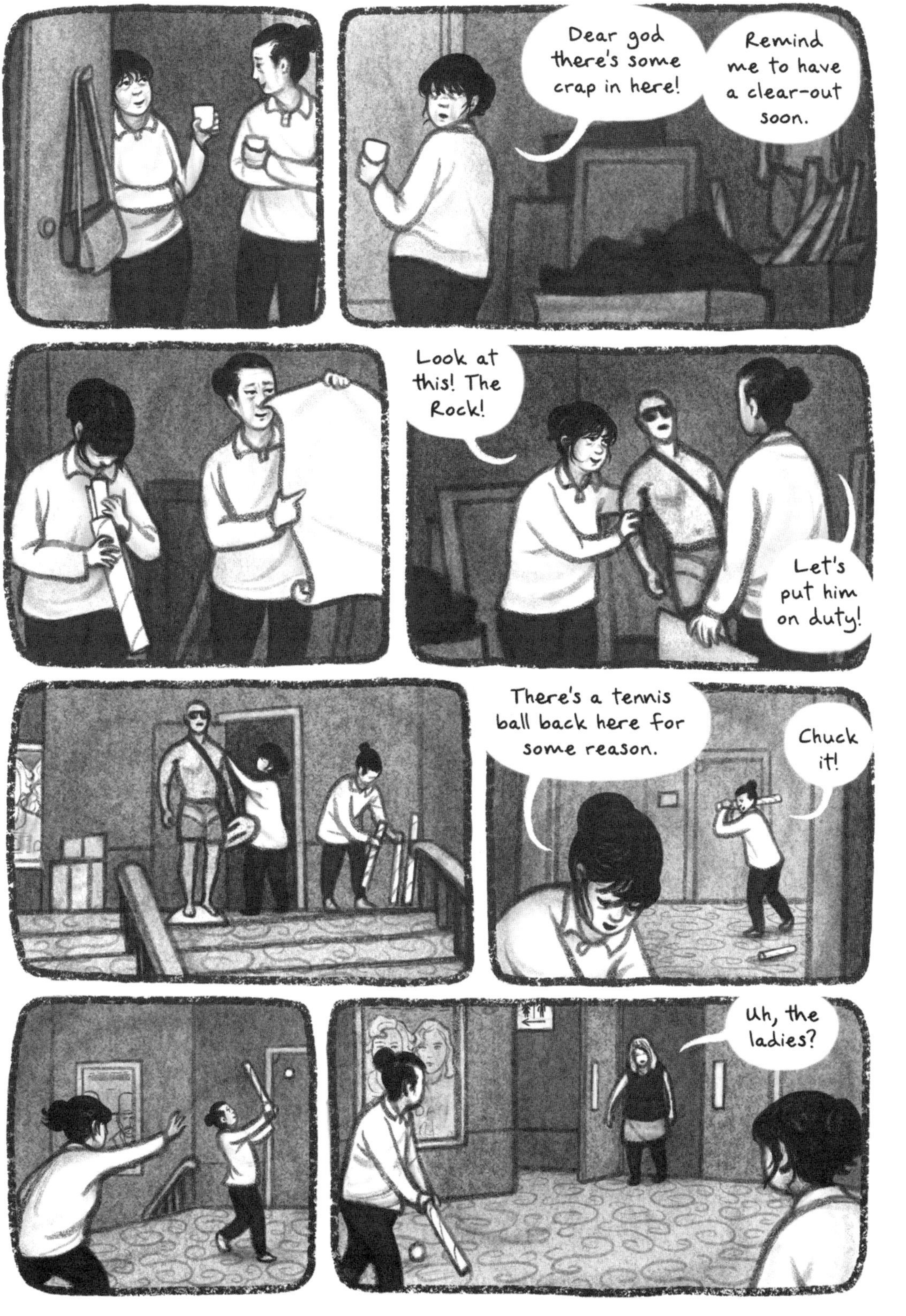
Dear god there's some crap in here!
Remind me to have a clear-out soon.
Look at this! The Rock!
Let's put him on duty!
There's a tennis ball back here for some reason.
Chuck it!
Uh, the ladies?

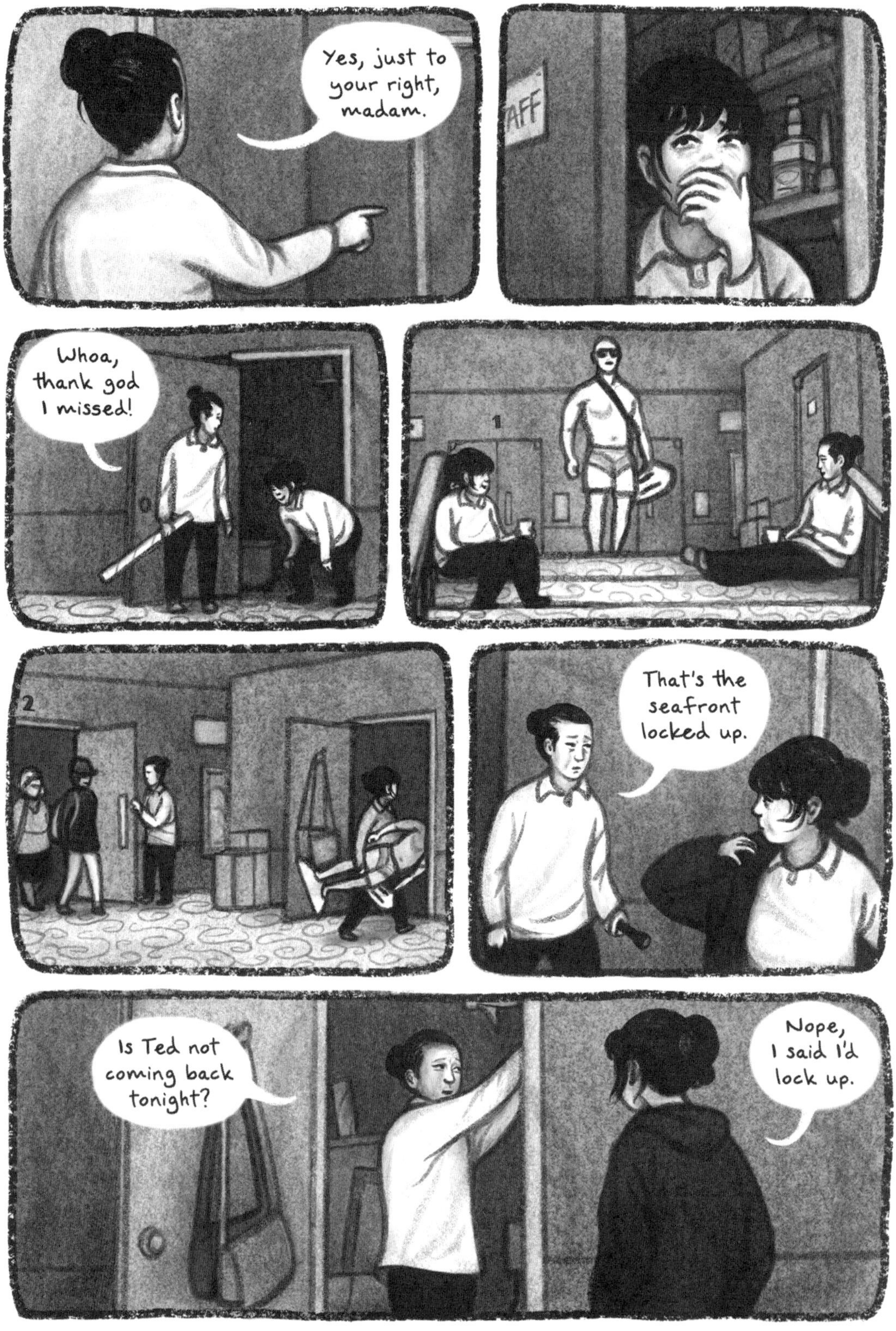
Yes, just to your right, madam.
STAFF
Whoa, thank god I missed!
1
2
That's the seafront locked up.
Is Ted not coming back tonight?
Nope, I said I'd lock up.

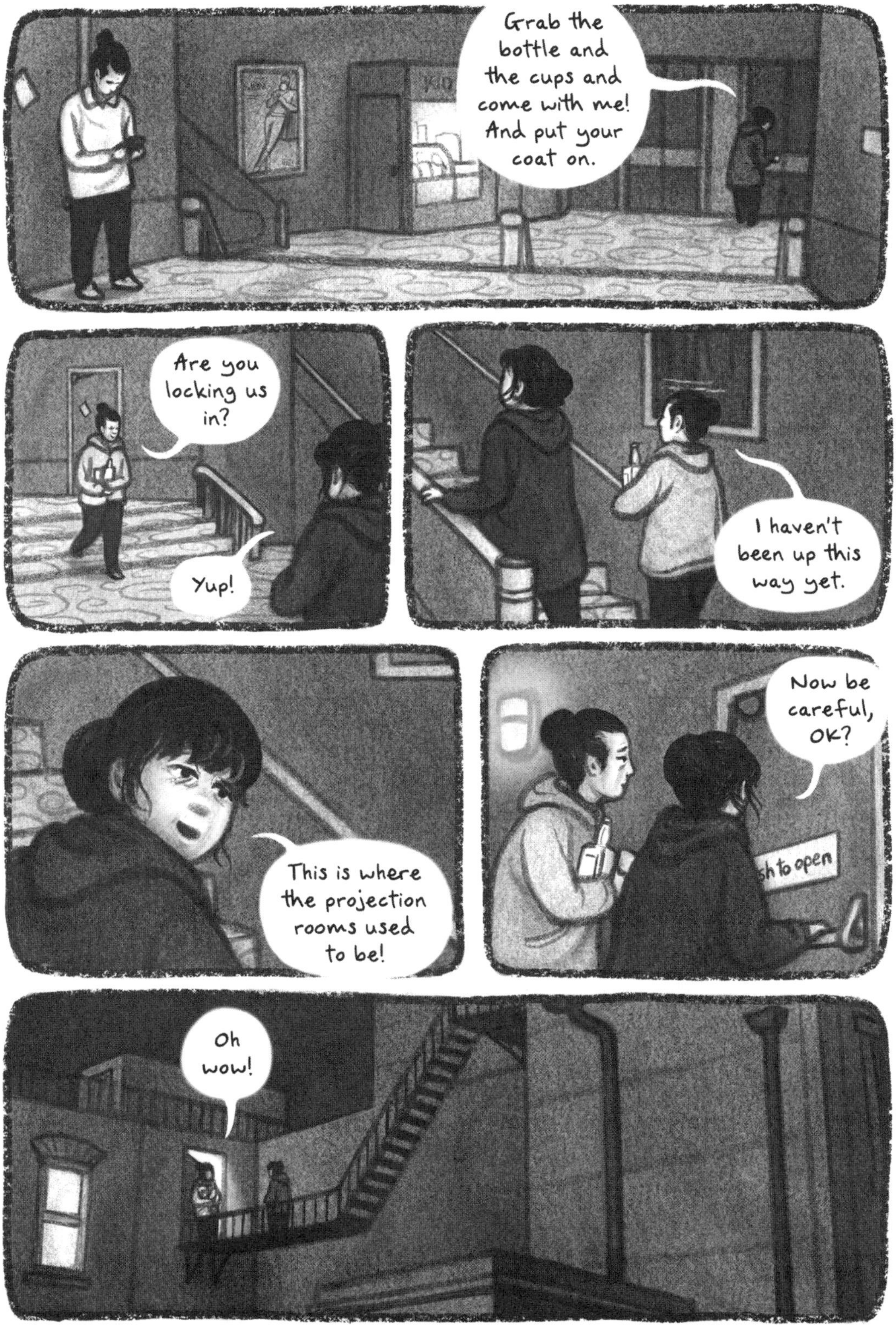
Grab the bottle and the cups and come with me! And put your coat on.
Are you locking us in?
Yup!
I haven't been up this way yet.
This is where the projection rooms used to be!
Now be careful, OK?
sh to open
Oh wow!

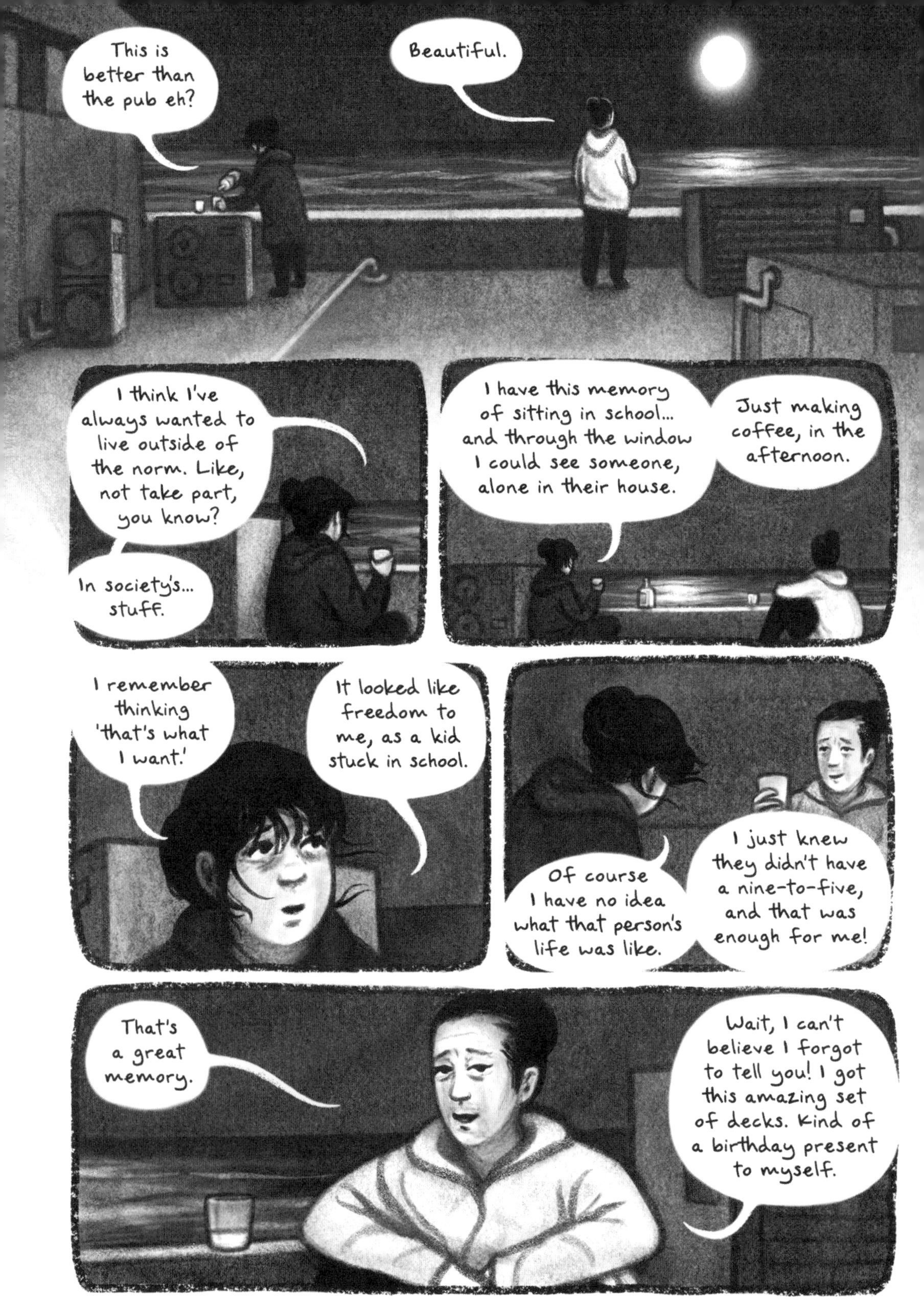

This is better than the pub eh?
Beautiful.
I think I've always wanted to live outside of the norm. Like, not take part, you know?
In society's... stuff.
I have this memory of sitting in school... and through the window I could see someone, alone in their house.
Just making coffee, in the afternoon.
I remember thinking 'that's what I want.'
It looked like freedom to me, as a kid stuck in school.
Of course I have no idea what that person's life was like.
I just knew they didn't have a nine-to-five, and that was enough for me!
That's a great memory.
Wait, I can't believe I forgot to tell you! I got this amazing set of decks. Kind of a birthday present to myself.

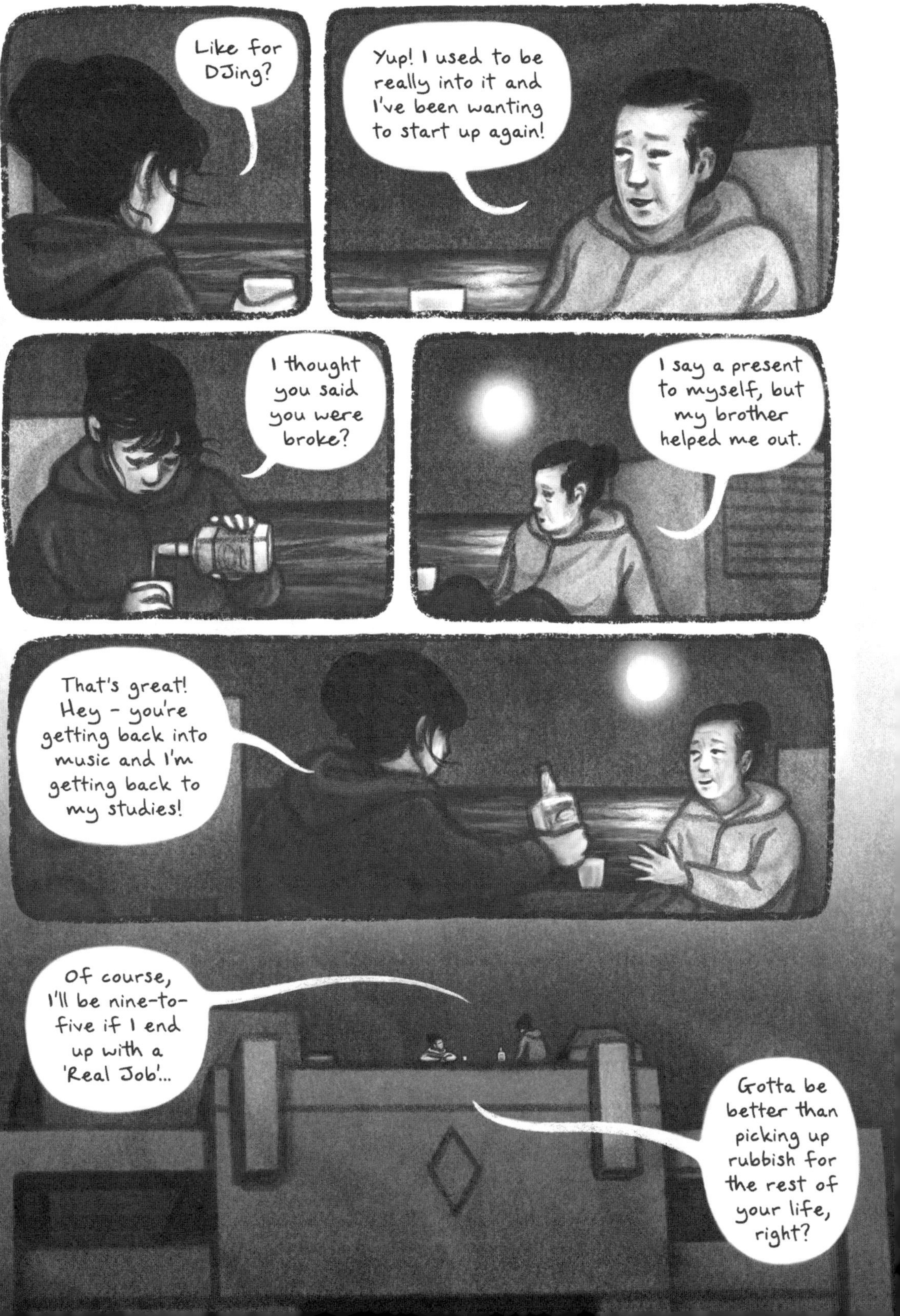
Like for DJing?
Yup! I used to be really into it and I've been wanting to start up again!
I thought you said you were broke?
I say a present to myself, but my brother helped me out.
That's great! Hey - you're getting back into music and I'm getting back to my studies!
Of course, I'll be nine-to-five if I end up with a 'Real Job'...
Gotta be better than picking up rubbish for the rest of your life, right?

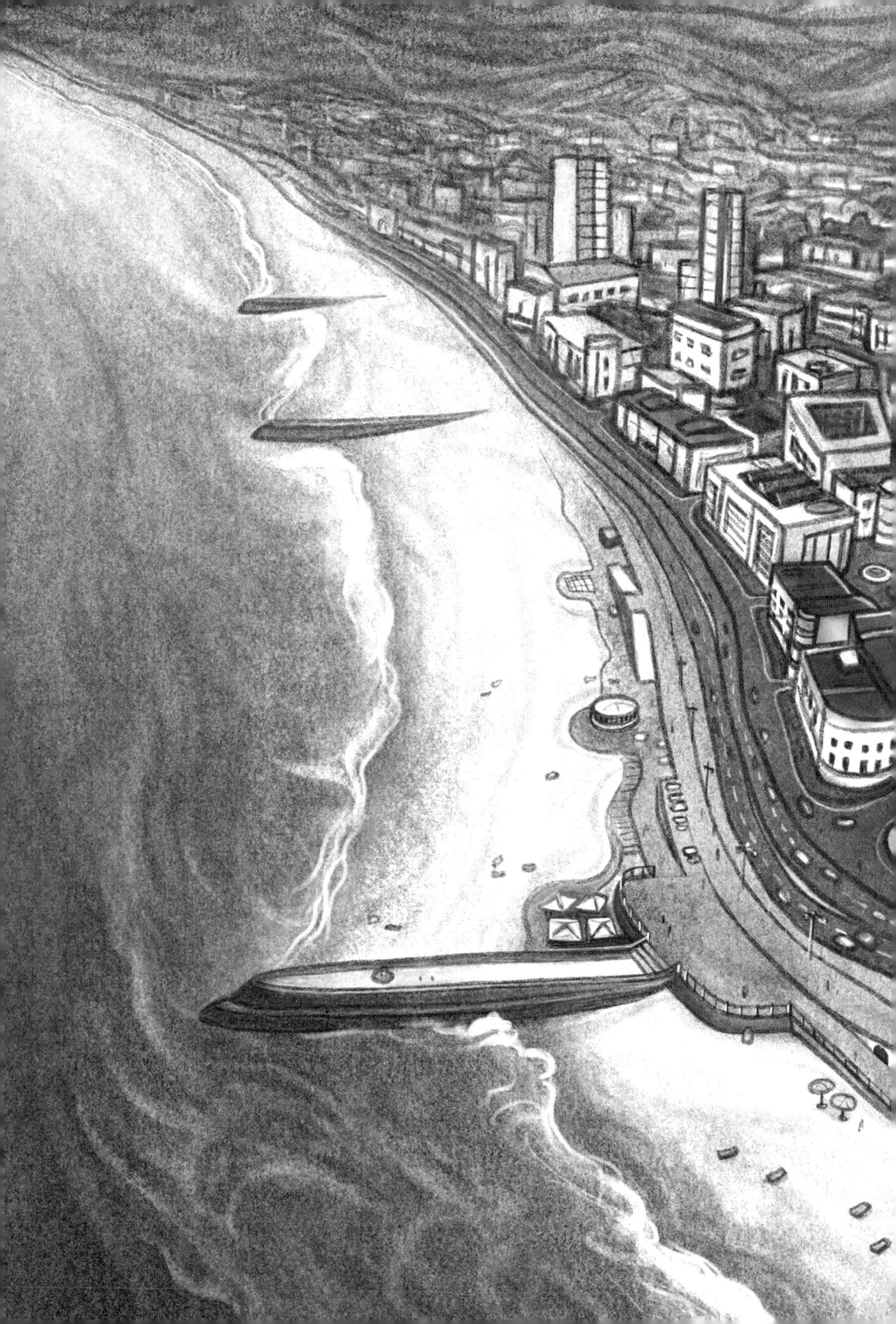

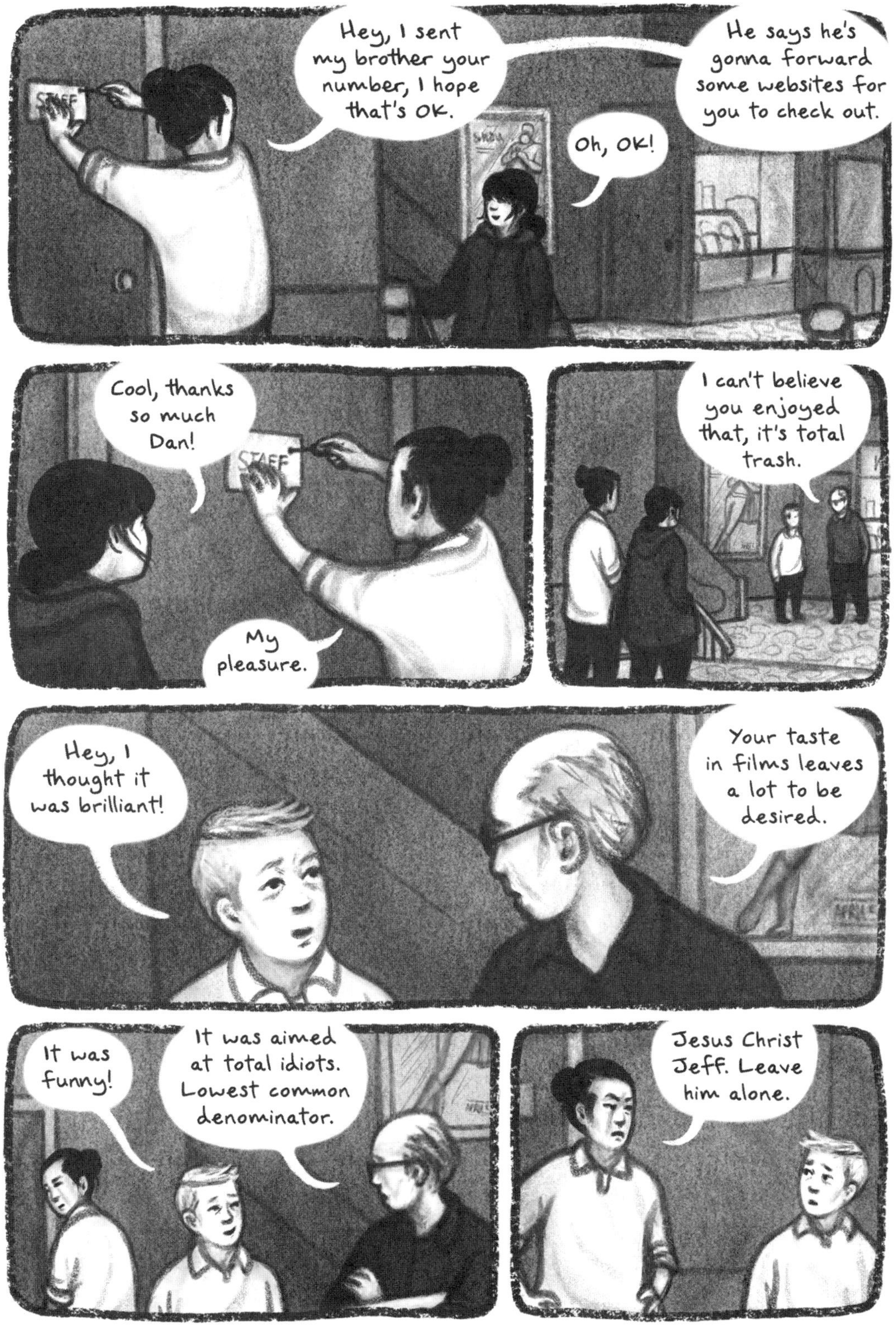
Hey, I sent my brother your number, I hope that's OK.
He says he's gonna forward some websites for you to check out.
Oh, OK!
STAFF
Cool, thanks so much Dan!
My pleasure.
I can't believe you enjoyed that, it's total trash.
Hey, I thought it was brilliant!
Your taste in films leaves a lot to be desired.
It was funny!
It was aimed at total idiots. Lowest common denominator.
Jesus Christ Jeff. Leave him alone.

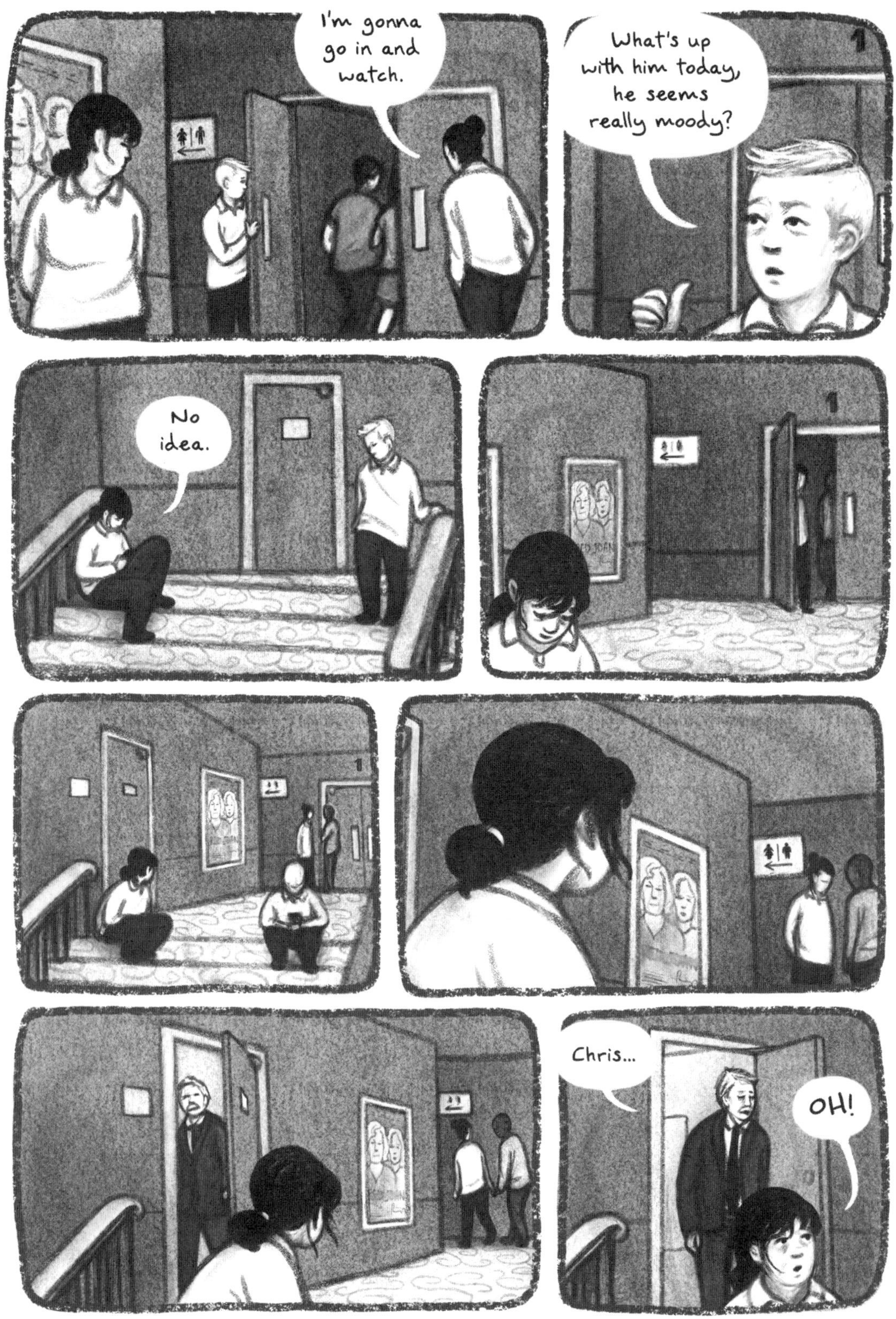
I'm gonna go in and watch.
What's up with him today, he seems really moody?
No idea.
Chris...
OH!

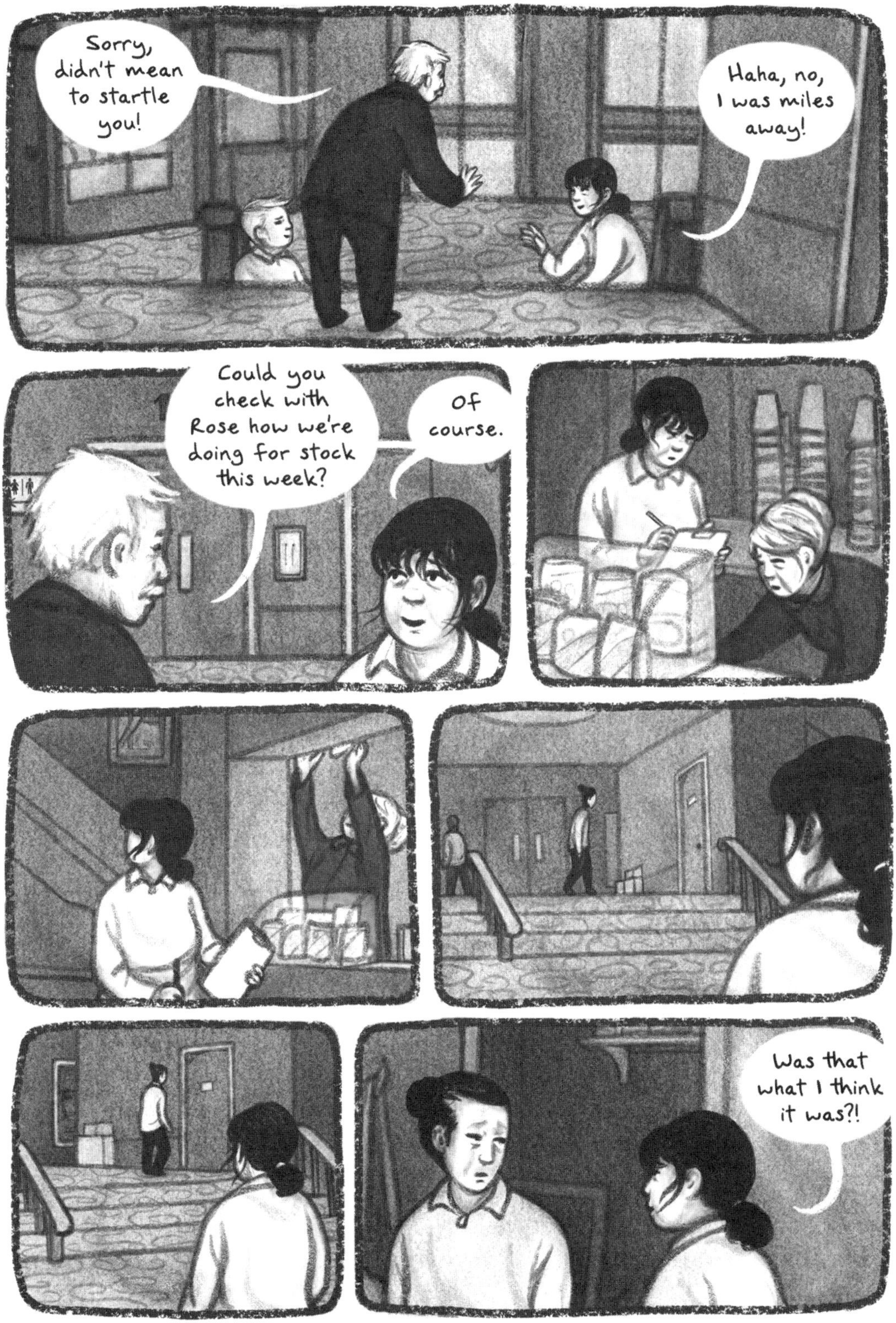
Sorry, didn't mean to startle you!
Haha, no, I was miles away!
Could you check with Rose how we're doing for stock this week?
Of course.
Was that what I think it was?!

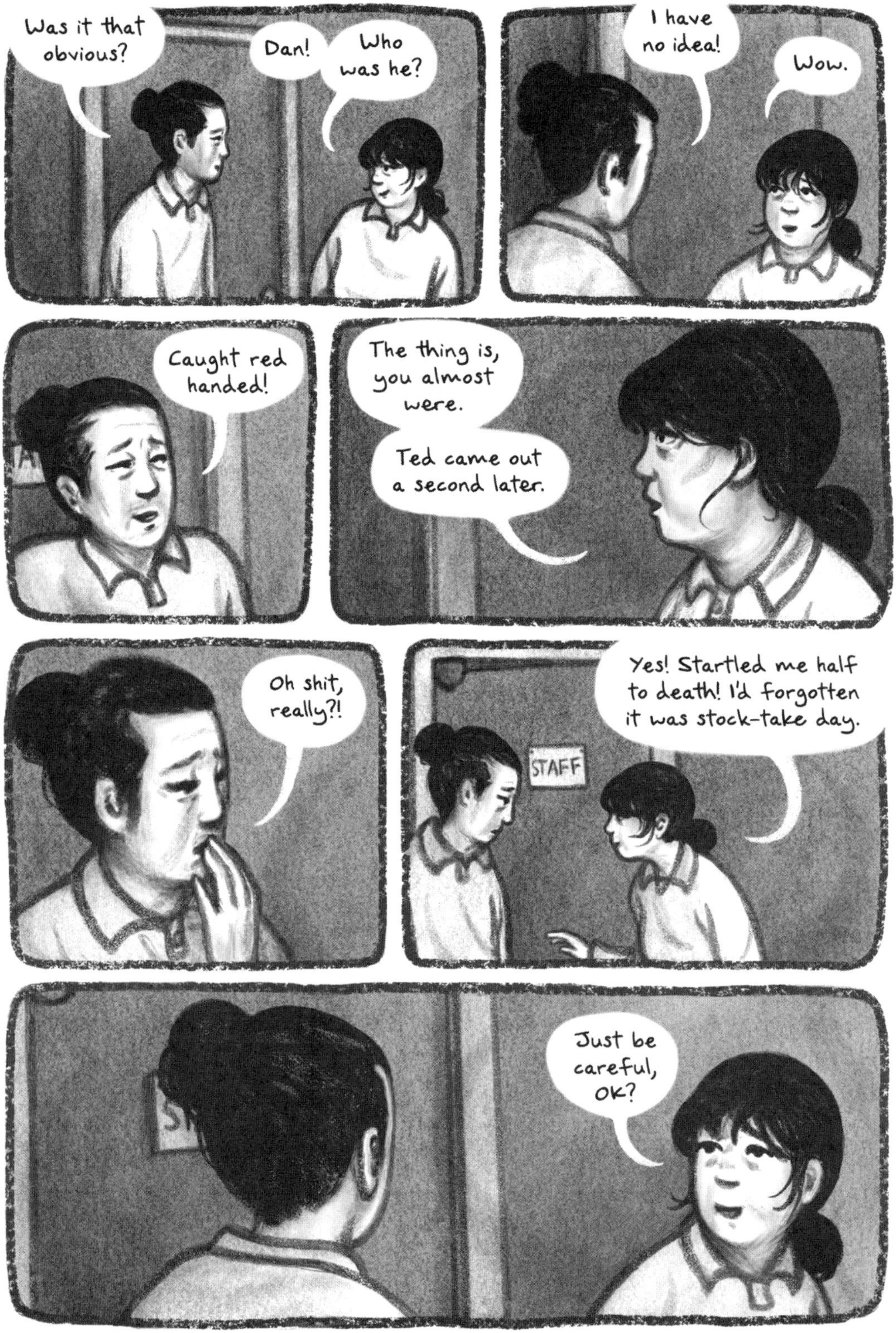
Was it that obvious?
Dan!
Who was he?
I have no idea!
Wow.
Caught red handed!
The thing is, you almost were.
Ted came out a second later.
Oh shit, really?!
Yes! Startled me half to death! I'd forgotten it was stock-take day.
STAFF
Just be careful, OK?

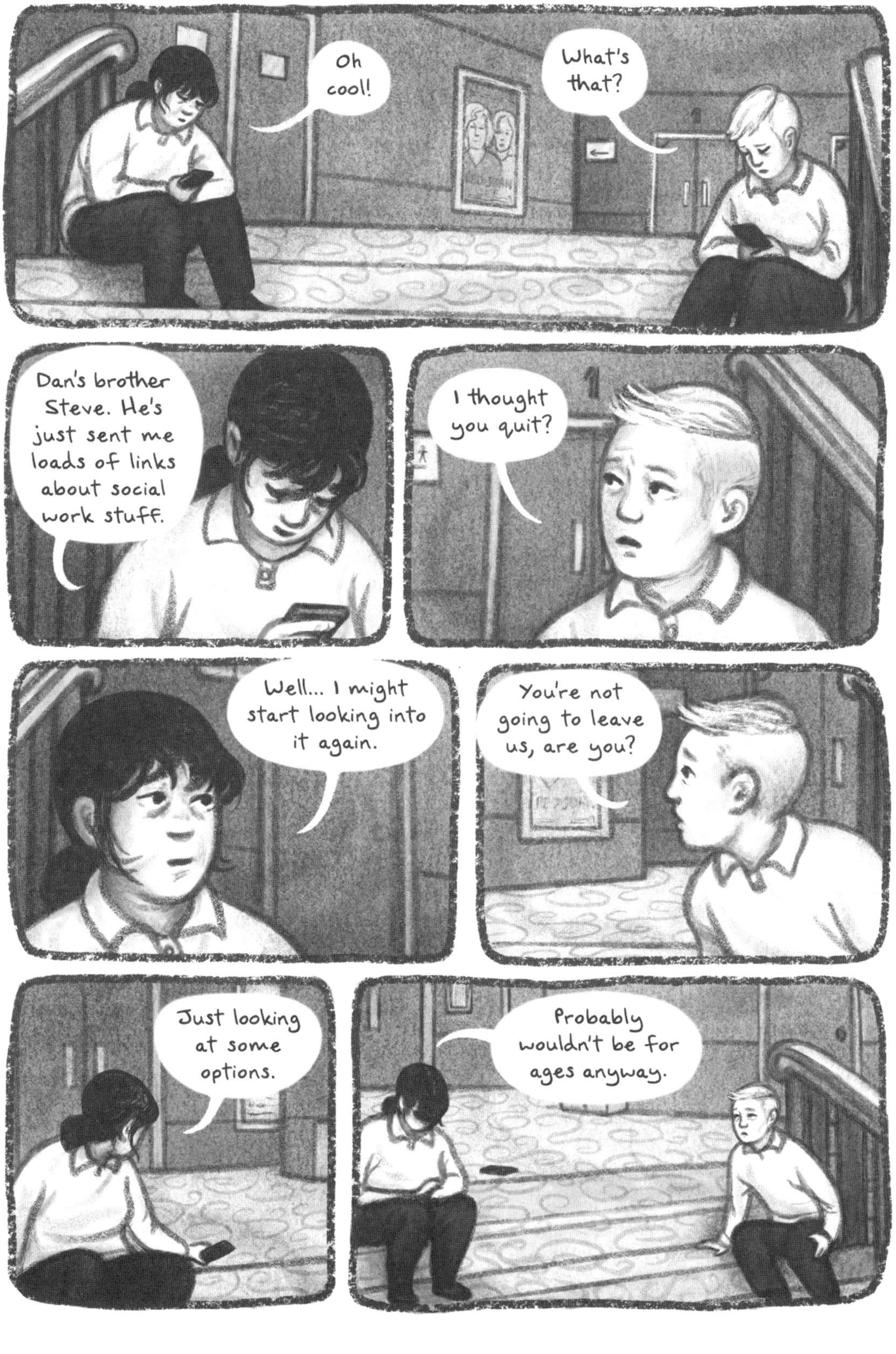
Oh cool!
What's that?
Dan's brother Steve. He's just sent me loads of links about social work stuff.
I thought you quit?
Well... I might start looking into it again.
You're not going to leave us, are you?
Just looking at some options.
Probably wouldn't be for ages anyway.

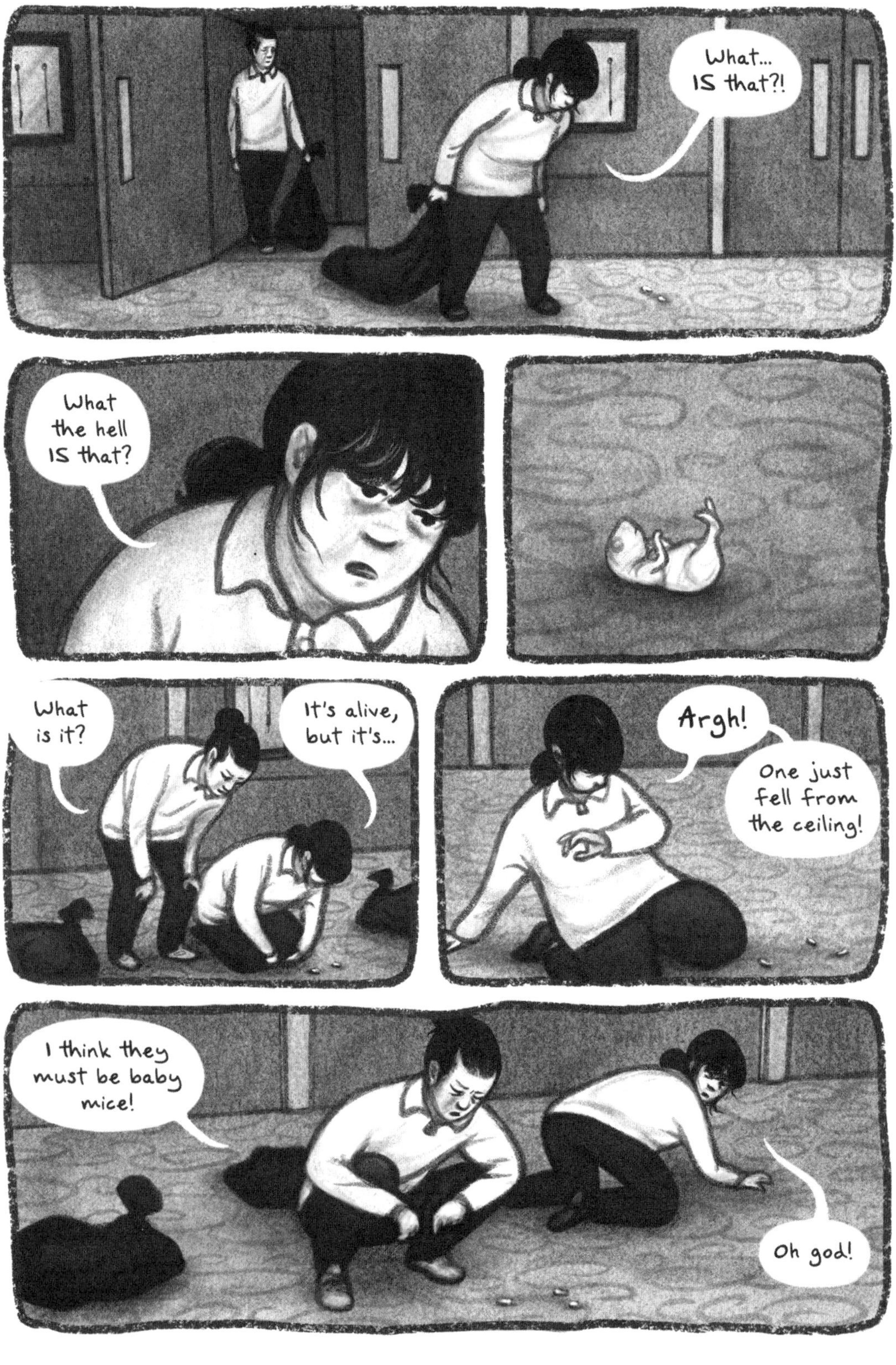
What... IS that?!
What the hell IS that?
What is it?
It's alive, but it's...
Argh!
One just fell from the ceiling!
I think they must be baby mice!
Oh god!

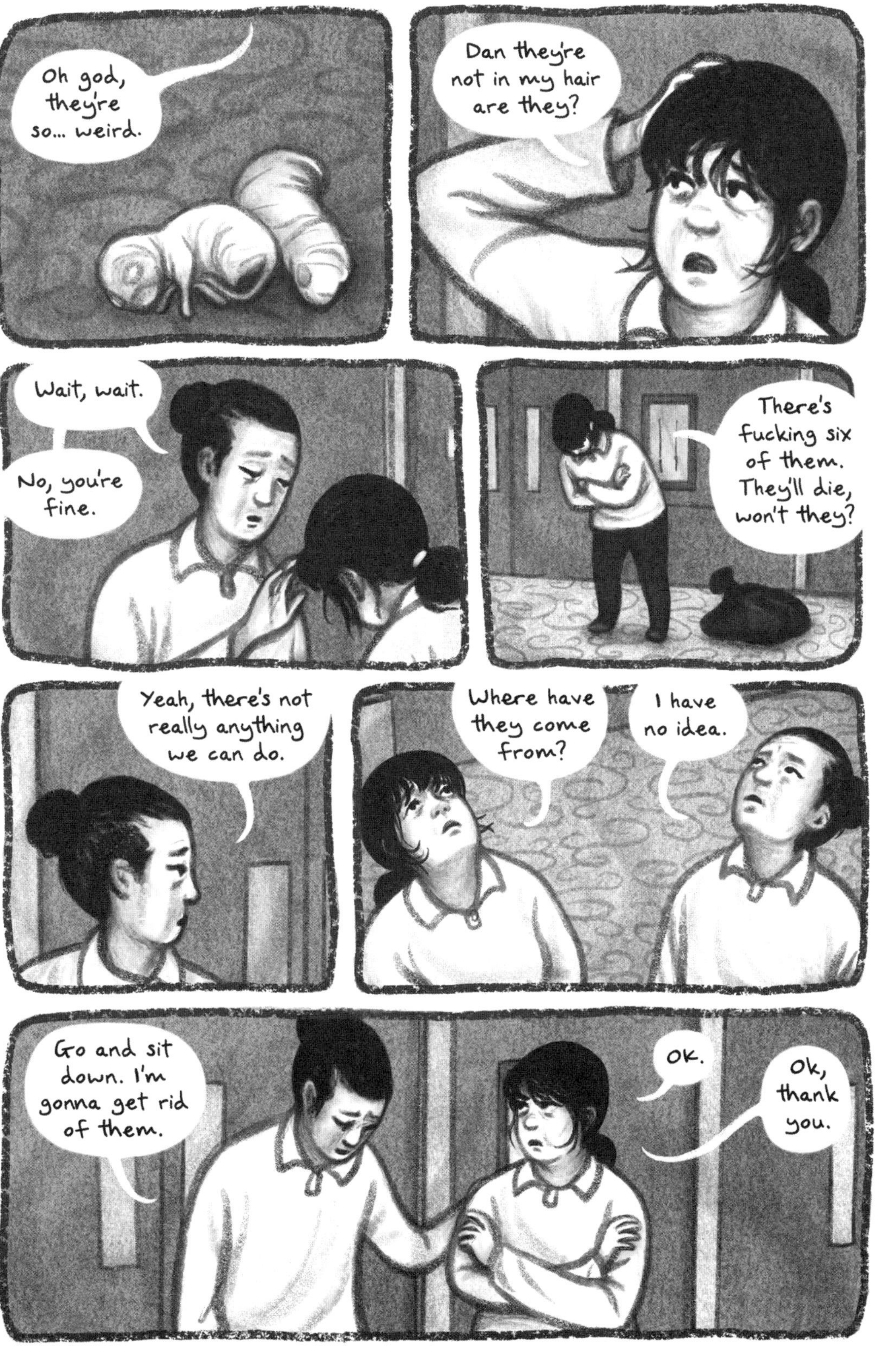
Oh god, they're so... weird.
Dan they're not in my hair are they?
Wait, wait.
No, you're fine.
There's fucking six of them. They'll die, won't they?
Yeah, there's not really anything we can do.
Where have they come from?
I have no idea.
Go and sit down. I'm gonna get rid of them.
OK.
Ok, thank you.

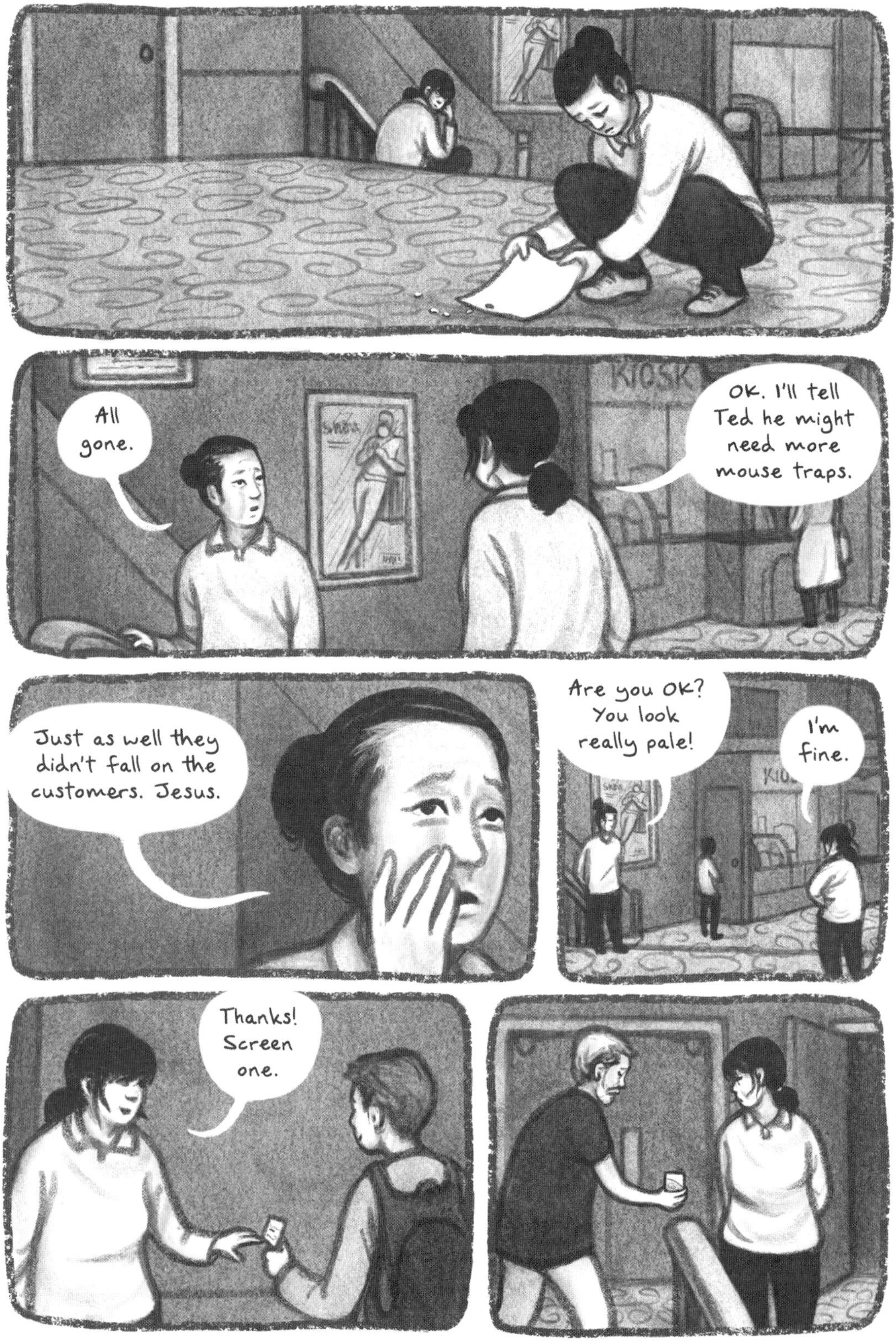
All gone.
OK. I'll tell Ted he might need more mouse traps.
KIOSK
Just as well they didn't fall on the customers. Jesus.
Are you OK? You look really pale!
I'm fine.
Thanks! Screen one.

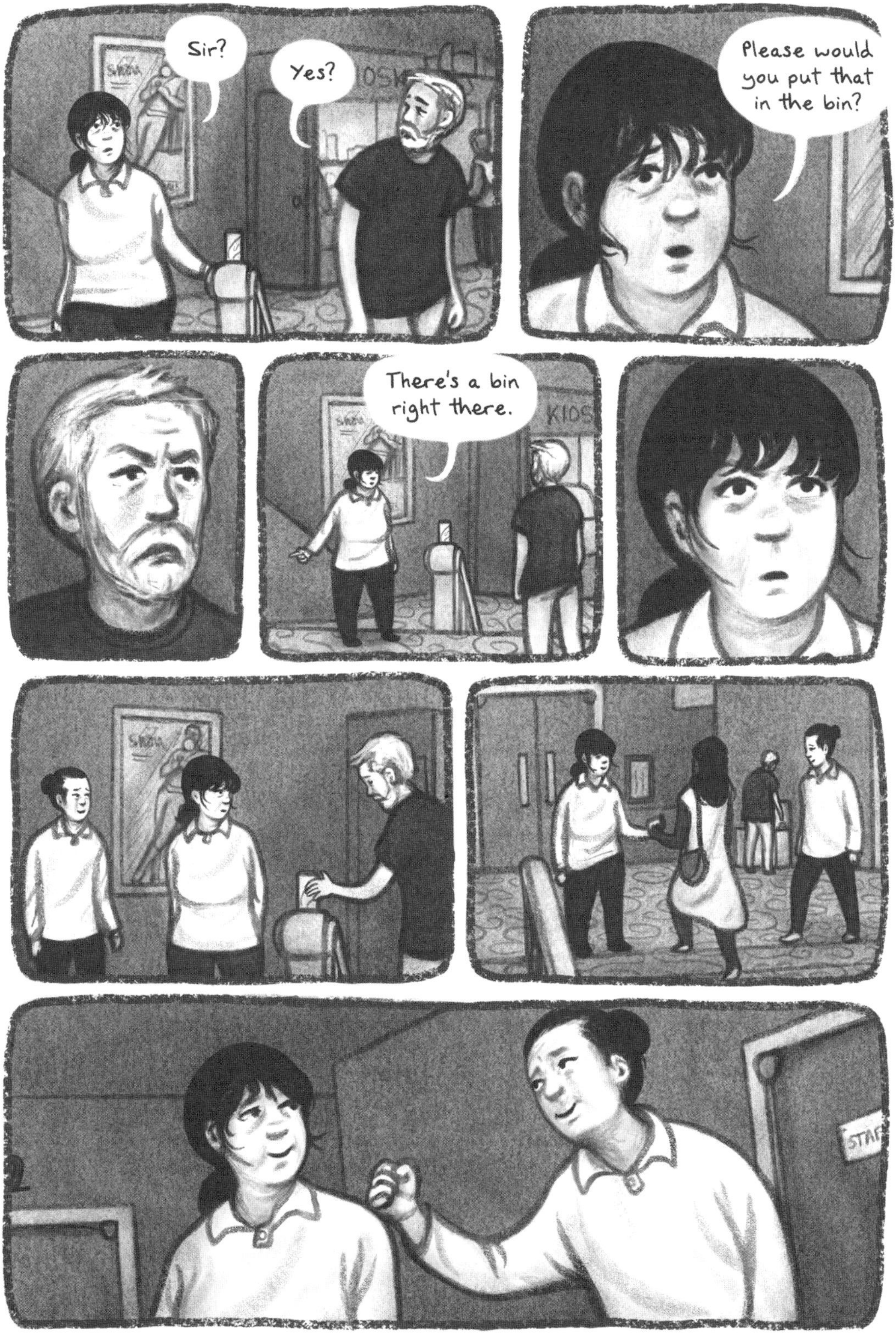
Sir?
Yes?
Please would you put that in the bin?
There's a bin right there.

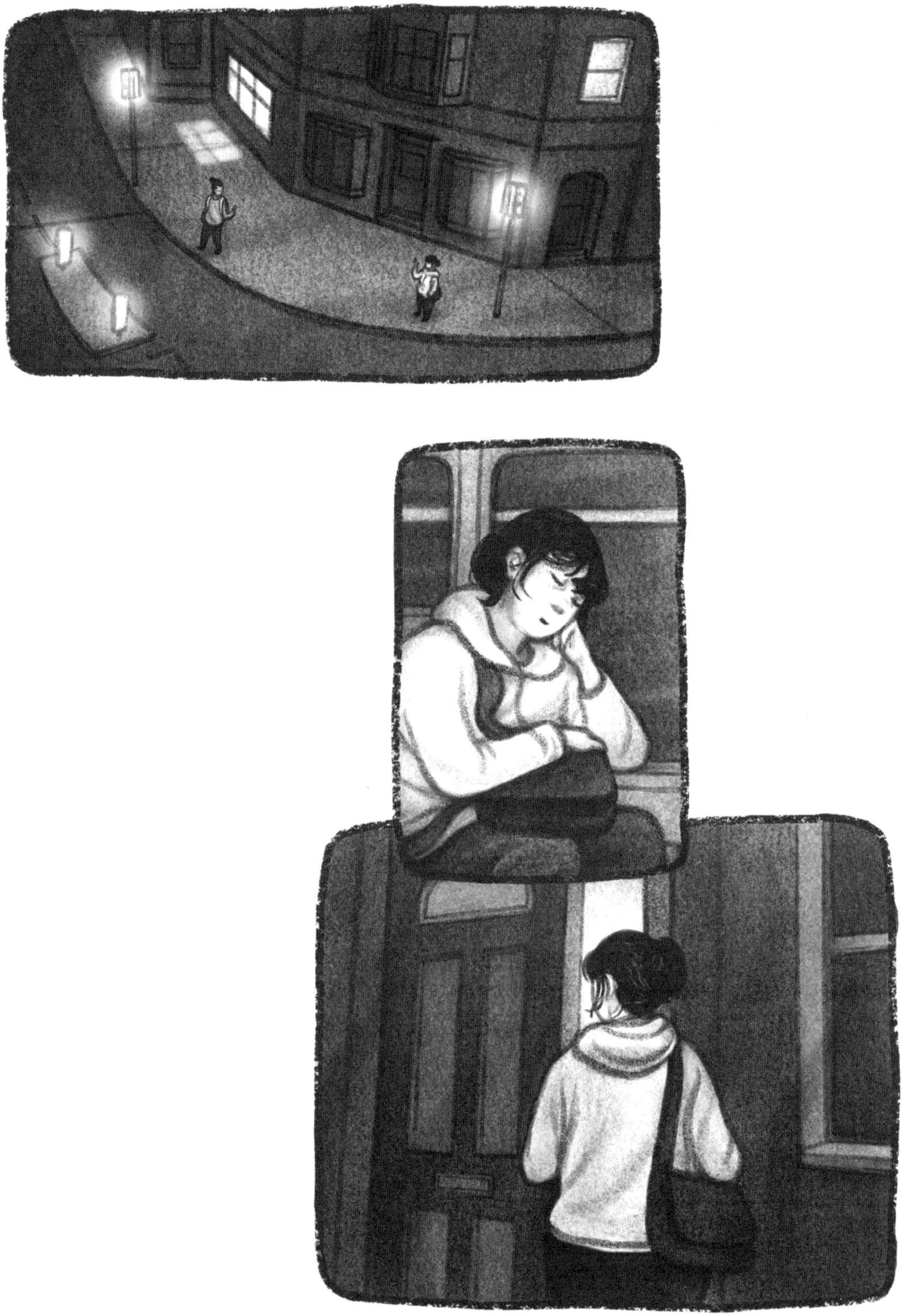

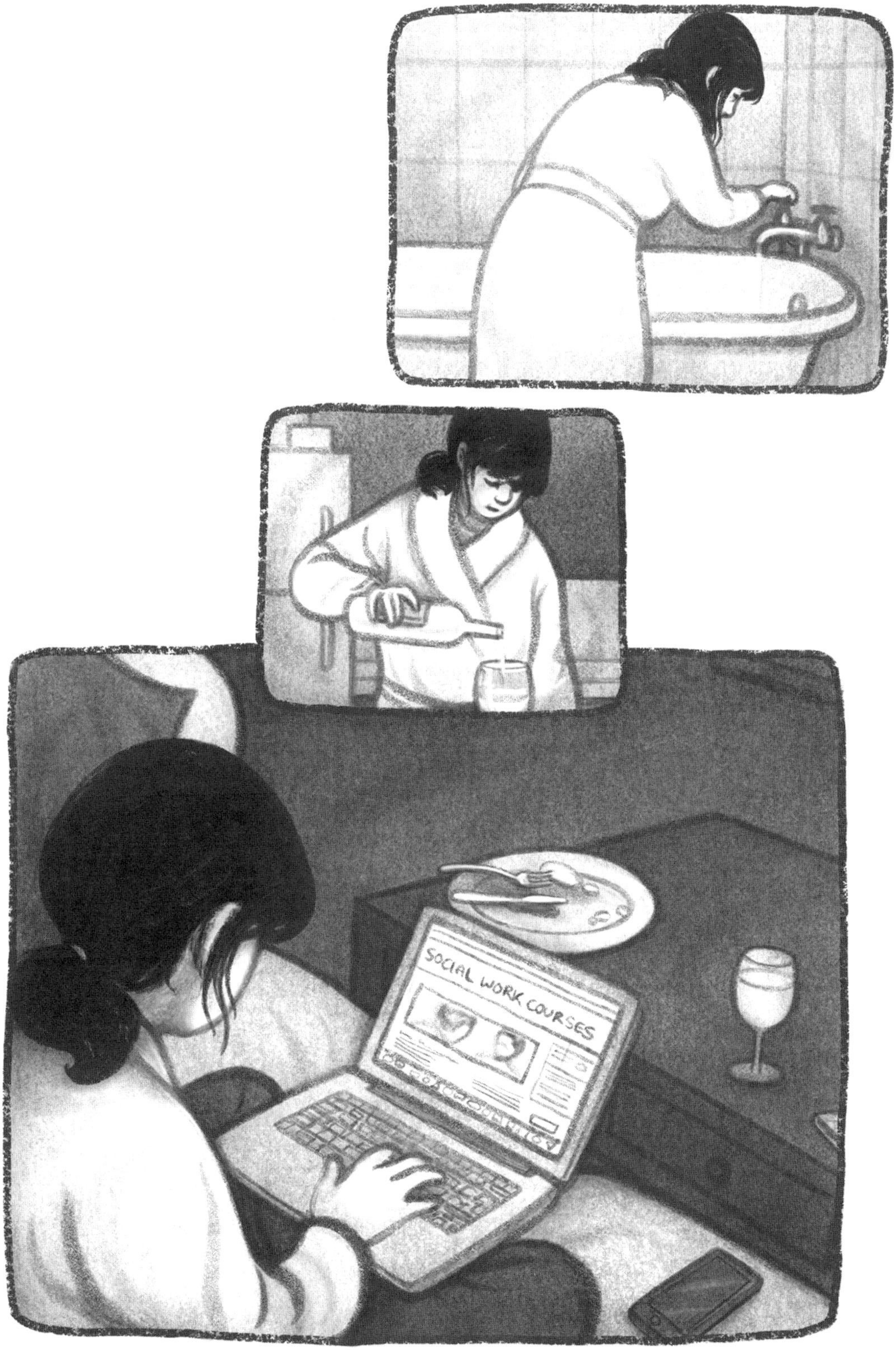
SOCIAL WORK COURSES

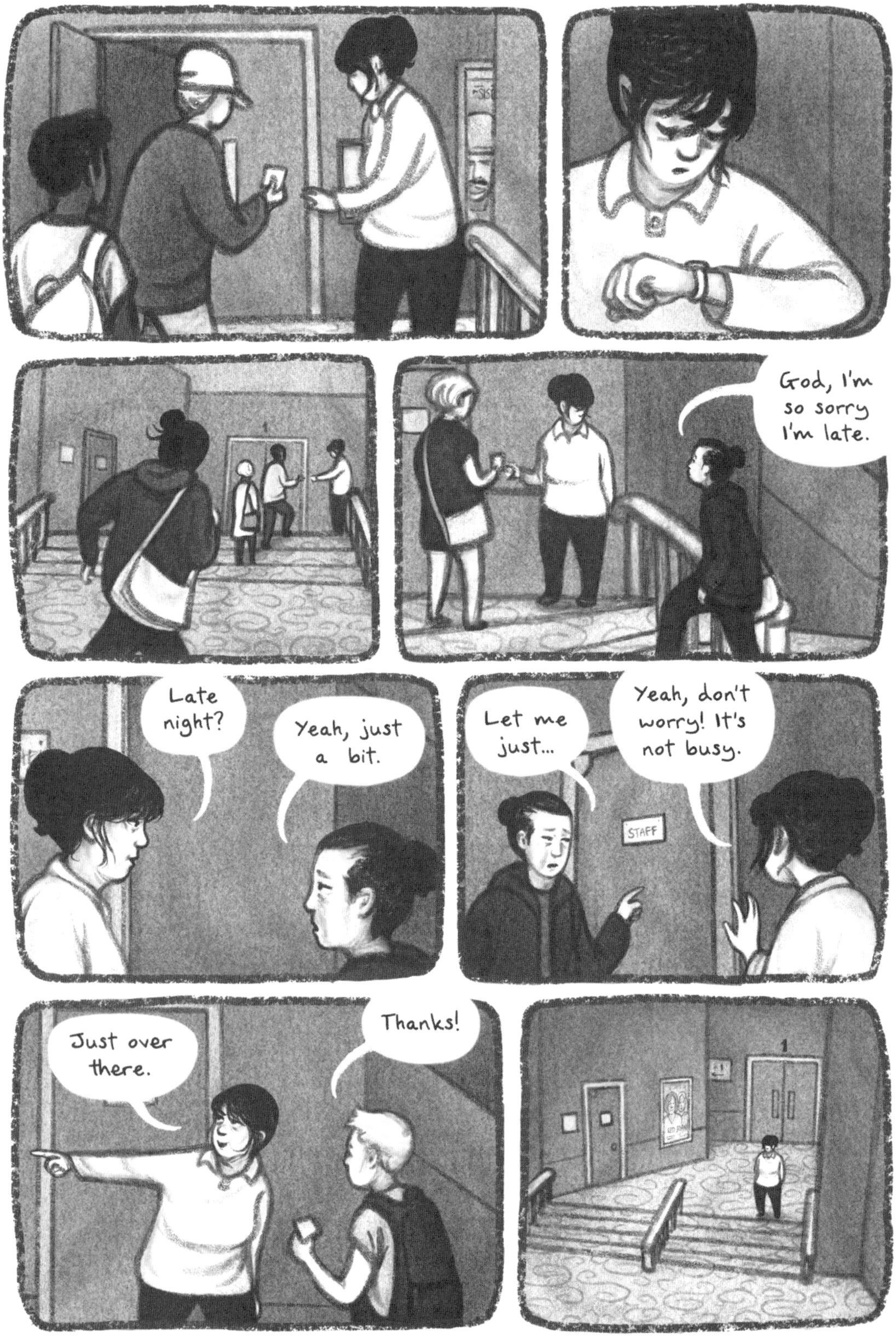
God, I'm so sorry I'm late.
Late night?
Yeah, just a bit.
Let me just...
Yeah, don't worry! It's not busy.
STAFF
Just over there.
Thanks!

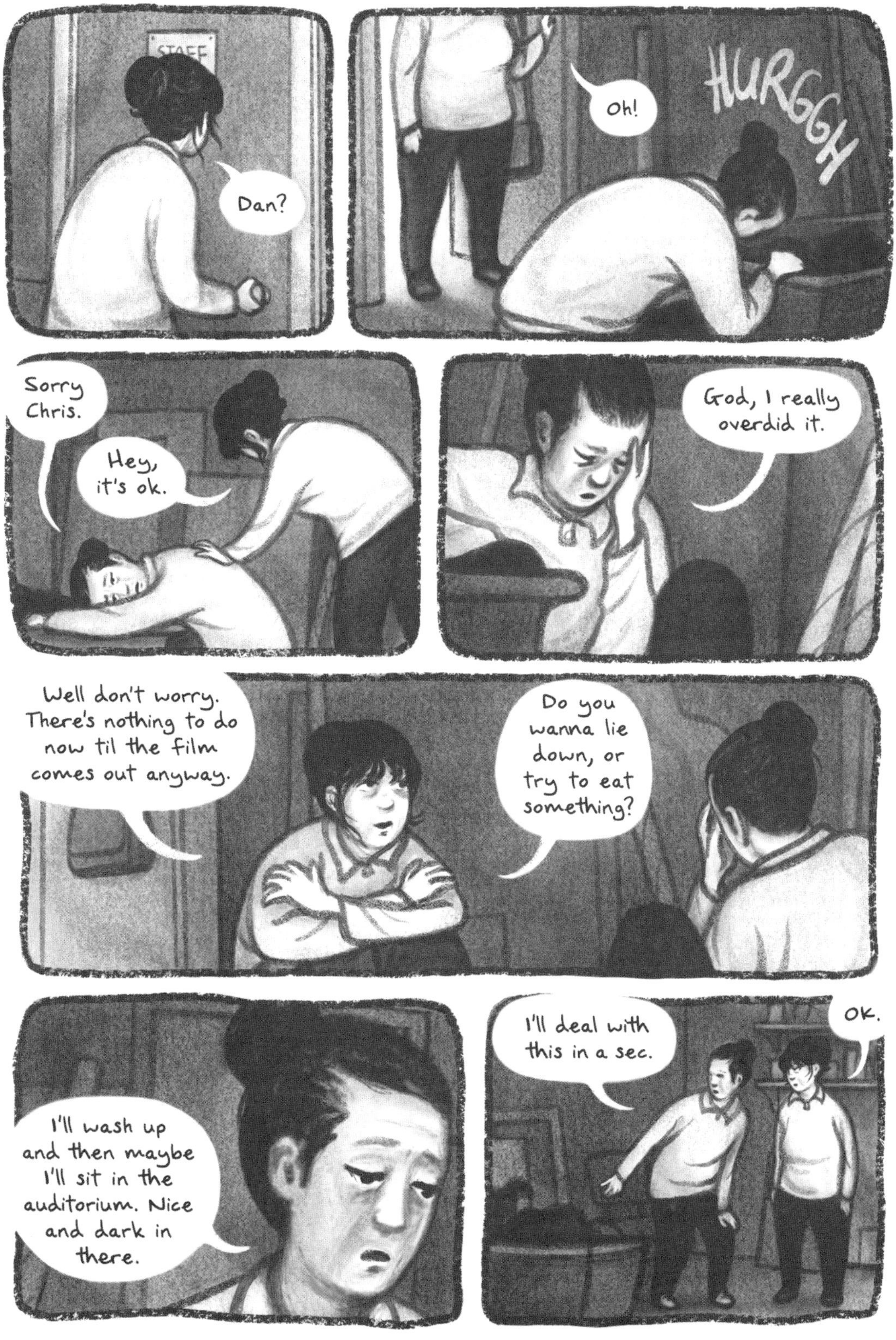

Dan?
Oh!
HURGGH
Sorry Chris.
Hey, it's ok.
God, I really overdid it.
Well don't worry. There's nothing to do now til the film comes out anyway.
Do you wanna lie down, or try to eat something?
I'll wash up and then maybe I'll sit in the auditorium. Nice and dark in there.
I'll deal with this in a sec.
Ok.

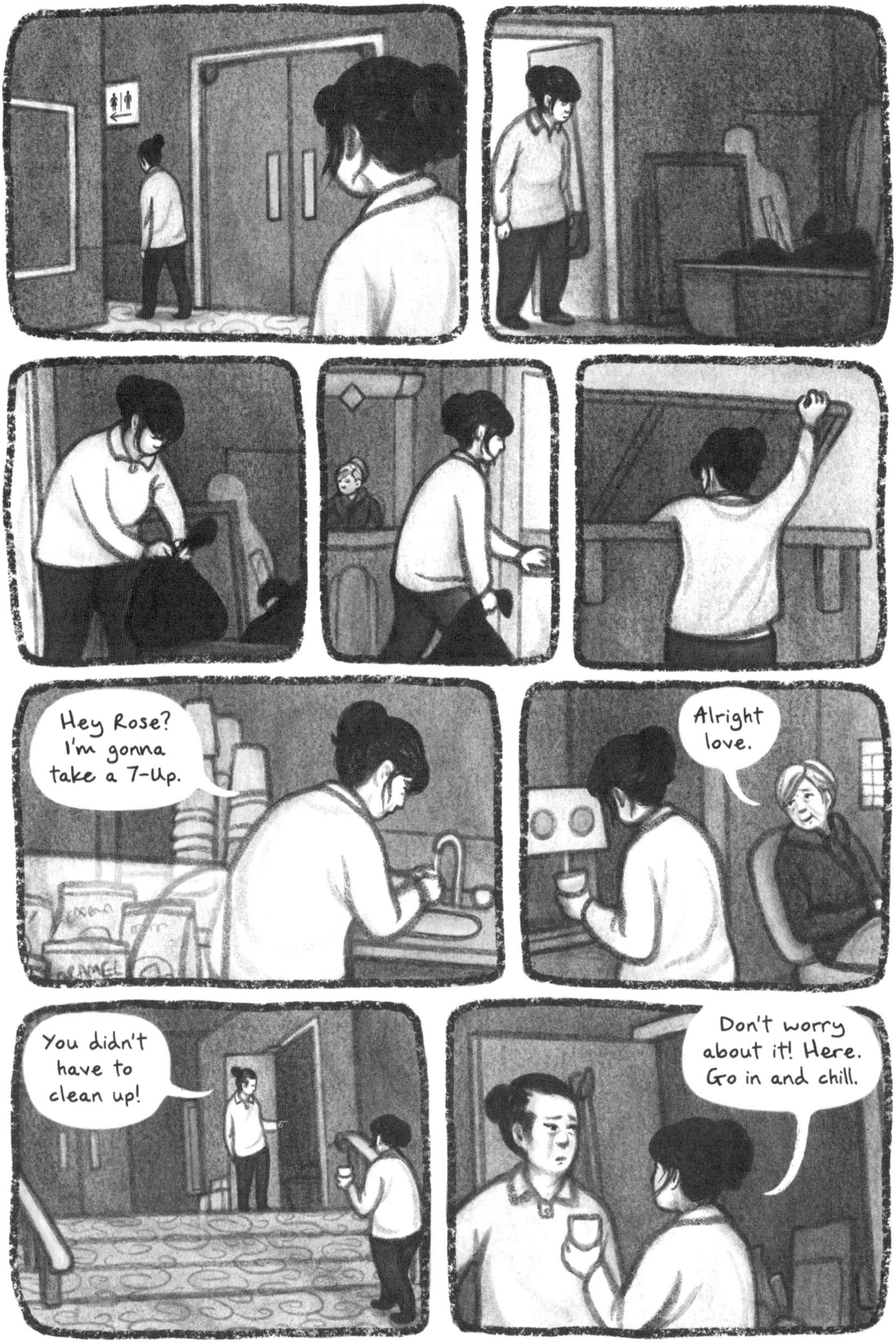
Hey Rose? I'm gonna take a 7-Up.
Alright love.
You didn't have to clean up!
Don't worry about it! Here. Go in and chill.

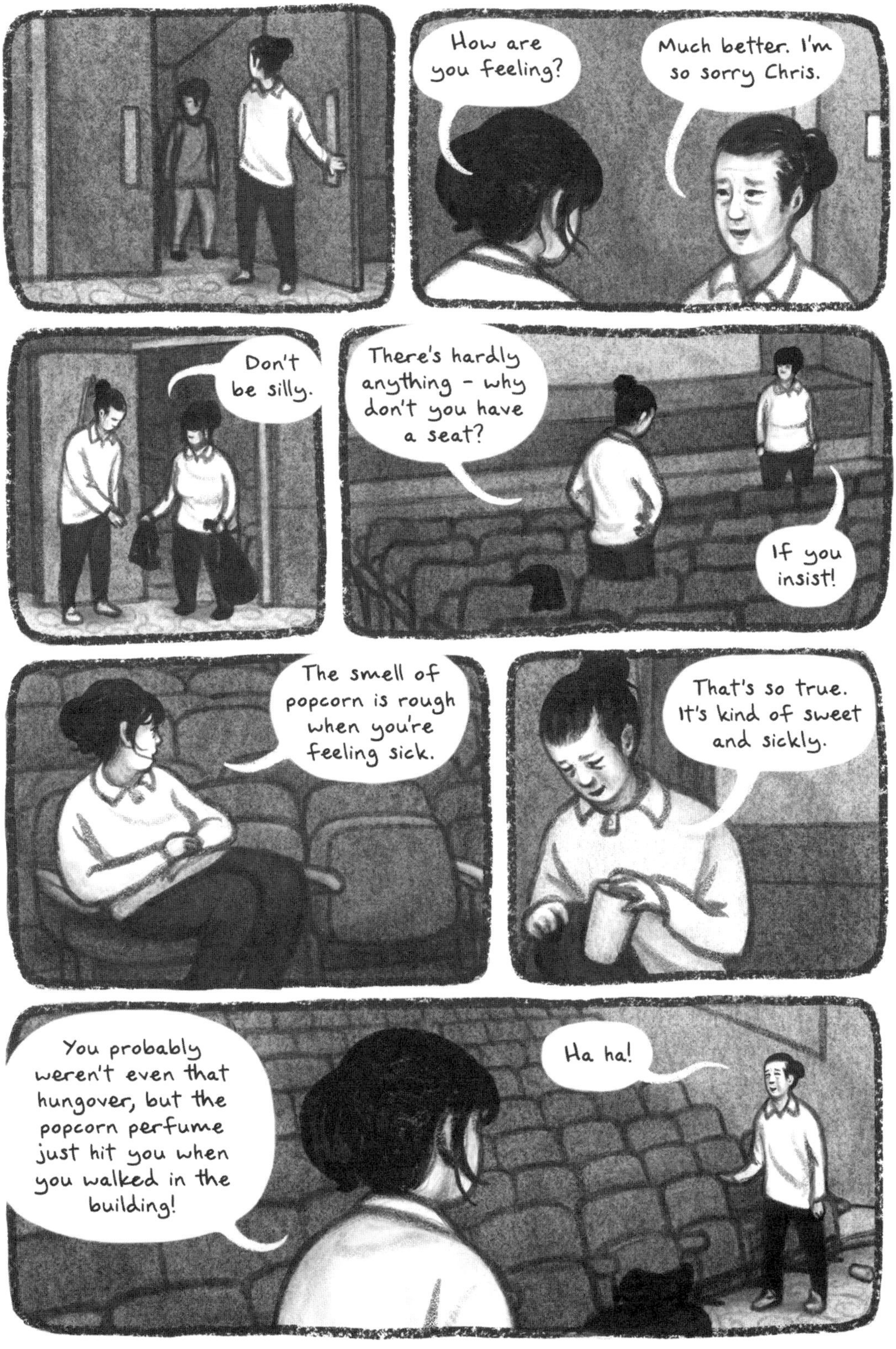
How are you feeling?
Much better. I'm so sorry Chris.
Don't be silly.
There's hardly anything - why don't you have a seat?
If you insist!
The smell of popcorn is rough when you're feeling sick.
That's so true. It's kind of sweet and sickly.
You probably weren't even that hungover, but the popcorn perfume just hit you when you walked in the building!
Ha ha!

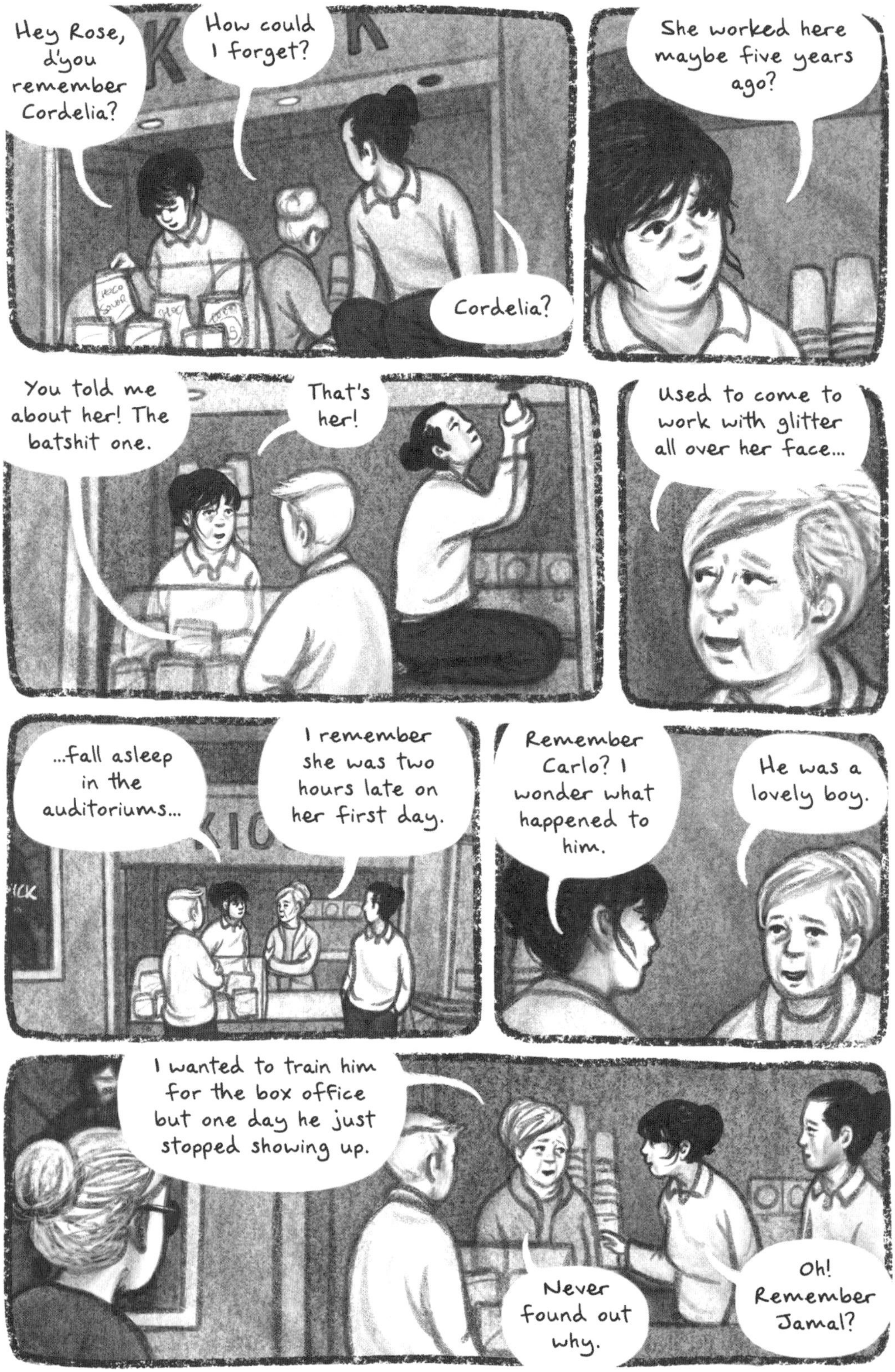

Hey Rose, d'you remember Cordelia?
How could I forget?
Cordelia?
She worked here maybe five years ago?
You told me about her! The batshit one.
That's her!
Used to come to work with glitter all over her face...
...fall asleep in the auditoriums...
I remember she was two hours late on her first day.
Remember Carlo? I wonder what happened to him.
He was a lovely boy.
I wanted to train him for the box office but one day he just stopped showing up.
Never found out why.
Oh! Remember Jamal?

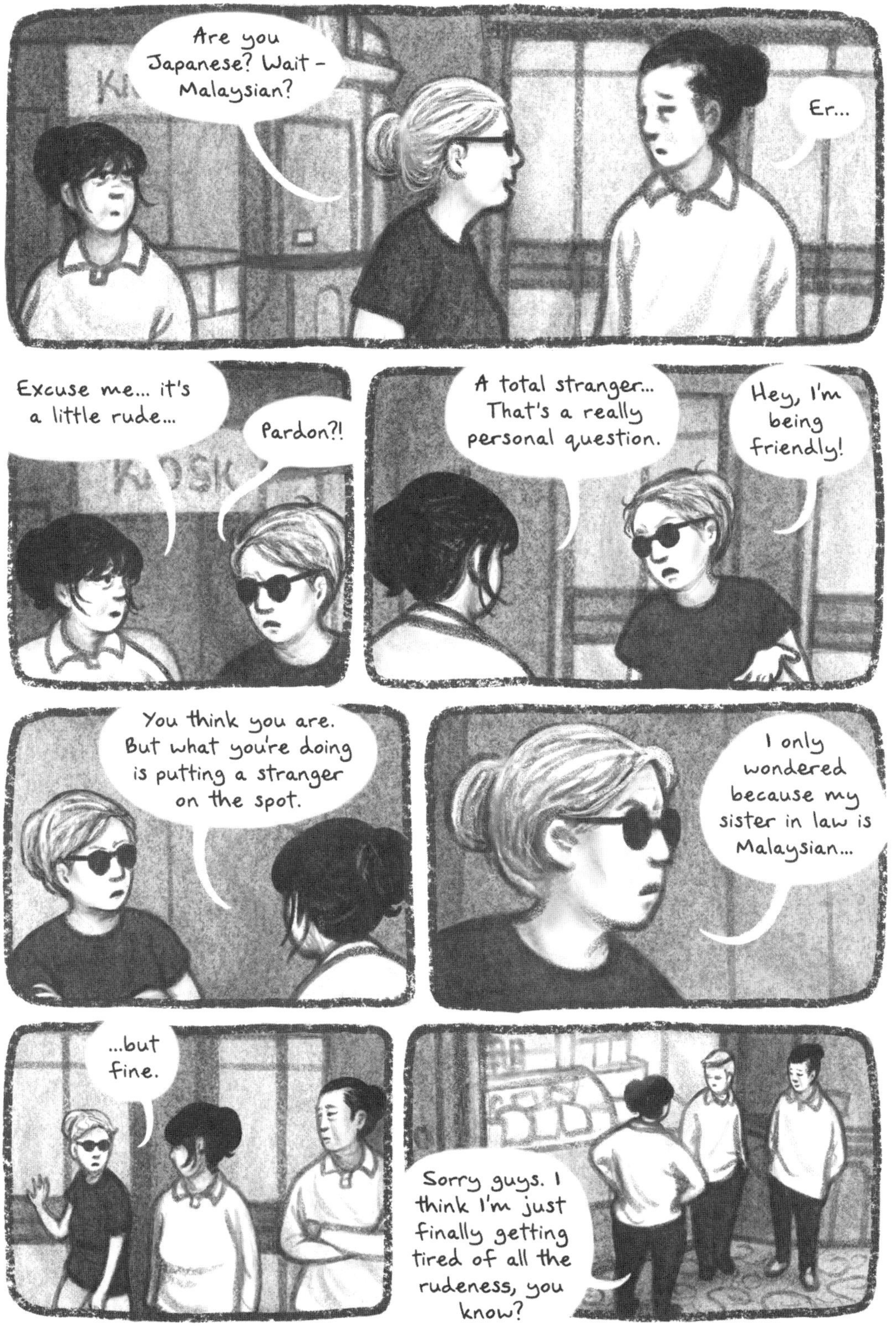

Are you Japanese? Wait - Malaysian?
Er...
Excuse me... it's a little rude...
Pardon?!
A total stranger... That's a really personal question.
Hey, I'm being friendly!
You think you are. But what you're doing is putting a stranger on the spot.
I only wondered because my sister in law is Malaysian...
...but fine.
Sorry guys. I think I'm just finally getting tired of all the rudeness, you know?

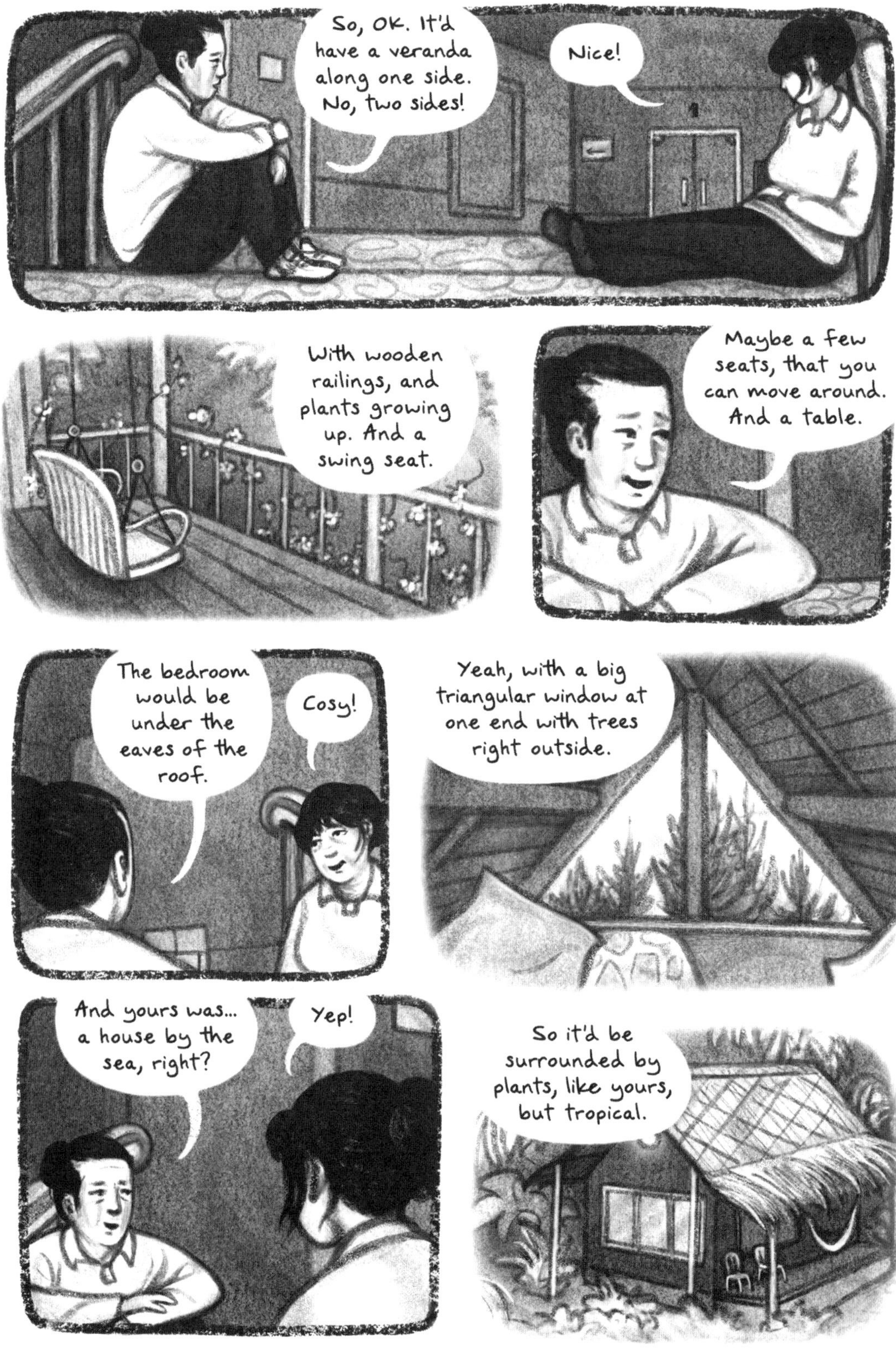
So, OK. It'd have a veranda along one side. No, two sides!
Nice!
With wooden railings, and plants growing up. And a swing seat.
Maybe a few seats, that you can move around. And a table.
The bedroom would be under the eaves of the roof.
Cosy!
Yeah, with a big triangular window at one end with trees right outside.
And yours was... a house by the sea, right?
Yep!
So it'd be surrounded by plants, like yours, but tropical.

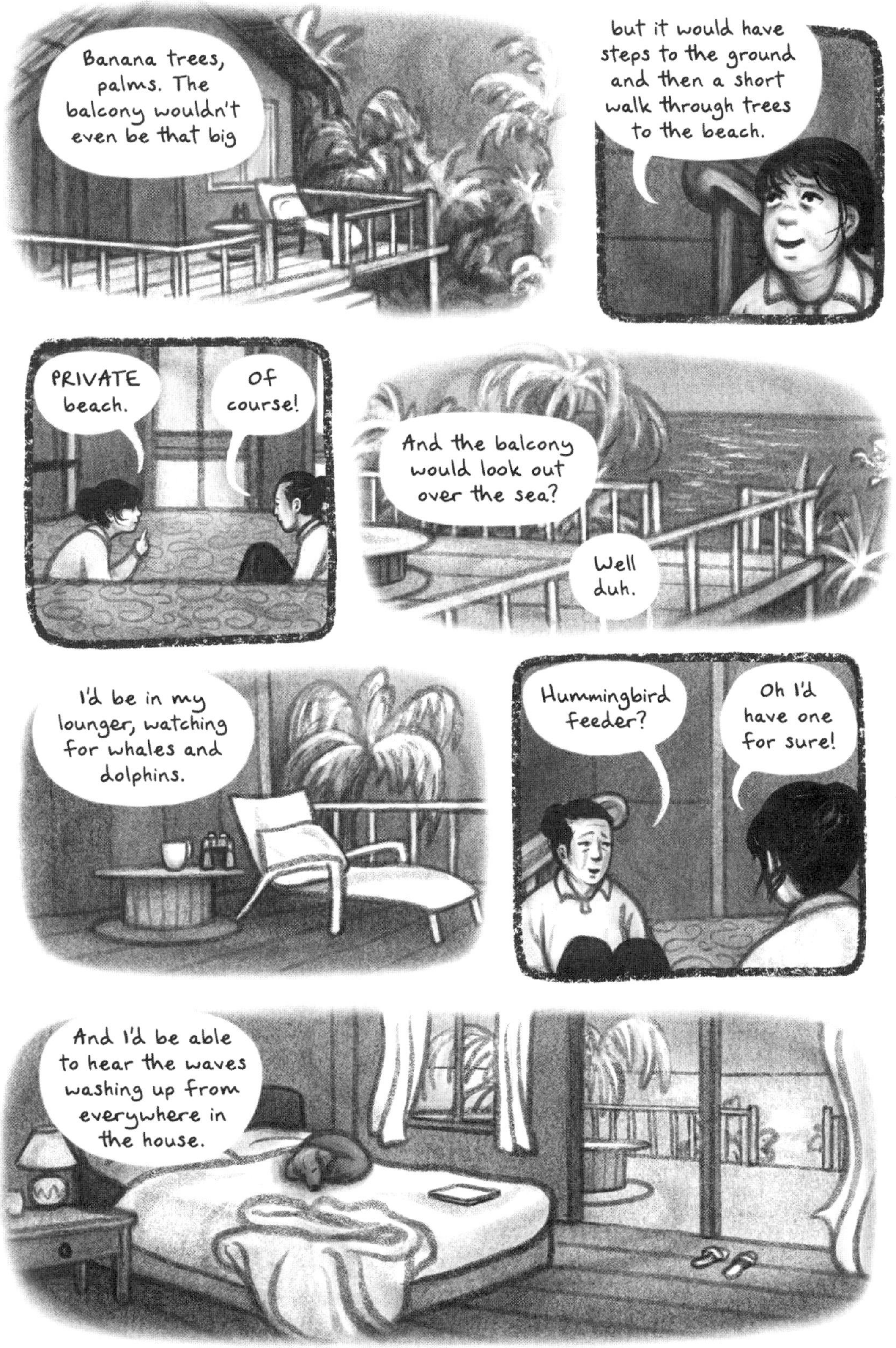
Banana trees, palms. The balcony wouldn't even be that big
but it would have steps to the ground and then a short walk through trees to the beach.
PRIVATE beach.
Of course!
And the balcony would look out over the sea?
Well duh.
I'd be in my lounger, watching for whales and dolphins.
Hummingbird feeder?
Oh I'd have one for sure!
And I'd be able to hear the waves washing up from everywhere in the house.

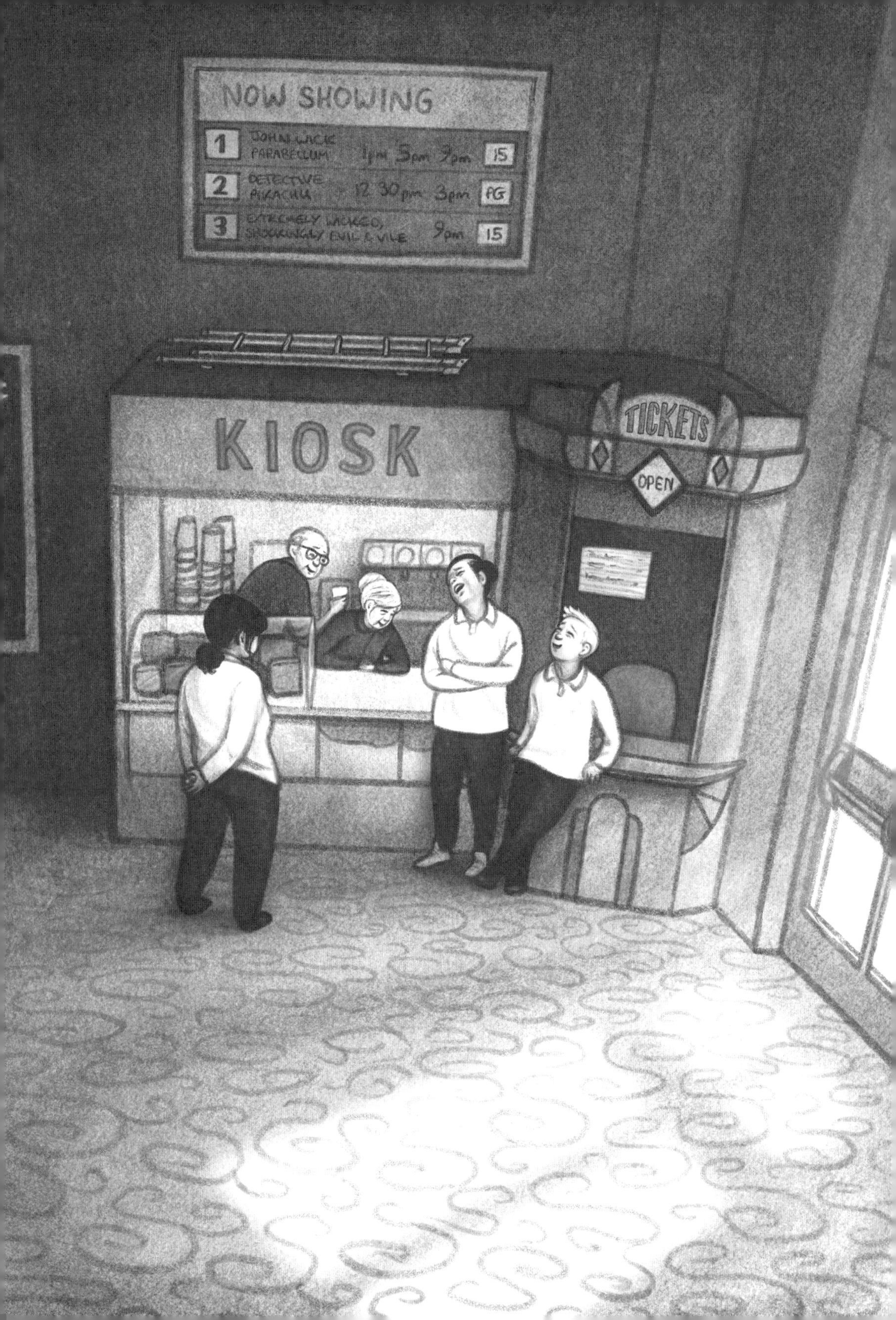
NOW SHOWING
1 JOHN WICK PARABELLUM 1pm 5pm 9pm 15
2 DETECTIVE PIKACHU 12 30pm 3pm PG
3 EXTREMELY WICKED, SHOCKINGLY EVIL & VILE 9pm 15
KIOSK
TICKETS
OPEN

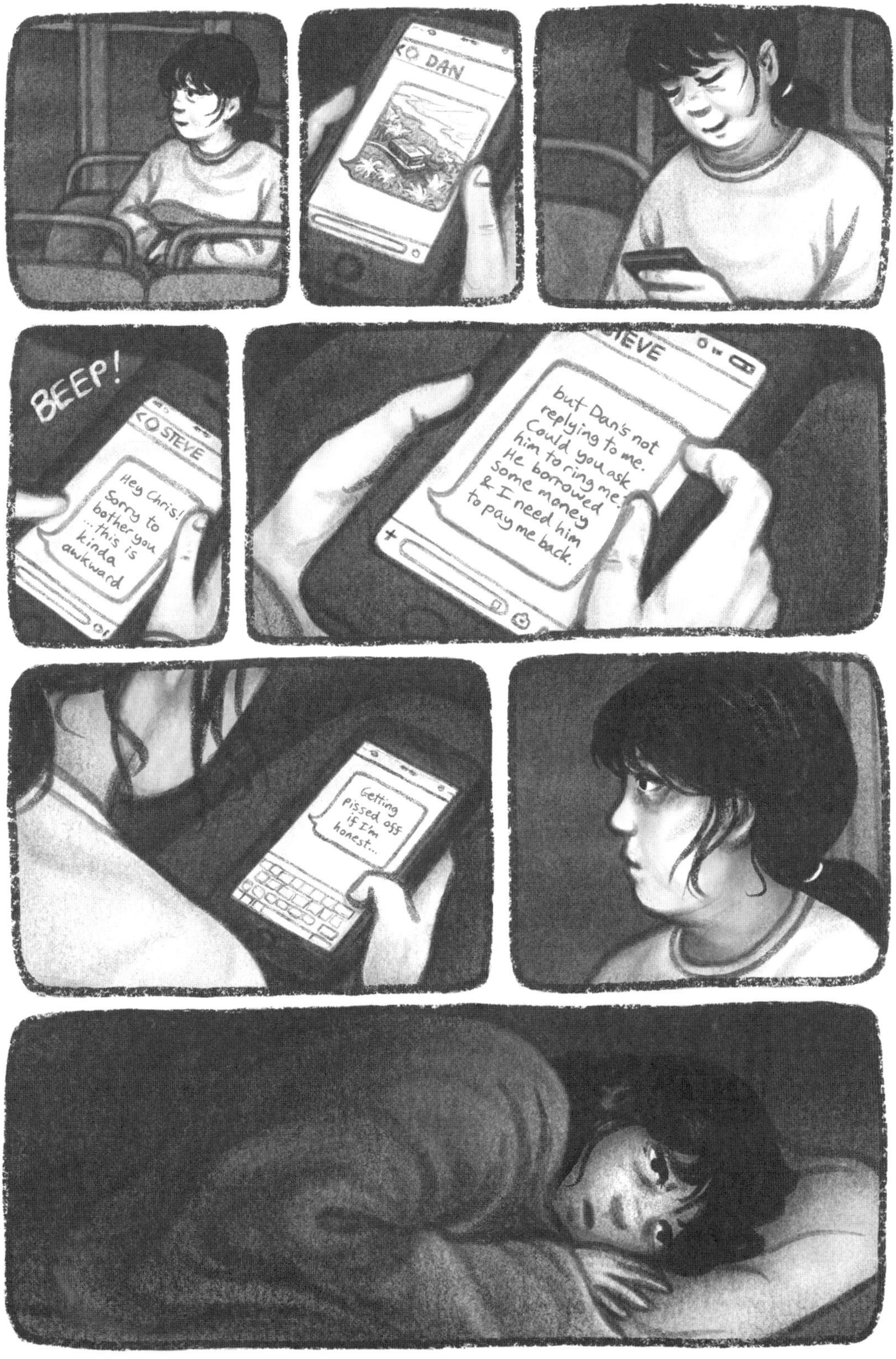

DAN
BEEP!
STEVE
Hey Chris! Sorry to bother you ...this is kinda awkward
but Dan's not replying to me. Could you ask him to ring me. He borrowed some money & I need him to pay me back.
Getting pissed off if I'm honest...

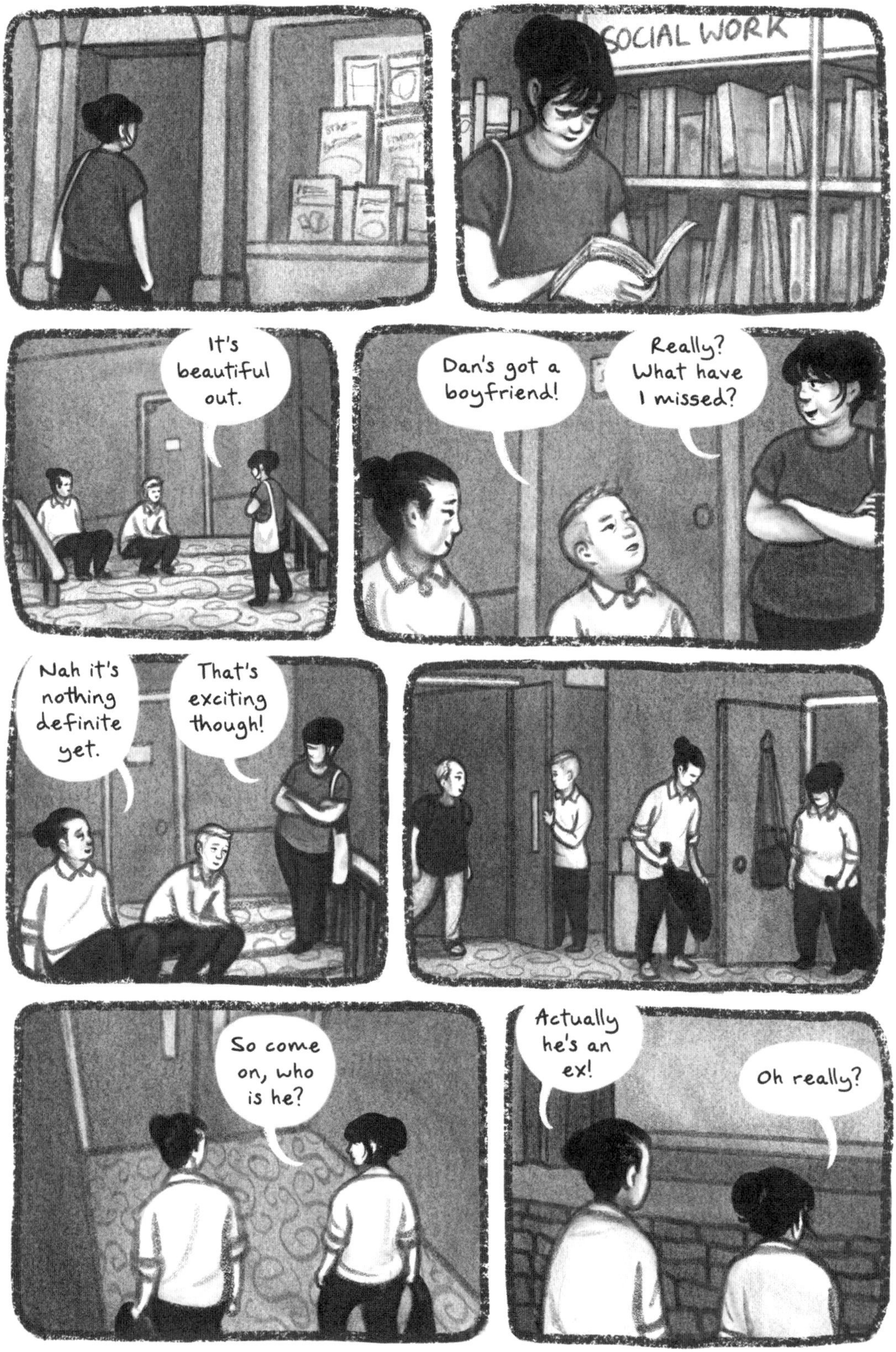
SOCIAL WORK
It's beautiful out.
Dan's got a boyfriend!
Really? What have I missed?
Nah it's nothing definite yet.
That's exciting though!
So come on, who is he?
Actually he's an ex!
Oh really?

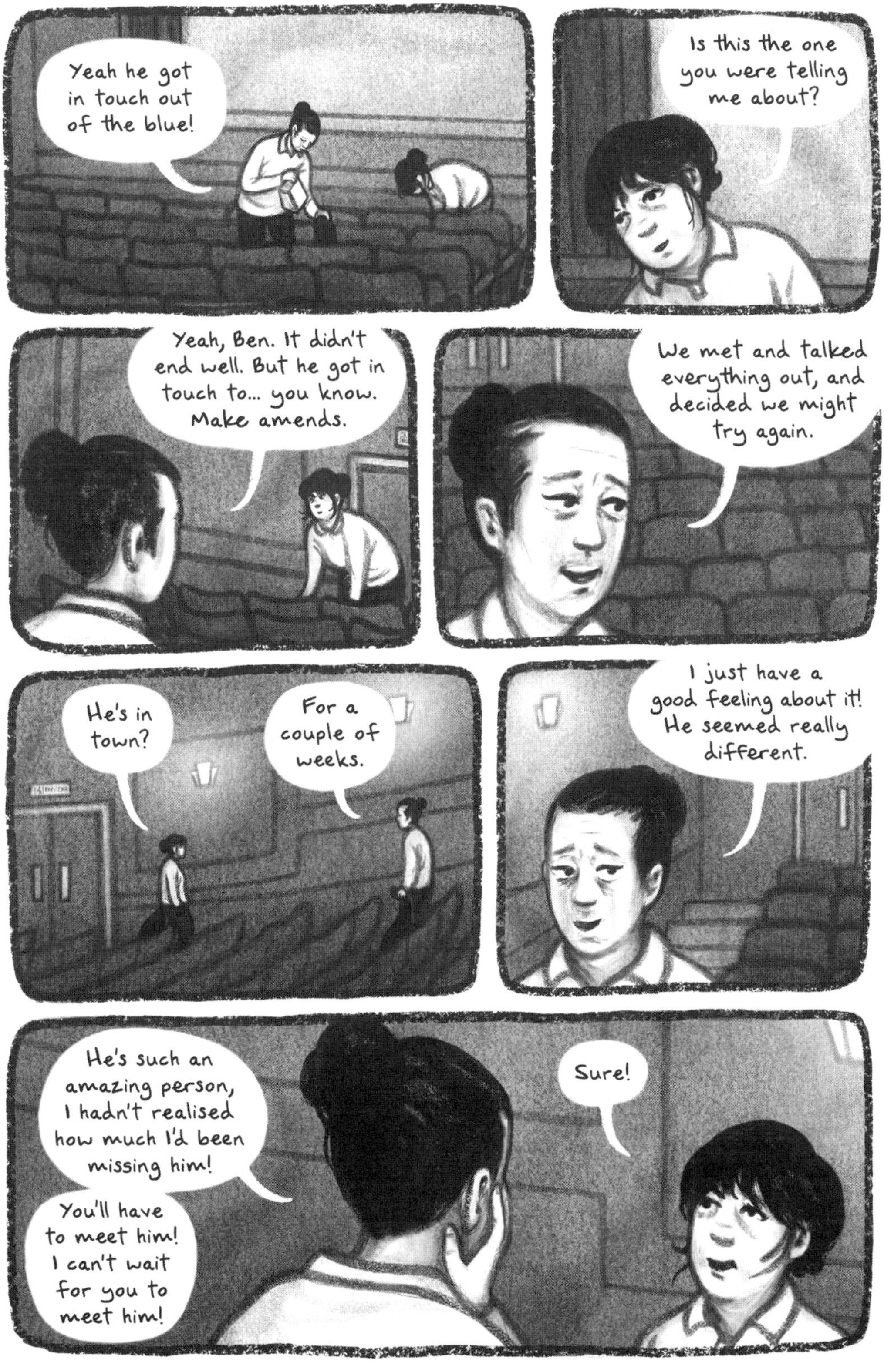
Yeah he got in touch out of the blue!
Is this the one you were telling me about?
Yeah, Ben. It didn't end well. But he got in touch to... you know. Make amends.
We met and talked everything out, and decided we might try again.
He's in town?
For a couple of weeks.
I just have a good feeling about it! He seemed really different.
He's such an amazing person, I hadn't realised how much I'd been missing him!
You'll have to meet him! I can't wait for you to meet him!
Sure!

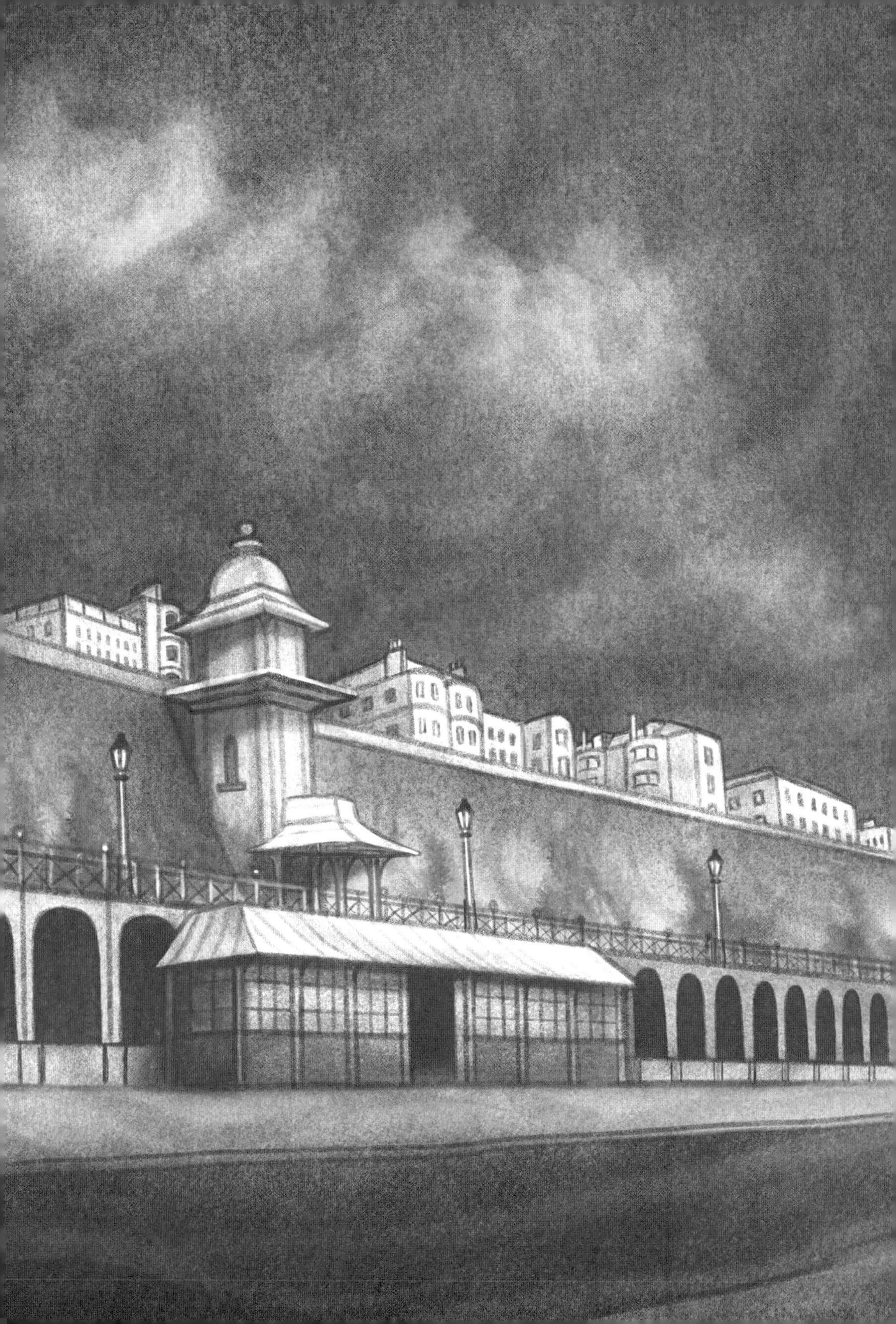

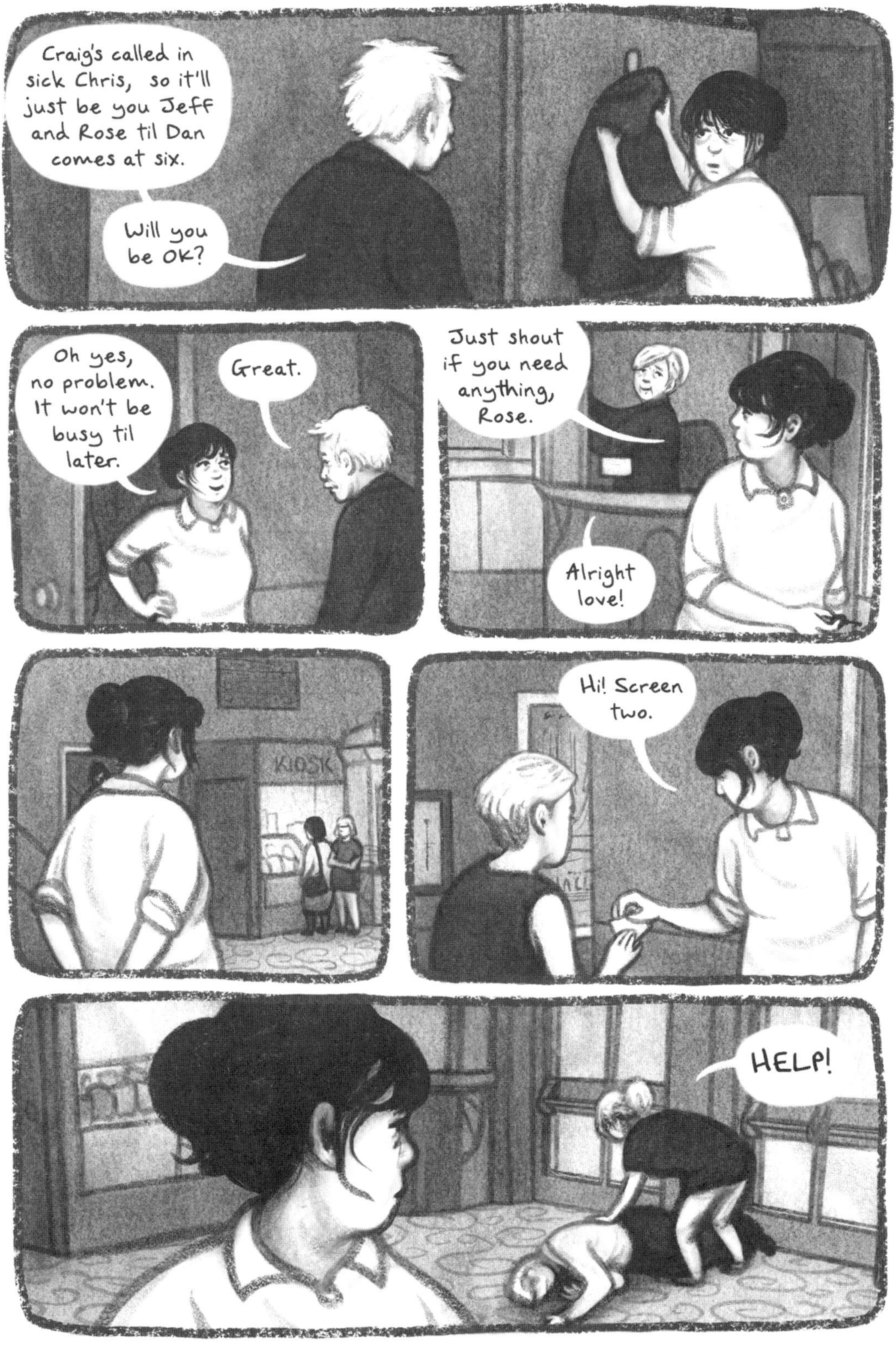
Craig's called in sick Chris, so it'll just be you Jeff and Rose til Dan comes at six.
Will you be OK?
Oh yes, no problem. It won't be busy til later.
Great.
Just shout if you need anything, Rose.
Alright love!
KIOSK
Hi! Screen two.
HELP!

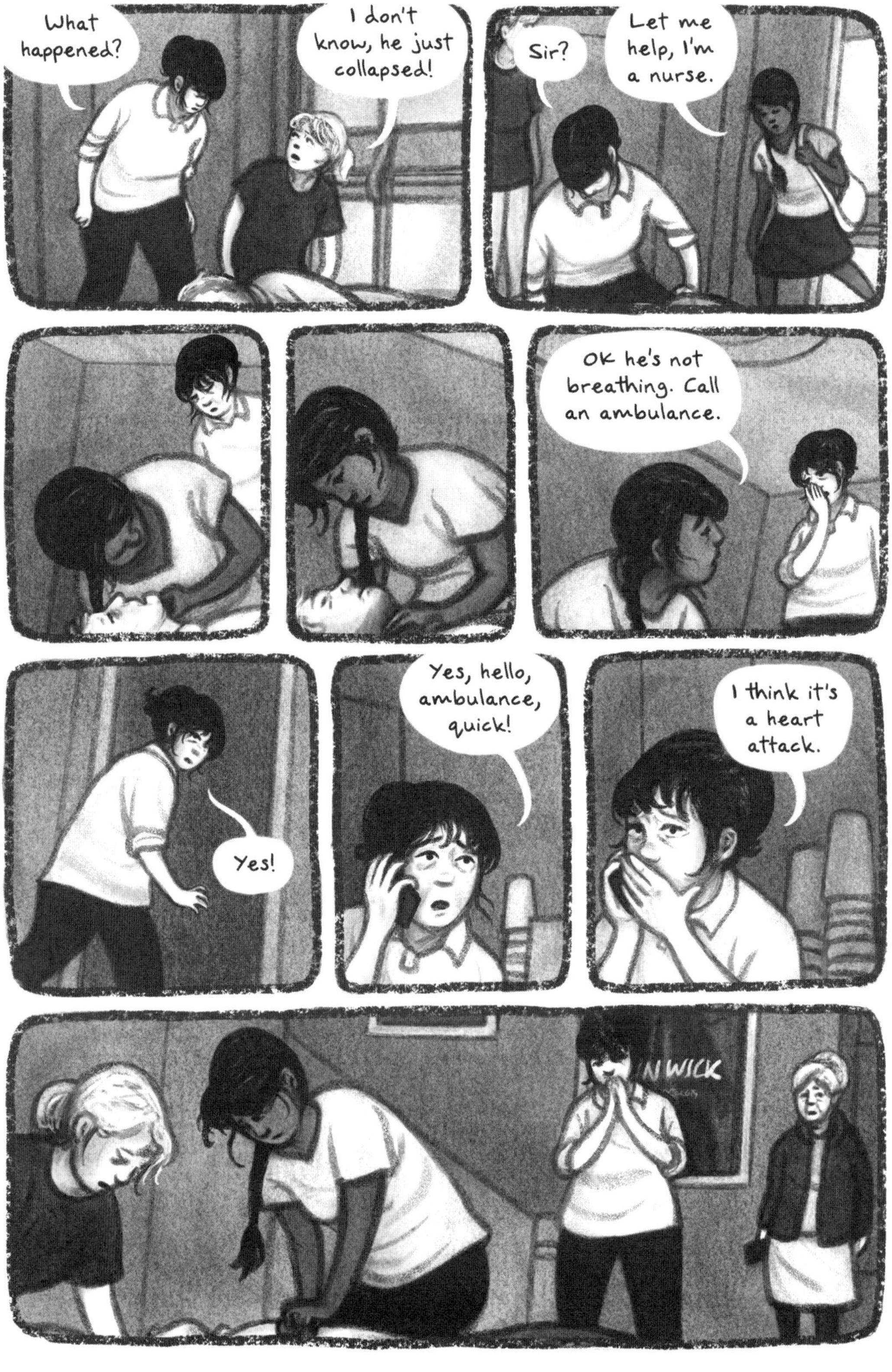
What happened?
I don't know, he just collapsed!
Sir?
Let me help, I'm a nurse.
OK he's not breathing. Call an ambulance.
Yes!
Yes, hello, ambulance, quick!
I think it's a heart attack.
N WICK

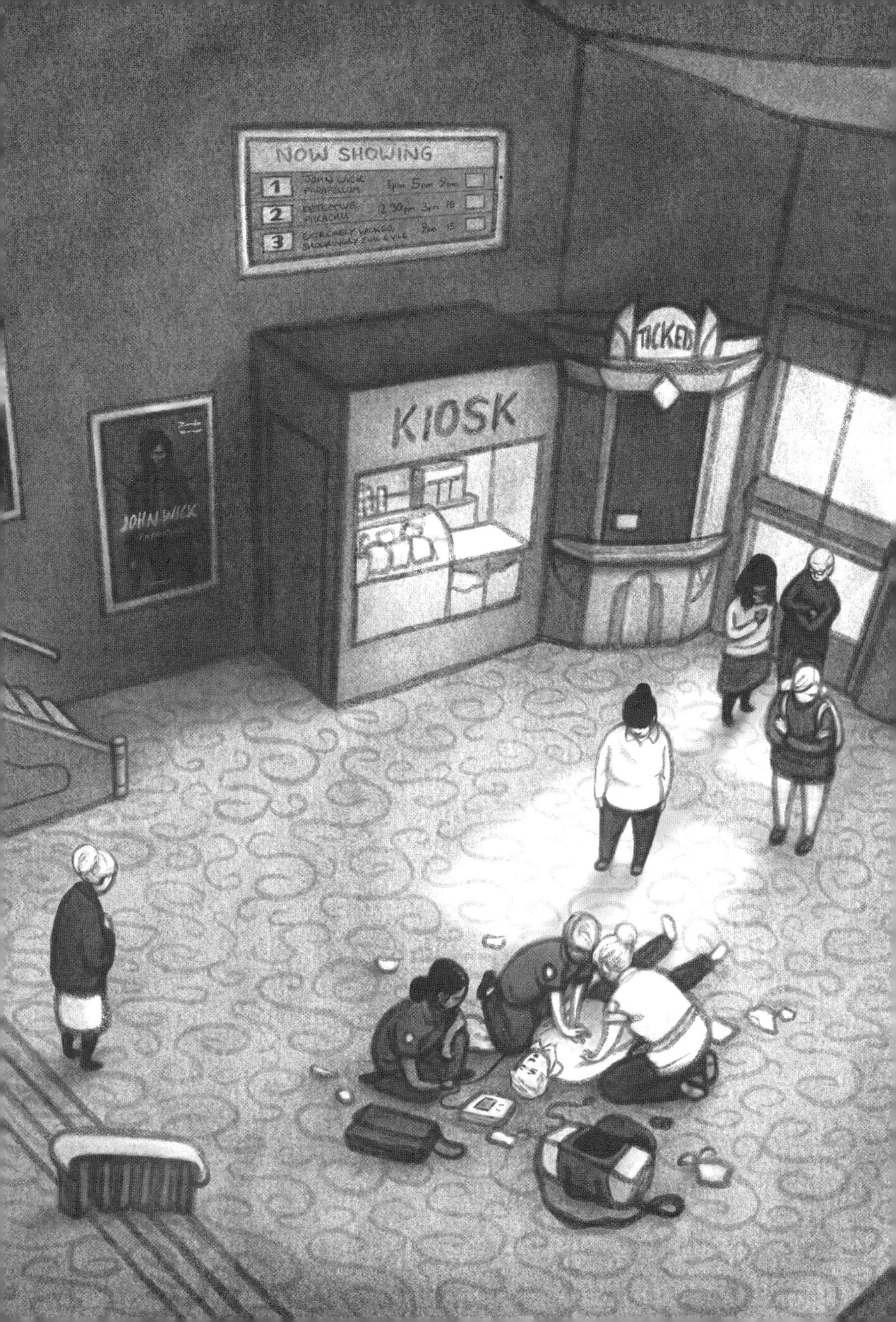
NOW SHOWING
1 JOHN WICK PARABELLUM 1pm 5pm 9pm
2 DETECTIVE PIKACHU 12.30pm 3pm PG
3 EXTREMELY WICKED, SHOCKINGLY EVIL & VILE 9pm 15
JOHN WICK
KIOSK

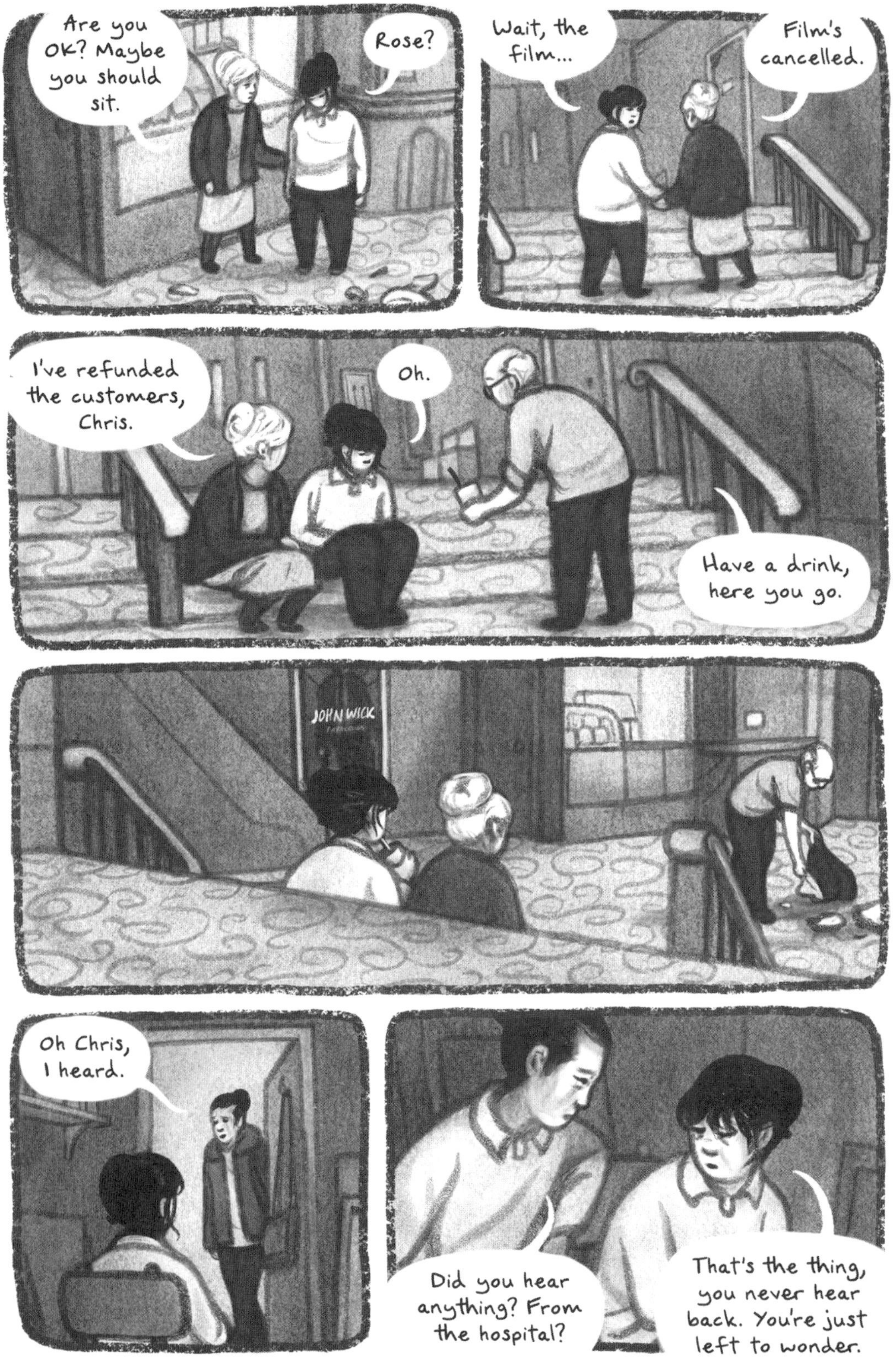
Are you OK? Maybe you should sit.
Rose?
Wait, the film...
Film's cancelled.
I've refunded the customers, Chris.
Oh.
Have a drink, here you go.
JOHN WICK
Oh Chris, I heard.
Did you hear anything? From the hospital?
That's the thing, you never hear back. You're just left to wonder.

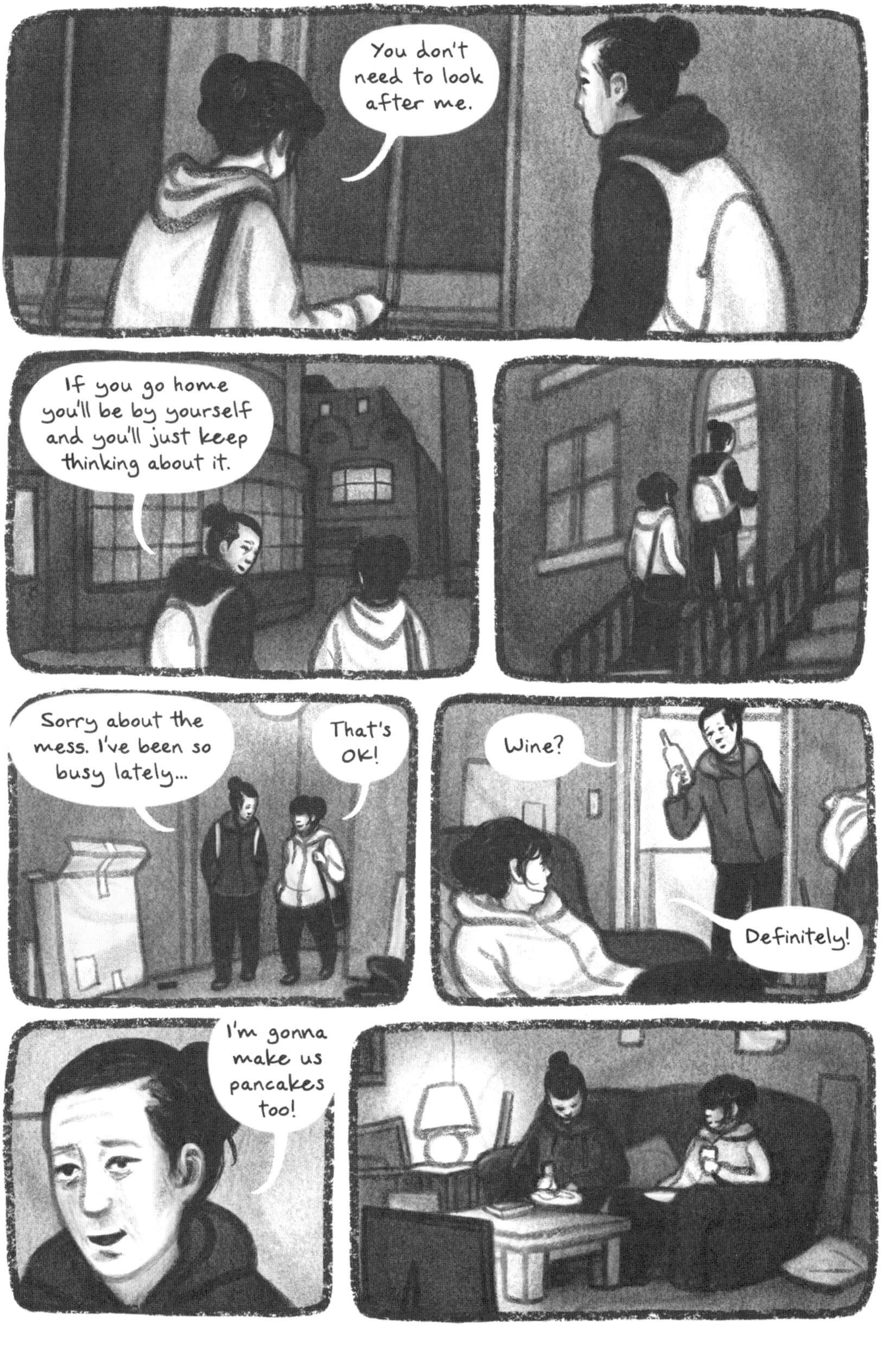
You don't need to look after me.
If you go home you'll be by yourself and you'll just keep thinking about it.
Sorry about the mess. I've been so busy lately...
That's OK!
Wine?
Definitely!
I'm gonna make us pancakes too!

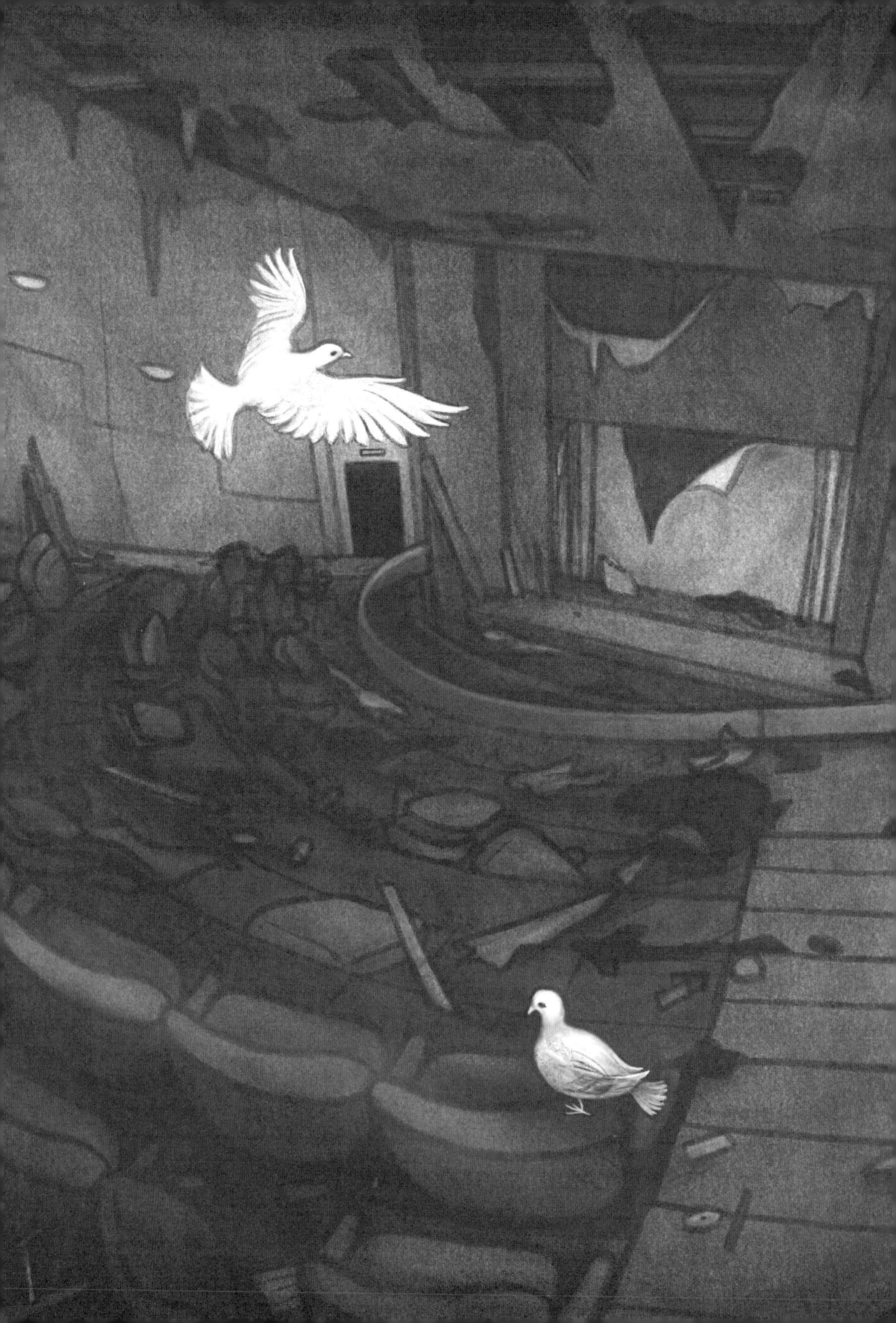

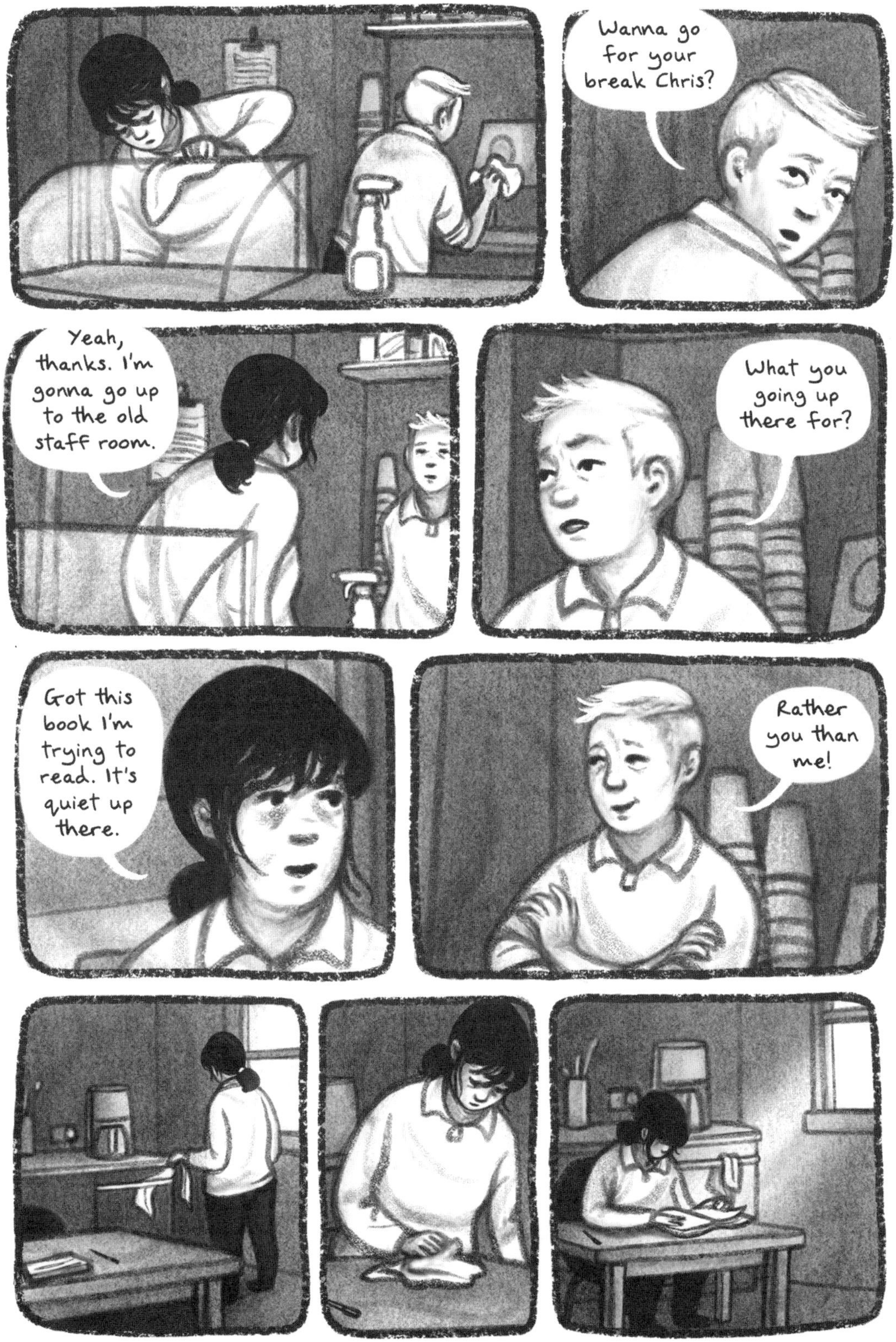

Wanna go for your break Chris?
Yeah, thanks. I'm gonna go up to the old staff room.
What you going up there for?
Got this book I'm trying to read. It's quiet up there.
Rather you than me!

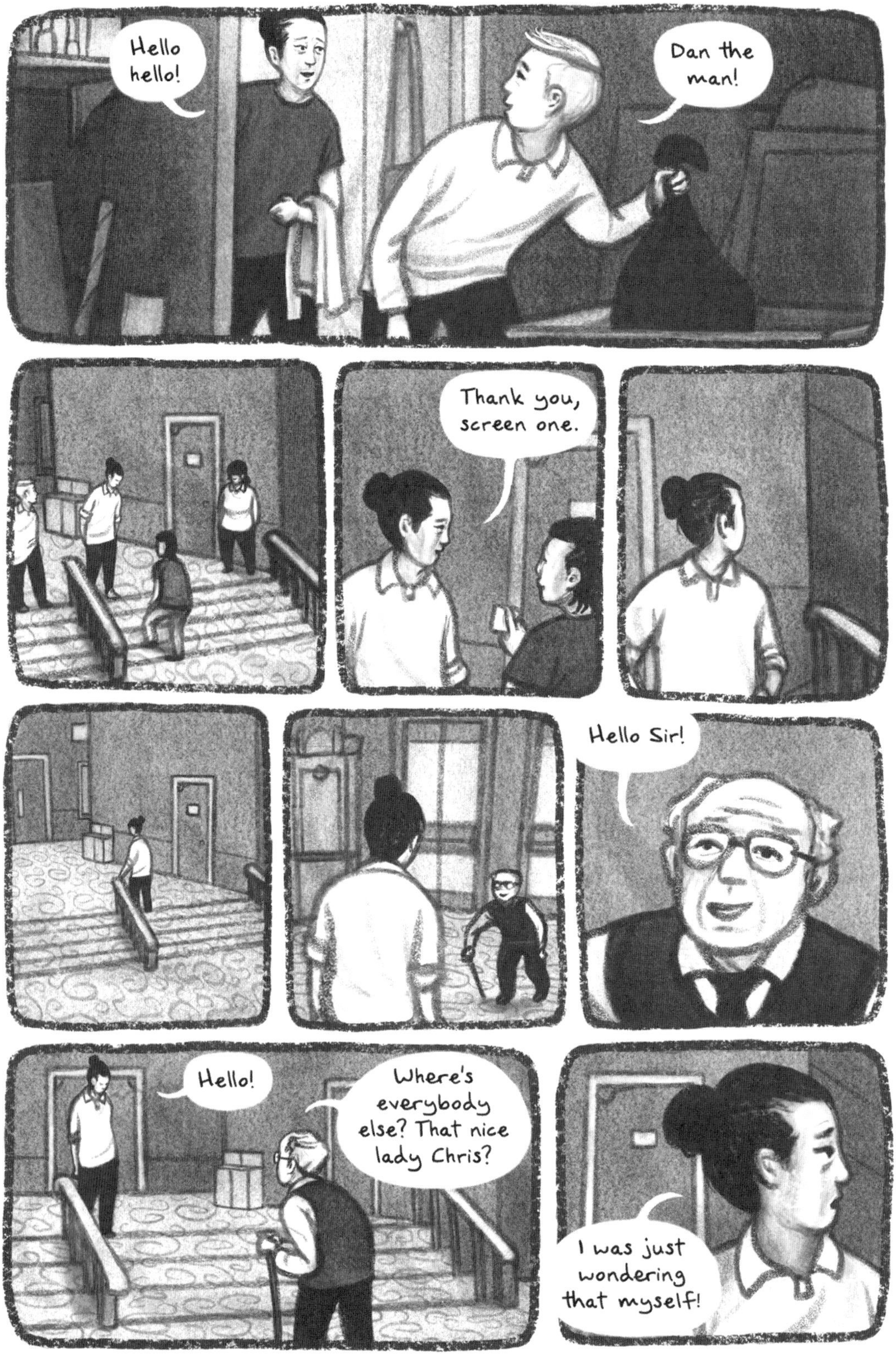
Hello hello!
Dan the man!
Thank you, screen one.
Hello Sir!
Hello!
Where's everybody else? That nice lady Chris?
I was just wondering that myself!

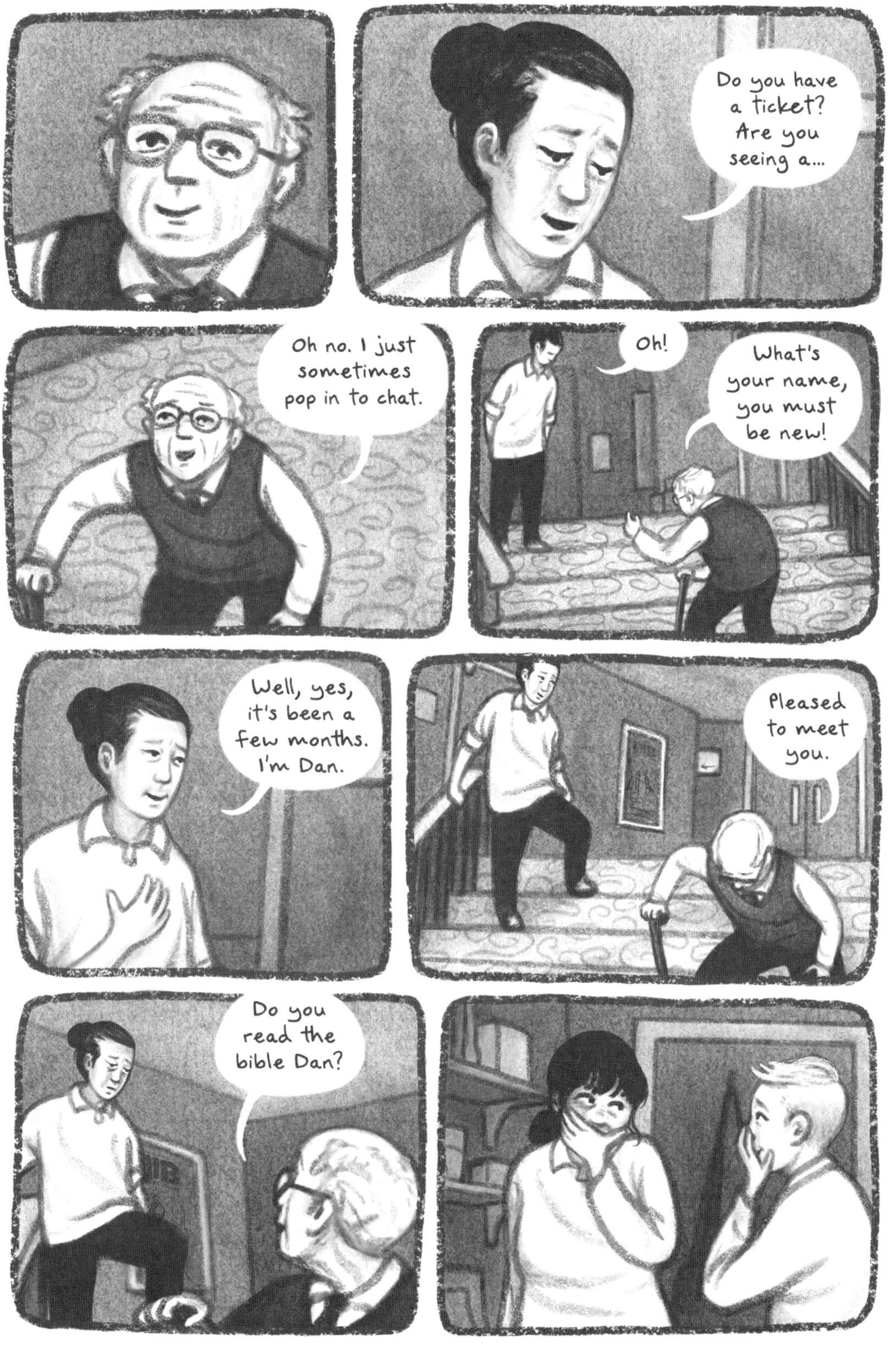
Do you have a ticket? Are you seeing a...
Oh no. I just sometimes pop in to chat.
Oh!
What's your name, you must be new!
Well, yes, it's been a few months. I'm Dan.
Pleased to meet you.
Do you read the bible Dan?

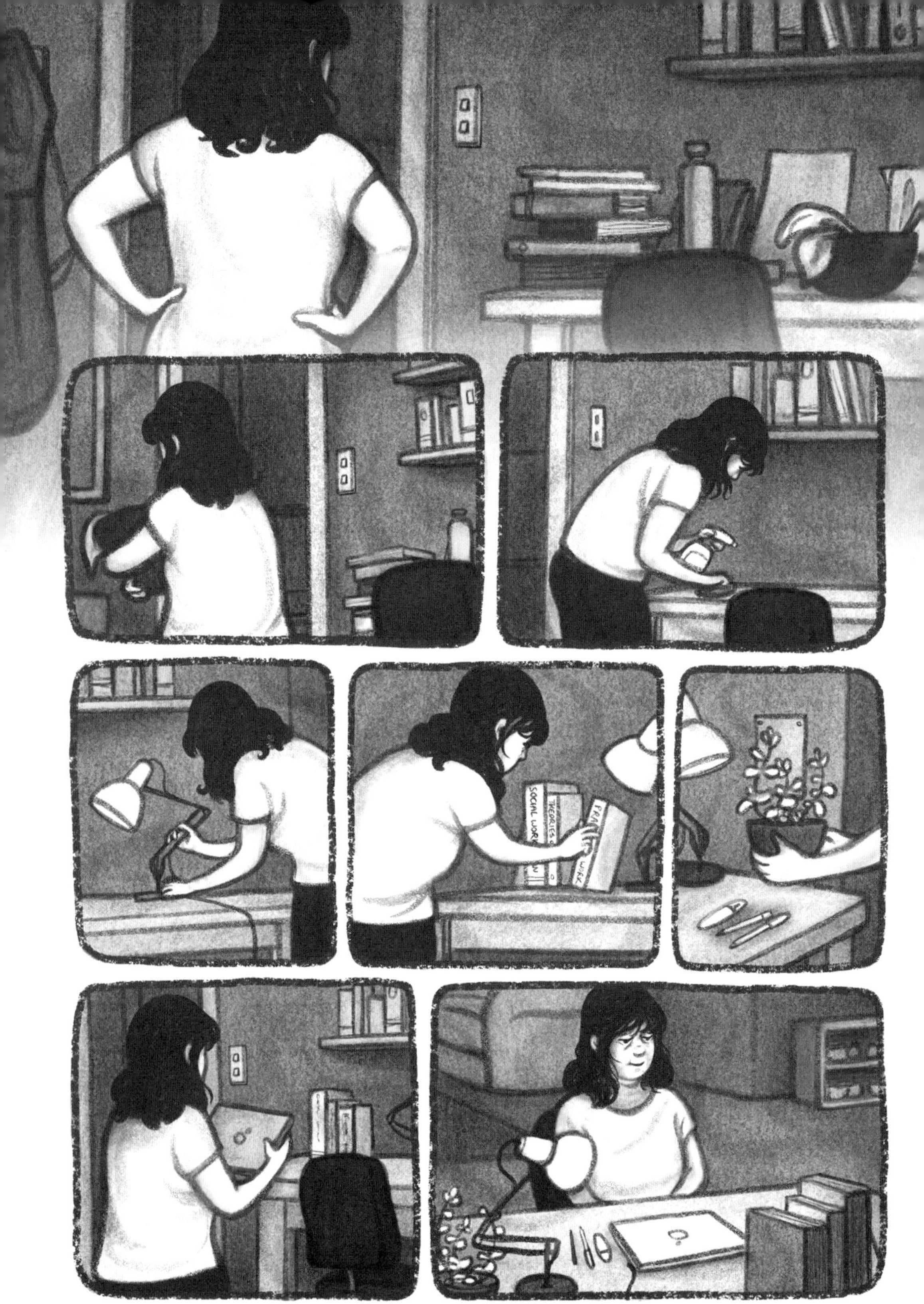
SOCIAL WORK
THEORIES

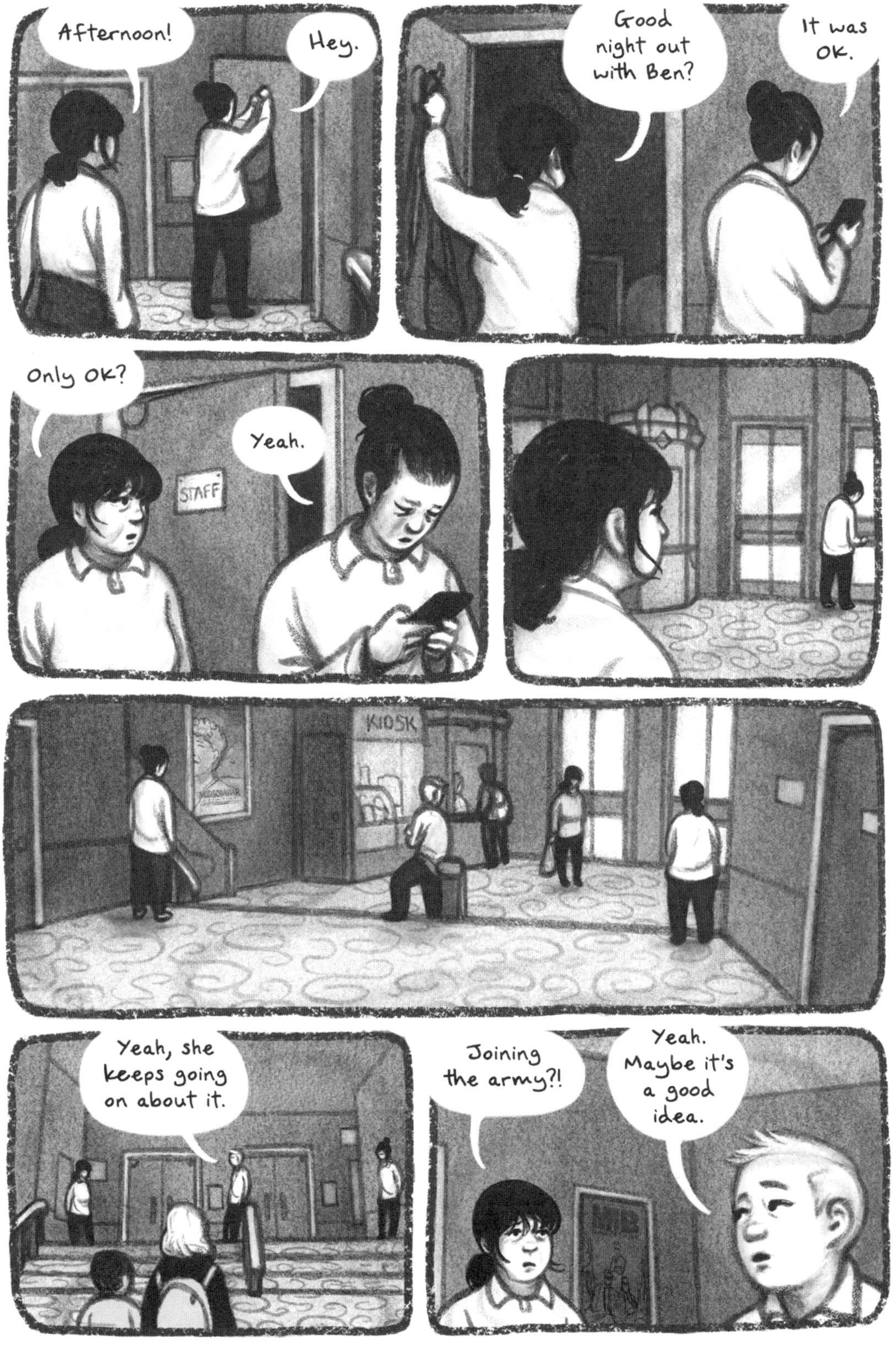
Afternoon!
Hey.
Good night out with Ben?
It was OK.
Only OK?
Yeah.
STAFF
KIOSK
Yeah, she keeps going on about it.
Joining the army?!
Yeah. Maybe it's a good idea.

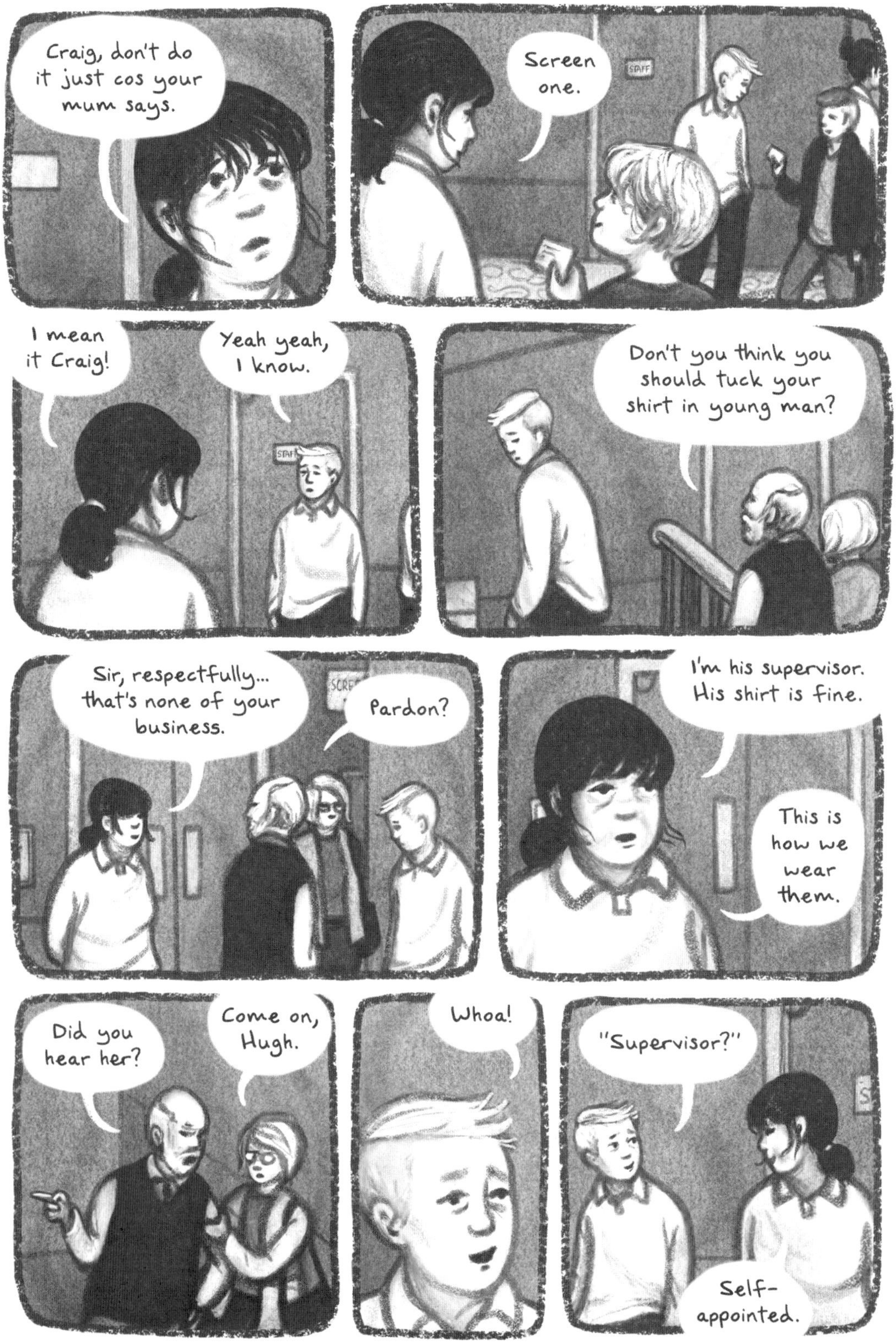
Craig, don't do it just cos your mum says.
Screen one.
STAFF
I mean it Craig!
Yeah yeah, I know.
STAFF
Don't you think you should tuck your shirt in young man?
Sir, respectfully... that's none of your business.
Pardon?
I'm his supervisor. His shirt is fine.
This is how we wear them.
Did you hear her?
Come on, Hugh.
Whoa!
"Supervisor?"
Self-appointed.

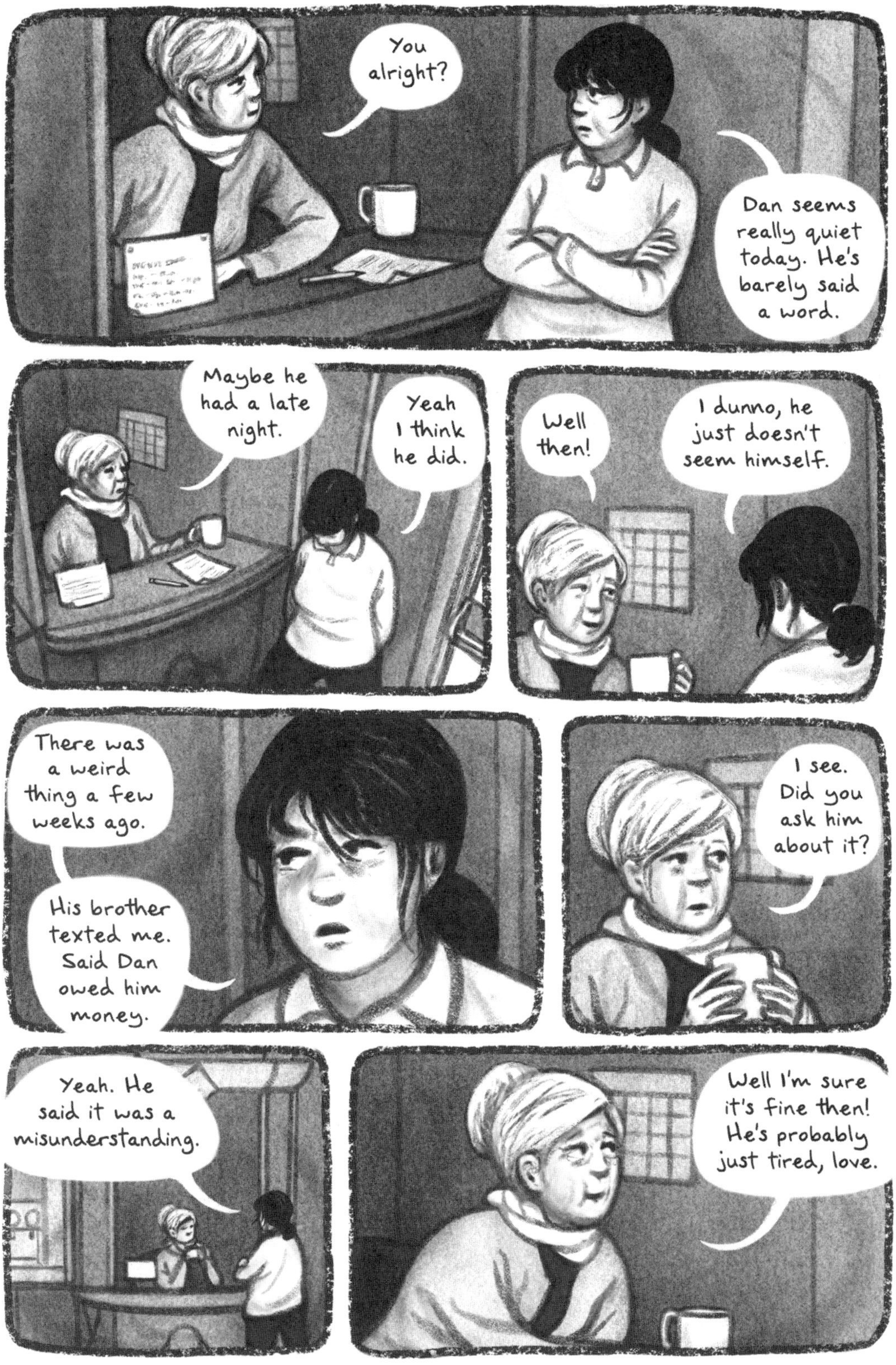
You alright?
Dan seems really quiet today. He's barely said a word.
Maybe he had a late night.
Yeah I think he did.
Well then!
I dunno, he just doesn't seem himself.
There was a weird thing a few weeks ago.
His brother texted me. Said Dan owed him money.
I see. Did you ask him about it?
Yeah. He said it was a misunderstanding.
Well I'm sure it's fine then! He's probably just tired, love.

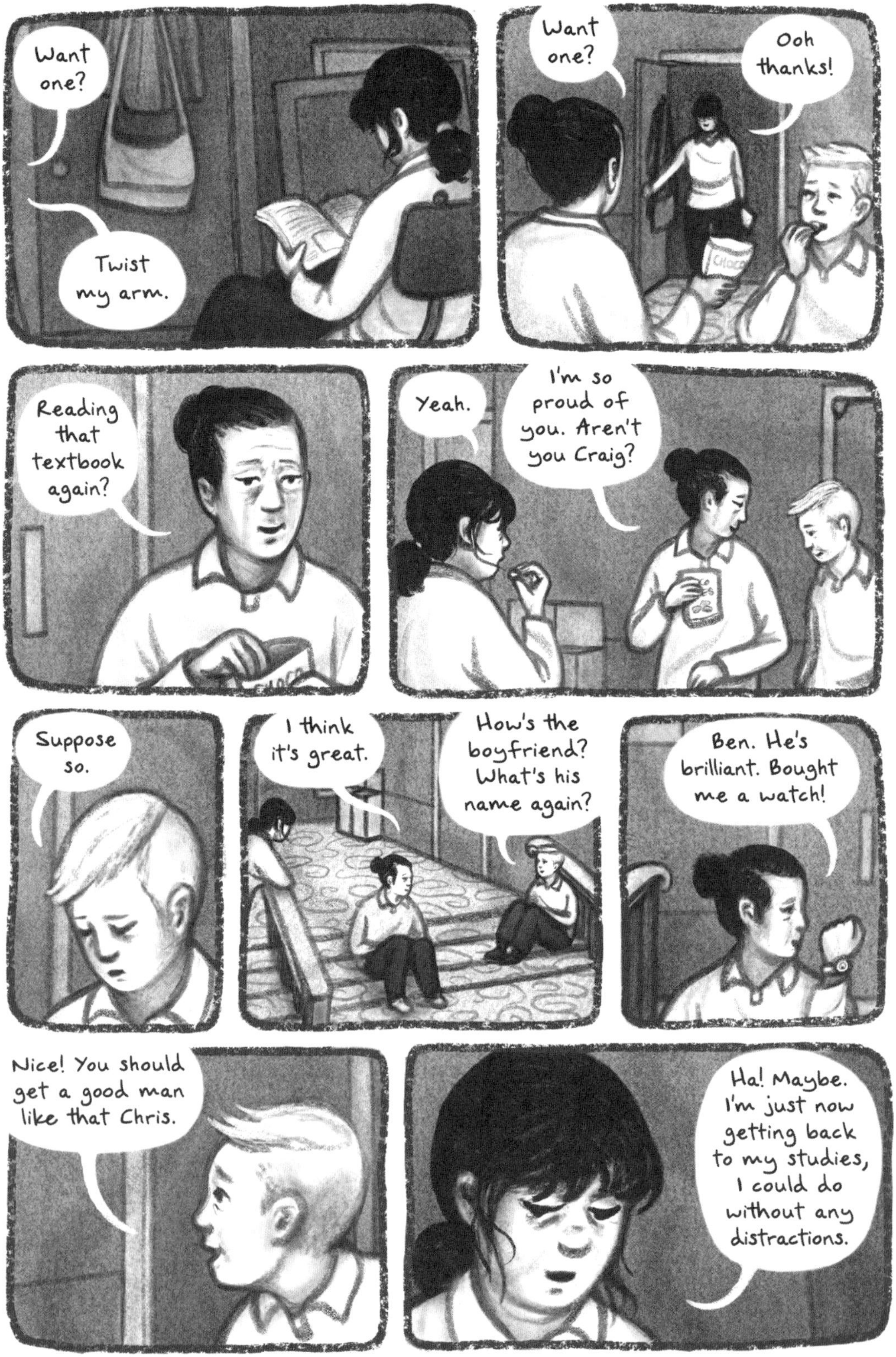
Want one?
Twist my arm.
Want one?
Ooh thanks!
Reading that textbook again?
Yeah.
I'm so proud of you. Aren't you Craig?
Suppose so.
I think it's great.
How's the boyfriend? What's his name again?
Ben. He's brilliant. Bought me a watch!
Nice! You should get a good man like that Chris.
Ha! Maybe. I'm just now getting back to my studies, I could do without any distractions.

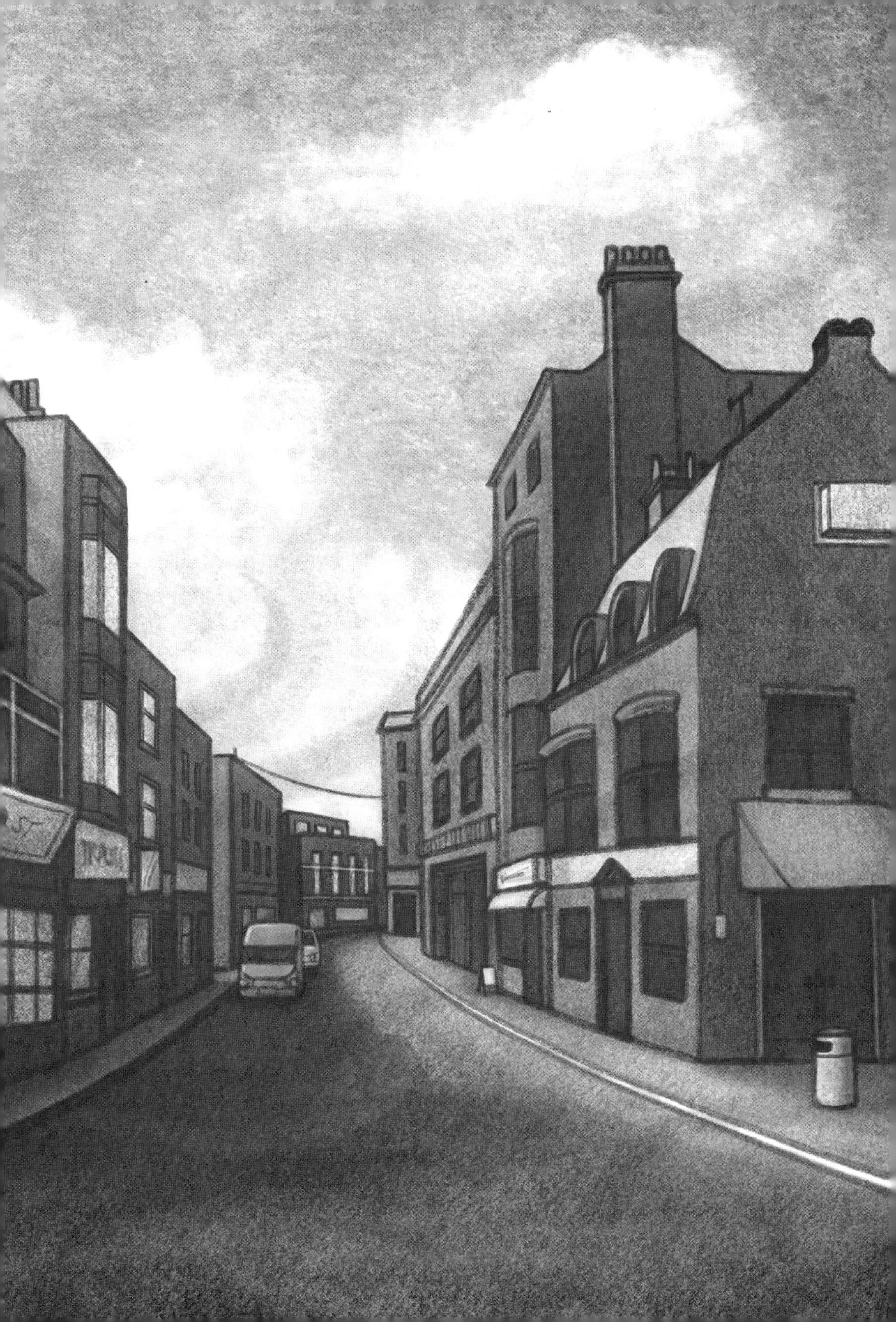

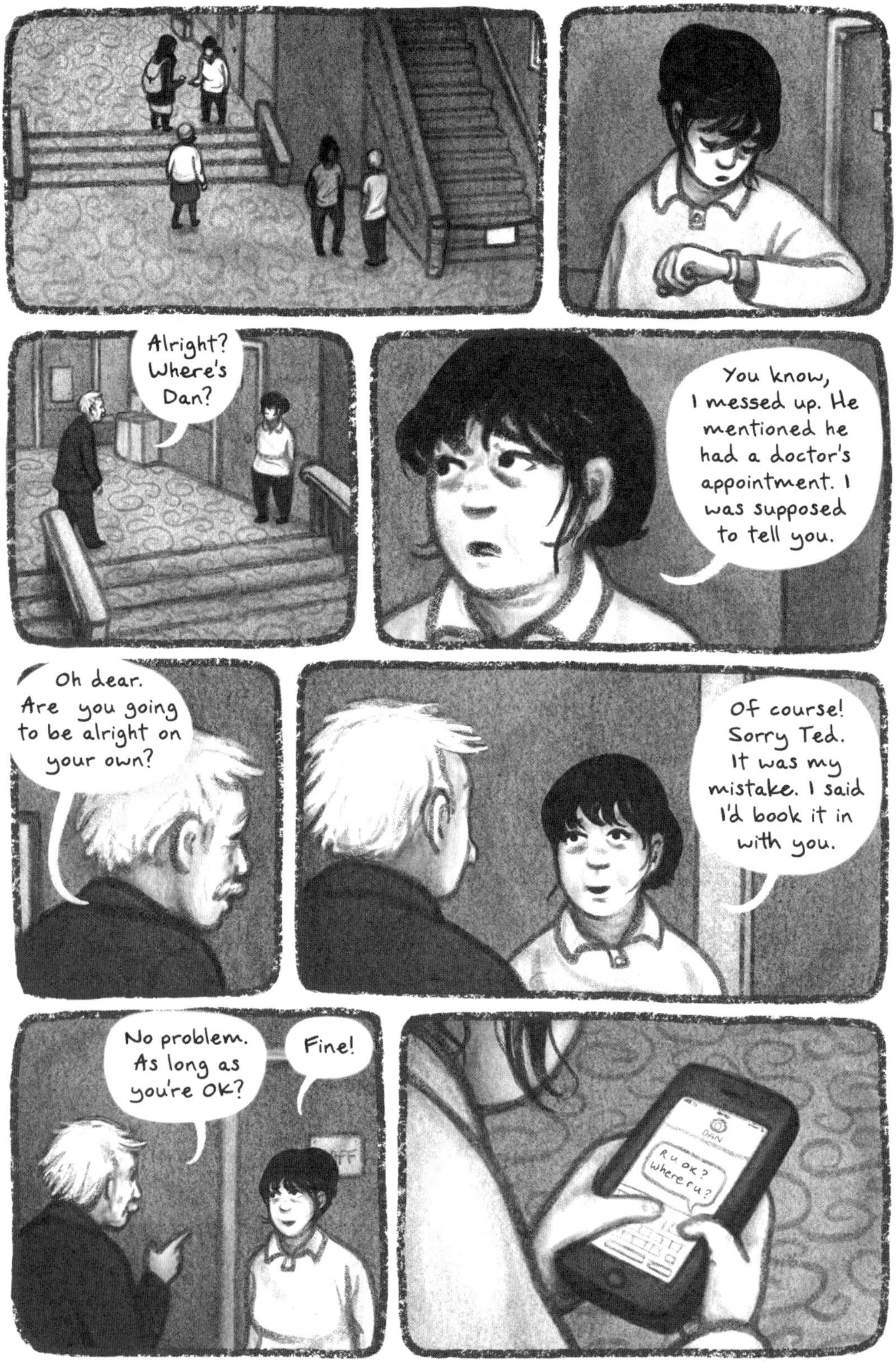
Alright? Where's Dan?
You know, I messed up. He mentioned he had a doctor's appointment. I was supposed to tell you.
Oh dear. Are you going to be alright on your own?
Of course! Sorry Ted. It was my mistake. I said I'd book it in with you.
No problem. As long as you're OK?
Fine!
DAN
R u ok? Where r u?

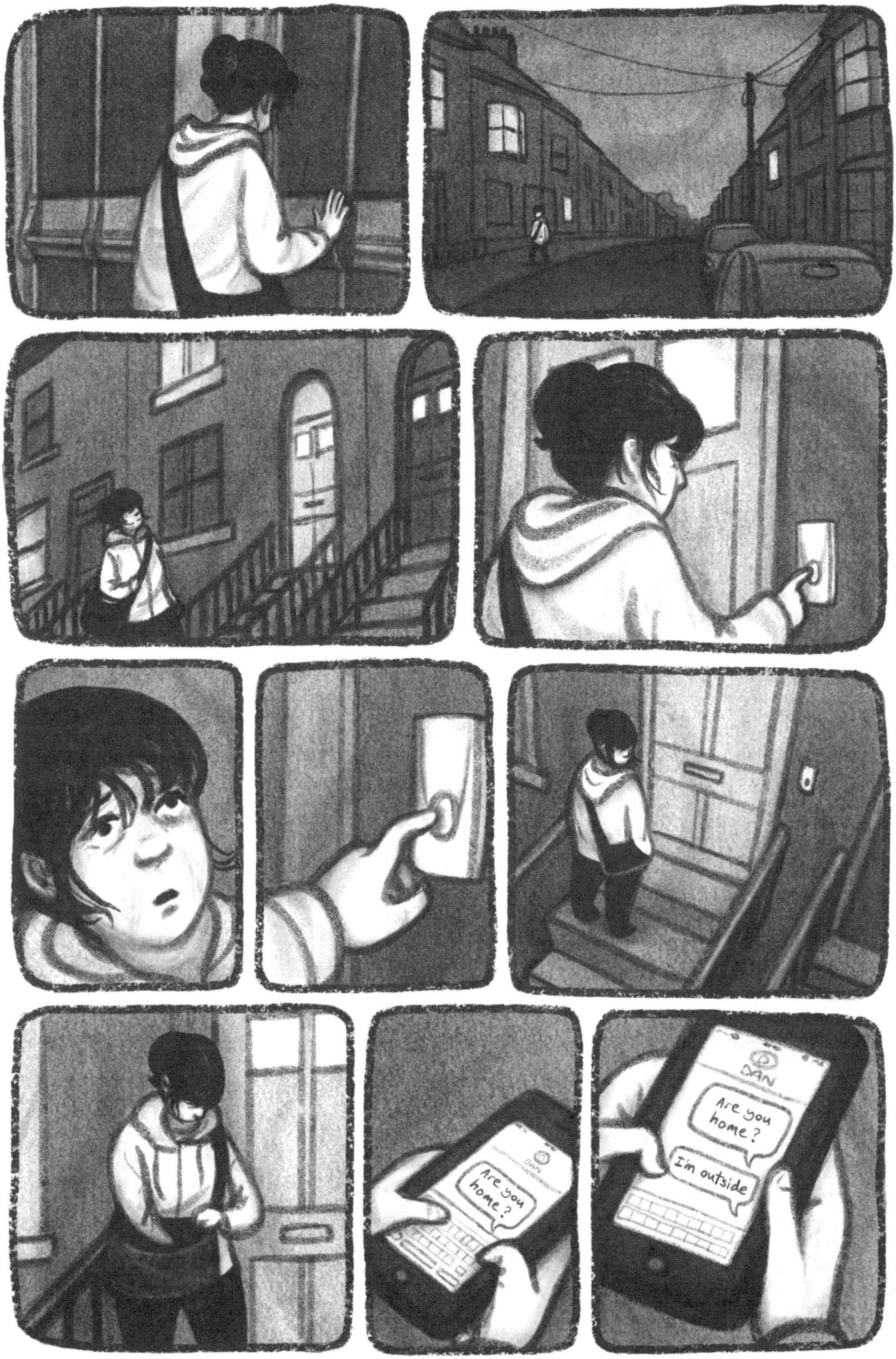
DAN
Are you home?
DAN
Are you home?
I'm outside

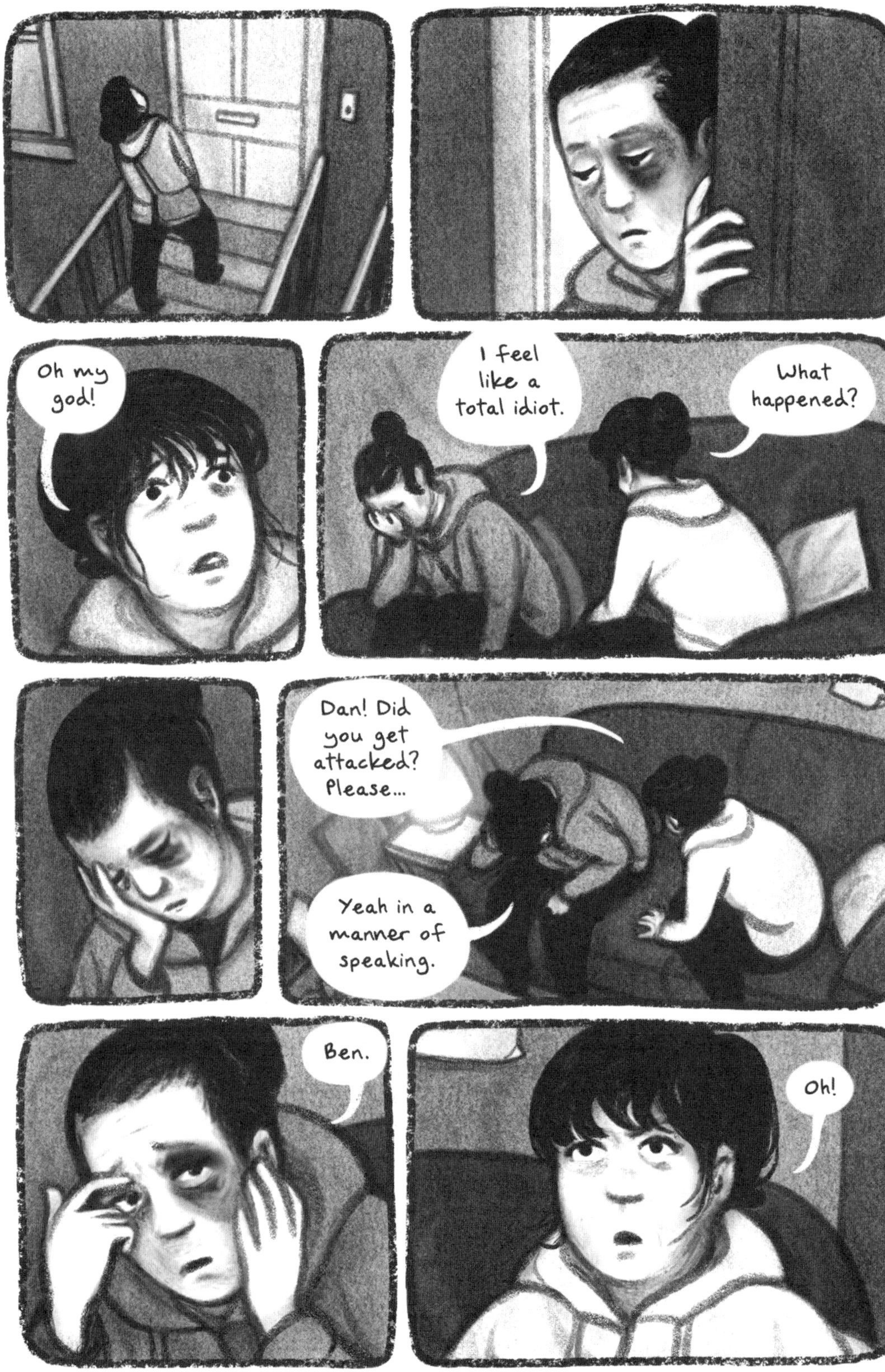
Oh my god!
I feel like a total idiot.
What happened?
Dan! Did you get attacked? Please...
Yeah in a manner of speaking.
Ben.
Oh!

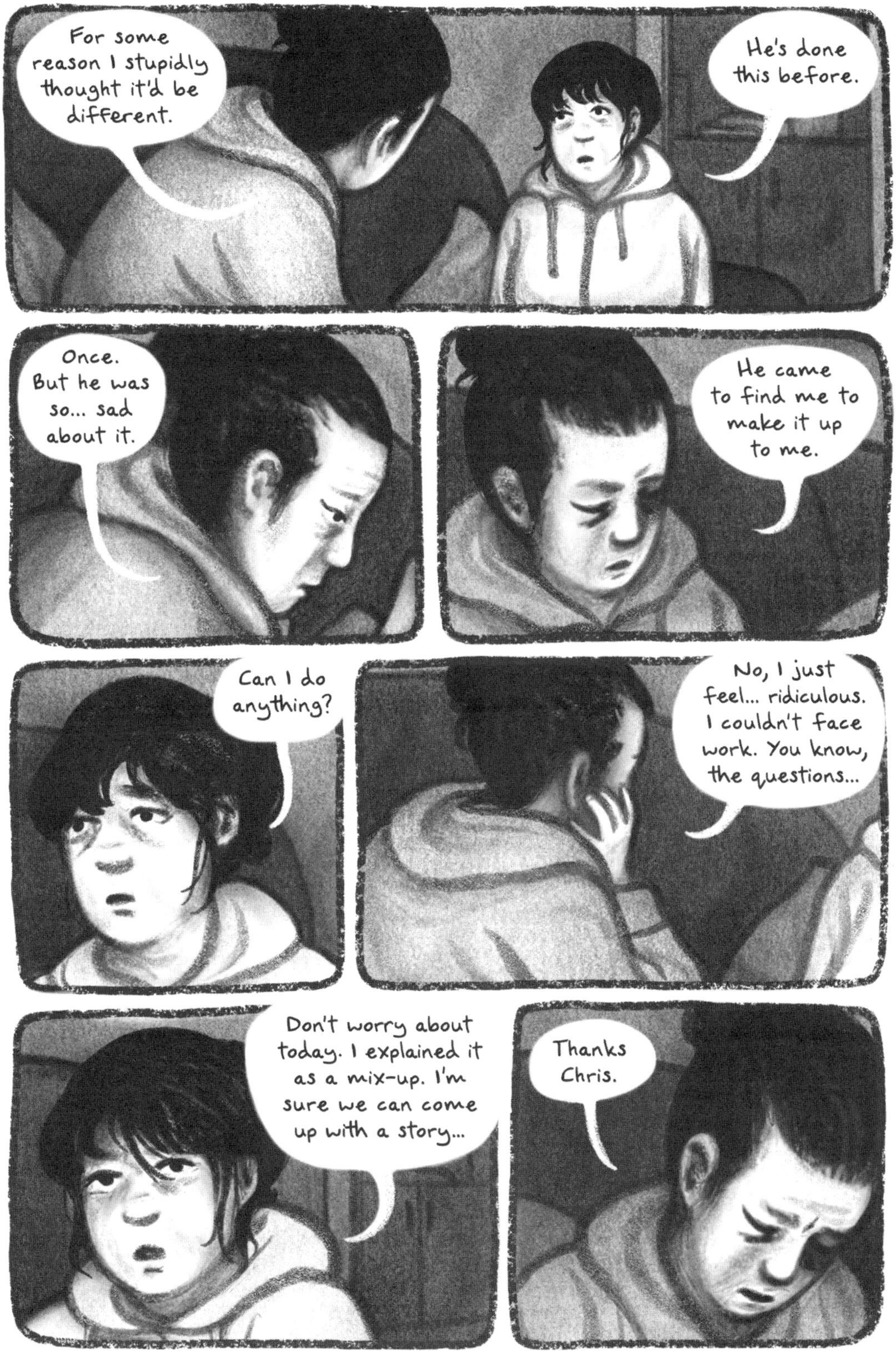
For some reason I stupidly thought it'd be different.
He's done this before.
Once. But he was so... sad about it.
He came to find me to make it up to me.
Can I do anything?
No, I just feel... ridiculous. I couldn't face work. You know, the questions...
Don't worry about today. I explained it as a mix-up. I'm sure we can come up with a story...
Thanks Chris.

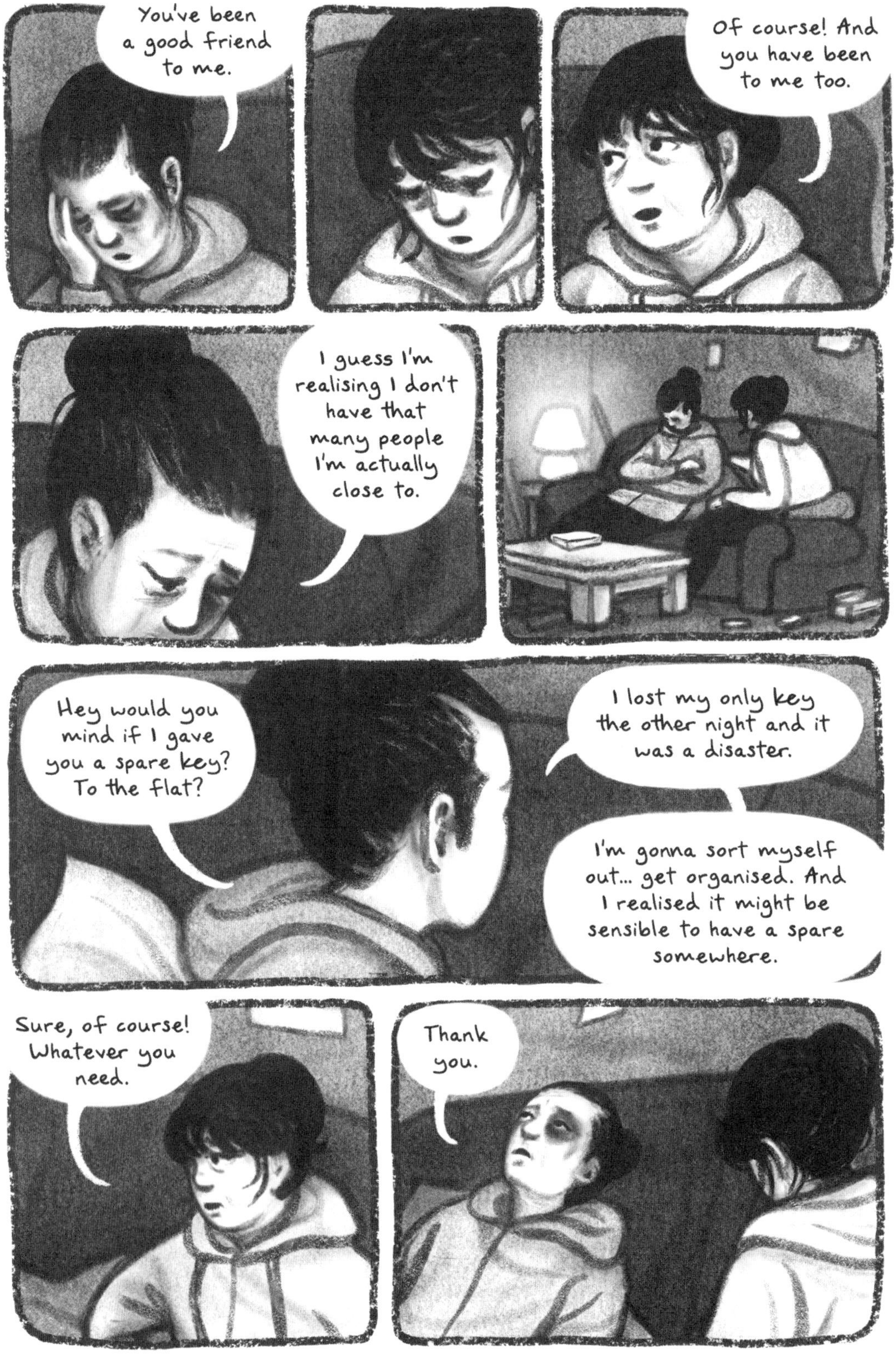
You've been a good friend to me.
Of course! And you have been to me too.
I guess I'm realising I don't have that many people I'm actually close to.
Hey would you mind if I gave you a spare key? To the flat?
I lost my only key the other night and it was a disaster.
I'm gonna sort myself out... get organised. And I realised it might be sensible to have a spare somewhere.
Sure, of course! Whatever you need.
Thank you.

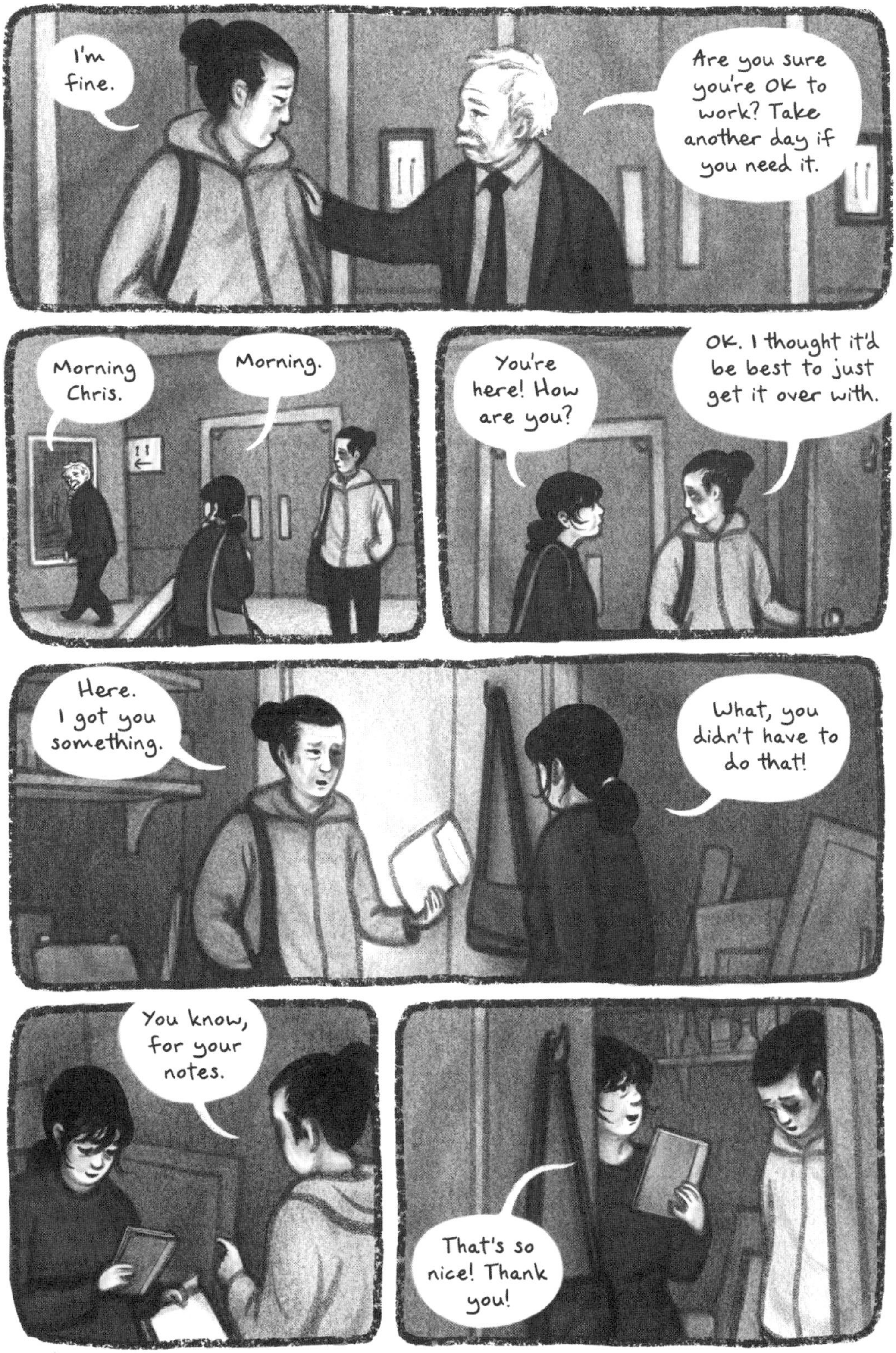
I'm fine.
Are you sure you're OK to work? Take another day if you need it.
Morning Chris.
Morning.
You're here! How are you?
OK. I thought it'd be best to just get it over with.
Here. I got you something.
What, you didn't have to do that!
You know, for your notes.
That's so nice! Thank you!

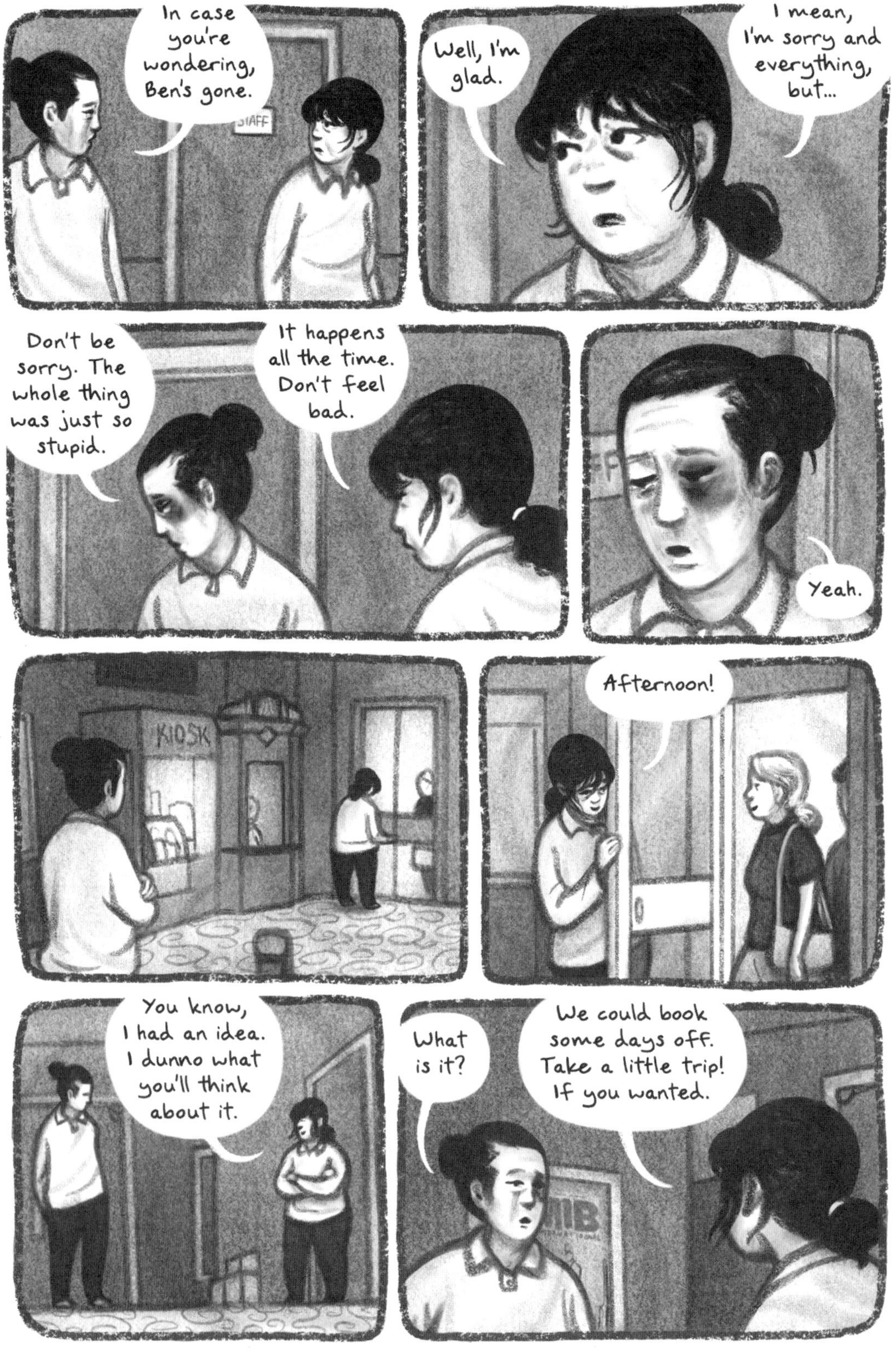
In case you're wondering, Ben's gone.
STAFF
Well, I'm glad.
I mean, I'm sorry and everything, but...
Don't be sorry. The whole thing was just so stupid.
It happens all the time. Don't feel bad.
Yeah.
KIOSK
Afternoon!
You know, I had an idea. I dunno what you'll think about it.
What is it?
We could book some days off. Take a little trip! If you wanted.

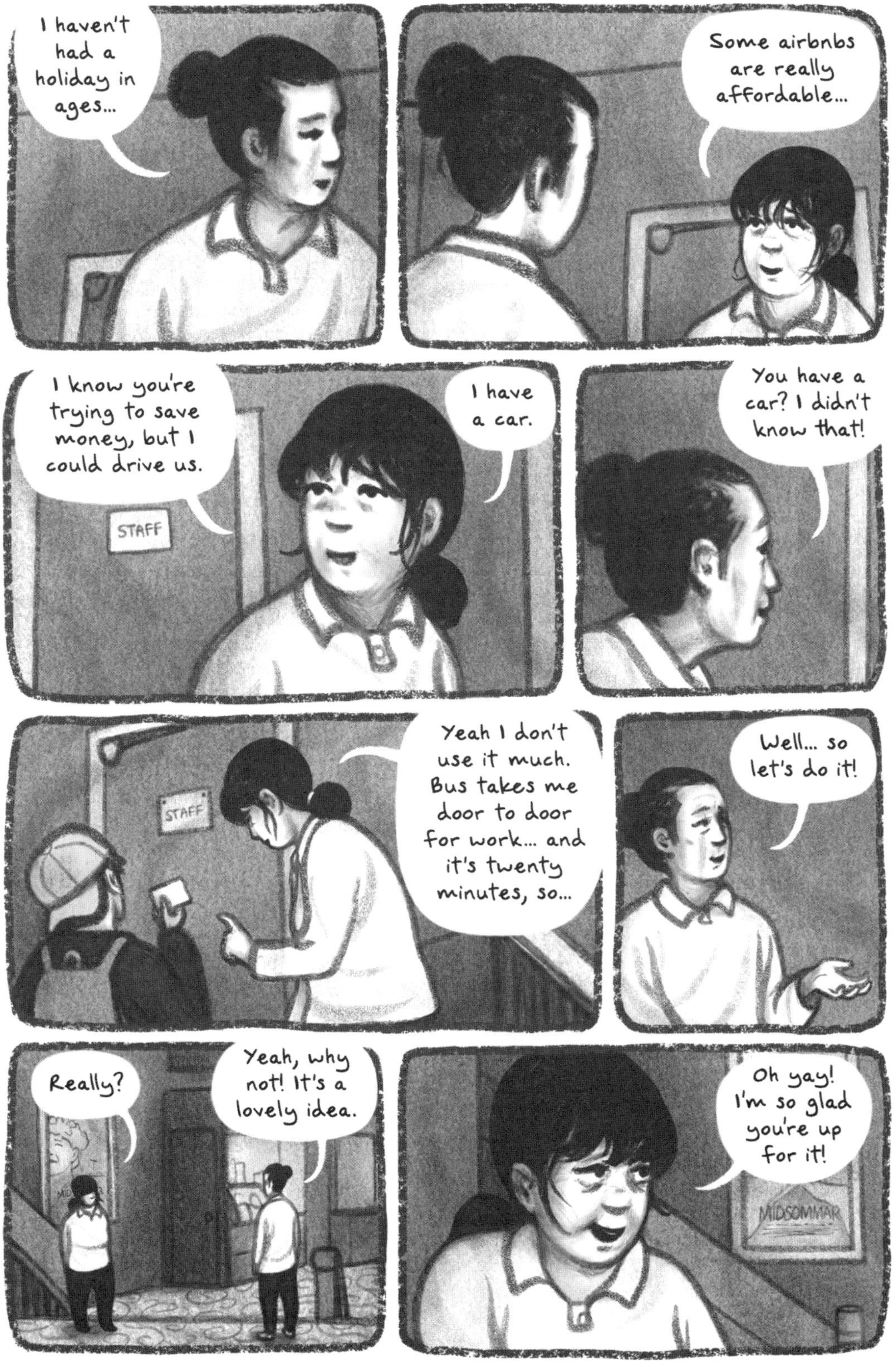
I haven't had a holiday in ages...
Some airbnbs are really affordable...
I know you're trying to save money, but I could drive us.
I have a car.
You have a car? I didn't know that!
STAFF
Yeah I don't use it much. Bus takes me door to door for work... and it's twenty minutes, so...
STAFF
Well... so let's do it!
Really?
Yeah, why not! It's a lovely idea.
Oh yay! I'm so glad you're up for it!
MIDSOMMAR

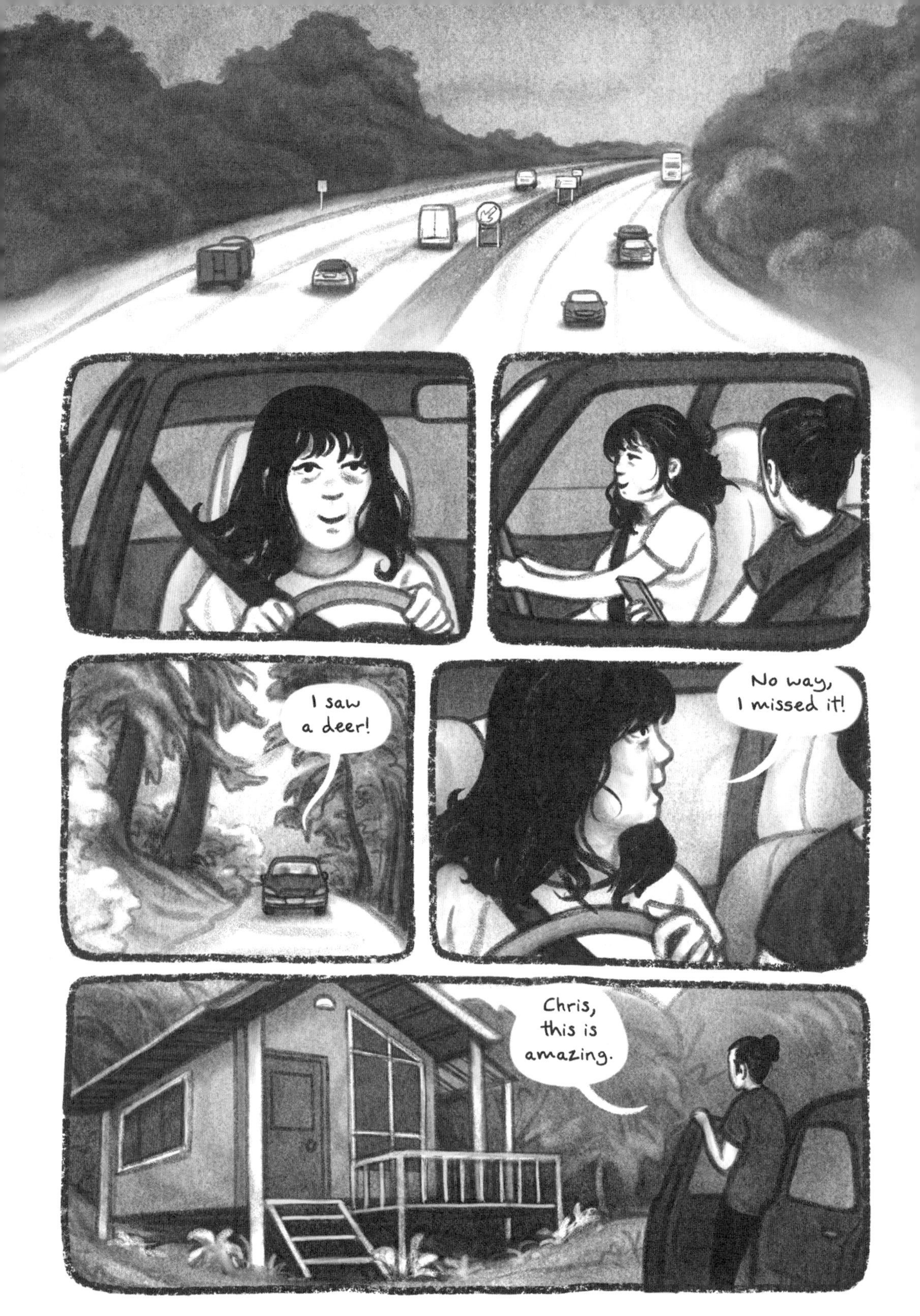
I saw a deer!
No way, I missed it!
Chris, this is amazing.

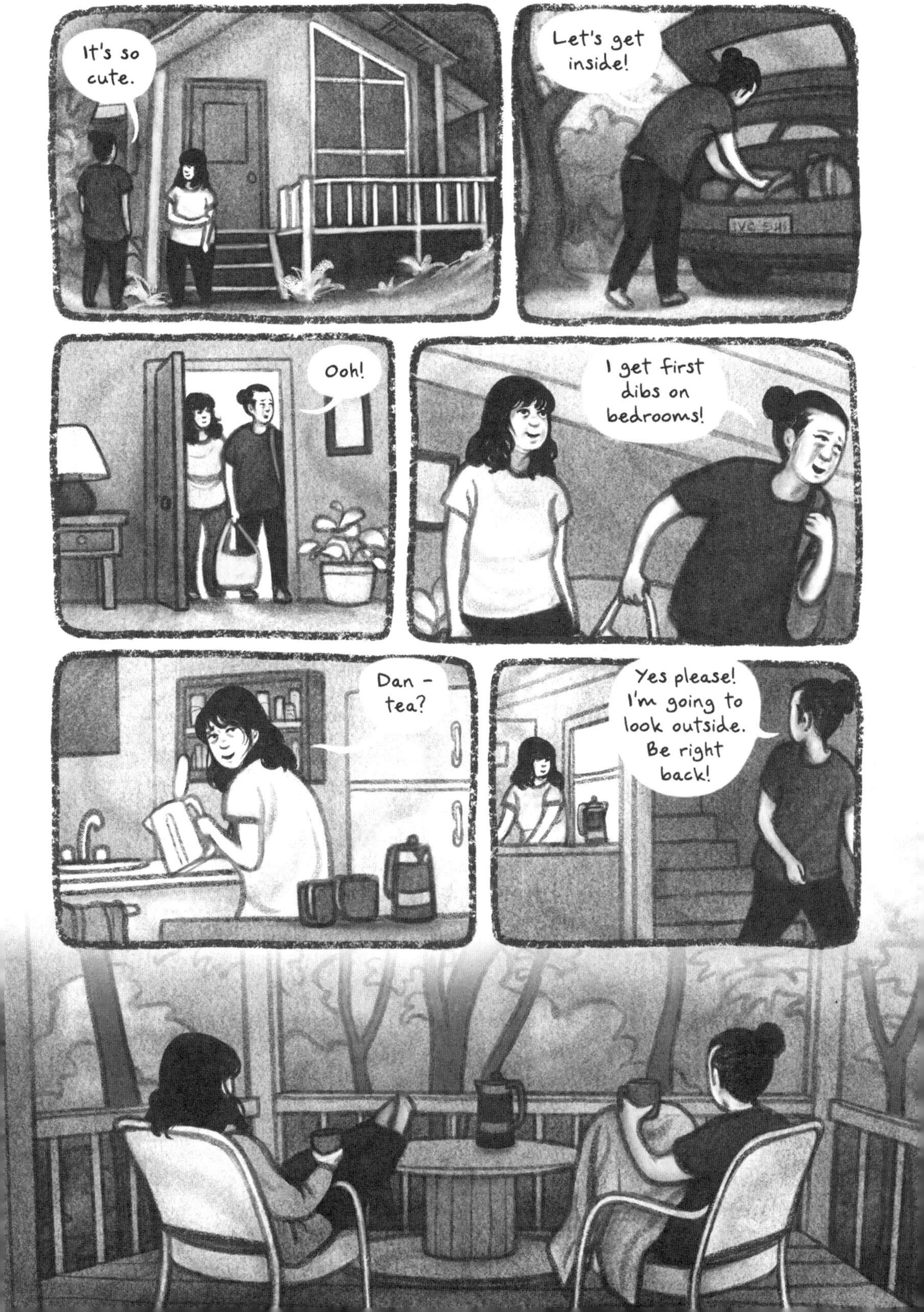
It's so cute.
Let's get inside!
Ooh!
I get first dibs on bedrooms!
Dan - tea?
Yes please! I'm going to look outside. Be right back!

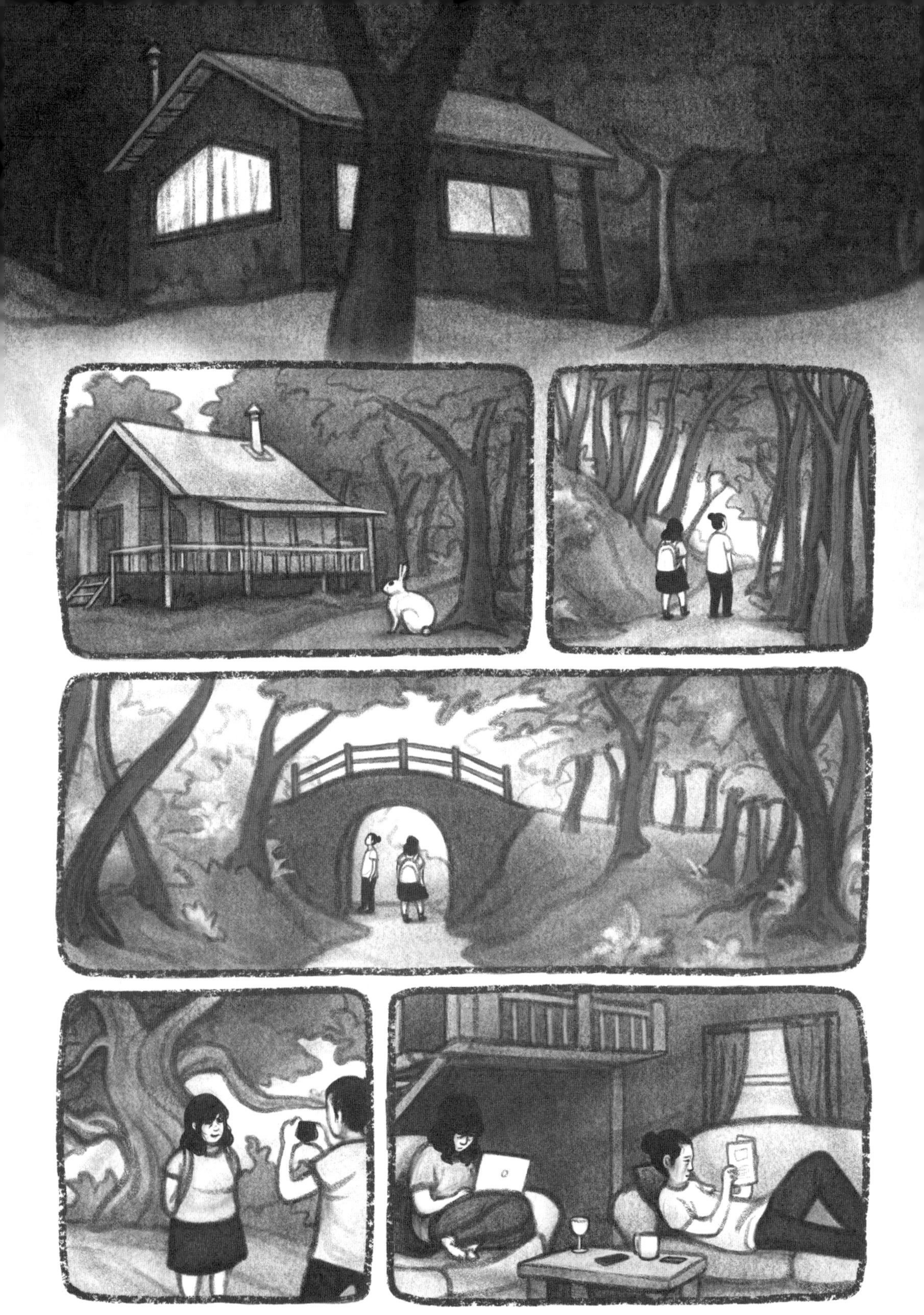

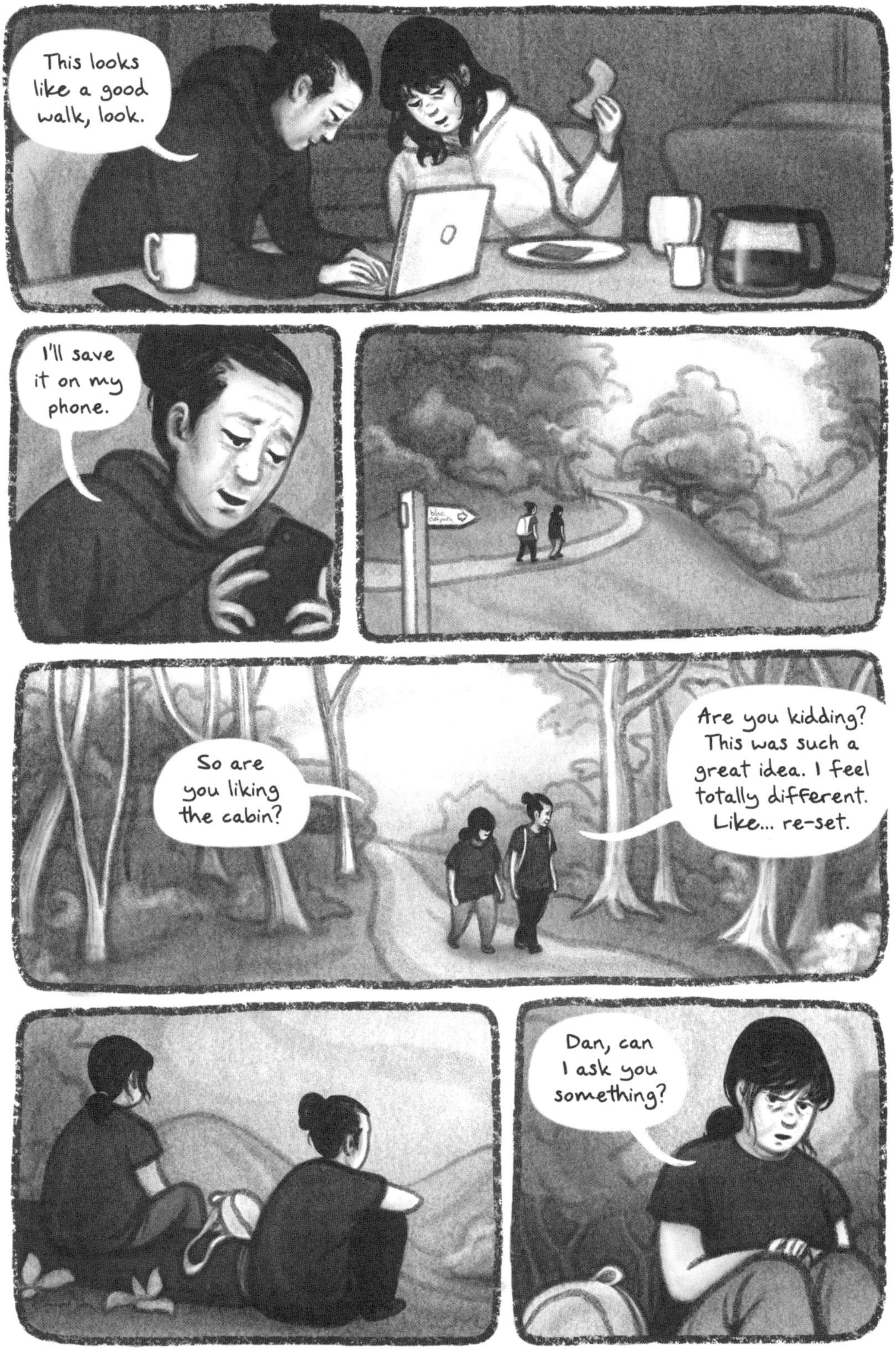
This looks like a good walk, look.
I'll save it on my phone.
So are you liking the cabin?
Are you kidding? This was such a great idea. I feel totally different. Like... re-set.
Dan, can I ask you something?

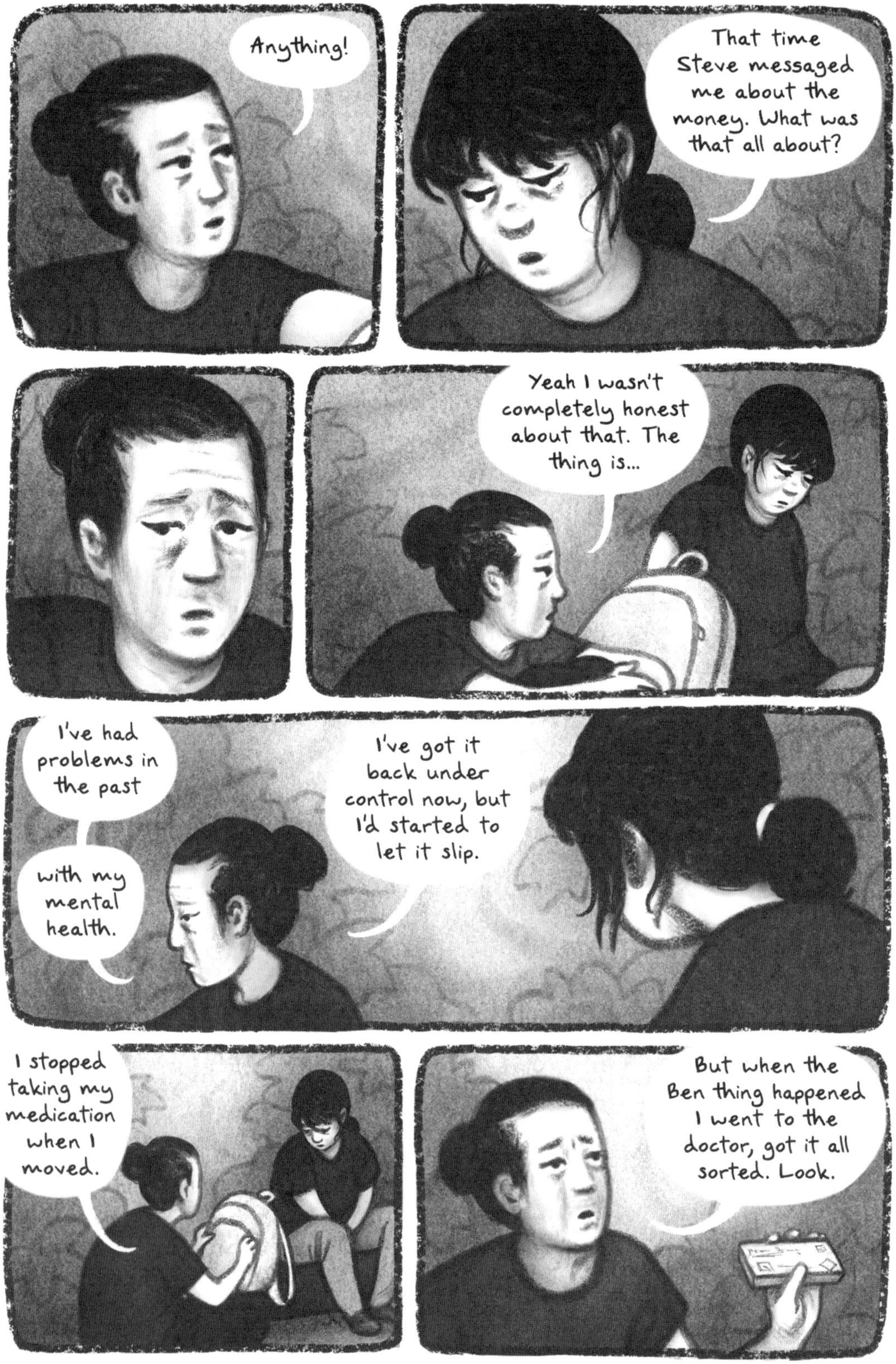
Anything!
That time Steve messaged me about the money. What was that all about?
Yeah I wasn't completely honest about that. The thing is...
I've had problems in the past
with my mental health.
I've got it back under control now, but I'd started to let it slip.
I stopped taking my medication when I moved.
But when the Ben thing happened I went to the doctor, got it all sorted. Look.

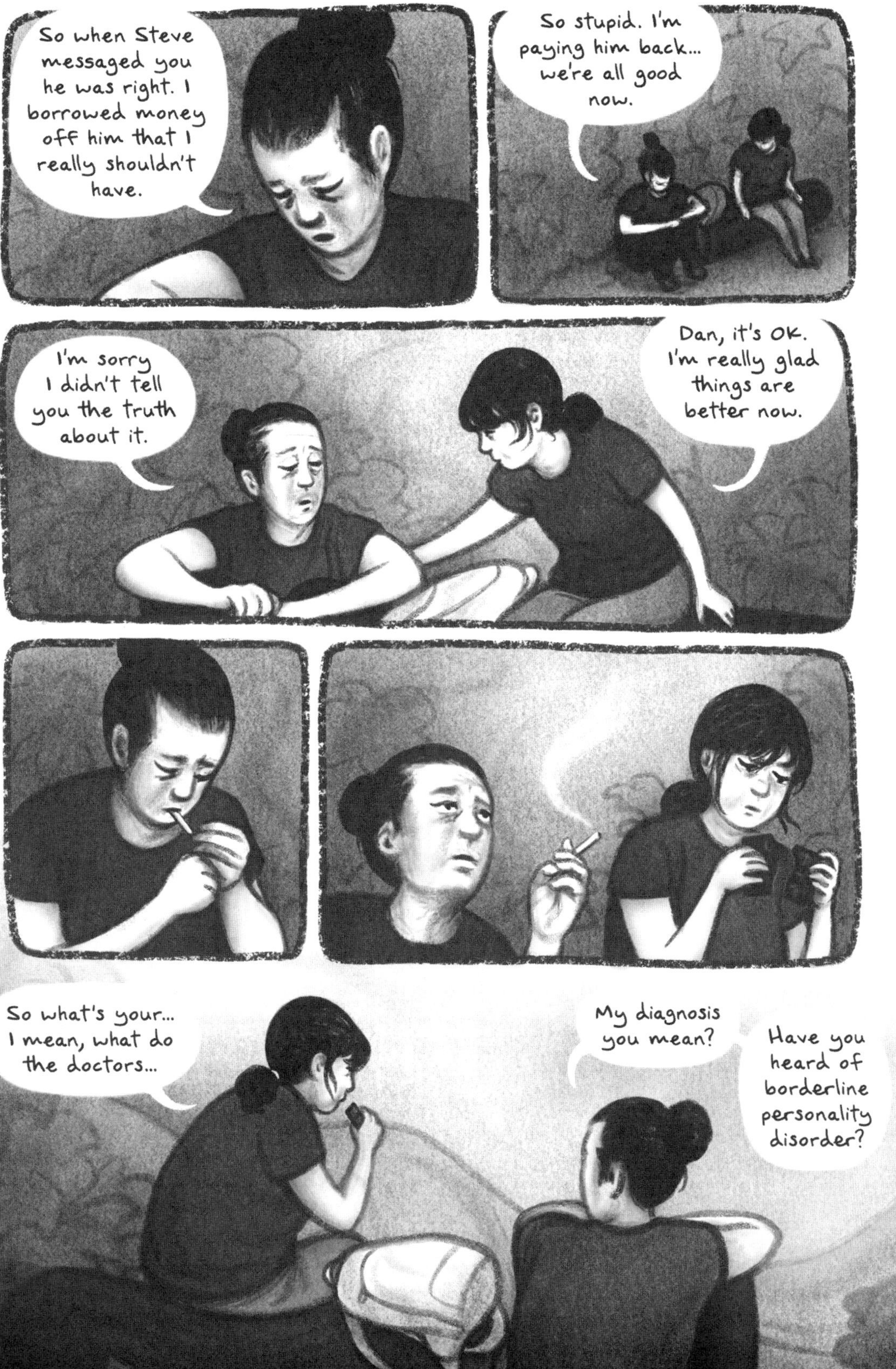

So when Steve messaged you he was right. I borrowed money off him that I really shouldn't have.
So stupid. I'm paying him back... we're all good now.
I'm sorry I didn't tell you the truth about it.
Dan, it's OK. I'm really glad things are better now.
So what's your... I mean, what do the doctors...
My diagnosis you mean?
Have you heard of borderline personality disorder?

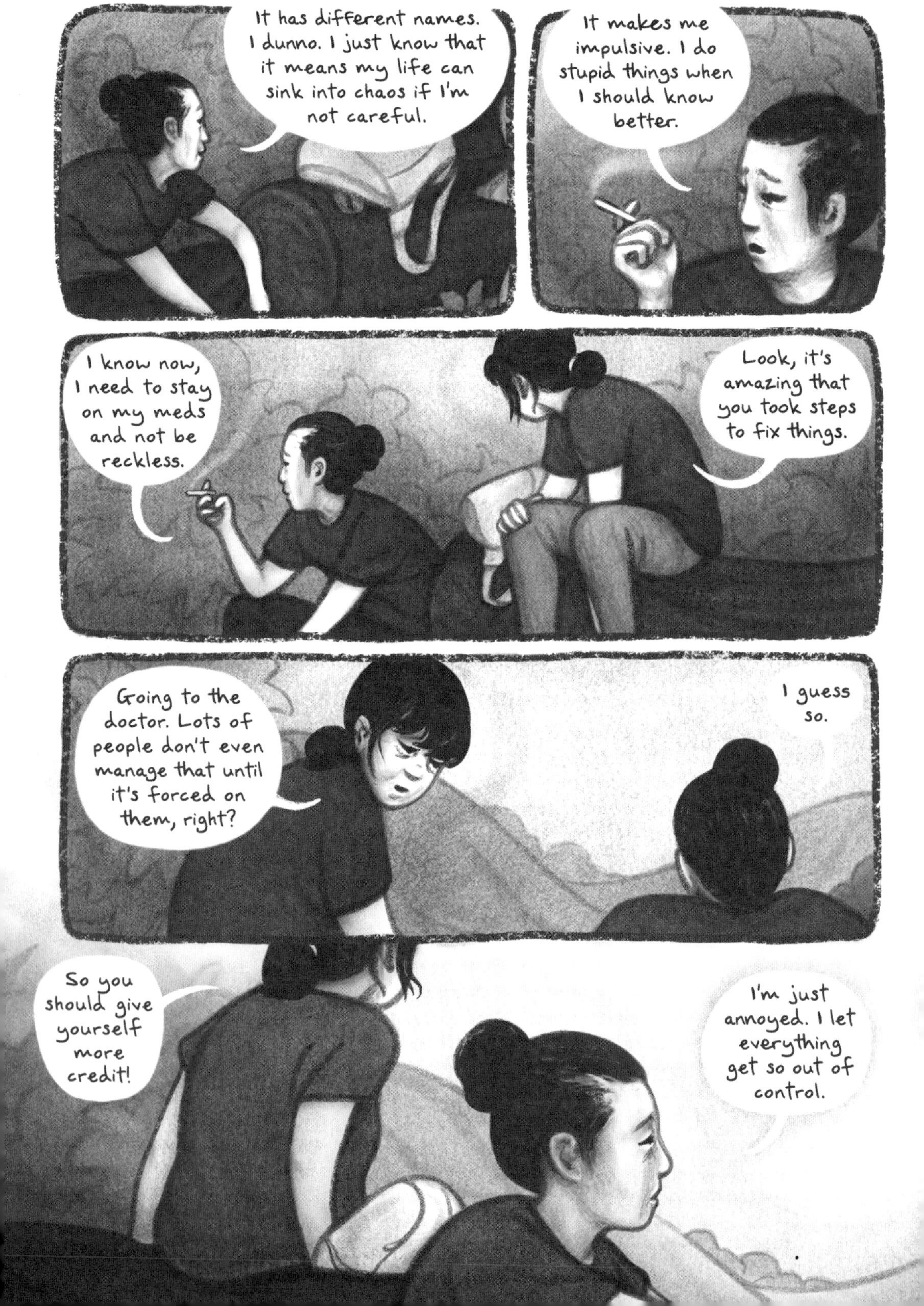
It has different names. I dunno. I just know that it means my life can sink into chaos if I'm not careful.
It makes me impulsive. I do stupid things when I should know better.
I know now, I need to stay on my meds and not be reckless.
Look, it's amazing that you took steps to fix things.
Going to the doctor. Lots of people don't even manage that until it's forced on them, right?
I guess so.
So you should give yourself more credit!
I'm just annoyed. I let everything get so out of control.

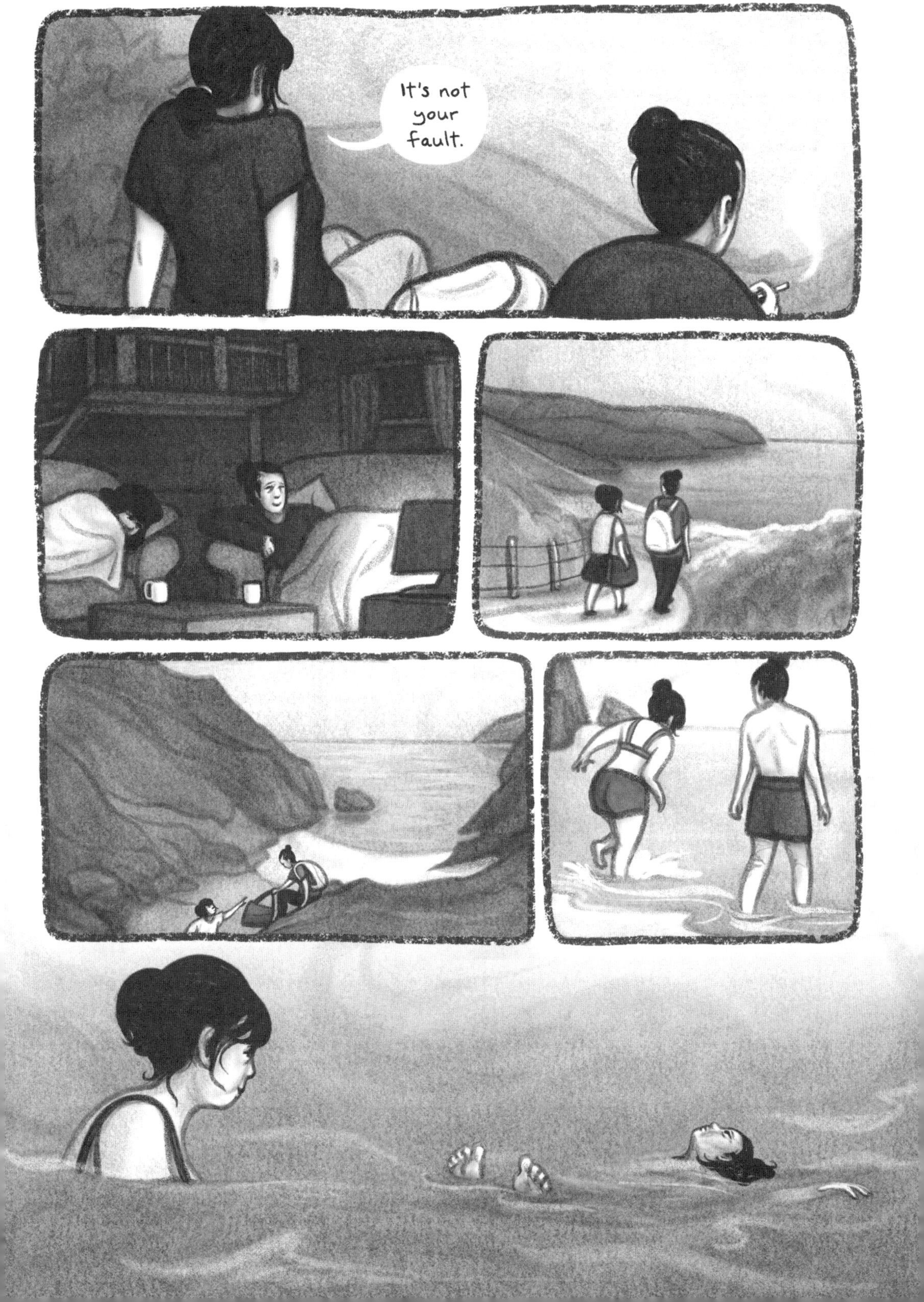
It's not your fault.

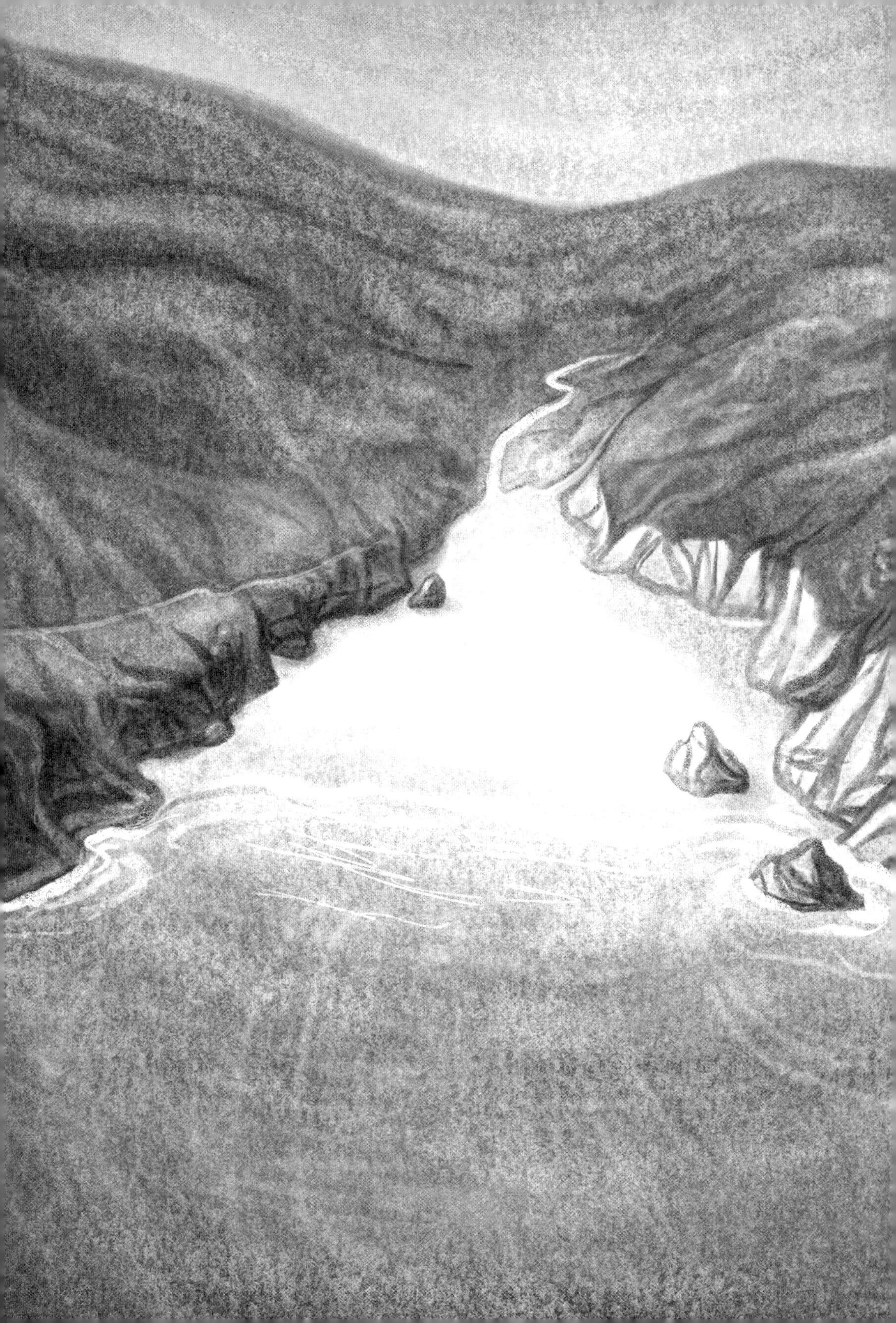

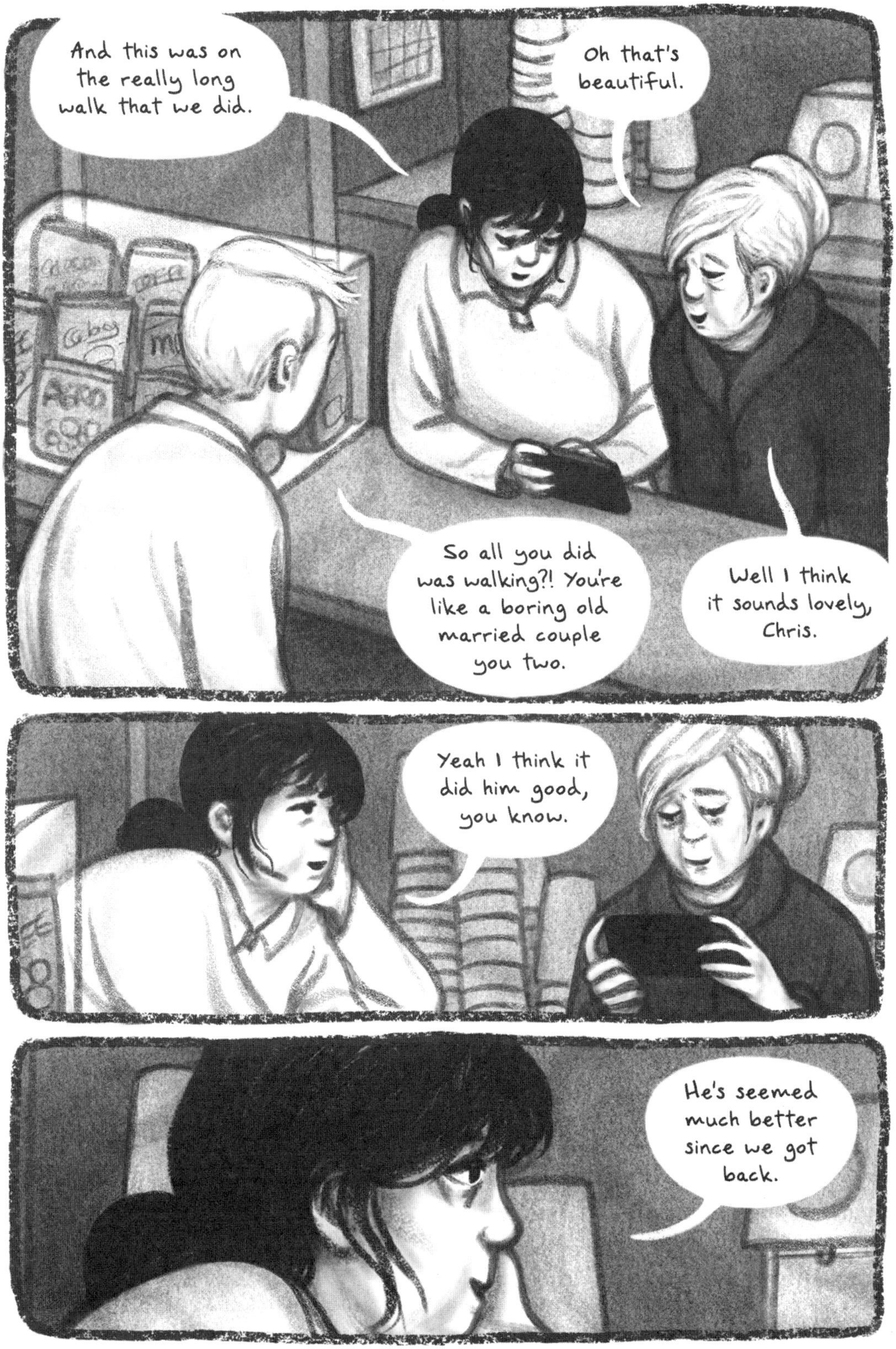

And this was on the really long walk that we did.
Oh that's beautiful.
So all you did was walking?! You're like a boring old married couple you two.
Well I think it sounds lovely, Chris.
Yeah I think it did him good, you know.
He's seemed much better since we got back.

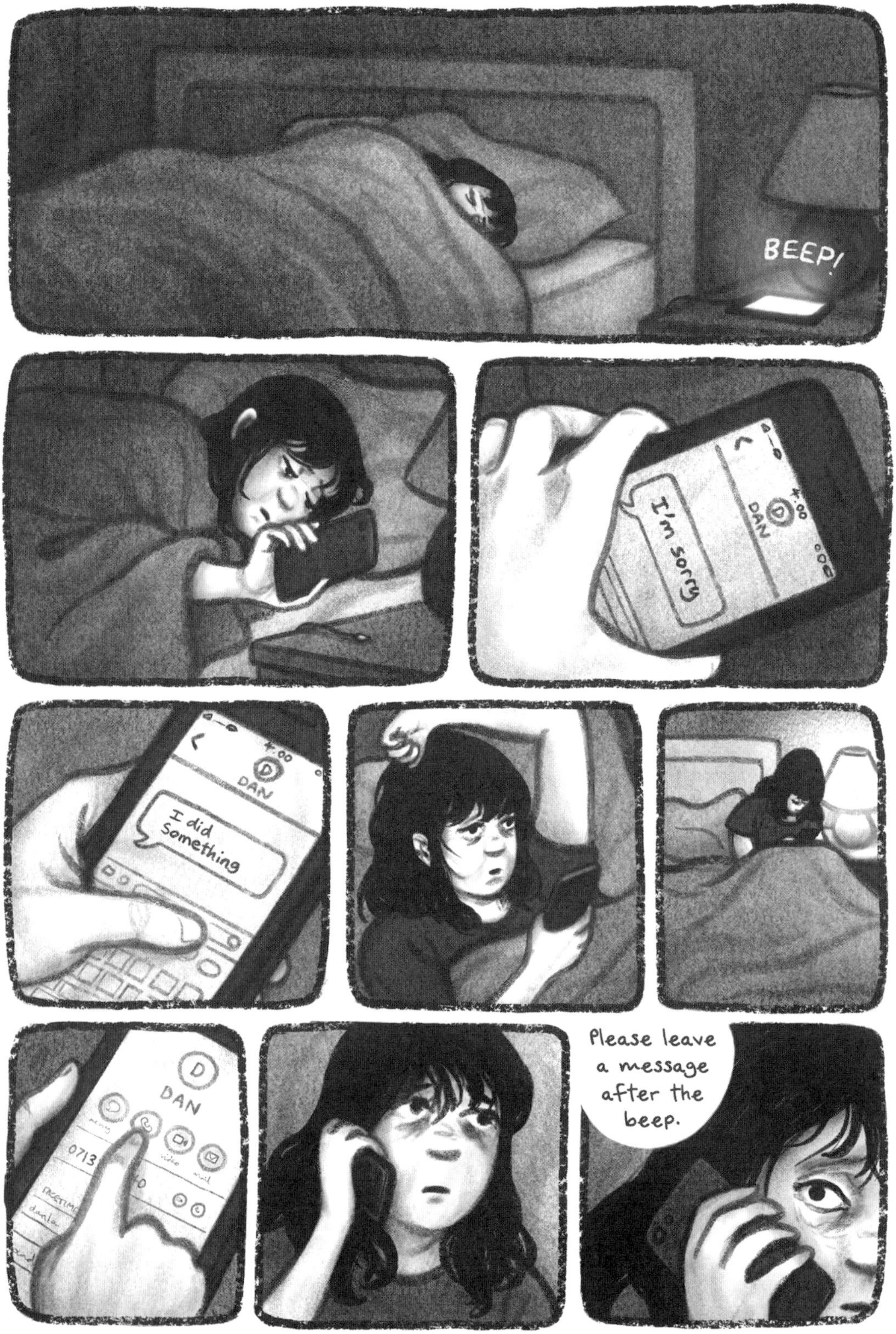
BEEP!
DAN
I'm sorry
DAN
I did something
DAN
Please leave a message after the beep.

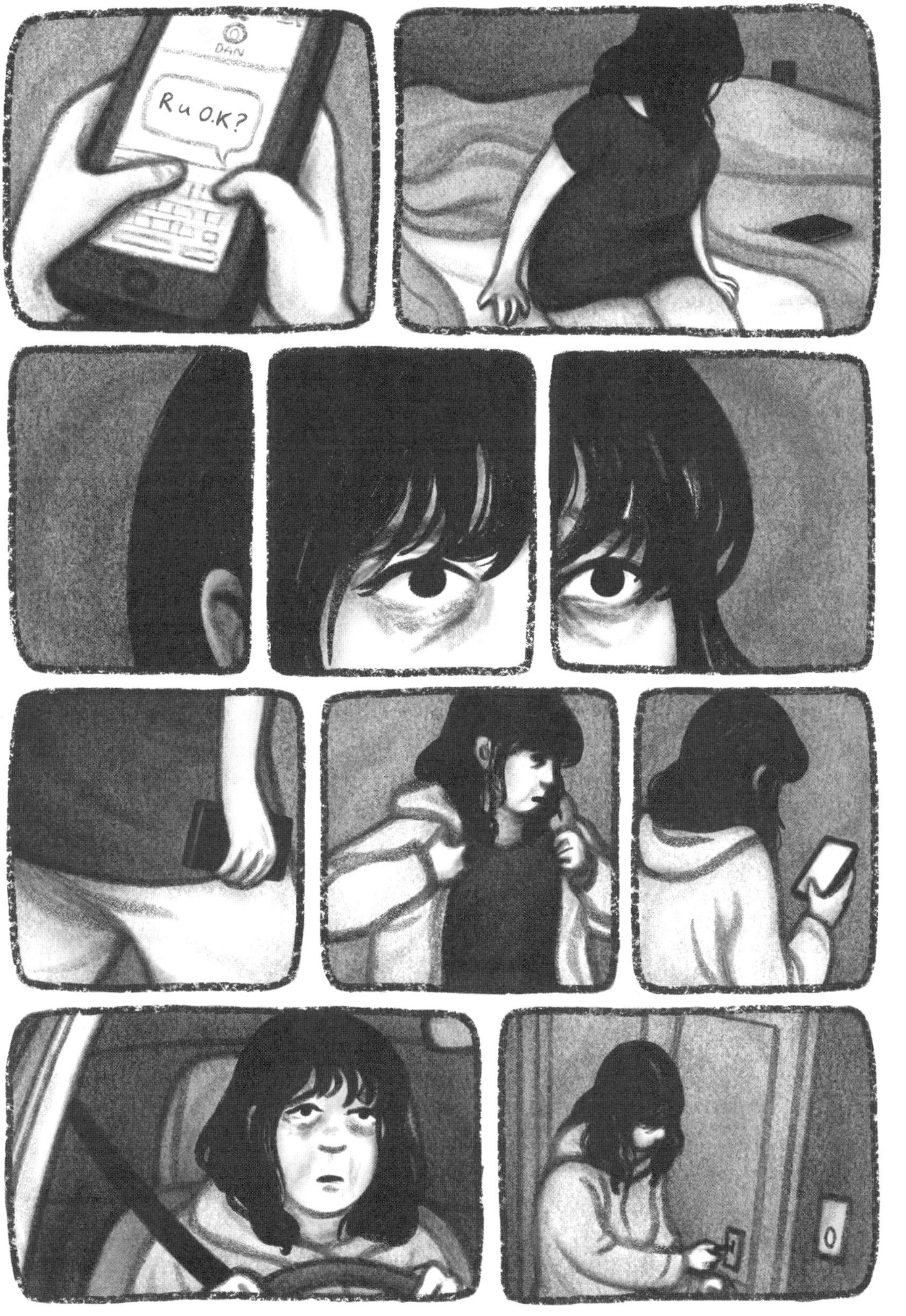
DAN
R u O.K?

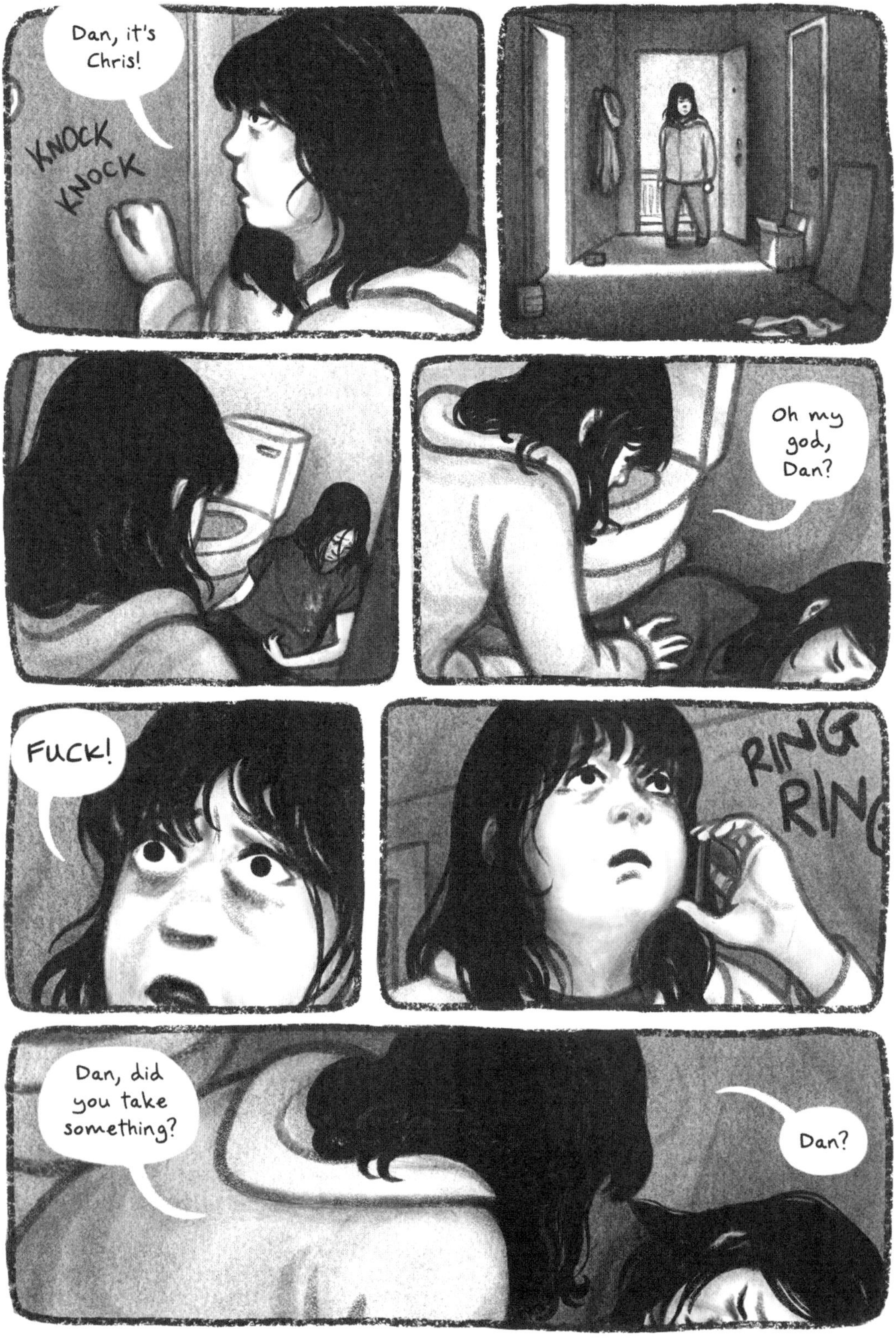
Dan, it's Chris!
KNOCK KNOCK
Oh my god, Dan?
FUCK!
RING RING
Dan, did you take something?
Dan?

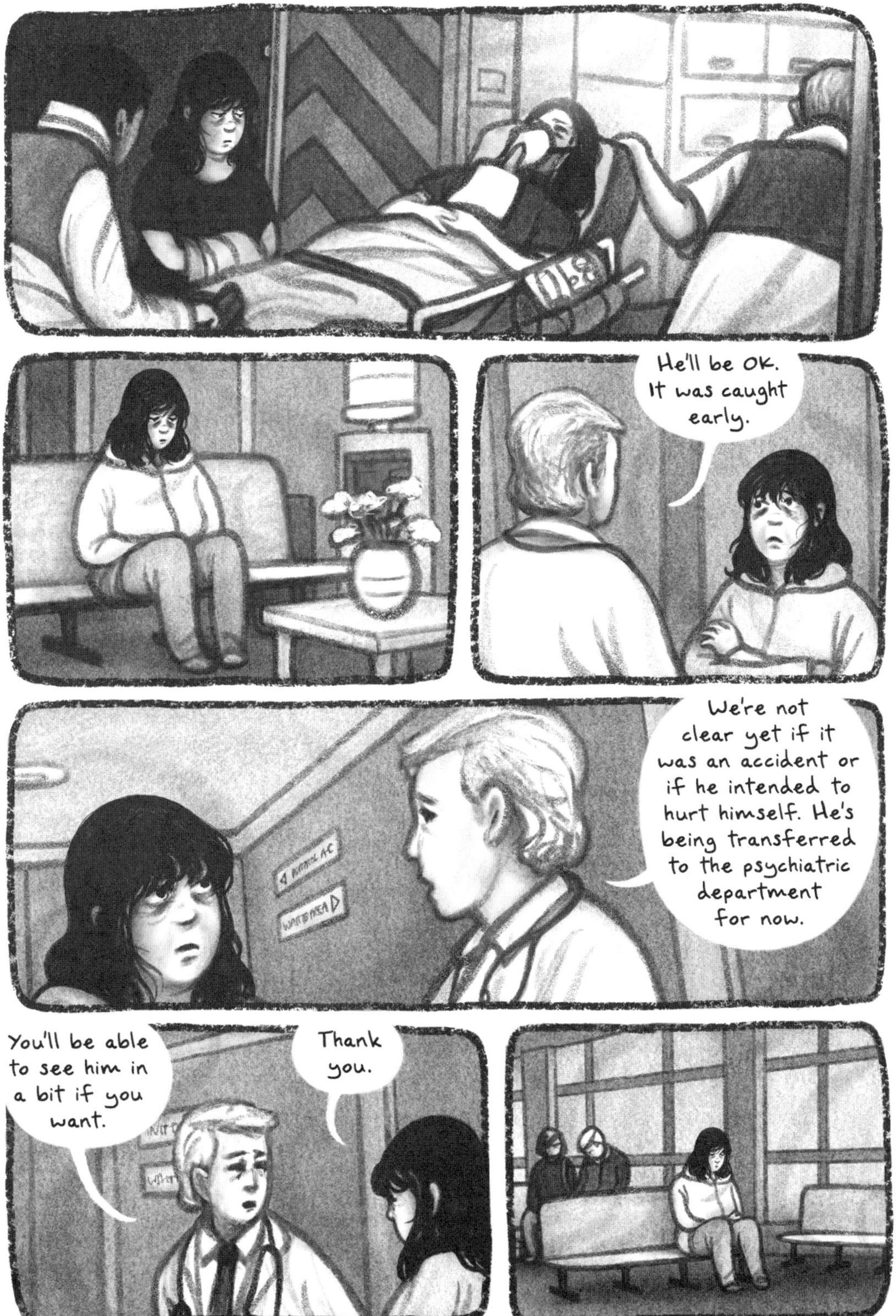
He'll be OK. It was caught early.
We're not clear yet if it was an accident or if he intended to hurt himself. He's being transferred to the psychiatric department for now.
You'll be able to see him in a bit if you want.
Thank you.

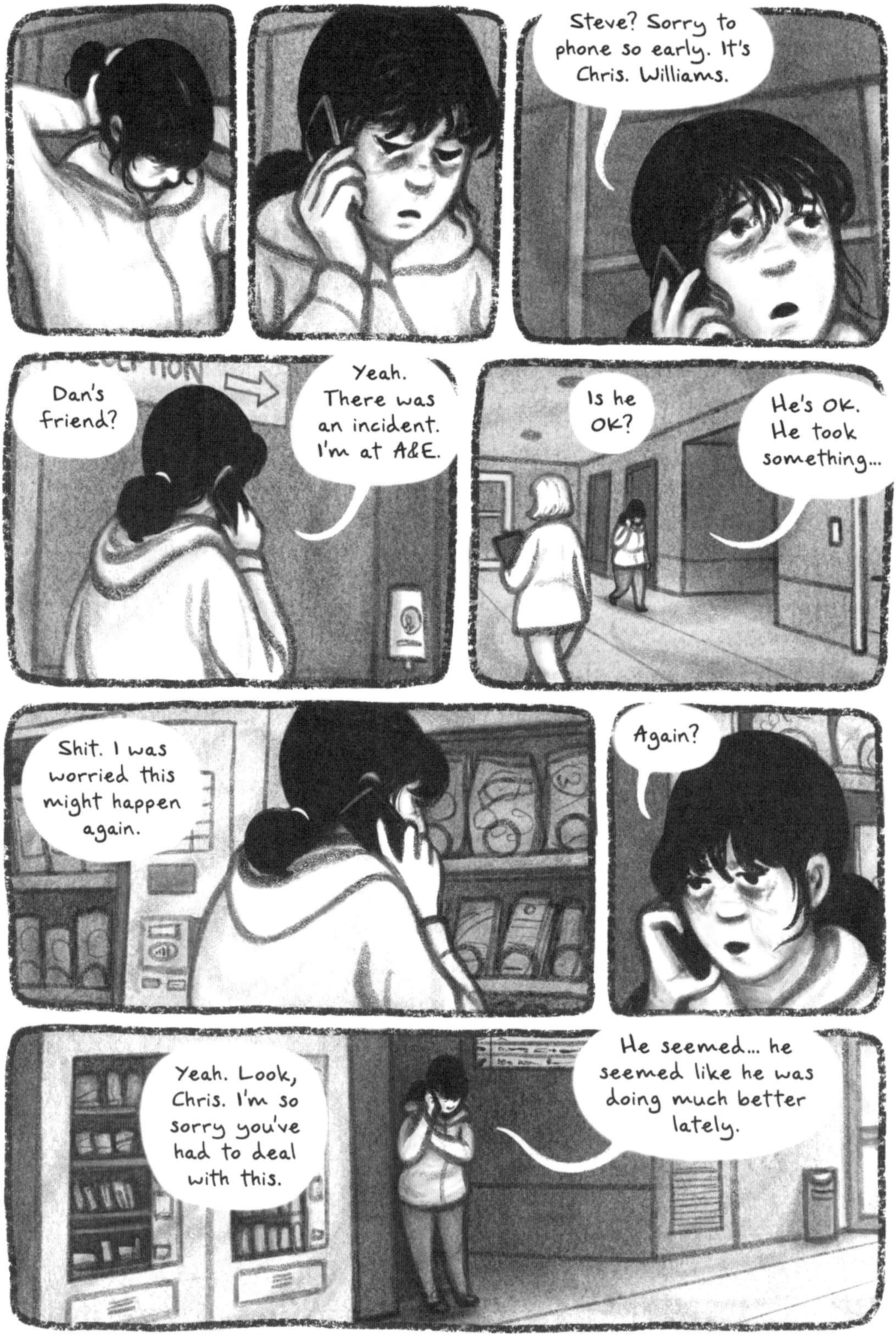

Steve? Sorry to phone so early. It's Chris. Williams.
Dan's friend?
Yeah. There was an incident. I'm at A&E.
Is he OK?
He's OK. He took something...
Shit. I was worried this might happen again.
Again?
Yeah. Look, Chris. I'm so sorry you've had to deal with this.
He seemed... he seemed like he was doing much better lately.

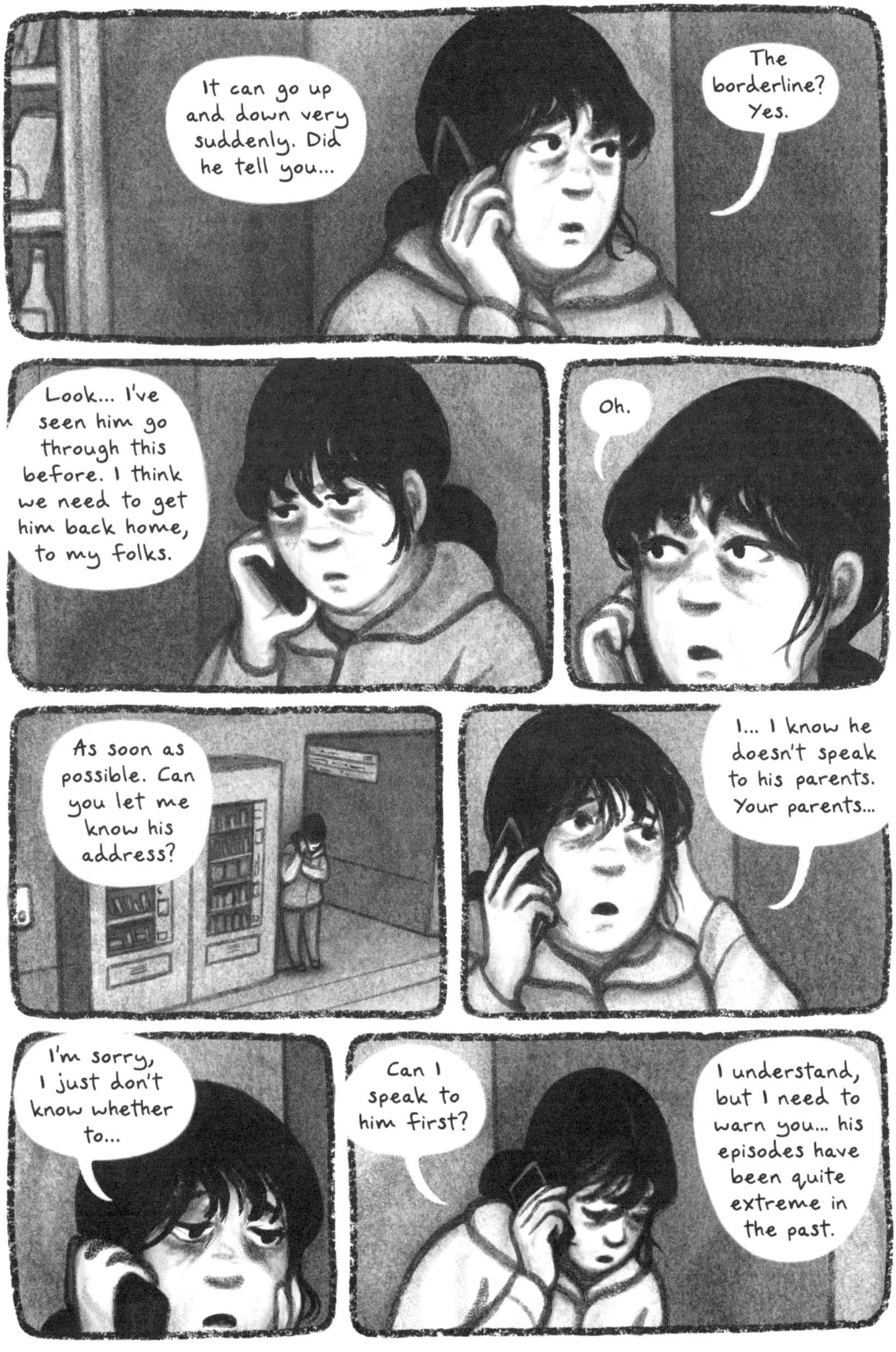
It can go up and down very suddenly. Did he tell you...
The borderline? Yes.
Look... I've seen him go through this before. I think we need to get him back home, to my folks.
Oh.
As soon as possible. Can you let me know his address?
I... I know he doesn't speak to his parents. Your parents...
I'm sorry, I just don't know whether to...
Can I speak to him first?
I understand, but I need to warn you... his episodes have been quite extreme in the past.

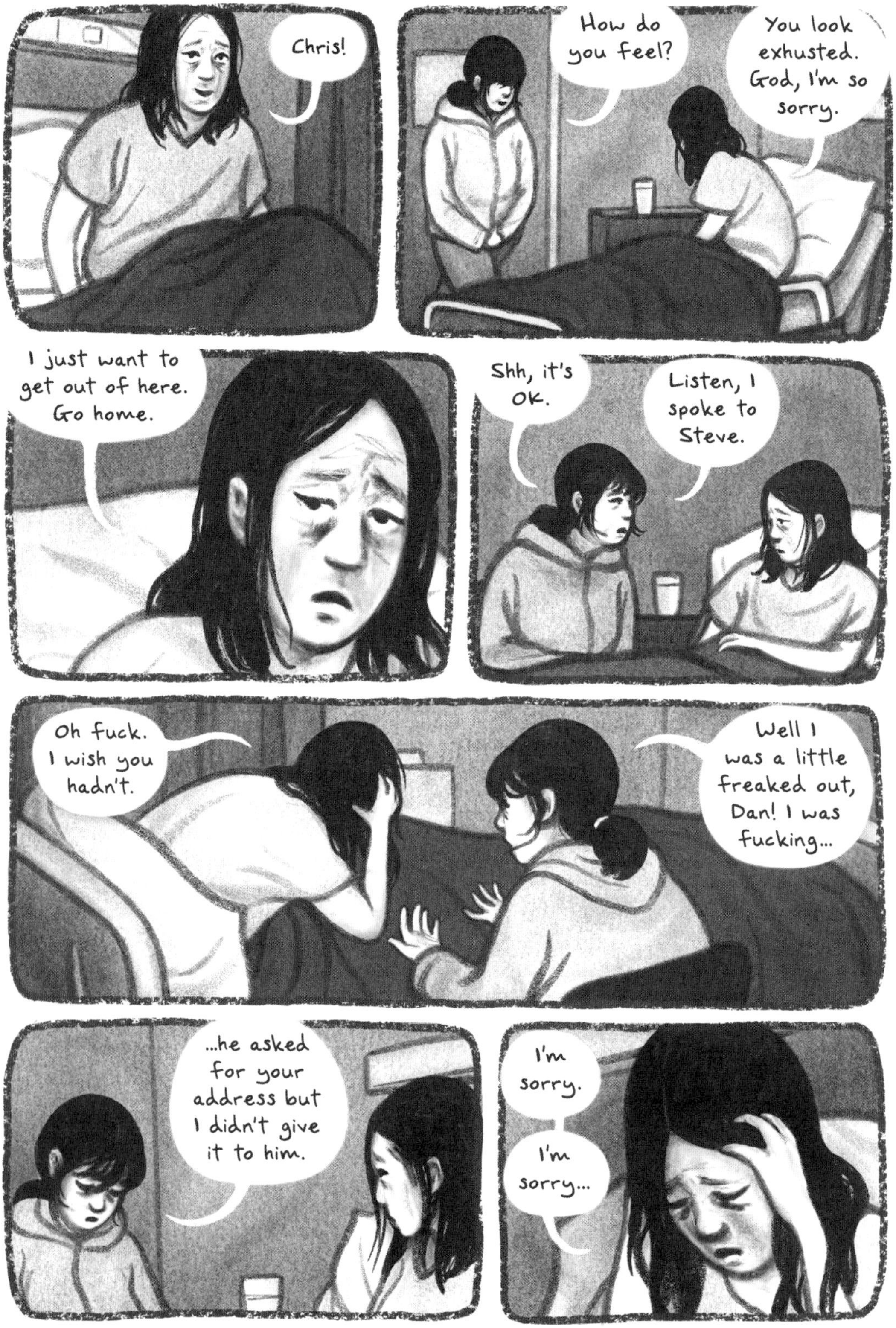
Chris!
How do you feel?
You look exhusted. God, I'm so sorry.
I just want to get out of here. Go home.
Shh, it's OK.
Listen, I spoke to Steve.
Oh fuck. I wish you hadn't.
Well I was a little freaked out, Dan! I was fucking...
...he asked for your address but I didn't give it to him.
I'm sorry.
I'm sorry...

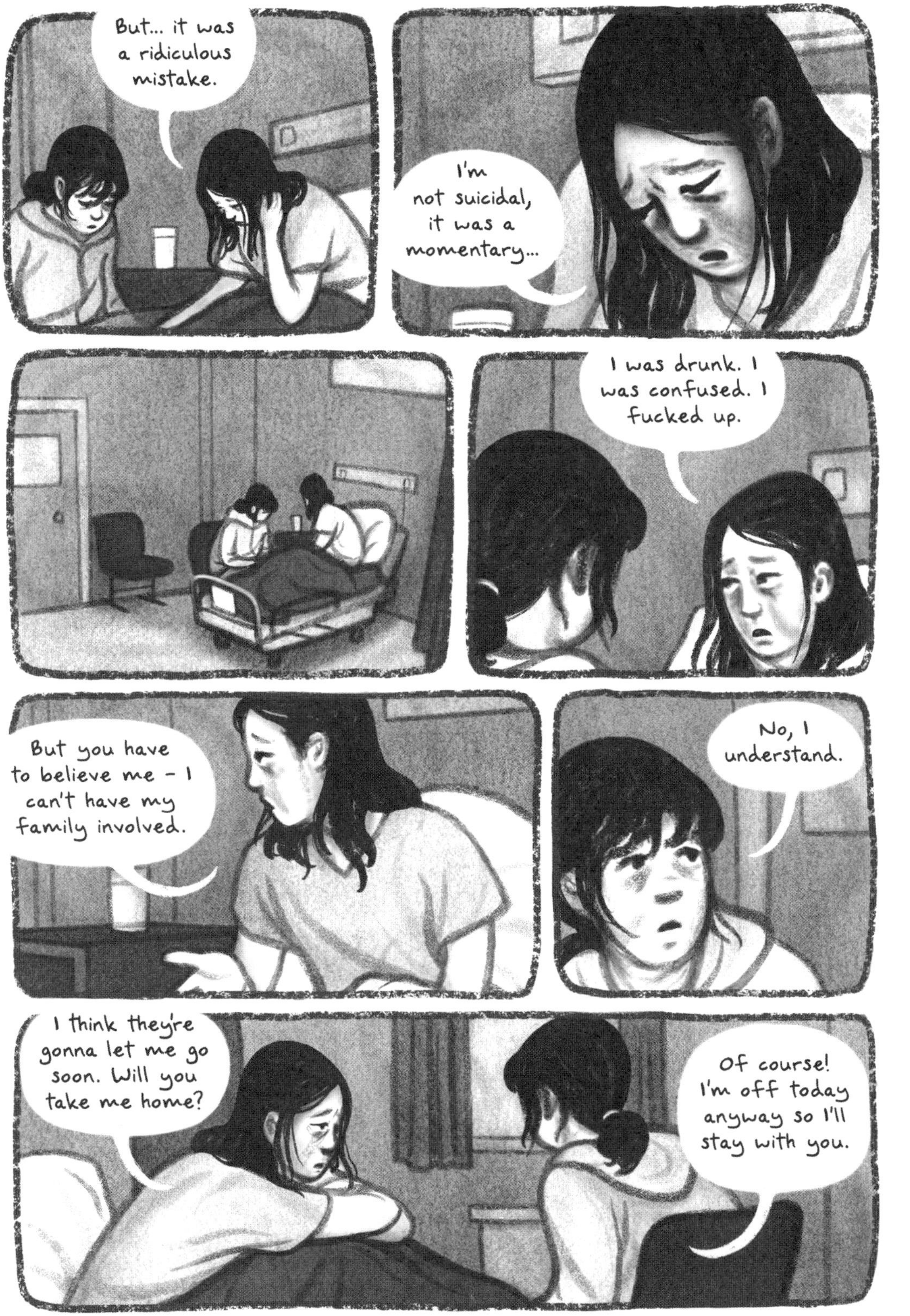
But... it was a ridiculous mistake.
I'm not suicidal, it was a momentary...
I was drunk. I was confused. I fucked up.
But you have to believe me - I can't have my family involved.
No, I understand.
I think they're gonna let me go soon. Will you take me home?
Of course! I'm off today anyway so I'll stay with you.

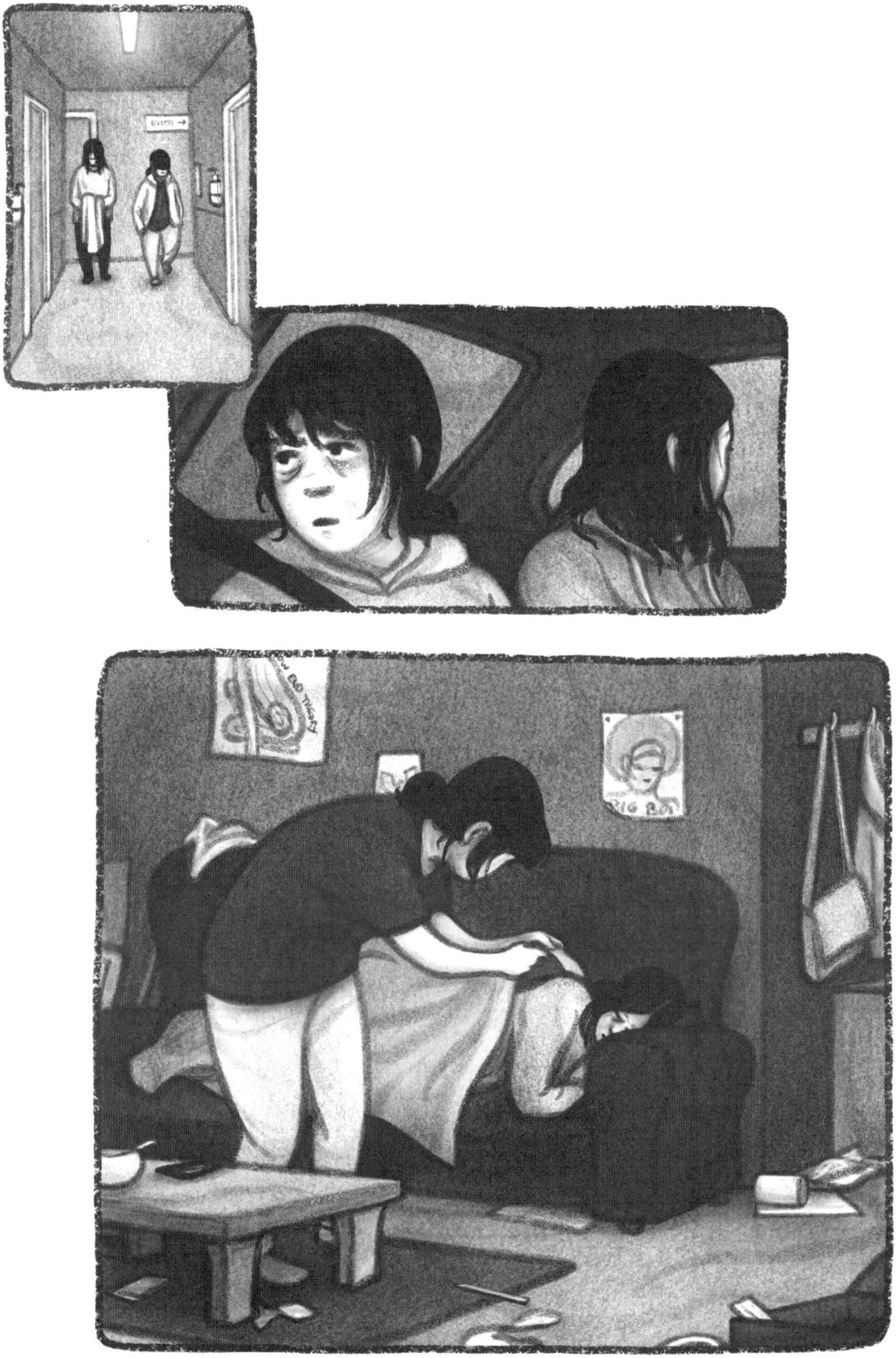

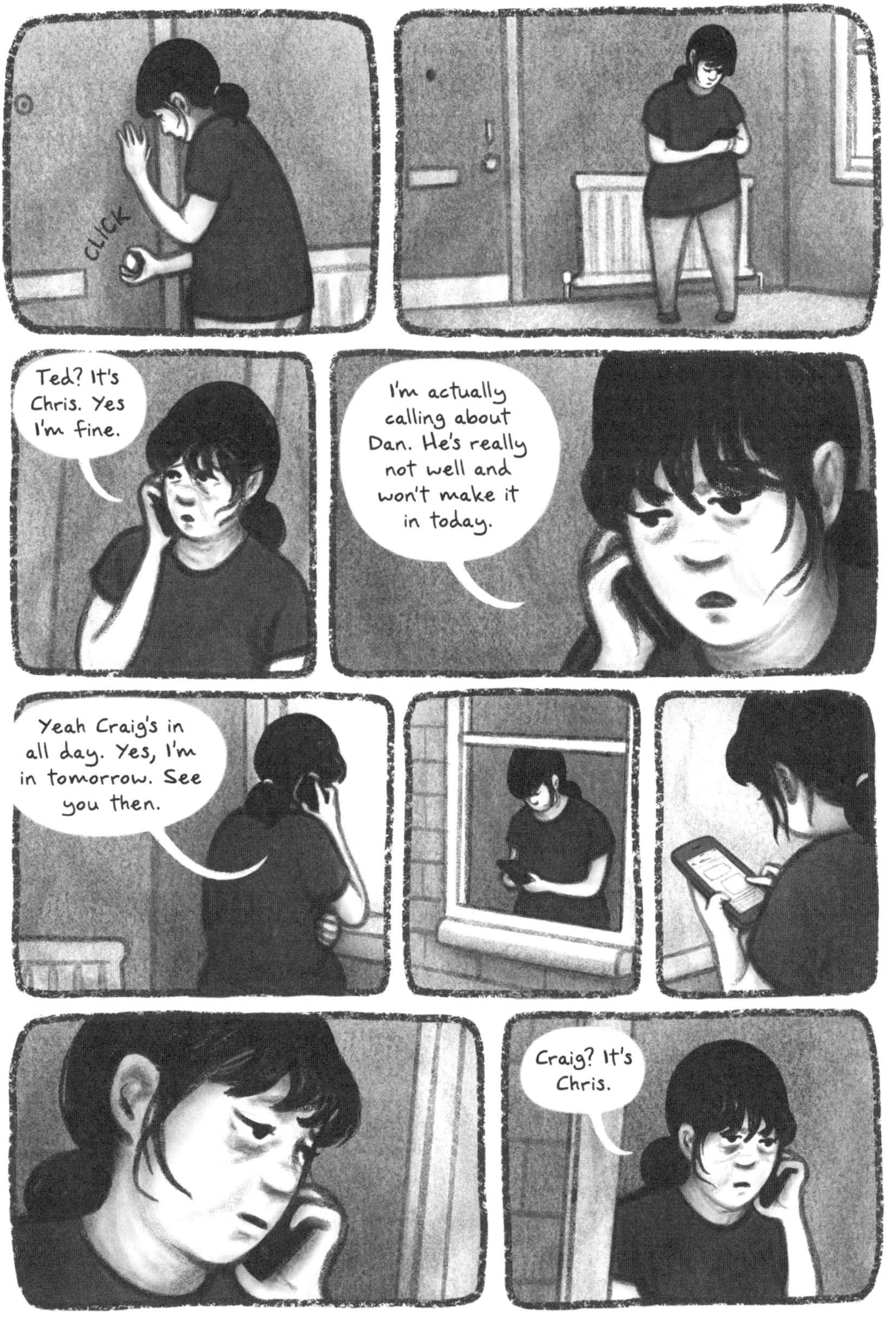
CLICK
Ted? It's Chris. Yes I'm fine.
I'm actually calling about Dan. He's really not well and won't make it in today.
Yeah Craig's in all day. Yes, I'm in tomorrow. See you then.
Craig? It's Chris.

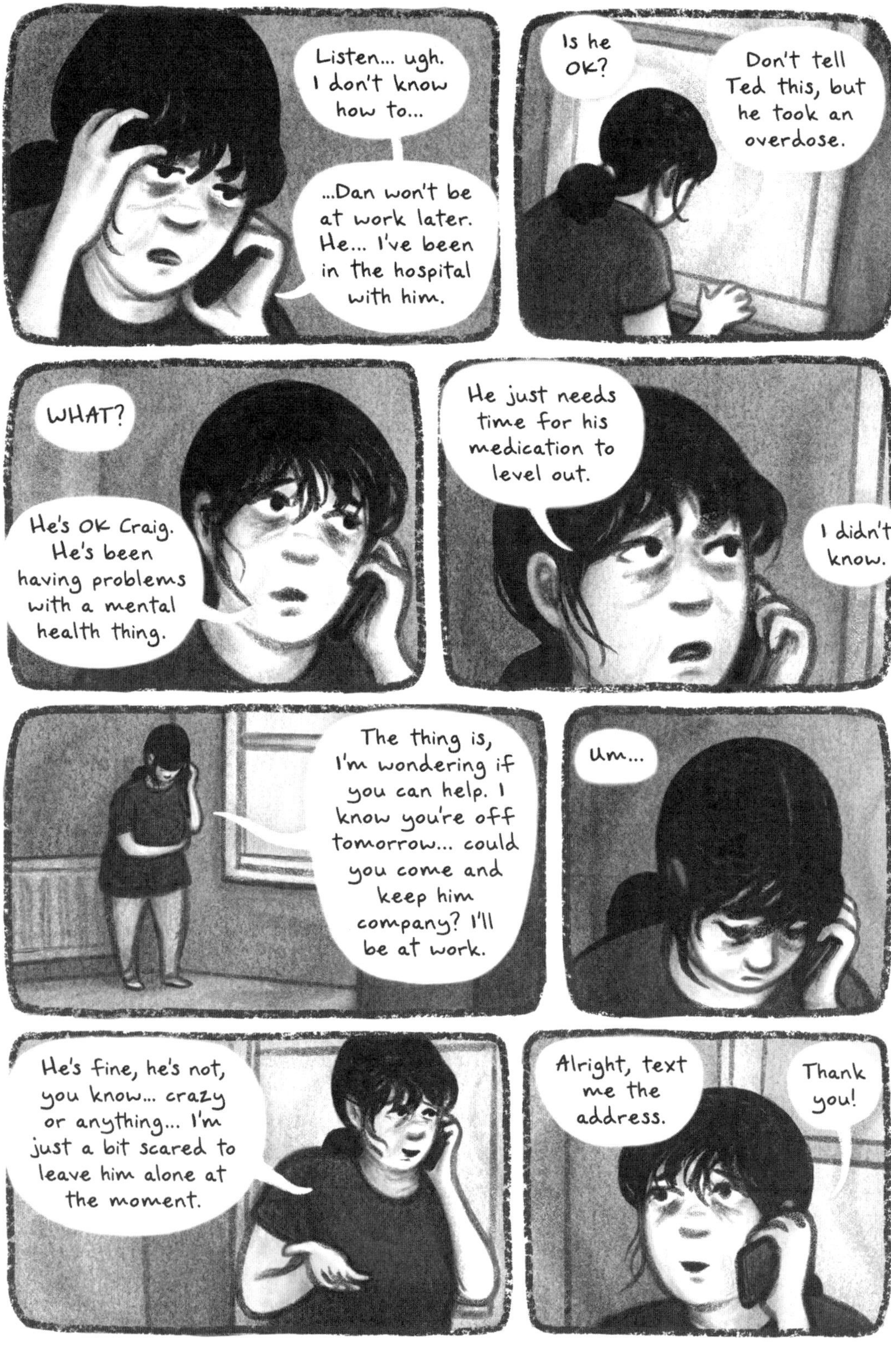
Listen... ugh. I don't know how to...
...Dan won't be at work later. He... I've been in the hospital with him.
Is he OK?
Don't tell Ted this, but he took an overdose.
WHAT?
He's OK Craig. He's been having problems with a mental health thing.
He just needs time for his medication to level out.
I didn't know.
The thing is, I'm wondering if you can help. I know you're off tomorrow... could you come and keep him company? I'll be at work.
Um...
He's fine, he's not, you know... crazy or anything... I'm just a bit scared to leave him alone at the moment.
Alright, text me the address.
Thank you!

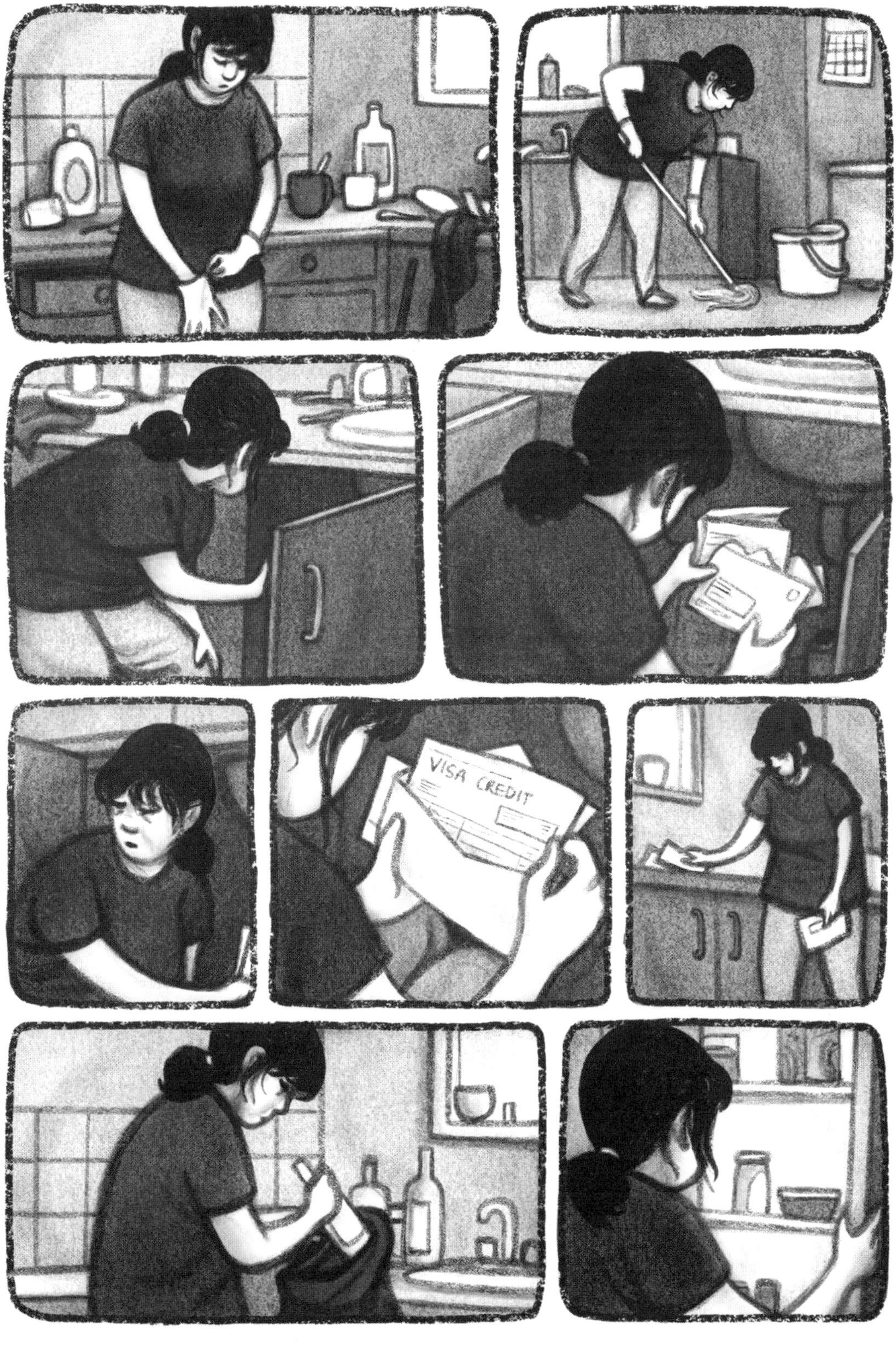
VISA CREDIT

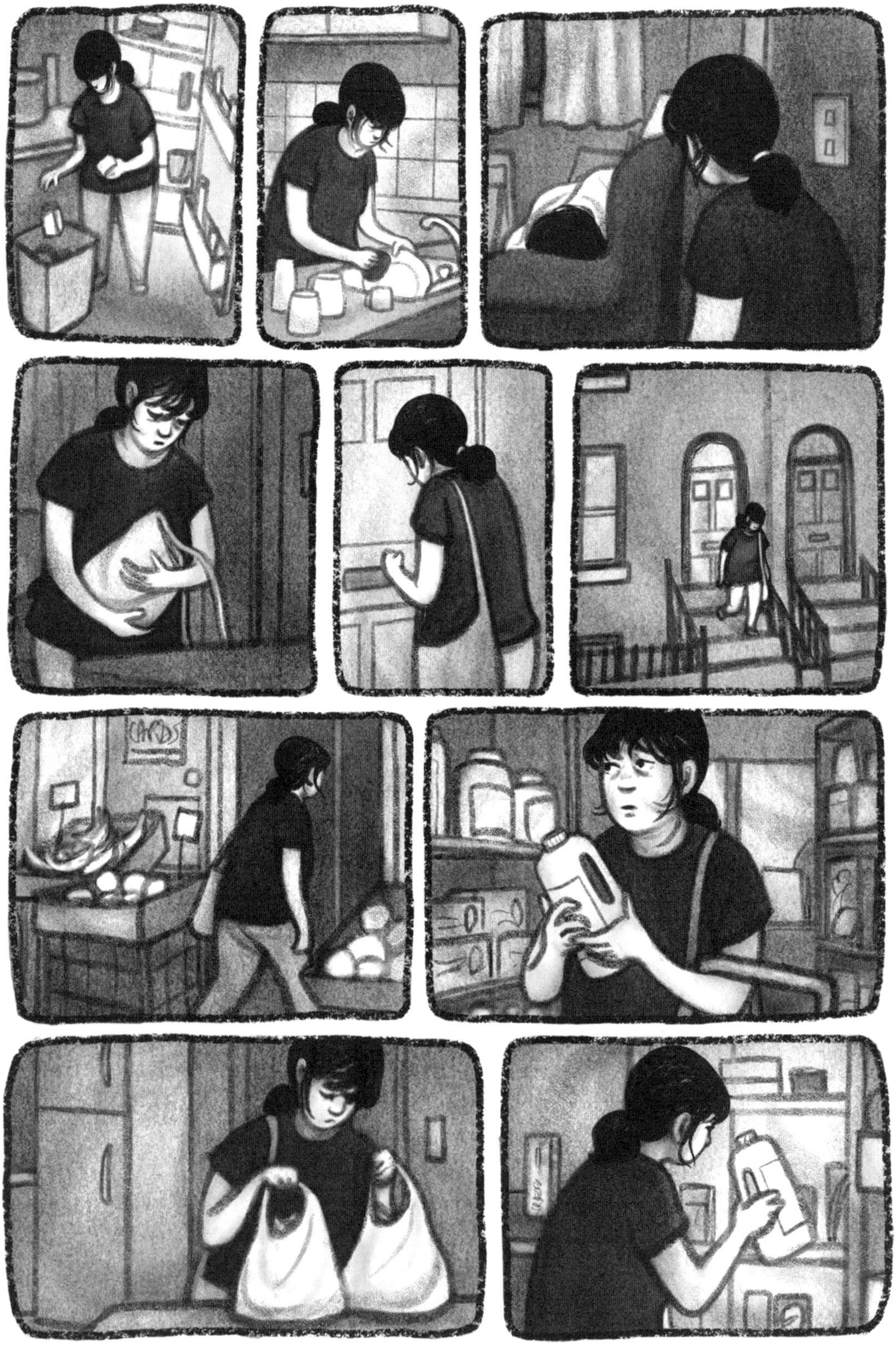

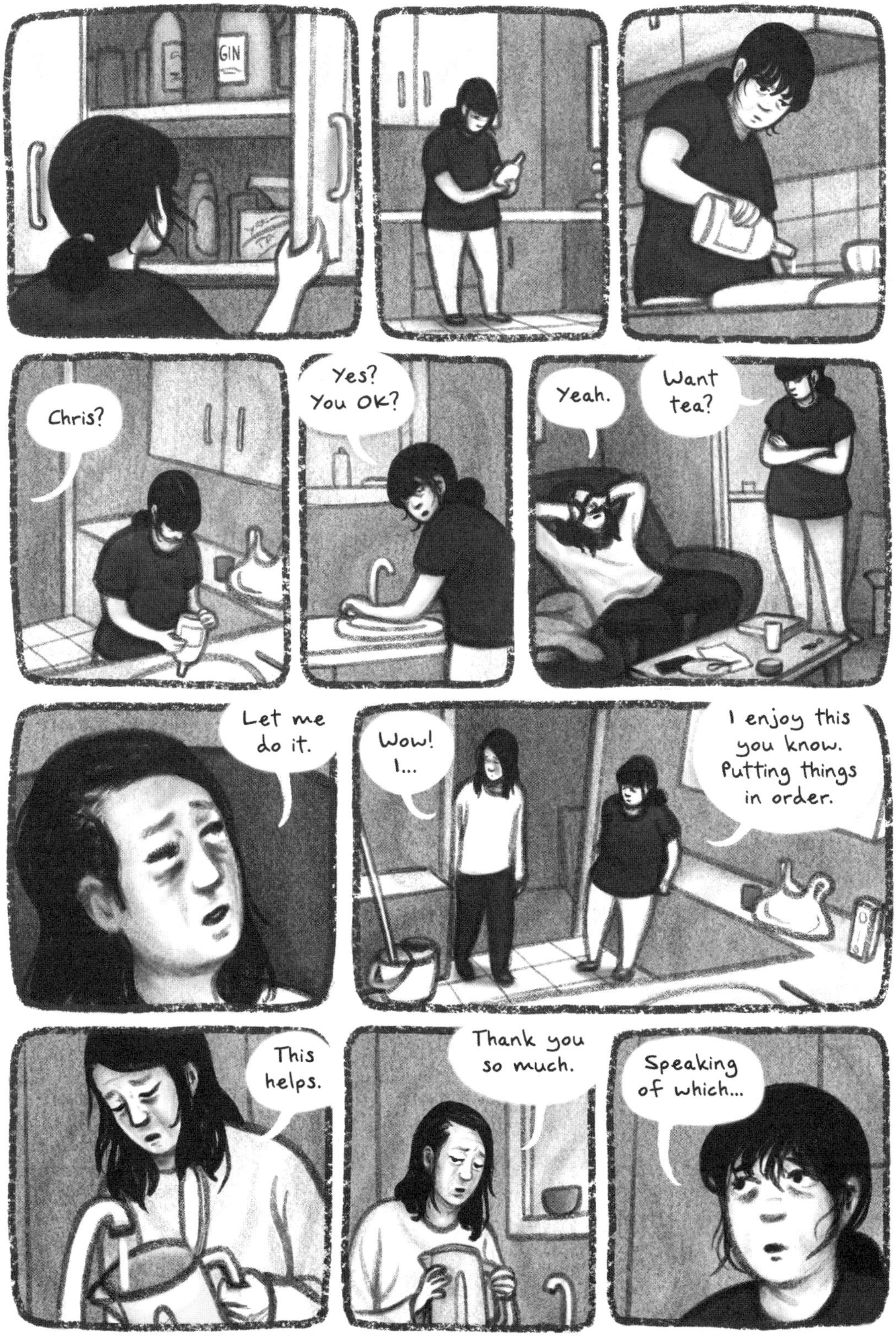
GIN
Chris?
Yes? You OK?
Yeah.
Want tea?
Let me do it.
Wow! I...
I enjoy this you know. Putting things in order.
This helps.
Thank you so much.
Speaking of which...

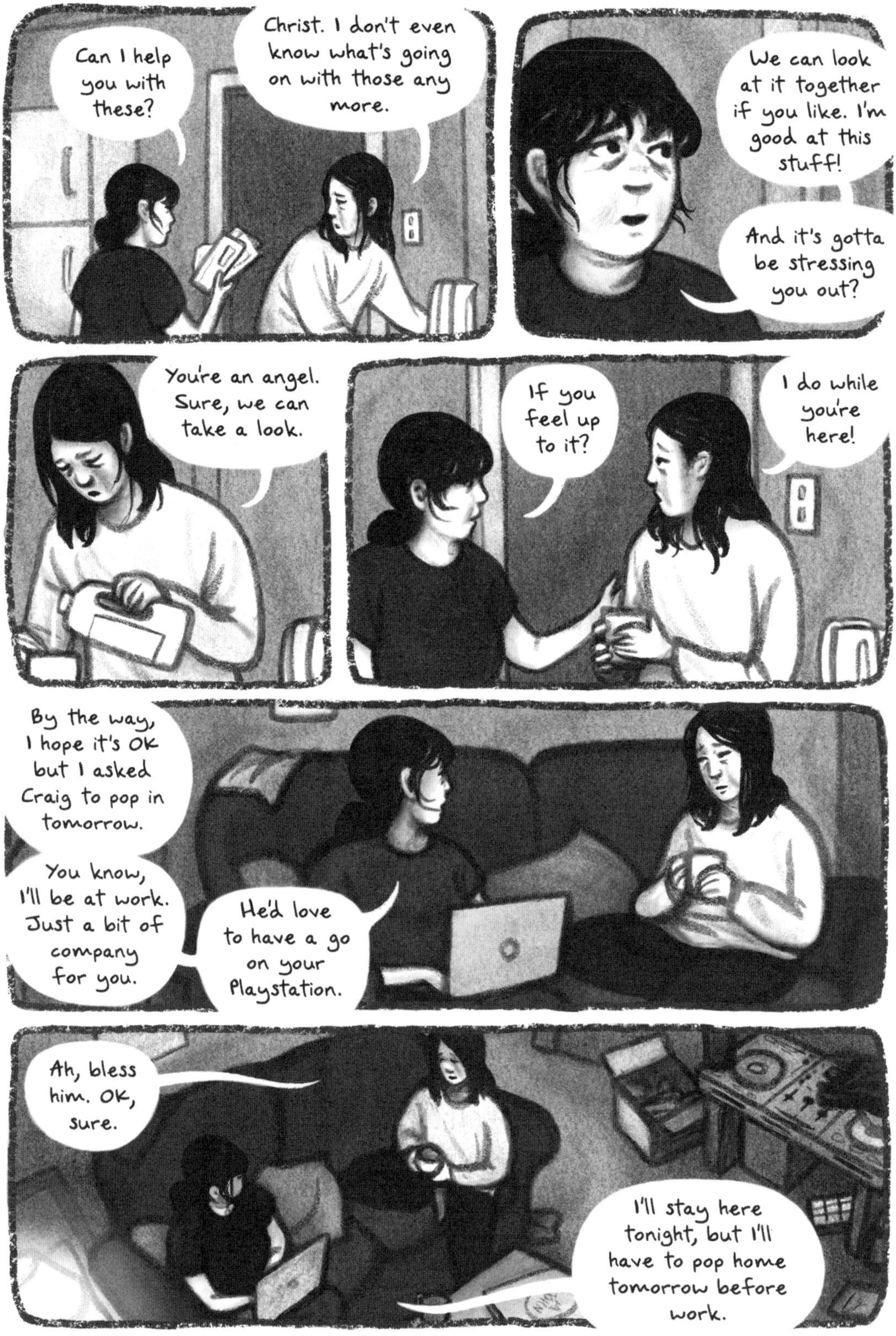
Can I help you with these?
Christ. I don't even know what's going on with those any more.
We can look at it together if you like. I'm good at this stuff!
And it's gotta be stressing you out?
You're an angel. Sure, we can take a look.
If you feel up to it?
I do while you're here!
By the way, I hope it's OK but I asked Craig to pop in tomorrow.
You know, I'll be at work. Just a bit of company for you.
He'd love to have a go on your Playstation.
Ah, bless him. OK, sure.
I'll stay here tonight, but I'll have to pop home tomorrow before work.

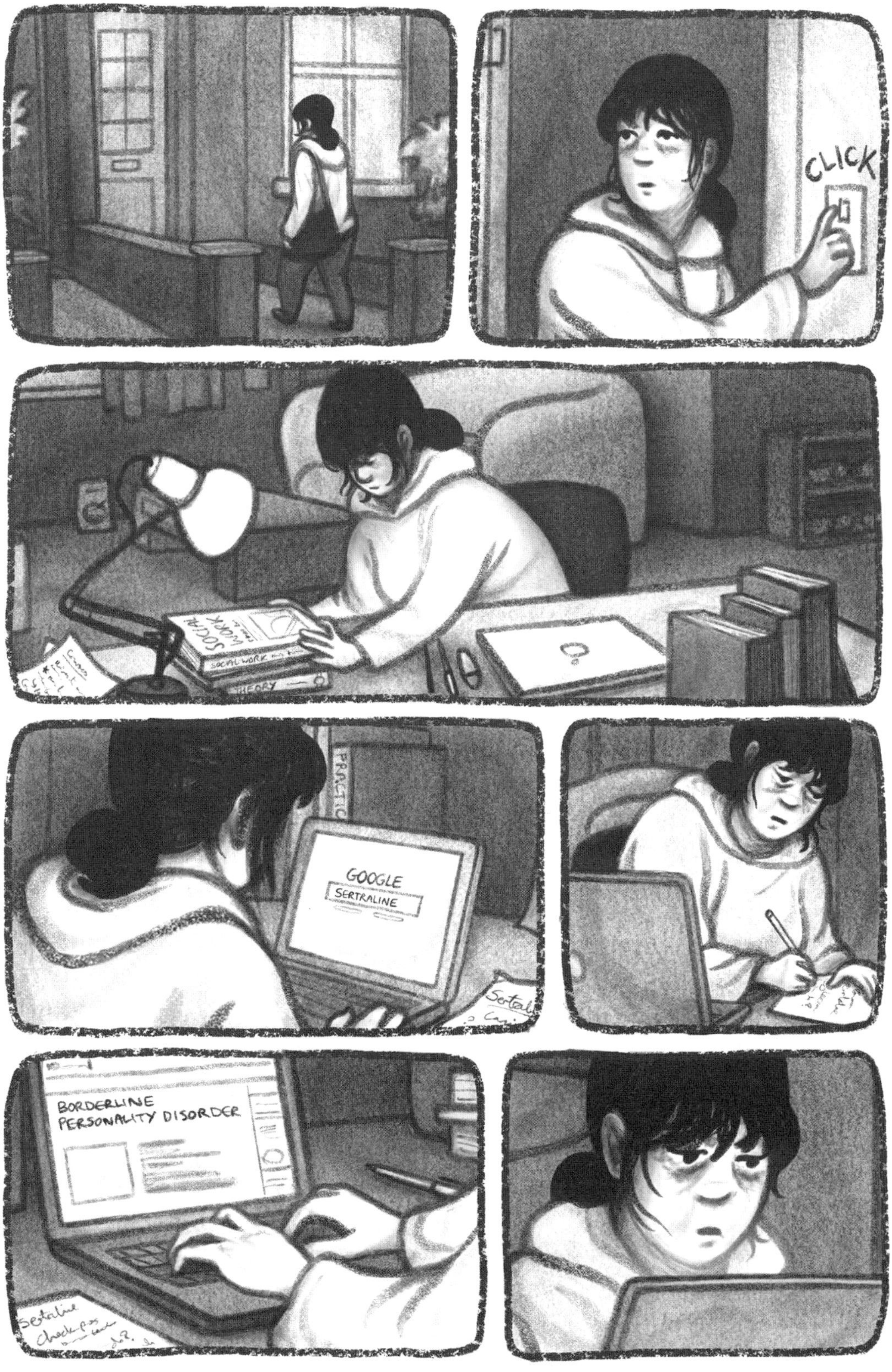
CLICK
GOOGLE
SERTRALINE
BORDERLINE PERSONALITY DISORDER

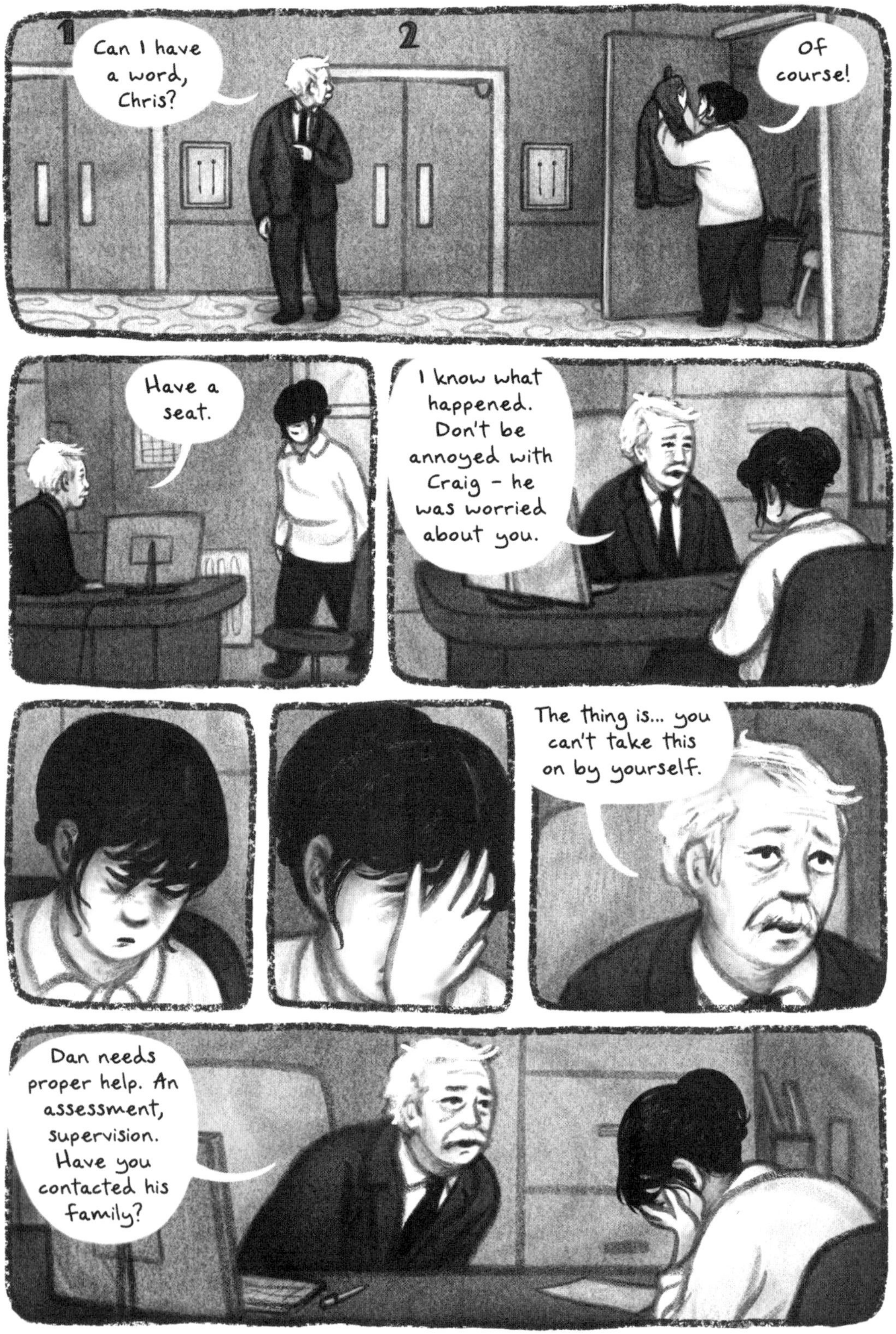
1
2
Can I have a word, Chris?
Of course!
Have a seat.
I know what happened. Don't be annoyed with Craig - he was worried about you.
The thing is... you can't take this on by yourself.
Dan needs proper help. An assessment, supervision. Have you contacted his family?

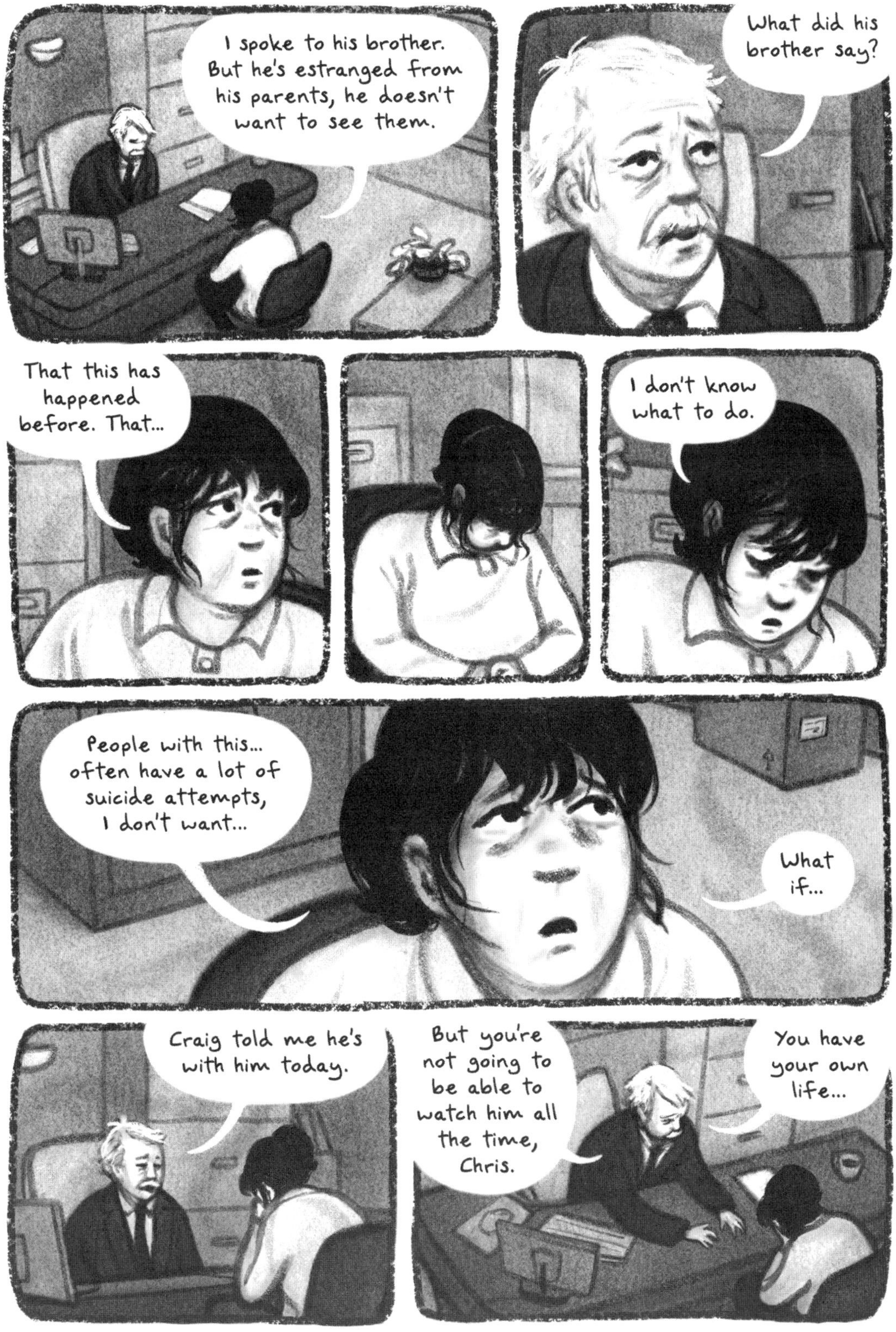
I spoke to his brother. But he's estranged from his parents, he doesn't want to see them.
What did his brother say?
That this has happened before. That...
I don't know what to do.
People with this... often have a lot of suicide attempts, I don't want...
What if...
Craig told me he's with him today.
But you're not going to be able to watch him all the time, Chris.
You have your own life...

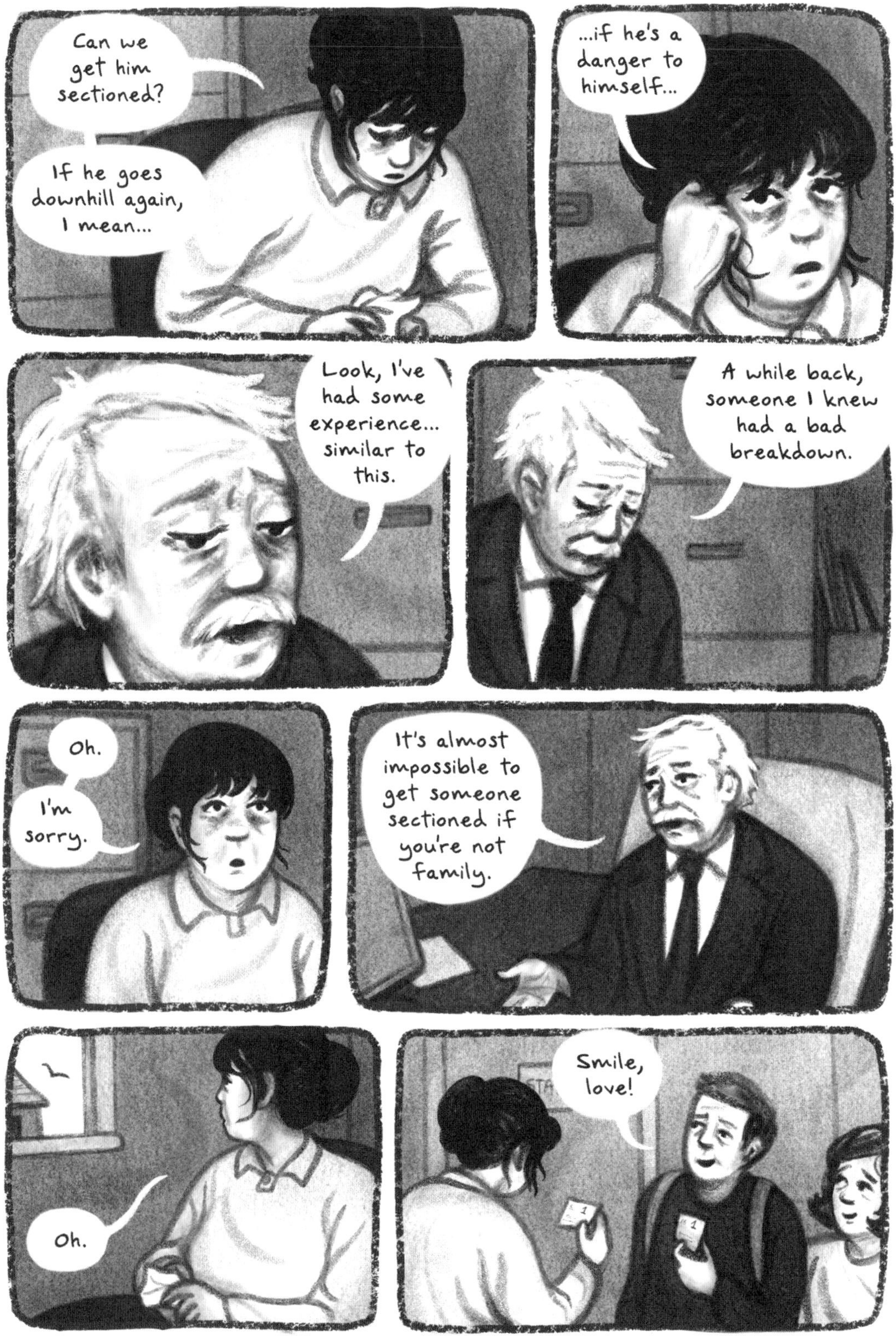
Can we get him sectioned?
If he goes downhill again, I mean...
...if he's a danger to himself...
Look, I've had some experience... similar to this.
A while back, someone I knew had a bad breakdown.
Oh.
I'm sorry.
It's almost impossible to get someone sectioned if you're not family.
Oh.
Smile, love!

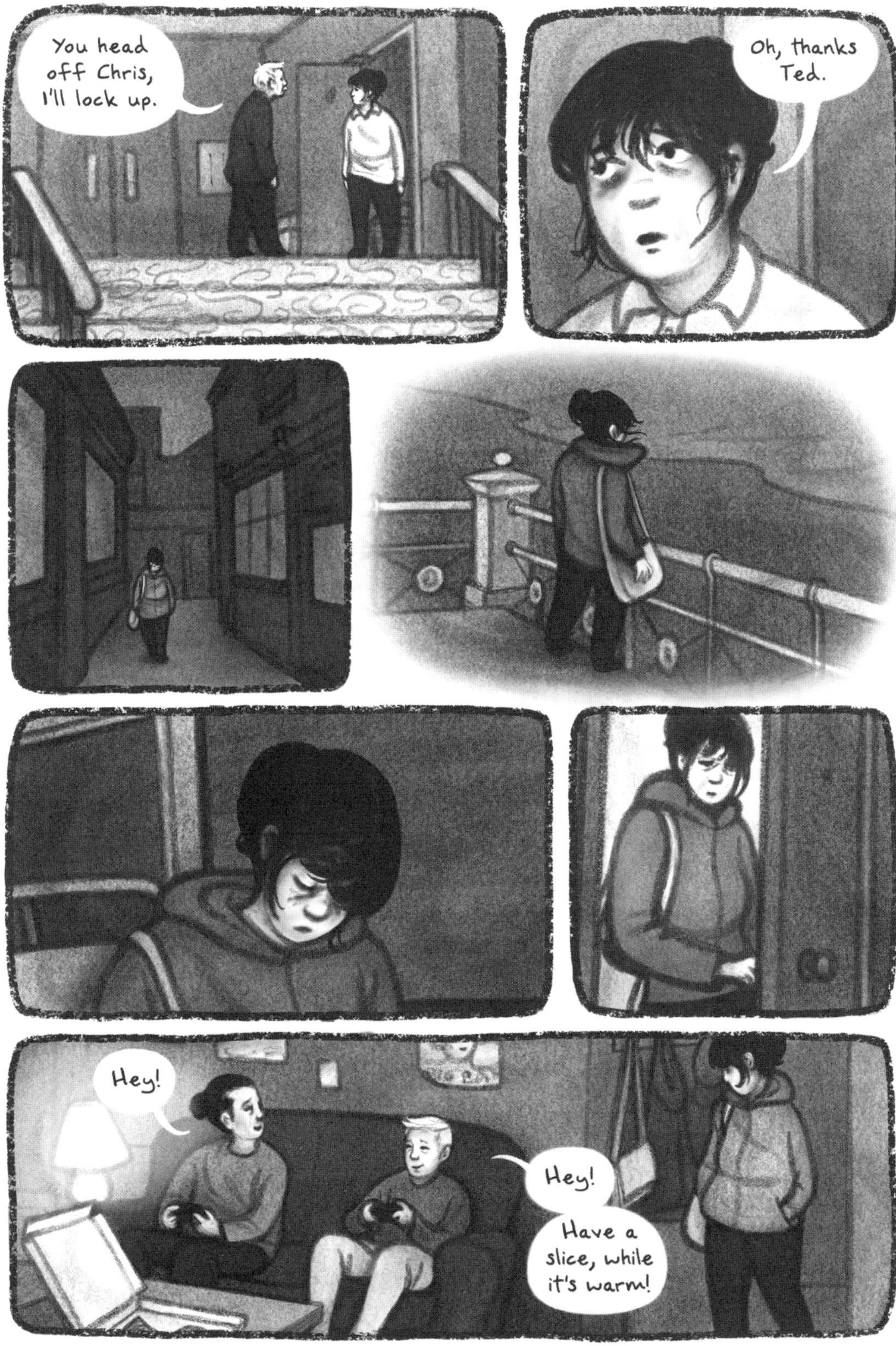
You head off Chris, I'll lock up.
Oh, thanks Ted.
Hey!
Hey!
Have a slice, while it's warm!

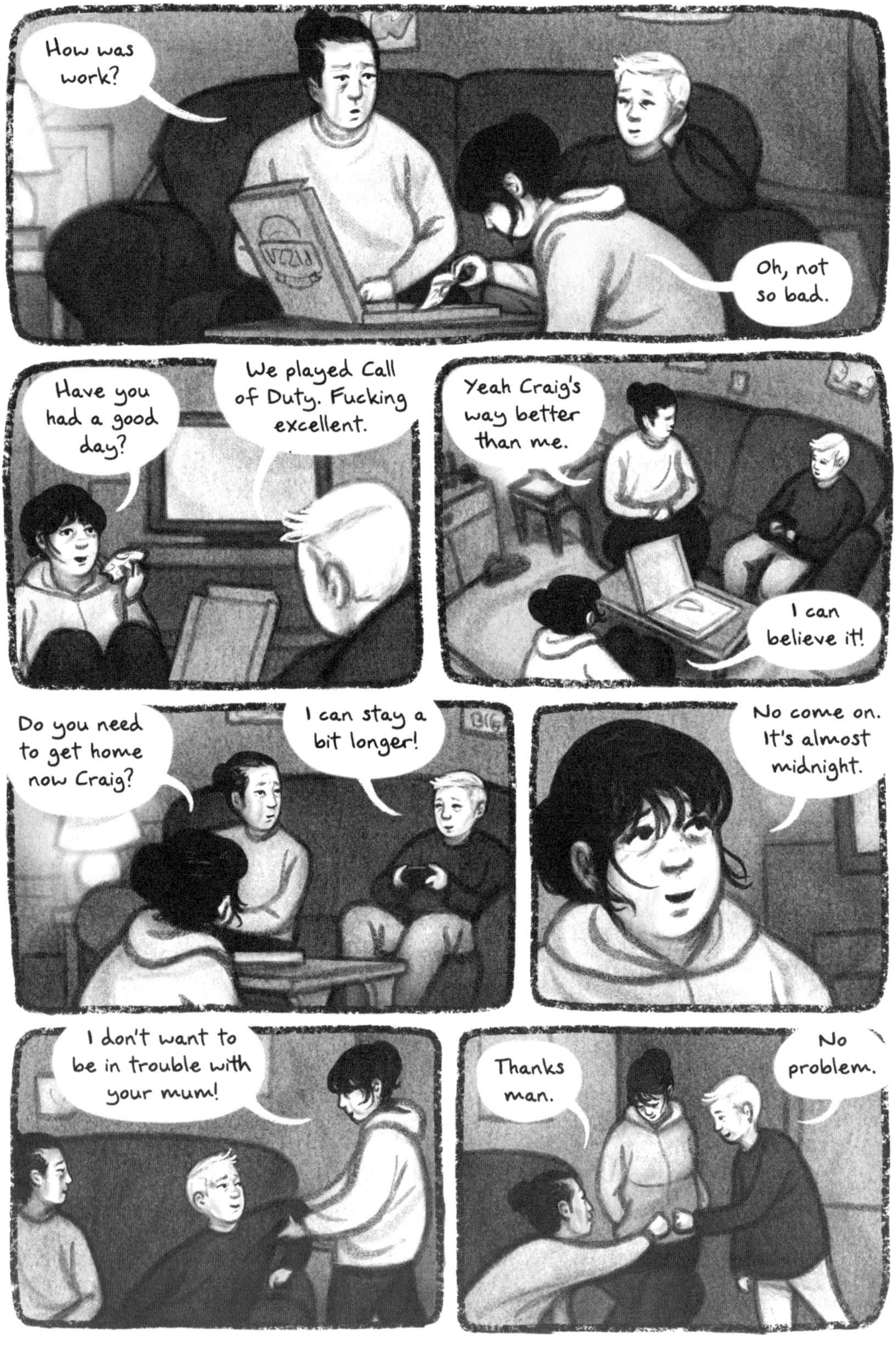
How was work?
Oh, not so bad.
Have you had a good day?
We played Call of Duty. Fucking excellent.
Yeah Craig's way better than me.
I can believe it!
Do you need to get home now Craig?
I can stay a bit longer!
No come on. It's almost midnight.
I don't want to be in trouble with your mum!
Thanks man.
No problem.

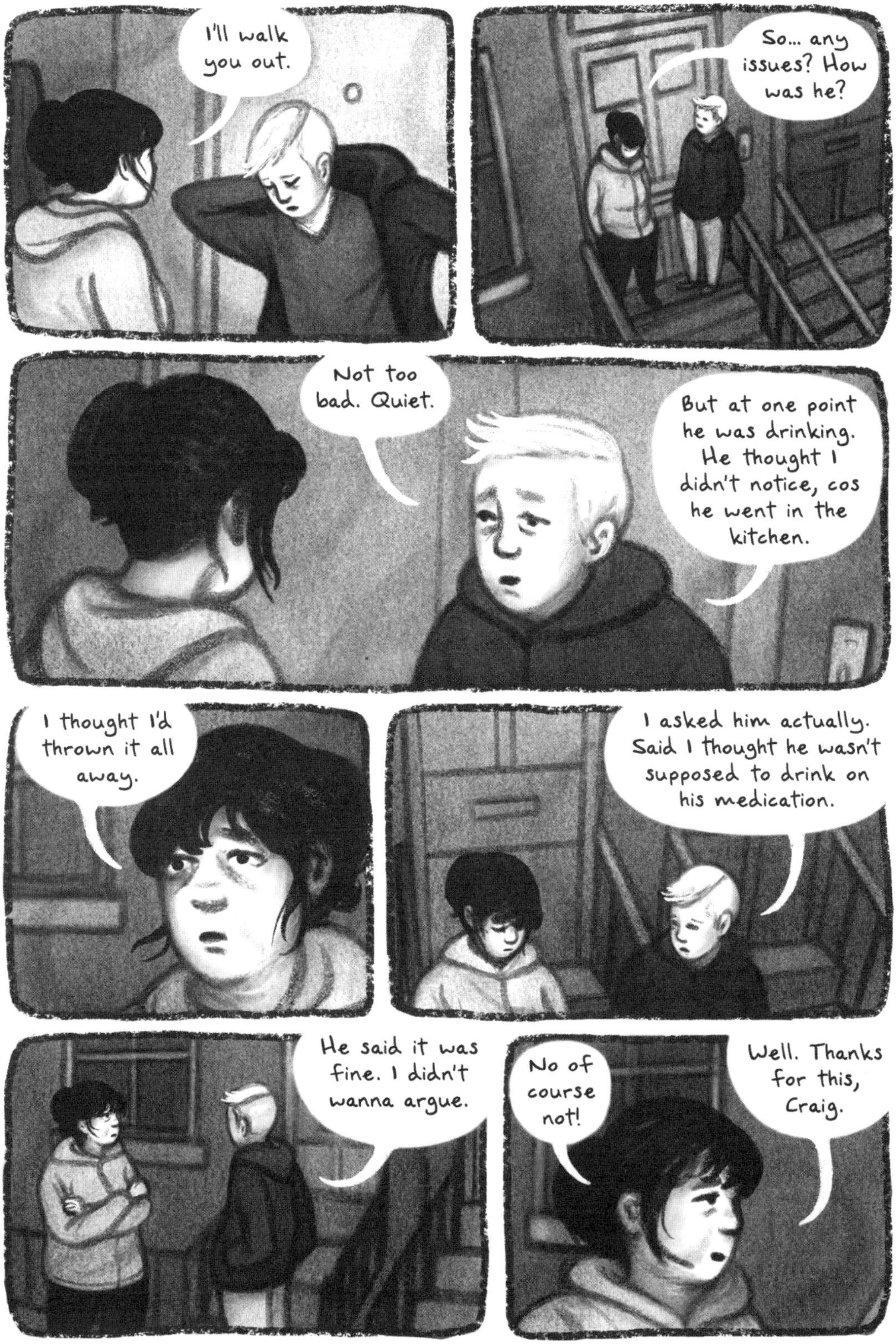
I'll walk you out.
So... any issues? How was he?
Not too bad. Quiet.
But at one point he was drinking. He thought I didn't notice, cos he went in the kitchen.
I thought I'd thrown it all away.
I asked him actually. Said I thought he wasn't supposed to drink on his medication.
He said it was fine. I didn't wanna argue.
No of course not!
Well. Thanks for this, Craig.

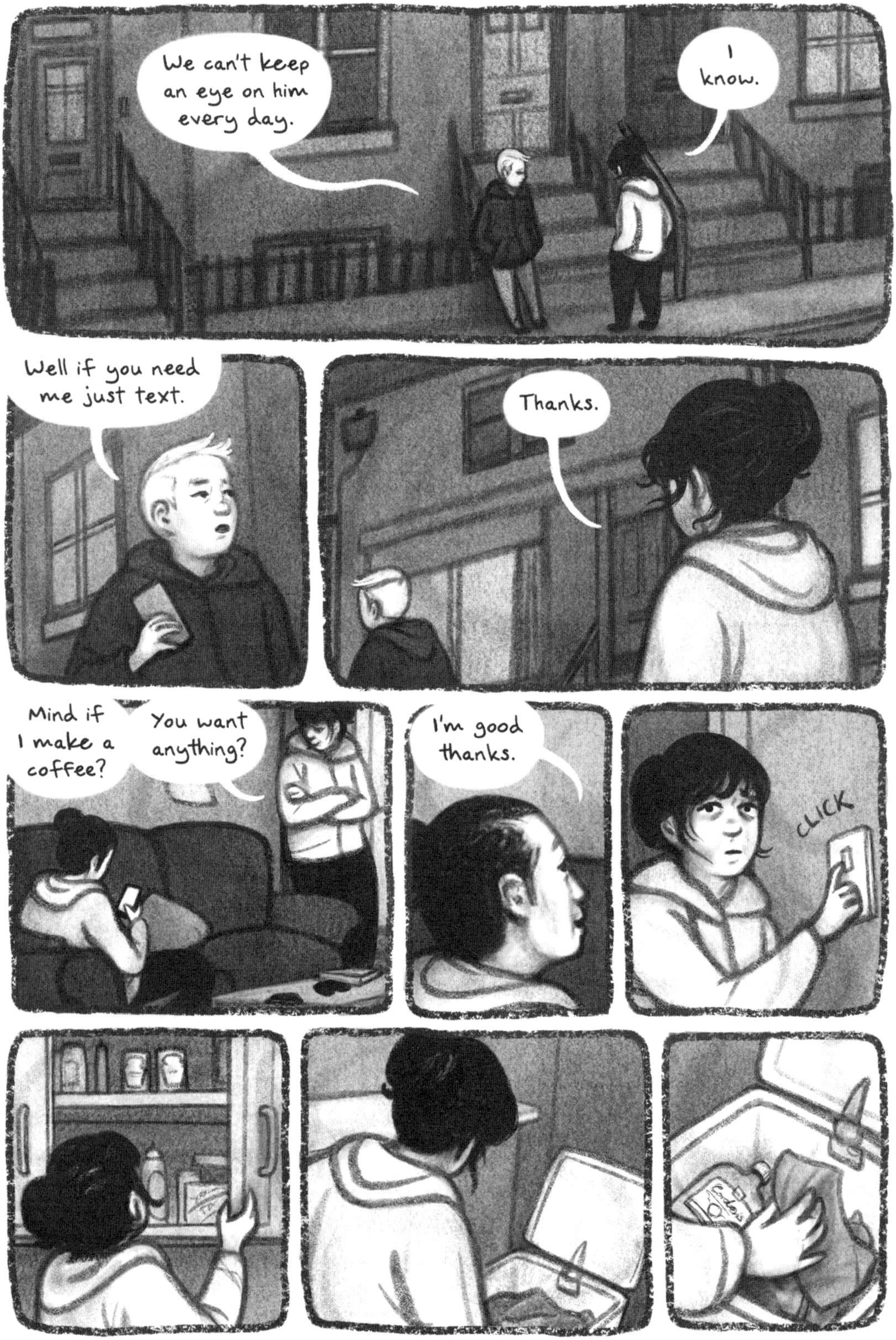
We can't keep an eye on him every day.
I know.
Well if you need me just text.
Thanks.
Mind if I make a coffee?
You want anything?
I'm good thanks.
CLICK

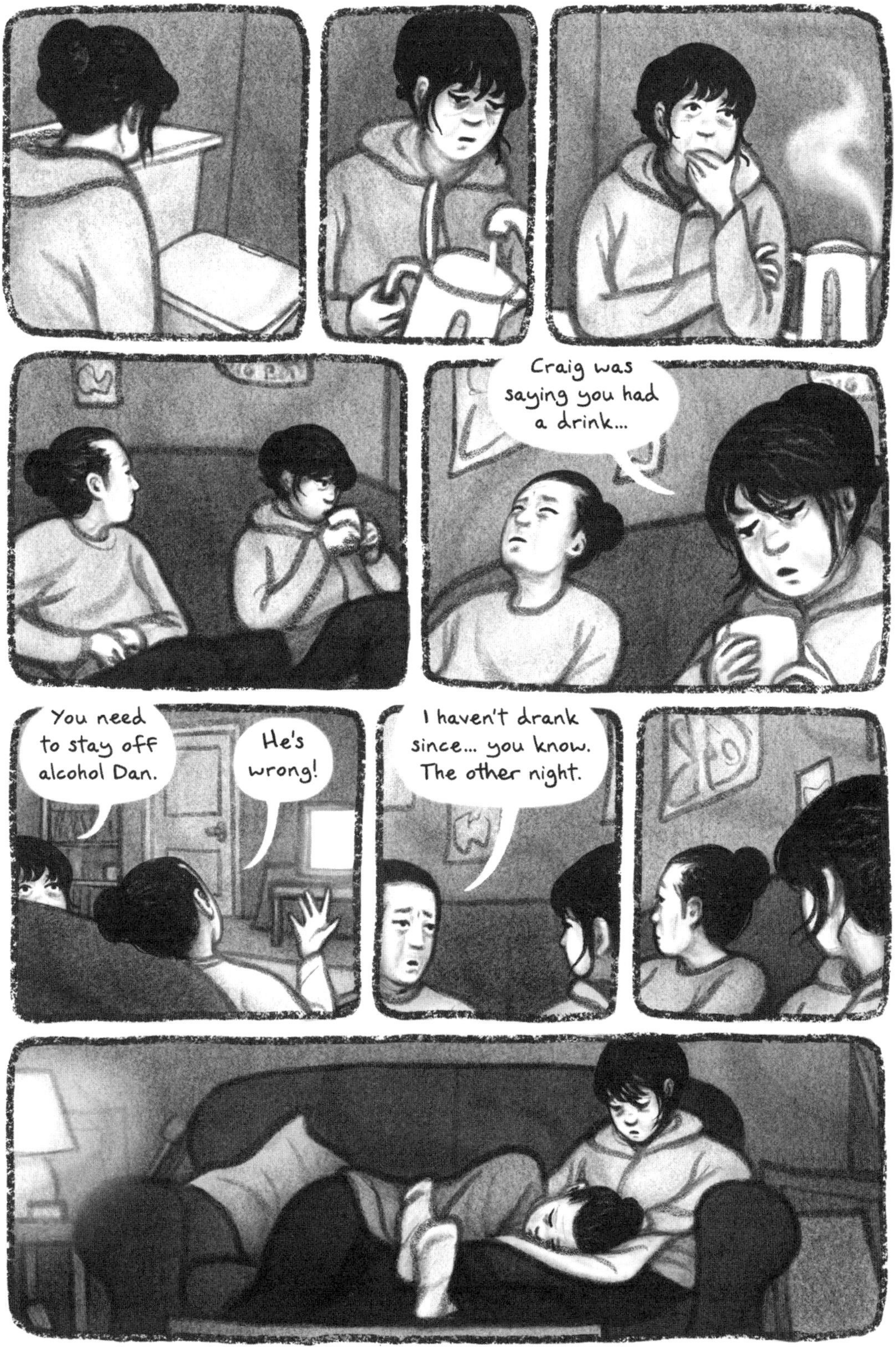
Craig was saying you had a drink...
You need to stay off alcohol Dan.
He's wrong!
I haven't drank since... you know. The other night.

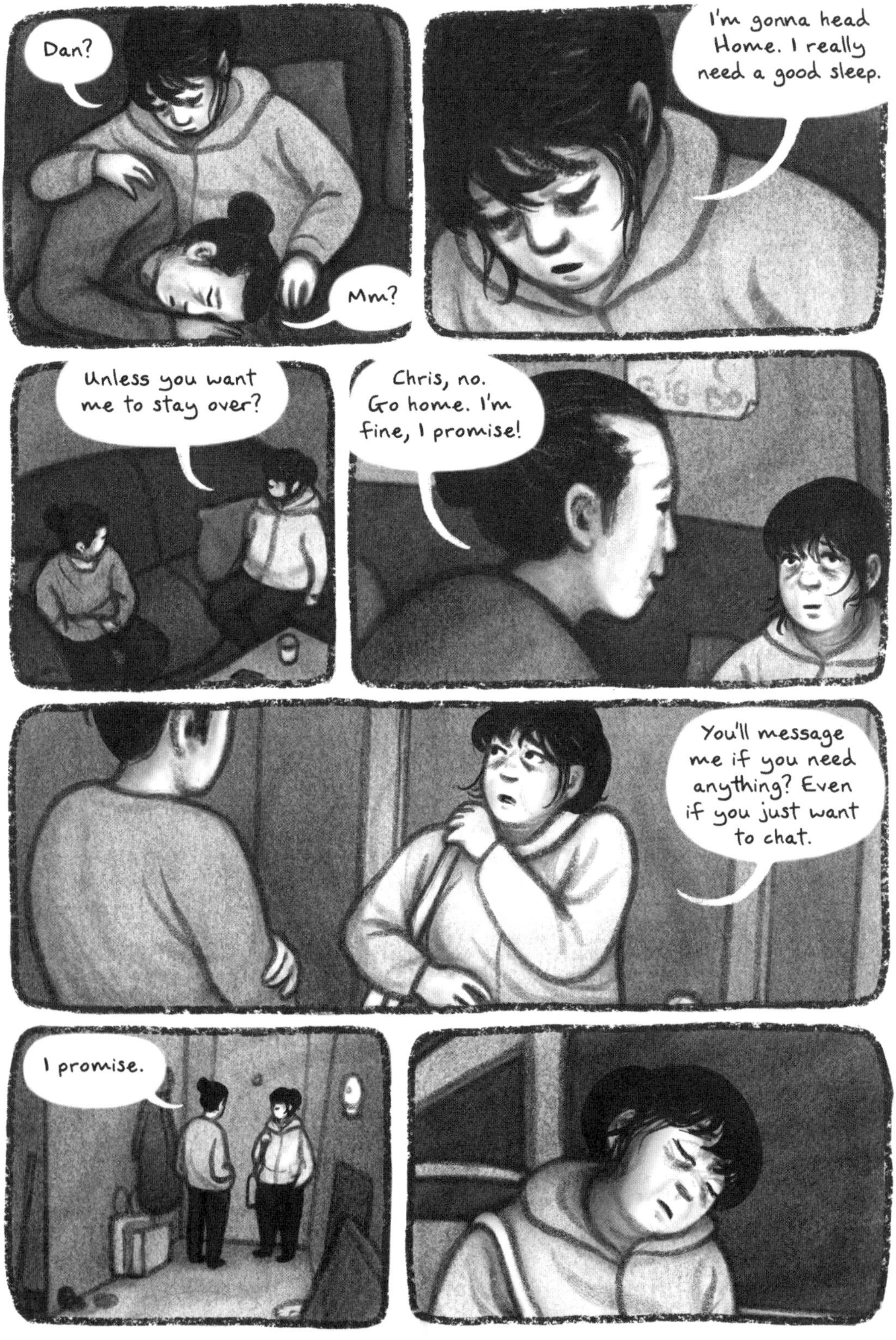
Dan?
Mm?
I'm gonna head Home. I really need a good sleep.
Unless you want me to stay over?
Chris, no. Go home. I'm fine, I promise!
You'll message me if you need anything? Even if you just want to chat.
I promise.

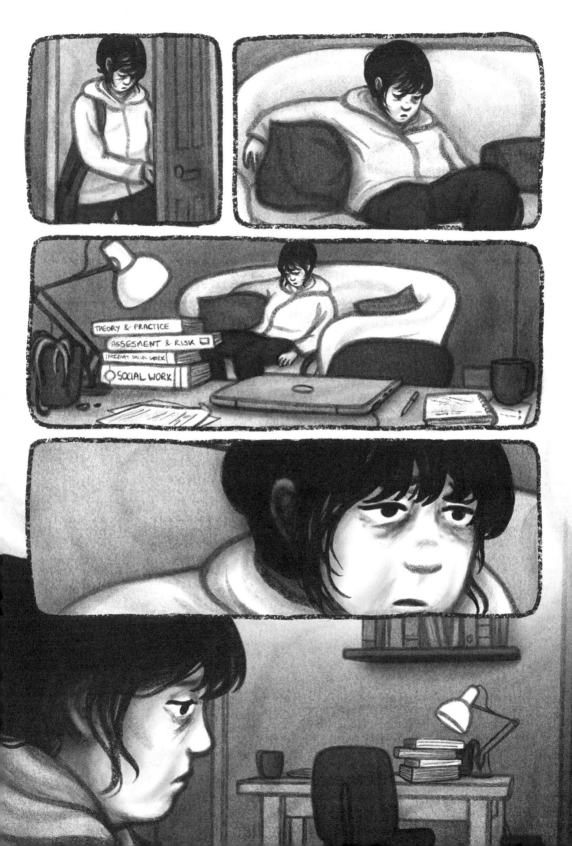

The books on the desk read:
THEORY & PRACTICE
ASSESMENT & RISK
INTERNAT SOCIAL WORK
SOCIAL WORK

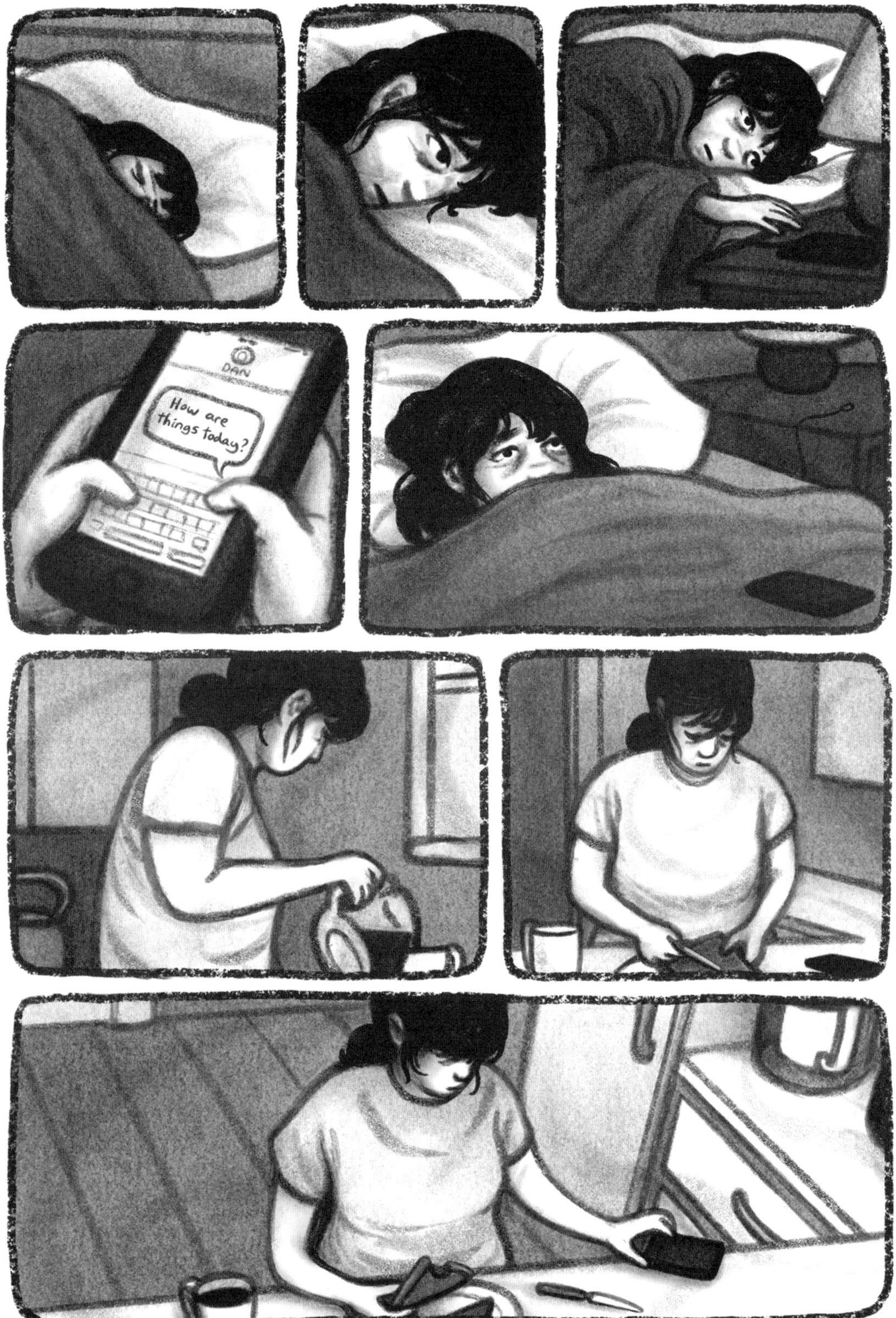
DAN
How are things today?

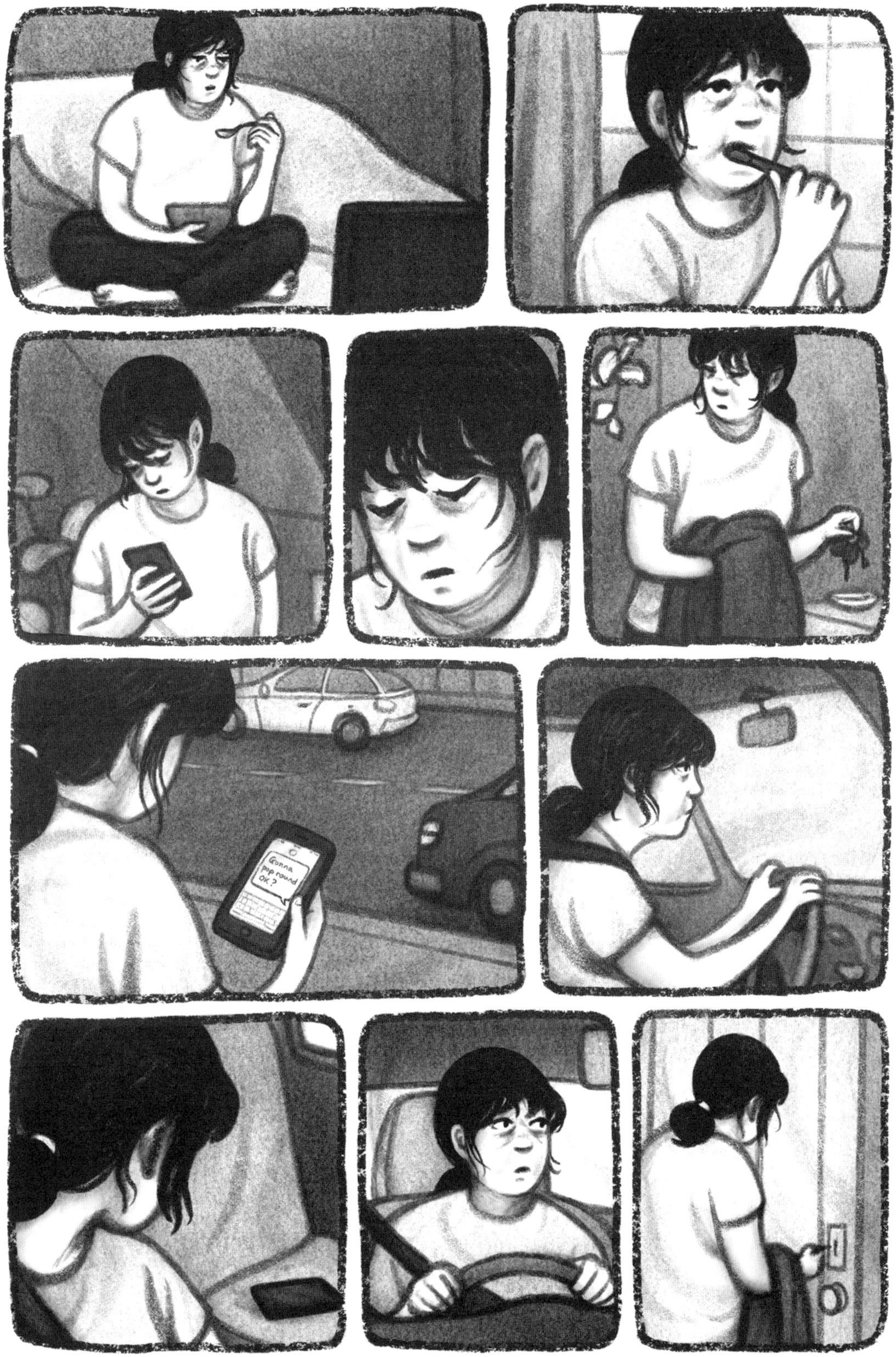
Gonna pop round OK?

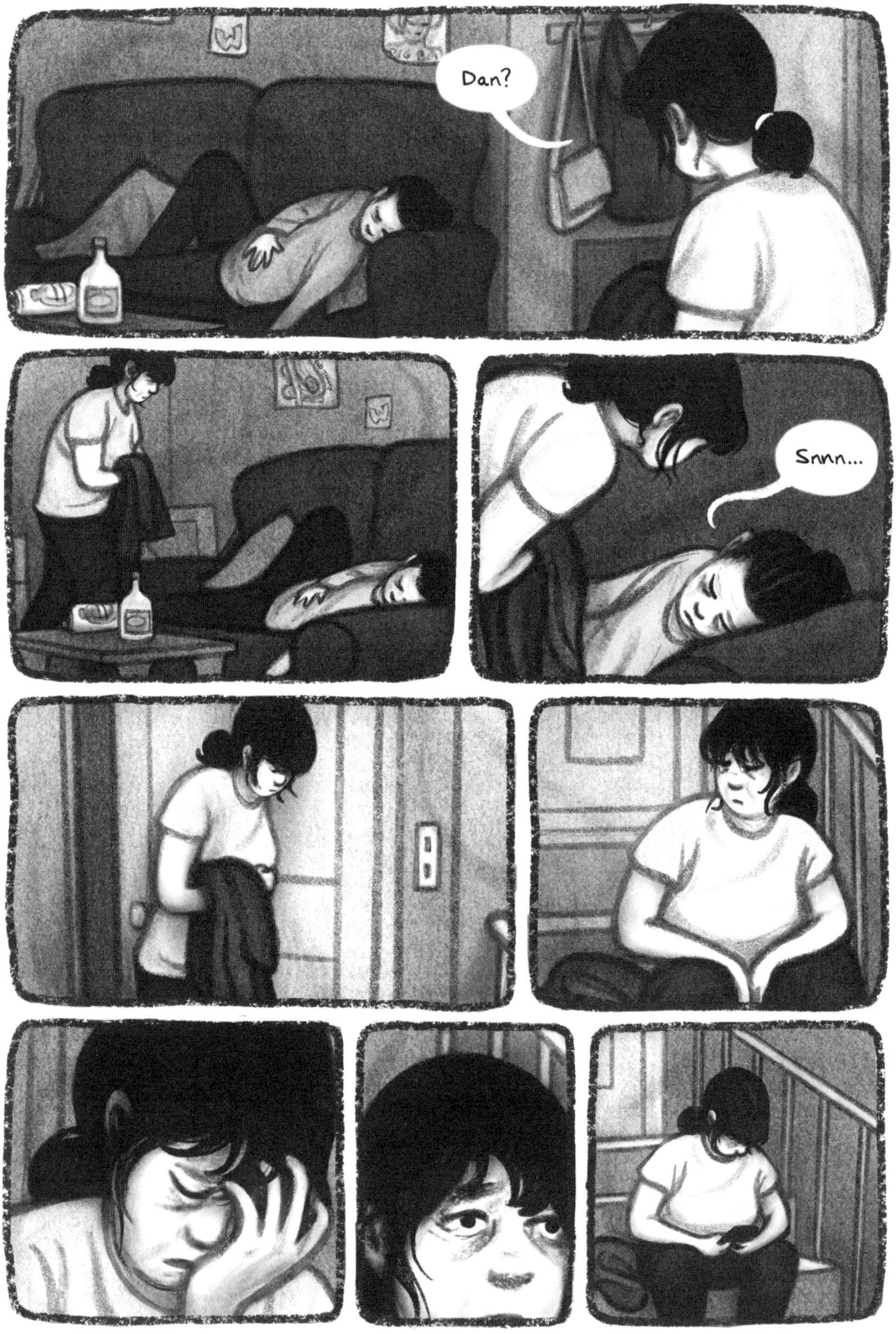
Dan?
Snnn...

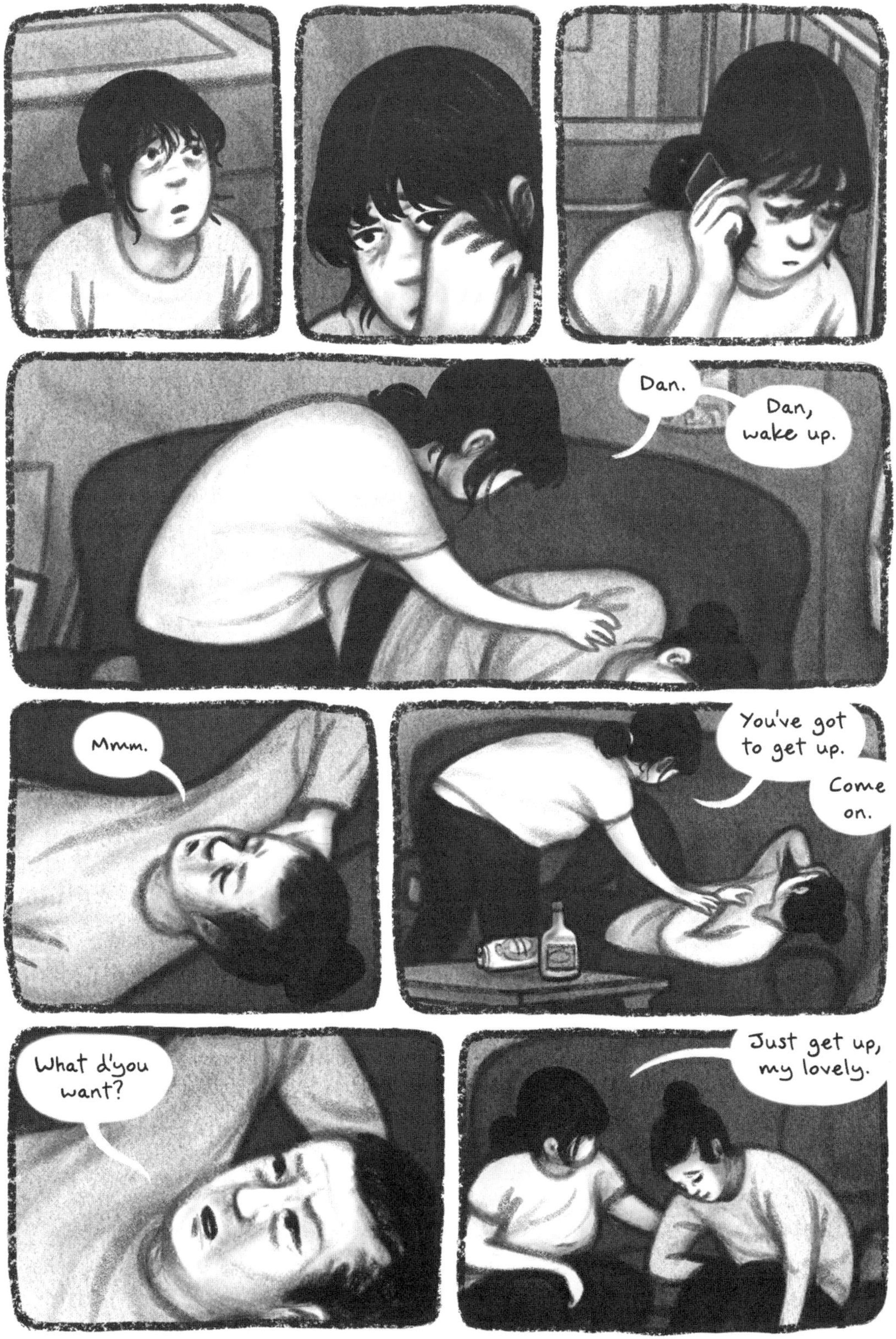
Dan.
Dan, wake up.
Mmm.
You've got to get up.
Come on.
What d'you want?
Just get up, my lovely.

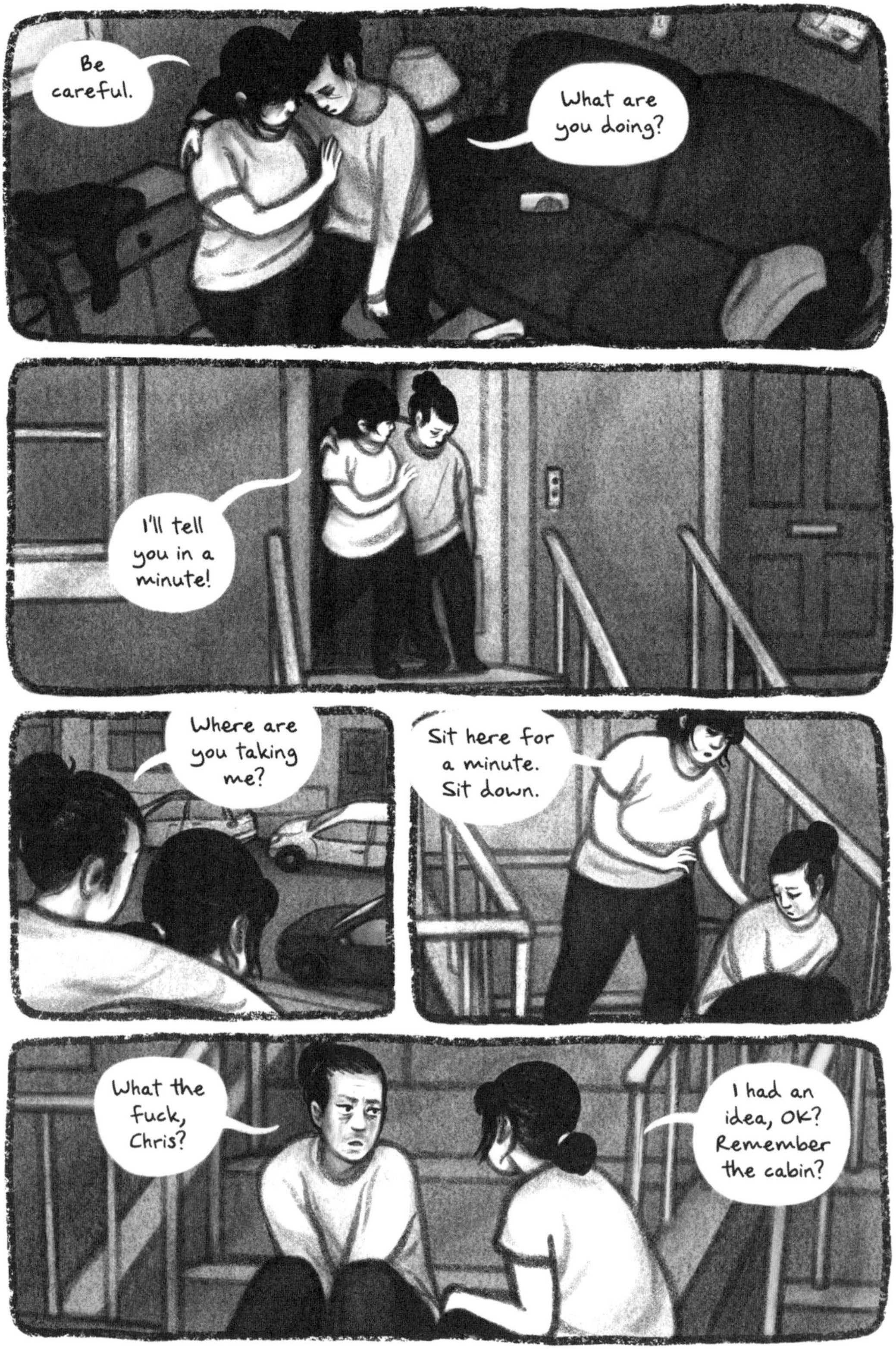
Be careful.
What are you doing?
I'll tell you in a minute!
Where are you taking me?
Sit here for a minute. Sit down.
What the fuck, Chris?
I had an idea, OK? Remember the cabin?

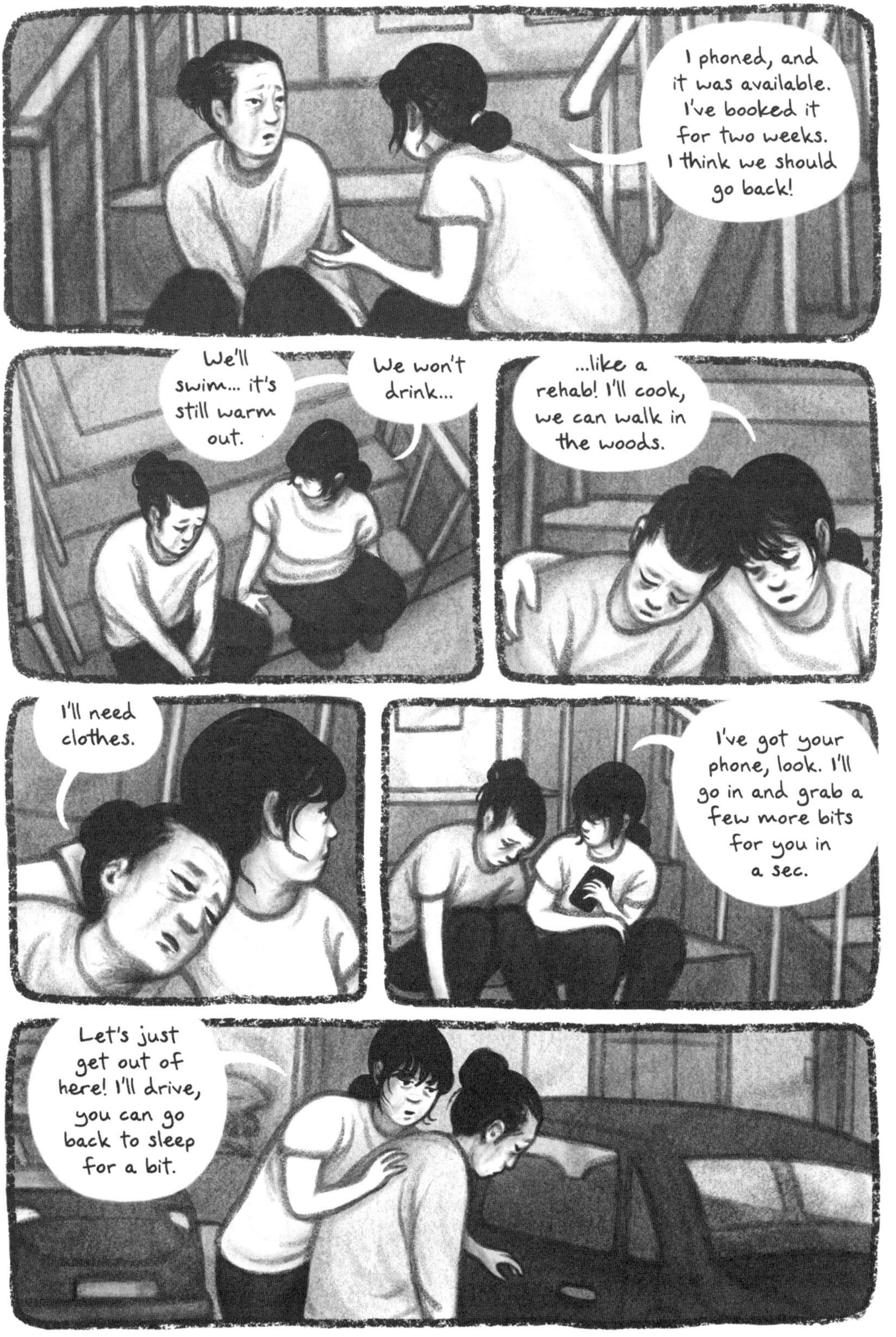
I phoned, and it was available. I've booked it for two weeks. I think we should go back!
We'll swim... it's still warm out.
We won't drink...
...like a rehab! I'll cook, we can walk in the woods.
I'll need clothes.
I've got your phone, look. I'll go in and grab a few more bits for you in a sec.
Let's just get out of here! I'll drive, you can go back to sleep for a bit.

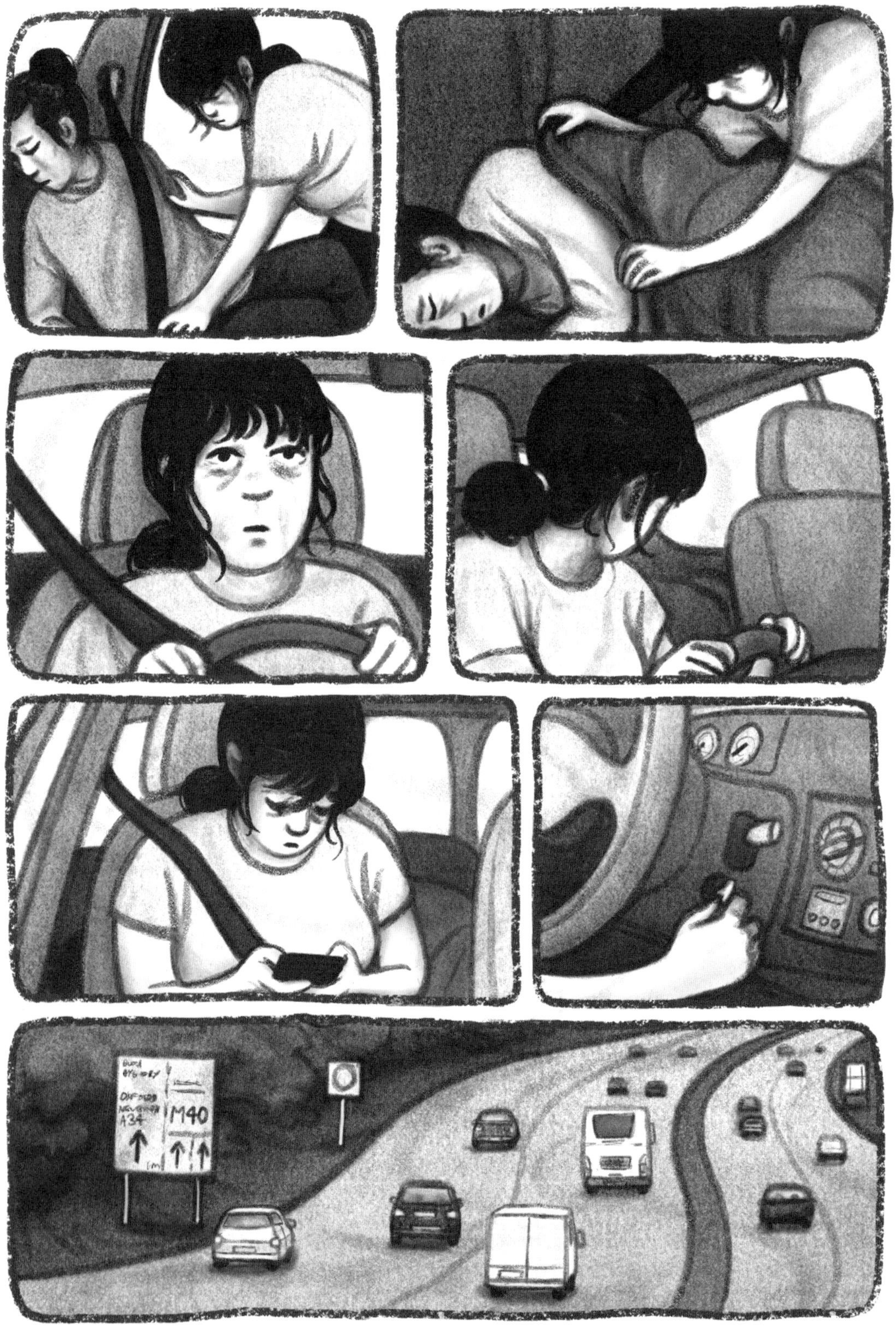
A34
M40

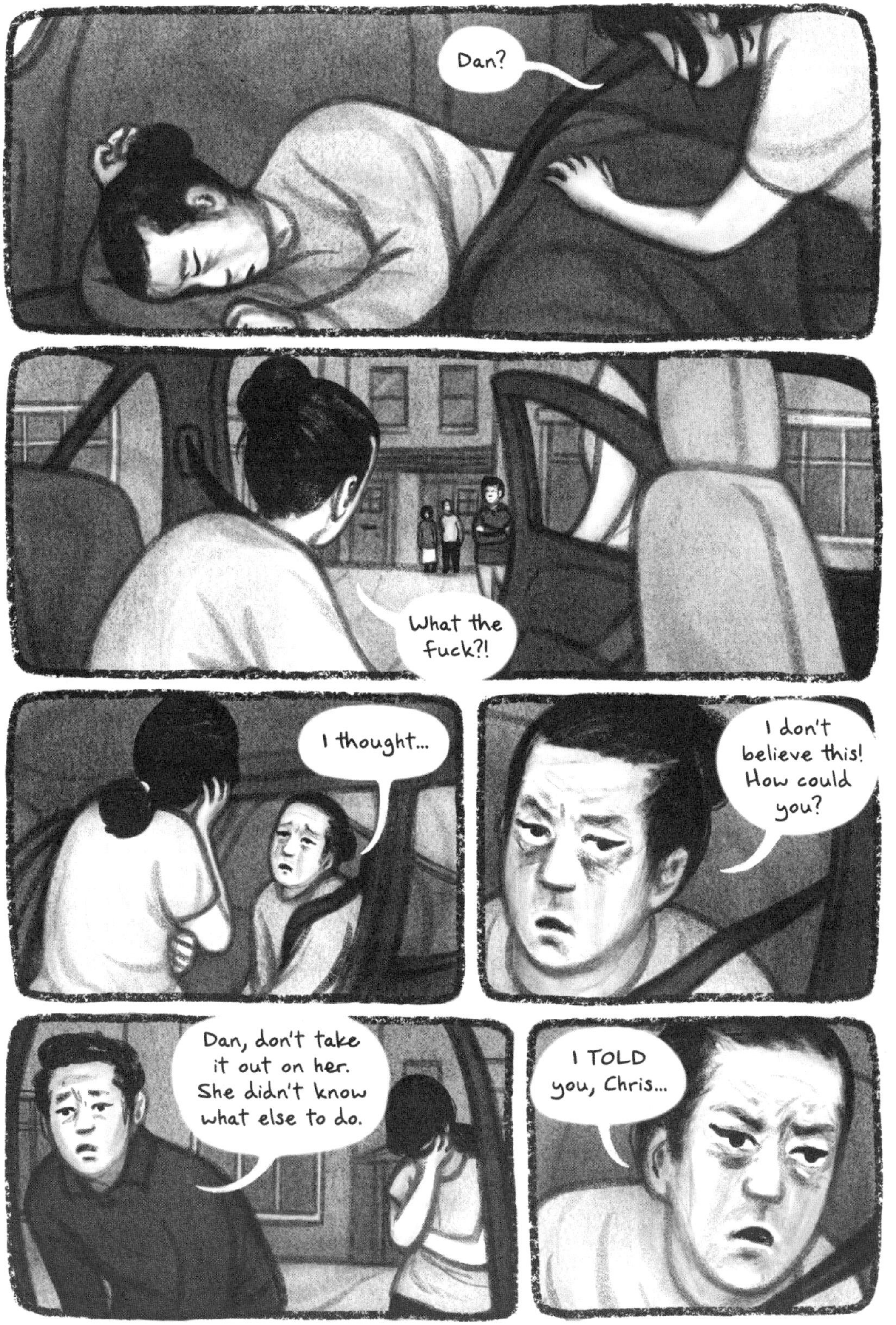
Dan?
What the fuck?!
I thought...
I don't believe this! How could you?
Dan, don't take it out on her. She didn't know what else to do.
I TOLD you, Chris...

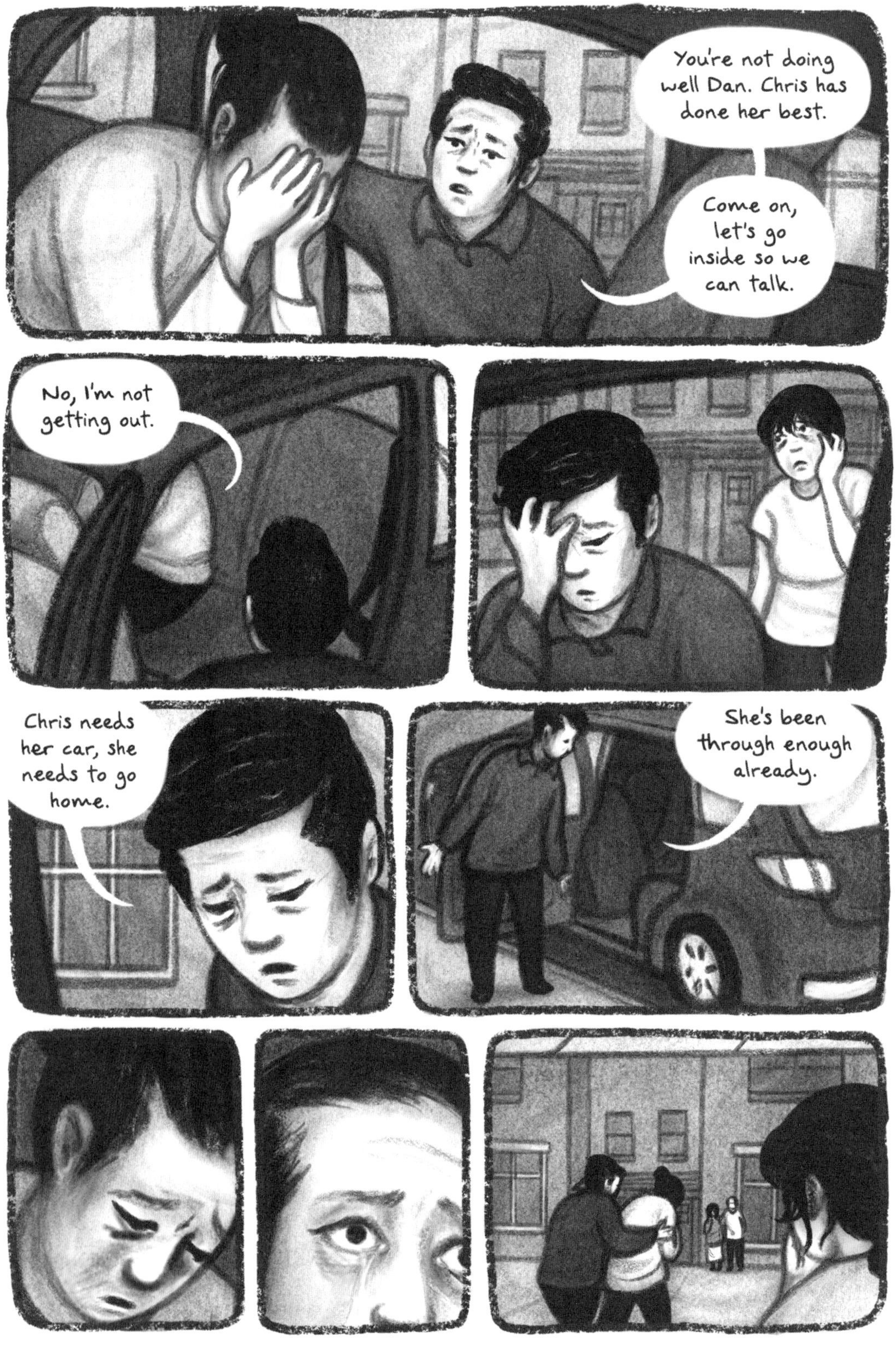
You're not doing well Dan. Chris has done her best.
Come on, let's go inside so we can talk.
No, I'm not getting out.
Chris needs her car, she needs to go home.
She's been through enough already.

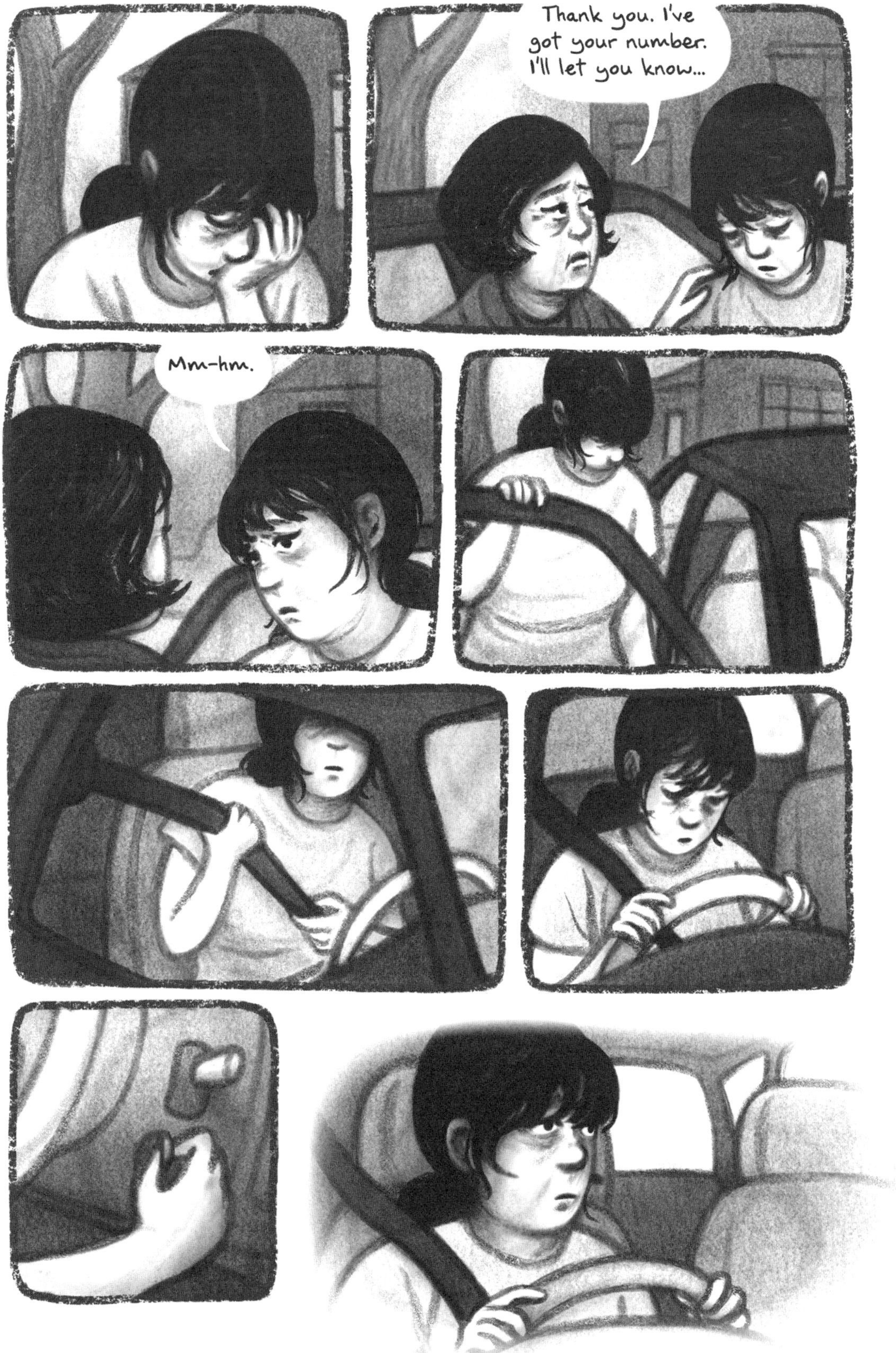
Thank you. I've got your number. I'll let you know...
Mm-hm.

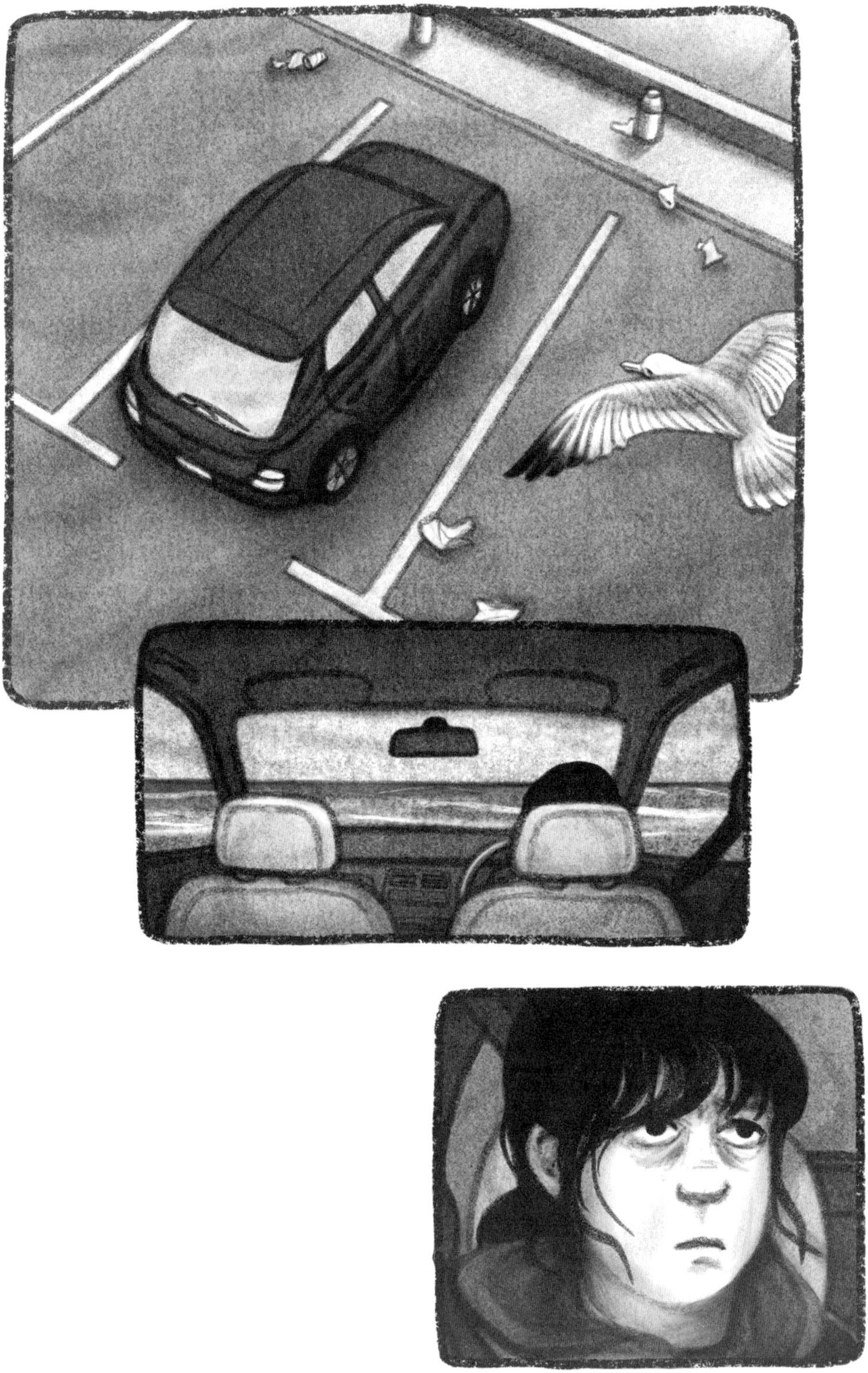

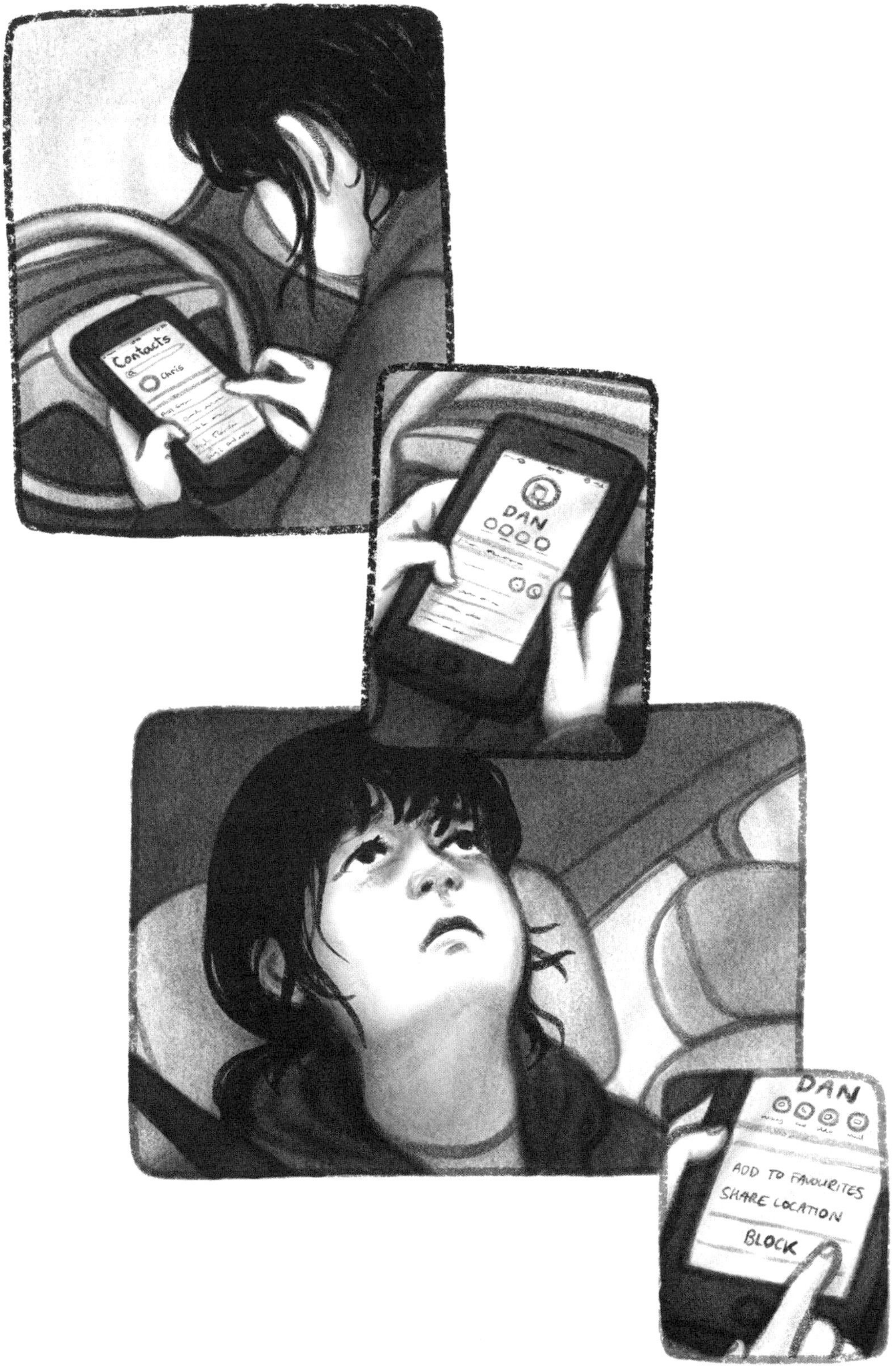
Contacts
Chris
DAN
DAN
ADD TO FAVOURITES
SHARE LOCATION
BLOCK

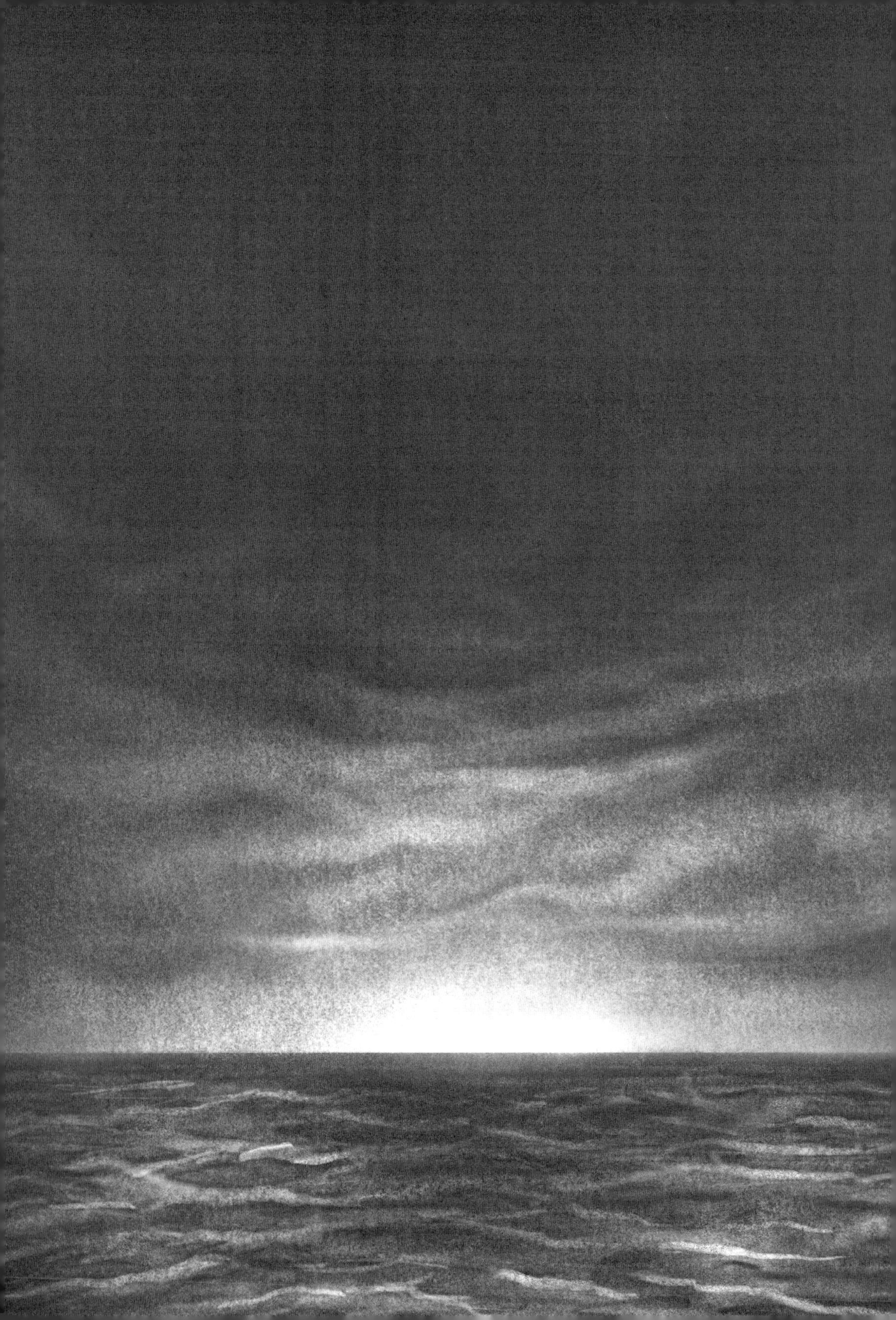

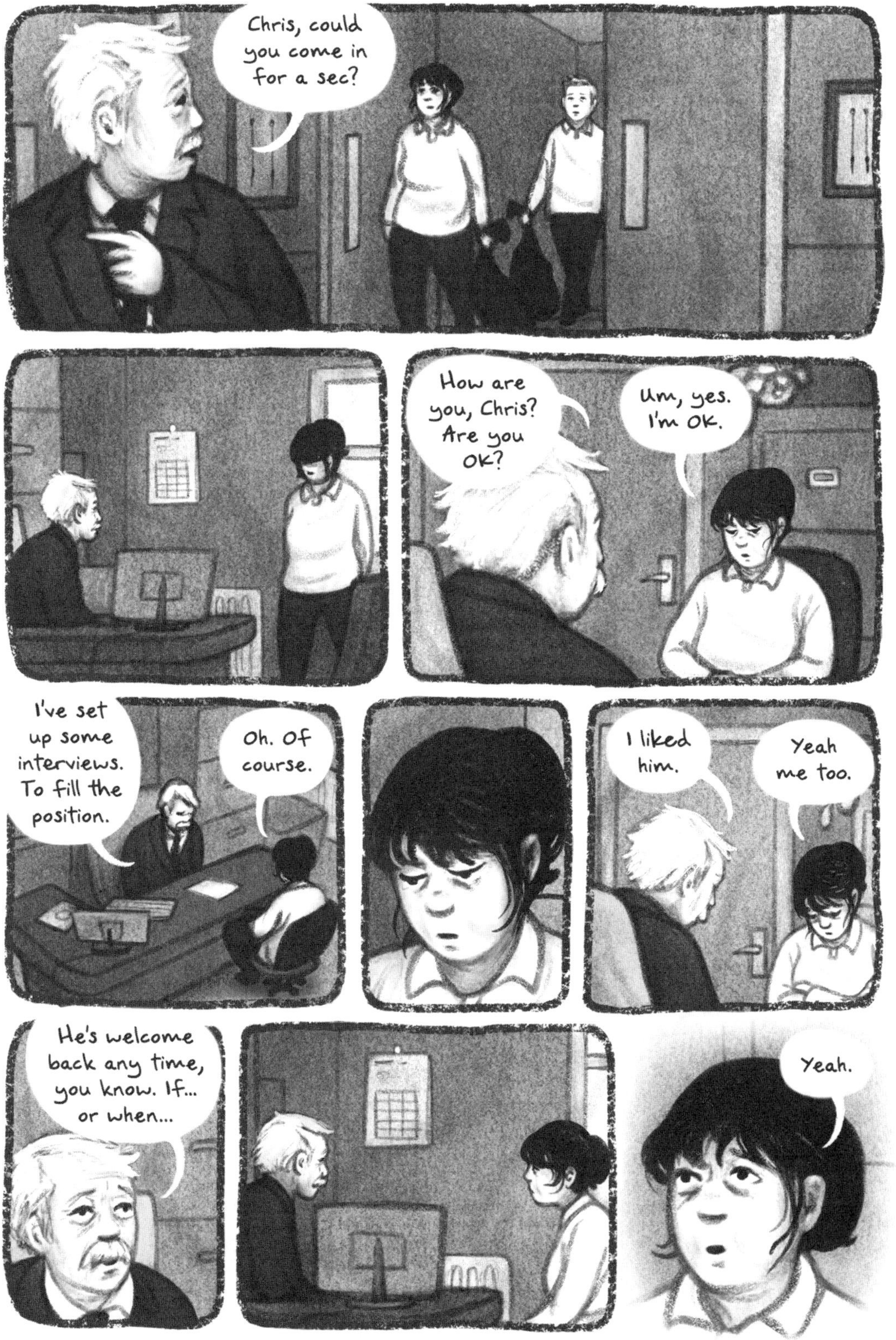
Chris, could you come in for a sec?
How are you, Chris? Are you OK?
Um, yes. I'm OK.
I've set up some interviews. To fill the position.
Oh. Of course.
I liked him.
Yeah me too.
He's welcome back any time, you know. If... or when...
Yeah.

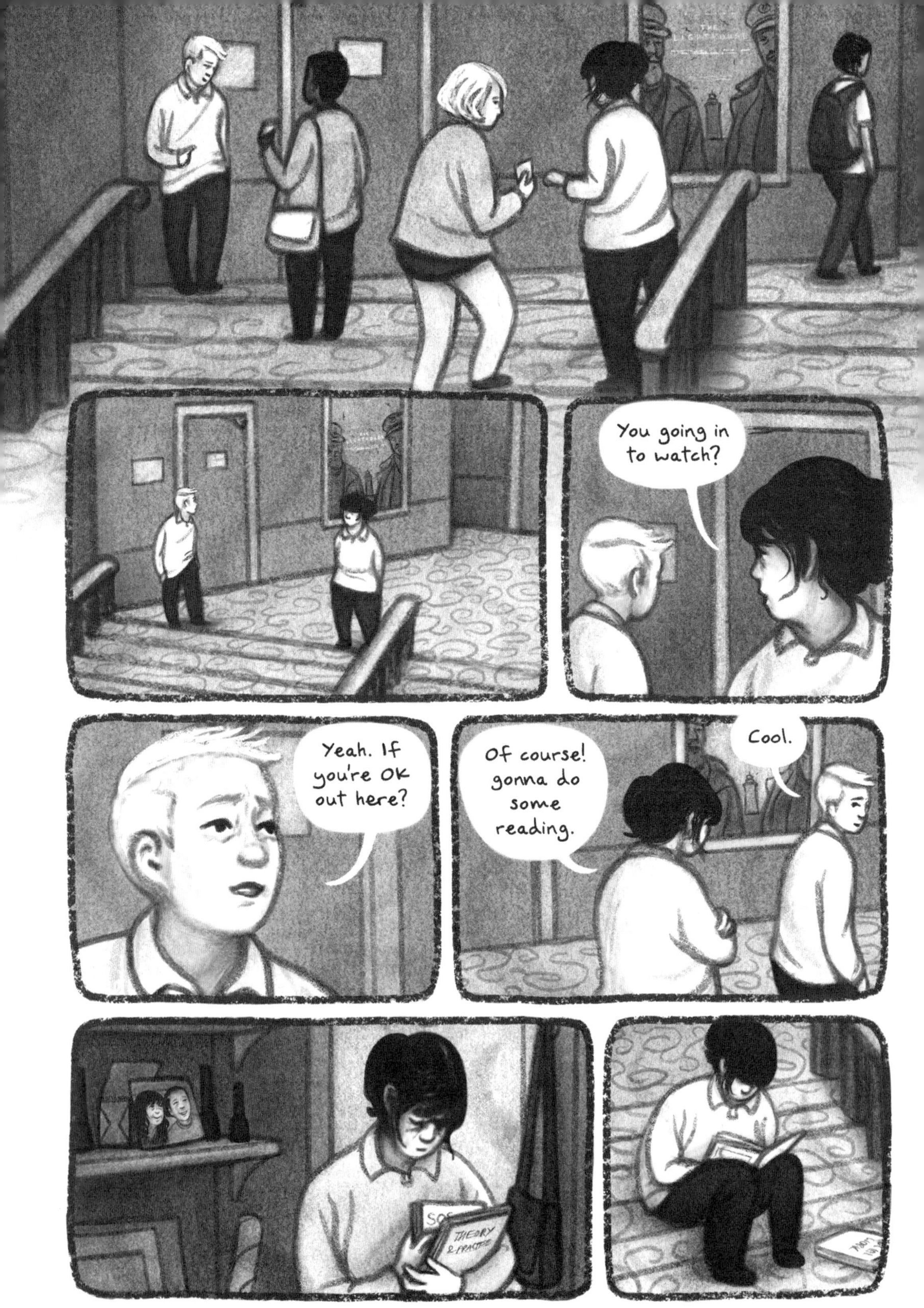
You going in to watch?
Yeah. If you're OK out here?
Of course! gonna do some reading.
Cool.
THEORY & PRACTICE

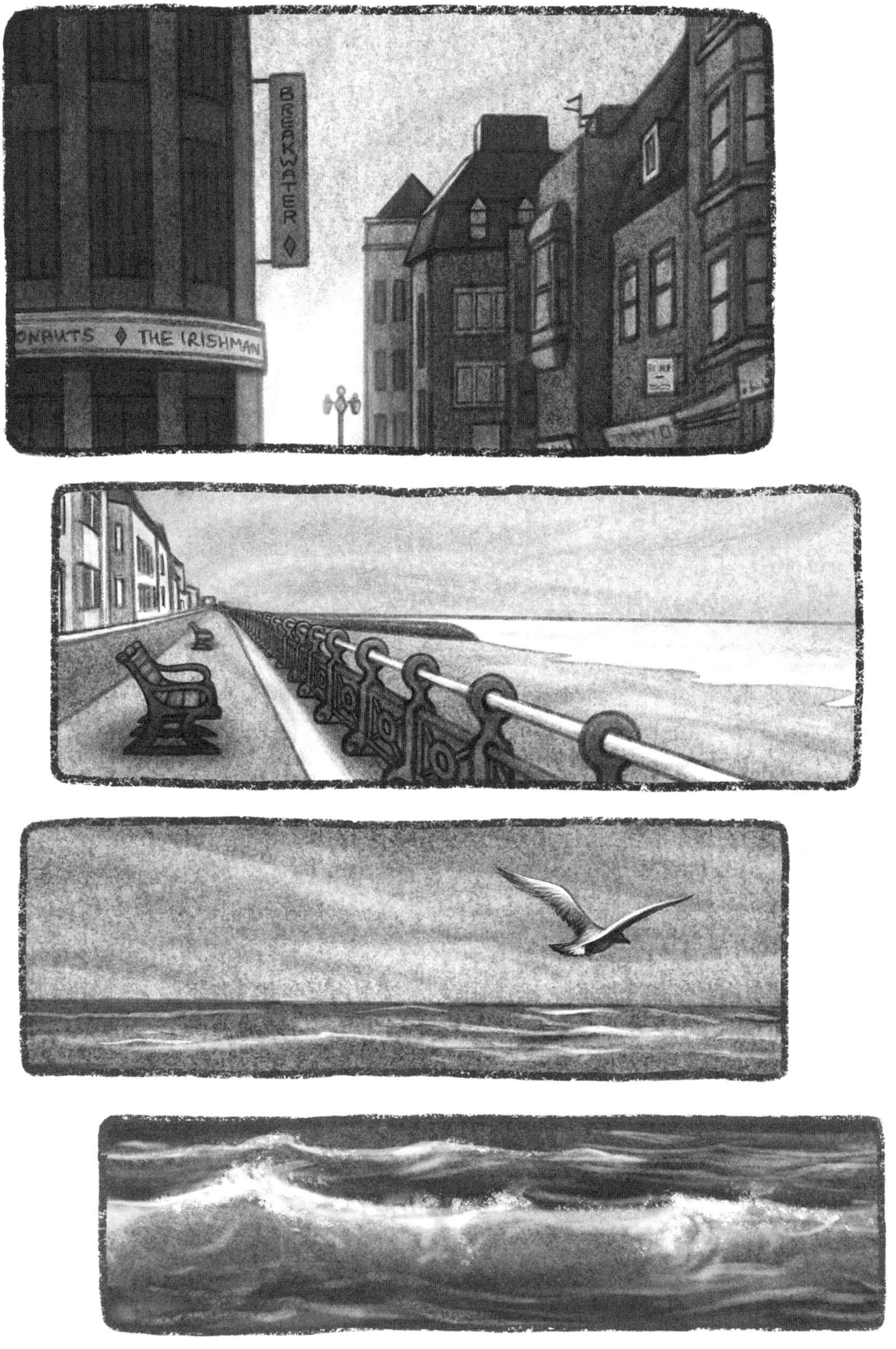
BREAKWATER
THE IRISHMAN

Published by Avery Hill Publishing, 2020

10 9 8 7 6 5 4 3 2 1

With thanks to Sergio Galaviz and Ricky Miller.

First published in the UK in 2020 by

Avery Hill Publishing
Unit 8
5 Durham Yard
London
E2 6QF

A CIP record for this book is available from the British Library
ISBN: 978-1910395578

Katriona Chapman is a comic artist and illustrator based in London UK.
www.katrionachapman.com

Avery Hill Publishing
www.averyhillpublishing.com